Outside the Lines

Outside the Lines

by

Melissa Sky

2023

OUTSIDE THE LINES

ISBN 13: 978-1-63679-403-7

This Trade Paperback Original Is Published By
Bold Strokes Books, Inc.
P.O. Box 249
Valley Falls, NY 12185

First Edition: April 2023

Credits
Editor: Barbara Ann Wright
Production Design: Stacia Seaman
Cover Design by Tammy Seidick

For the dark gift of time and its indiscriminate dust
For the obscure simplicity of love and its redemption
For all those who find themselves outside the lines
And the families we make for ourselves
For my son, Liam, who brings me laughter
And my lover, Cogie, who brings me peace

My deepest gratitude to all who have sustained me
in the wild joy of creating

Chapter One

Death, Thou Shalt Die

Every day of your life is just another day. Until it isn't.

And you can never know when it's your last everyday day. You can only know that afterward, when you look back, and all those mundane things you used to do are infused with a tender, precious meaning you didn't know lived there alongside you.

You just can't know. Until the big change comes. Whatever it is.

❖

My last everyday day, I was paying attention to the wrong things. As usual. Distracted. Daydreaming. "Head in the clouds," as my mother used to lovingly scold. I was supposed to be hurrying home from delivering a care package to Mr. Hernandez, an elderly widow that my mother had been taking care of ever since his wife died years ago. He was too frail to walk the five kilometers to my mother's food stall, so off I was sent with his daily free meal. Not that my mother would allow him to believe it was free. He paid us random belongings he felt he could part with: a can of nails, his wife's old slippers, a pile of outdated pamphlets. Bartering was common in the Freelands, but Mr. Hernandez took it to a whole other level. His place was a wonderland of bizarre, dusty old junk and treasures. It was a ramshackle mishmash, just like his mind; his rambling stories ran the gamut from the oft repeated, boring tale of how he met his wife to lively, unexpected accounts of the romantic dalliances and bad choices of his youth.

I was returning home with a random key and a solitary knitting needle as payment when I was stopped in my tracks by the sight of a child and dog playing in the street. It was nothing exceptional. Nothing particularly special. But I'd always been one to stop for beauty whenever it showed its elusive face. It was amazing how much beauty I could find in the ugliness of life if I just looked hard enough. After all, maybe beauty was just a matter of squinting. Of selective focus. Knowing which details to hold on to and which to let go.

I stopped. I squinted. My fingers already itched for my pencil, my mind already sketched the broad outlines before I grabbed my sketchbook from my bag.

A bold stroke here, and there, a child squealing with delight.

Some dragging of the nib across the smooth possibility of the page, tiny feet pattering.

A bit of scratching, a touch of smudging, shapes emerging out of nothingness, the dog's playful scampering.

I could have drawn the scabs on the child's knobby knees and the filth on his bare feet. I could have focused on the bald spots among the dog's mangy fur. But I didn't. I fixed on the way the child's laughter sparkled in his eyes. On the riotous, wild enthusiasm that vibrated through the pup's entire frame. The tender curve of the child's belly. The frenetic thrill of the animal's wagging tail.

I scribbled madly, rushing, knowing this moment would be fleeting. And indeed, a few minutes later, the child's older sibling appeared. He shooed away the stray. Harsh words and rough tugging burst the bubble.

But it had been there. I'd seen it.

My sketchbook preserved such bubbles of beauty. Ephemeral, shimmering, fragile moments of wholeness and light. I captured them between these pages. I drew the beauty that drew me in. Then I added an opalescent bubble frame afterward. Some curving lines of dainty, luminous color from the few treasured stubs of colored pencils in my possession. I didn't know why I obsessively drew these bubbles. But my sketchbook was full of them.

Perhaps because nothing fragile survived long here.

"Shoulda known!"

A voice ripe with amusement disrupted my reveries. I didn't have to look up to know it was Rake, my best friend since forever.

I did look up, though, because she was always a pleasure to look at. A wildflower blooming with abandon amongst all the rubble and detritus of the Freelands. Her clothes never matched and were always an eccentric but surprisingly stylish mix of odds and ends from both genders and all time periods. Her hair was shaved on one side and dyed a bright purple on the other. She exuded vibrancy, strength, and a queer kind of beauty. Not to mention a suave charm that made her very popular with pretty much everyone, from children to little old ladies.

We couldn't possibly have been more different, and yet we fitted. She was bold; I was timid. She was earthy; I was whimsical. She made fun of me constantly and I…well, I not so secretly loved it. Being with her, I felt safe and yet strangely on edge. An odd, delicious sensation. What she got from me, I'm not really sure. But I'd been following her around ever since I was a little kid, this awkward, freckle-faced ginger waif just hanging around the punky, cool, older kid.

Rake sauntered toward me, her jaunty, teasing energy already shifting my emotions before she even reached me. What was it about her that both unsettled me and made me feel at home? It was maddening and intoxicating and comforting all at the same time.

She leapt playfully beside me and tore the sketchbook from my hands. I didn't bother resisting. Rake always got what she wanted, and she'd seen pretty much all my sketches anyway. Besides, those precious stubs of pencil crayons? Totally gifts from her, so I couldn't exactly complain when she insisted on seeing my work.

She grabbed the chain around her neck and held it up to her right eye, pretending there was a monocle attached to its end, then mimicked being some kind of fancy art critic with a stuffy elitist voice. It was an old joke between us whenever she looked at my drawings.

"Yes, yes, I see real development in the use of texture. Quite an invigorating sense of energy in the lines. Designed to cultivate delight in the most hardened viewer. Very impressive. Though I'm not sure your mother would agree." With this, she clapped shut the sketchbook and handed it back. Sort of. She held it out of reach the first few times just to laugh at my frustration.

When I finally wrestled it free and stowed it safely back in my bag, I realized I must be way later than usual if my mom had sent Rake after me. Indeed, looking around, I recognized that my mom would be closing up soon. "Sorry, I got distracted."

"Shocker. That never happens," Rake drawled.

"Did my mom send you to find me?"

"Yep, didn't want her wayward daughter out all alone after dark."

"I'm not wayward," I protested, speeding up as we started home.

Rake responded by clearing her throat and beginning to imitate Mrs. Flores, our childhood teacher. "Wayward. Part of speech: adjective. Linguistic origin: probably Latin because most words are. Meaning: difficult to control or predict. Now who can use it in a sentence?" She was wrapping an imaginary sweater tightly across her chest, looking up at nothing in particular, and pacing the way Mrs. Flores used to do. I had to laugh. Rake was good at impressions. She had a real knack for noticing and portraying a person's gestures, facial expressions, and patterns of speech, all those intimate little idiosyncrasies that made someone unique. She was perceptive. Like me. Just in a different way.

While there weren't official schools in the Freelands—there wasn't anything official out here—there were still people who acted as makeshift teachers, educating the community's children for whatever their families could spare, sharing whatever knowledge they deemed important for the collective future of the offspring of the ghetto. In our neighborhood, the Barrio, so nicknamed for its significant Latino population, most kids went to Mr. Brown, a kind, older Black man who focused on practical stuff kids would need to know how to *do*. But not Rake and I. My mom had insisted on Mrs. Flores. She wanted me to get what she called a "classic" education. Mrs. Flores was ancient and strict but really, really smart. She knew oceans and oceans of completely irrelevant, fascinating things. Her curriculum? Nothing useful. Everything magical. She was the first to encourage my drawing, so, of course, she had a special place in my heart. As for Rake, she popped by Mrs. Flores's classes from time to time, but Rake had never taken anything there very seriously. She said she preferred to learn from "life itself." A pretentious but sort of endearing stance.

We rounded the corner, and there stood my mom's familiar Mexican food cart, packed up and ready to wheel home. Customers still hung about, gossiping and laughing with her, a generous, hard-working, middle-aged, petite woman who was just always there, both loving and annoying me, predictable as the sunrise.

She gave me an indulgent if exasperated smile when she caught sight of me. "Amara, my girl, what kept you this time?"

"Do you have to ask?" Rake teased, sidling up to my mom and turning to study me, shaking her head slightly as though she was also an adult, unsure what to do with this teenager who was clearly the very definition of wayward.

I'd actually never been sure which of us Rake was closer to. Just like the food stall, she'd been around as long as I could remember. My mom had sort of taken her under her wing after Rake's mother had disappeared. Rake's father had died long ago in a turf skirmish. So it had just been her and her mom for years. Then, just like that, her mom hadn't come home one day. It happened a lot in the Freelands.

Especially to women. There were plenty of wild rumors as to why, most of them involving Hydra, the Old Blood enclave. But there were always wild rumors about the enclave. It was impossible to know what was really true. A person was either in or out, and there weren't many ways in for us New Bloods.

So Rake was kinda like a sister. Though that felt wrong. I mean, we didn't even live together. Rake crashed with a bunch of other orphans in an outrageously graffitied old building a few blocks away, and she seemed to like it that way.

In any case, my mom and her were really close. Like, freakishly in tune to the point where sometimes, I felt like the newcomer to their cozy family unit. And it was so exactly like my mom to take Rake in. She was always helping others. And she actually did really well for herself, despite constantly giving handouts. She knew how to offer what was needed and how to receive what could be offered in return, all with impeccable grace. So she fed everyone. Literally, everyone was welcome at her stall, where they would be sure to receive a radiant smile, an ample helping of delicious Mexican street food, and good-natured neighborhood gossip as well. Those who couldn't pay found other means. Someone was always doing something for Mama Maria.

In the Barrio, we took care of our own and prided ourselves on it. But if I was being honest, the Freelands might have been free, but they weren't much else. As Rake said in her darker, more cynical moments: "We're free all right. Free to die in the gutter."

Now Rake asked if she could steal me for a few hours, and my mom agreed, which only annoyed me. "I thought the whole reason you sent Rake after me was because you didn't want me out after dark."

"I don't want you out *alone* after dark. Rake can handle anything that comes up."

Her utter confidence in Rake irritated me more, and I mumbled, "I can handle things too." But this just inspired looks that all but shouted, "Isn't she so cute and clueless?"

Ugh. Sometimes I hated their weird telepathic bond.

Still, my mom was right. Rake could handle anything. Not like me, who was awkward, easily flustered, and overwhelmed. Rake understood people, and she understood the game. She smoothed the path for me wherever we went. And I *did* feel safe with her. The Freelands could be dangerous, especially outside our own neighborhood where folks didn't know us. More people knew Rake, just like they knew my mother. Whereas they probably didn't know my name, but they would know my face. I was Maria's girl or that weird, quiet ginge always hanging around Rake.

As if to prove my mother right, on the way to the park, we passed a couple of guys I didn't recognize who were posturing and talking too loudly. Street rats. They popped up everywhere. I didn't like their energy and quickened my pace, but Rake slowed. When they threw some crude insults our way, she upped the ante and threw them right back with a clever twist. The guys laughed, and she smiled wide, sauntering away.

Typical.

It was getting late, so I didn't expect to see any kids lingering, but Jasper and Lana were still at the park. Their dad was a handyman. Good at fixing almost anything. He had helped out around our place more than once in exchange for Maria's legendary churros.

Jasper was heading from the swings for the slide, so Rake started running for the slide too, edging in front of him and being obnoxious. She had no shame about messing with a five-year-old. She slid down enthusiastically, then popped up, swung around, and began running back *up* the slide.

Jasper was the at the top by then, ready for his turn to go down. "You can't do that. It's not your turn, and you're not allowed to go up the slide part. My daddy says it's dangerous."

"Oh, it *is* dangerous," she returned, stepping onto the raised side rails of the slide and teetering with exaggeration. "You might fall off and break your noggin like this." She fell dramatically, and he laughed while his sister and I looked on, only one of us smiling.

"It's time to go, Jasper. It's getting late," Lana said, looking sternly in Rake's direction.

"Just a few more minutes. I wanna try breaking my noggin too."

Lana's nine-year-old's death glare was making me sweat, but Rake was oblivious. "Oh, but you have such a fine noggin, Jasper. We don't want to break yours. Mine's already damaged, so it's different." She leaned in close and stage-whispered loudly enough for everyone to hear, "Don't say anything, but I don't think your sister likes me very much."

Jasper giggled and bounced excitedly while Lana continued to throw daggers with her eyes.

"How 'bout if you run up the slide twice with me as a spotter, then head on out before it gets dark?"

This seemed to satisfy both siblings, and after doing it twice, then whining and cajoling his way into a third and fourth time, they finally headed home. Rake ran up the slide one more time, then leaned against the rails at the top, pulled a joint out of a little metal case, and lit up. She didn't bother asking if I wanted any. She knew better.

While I waited for her to finish, I lay on the end of the slide and stared at the last remnants of the daytime sky, feeling relaxed and happy with my hands folded across my chest. Mrs. Flores said this was "golden hour," a phrase that stayed with me. I'd noticed how the quality of the light shifted just before sunset, how everything became suffused in a warm, soft, orange glow. But I hadn't had the words for it before Mrs. Flores gifted them to me.

I just lay there and enjoyed being and doing nothing. I thought about the beauty of this final reddish blush of day. The sun's good night kiss.

"I betcha anything that girl ends up a BabyDoll."

Startled out of my reverie, I tried to catch up. "Who? Lana?"

"Yeah. She'll make the perfect BabyDoll. Good looks. Rigid adherence to authority. Gullible. No mind of her own…"

Rake started listing the qualities for good candidates. I knew better than to interrupt or to betray my curiosity about that life. She was virulently anti-enclave, even before her mother had disappeared, though her political rants had intensified afterward. As far as she was concerned, the Hydra enclave was the very definition of evil. There wasn't anything she wouldn't put past them. And while I acknowledged that it was pretty damn selfish of them to hoard the Remedy for themselves, I didn't take it as personally as she did.

When the Asenescence Corporation had developed a cure for human aging, perhaps the single greatest scientific achievement of all time, it should have been a moment of worldwide celebration. No more aging? Surely that meant the end of physical and mental deterioration. No more senility. No more frailty. No more slow descent into indignity. What an advancement!

But while the creation of the Remedy might have been the pinnacle of human achievement, its distribution had been the height of human failure. It *wasn't* really distributed. Not even to the uber-wealthy who could afford it. Asenescence had set itself up as the arbiter of immortality, choosing who deserved to live forever.

Sort of. Humans could still die. Of accidents, murder, suicide, and some diseases, even with the Remedy. But they no longer aged from the moment they took it, and the vast majority of terminal diseases were age-related. Some FirstGen Old Bloods were into their second century of life now. All thanks to a bunch of scientists who'd studied the regenerative properties of these weird little green jellyfish-like blobs called hydras.

They creeped me out whenever I saw images of their freaky, tiny, gelatinous bodies. Evidently, they basically lived forever, and if chopped up, they could respawn from the pieces. Gross. And amazing. And gross.

As for the rest of us, well, life went on. We were born, we grew up, we worked, we fell in love, we reproduced, we got old and we died. New Bloods: considered mere children to the Old Bloods.

But children had their uses.

Or did they? Eventually, Hydra banned human reproduction in the enclave. That hadn't gone over well at first, but eventually, the Old Bloods had fallen in line. I mean, how many babies could they really want to carry over centuries? And resources were limited. The LastGen would be about my age now. Who knew if they even still had things like playgrounds on the inside now? What would be the use?

But they had some use for us. One of very few ways a New Blood could enter the enclave was to work as a BabyDoll, an insulting and ridiculous name for a glorified slave, according to Rake and her ilk. But I could understand why so many people out here dreamed of it. Sure, BabyDolls had to be sterilized, but that wasn't such a big deal when the trade-off was a life of luxury, predictability, cleanliness, and order. Everything the Freelands wasn't. Sure, they had to work, but they would have to work out here too. The outfits *were* undeniably cute, and then there were the rumors of their lives…

Rake was getting animated and paranoid, her trip taking a negative turn. I hated when she got like this, so I suggested a change of scenery and invited her to join me in our favorite climbing tree. It had low-hanging branches made for climbing. When we were kids, I'd thought we were so impressively brave and daring for tackling it, but realistically, our favorite branch was only eight feet up, hardly high enough to break anything should we fall.

Rake cajoled me into snuggling in the crook of the best branch, a sturdy one with others close by so we could rest our feet and arms. She leaned against the trunk, content while I fidgeted, trying to figure out how to position myself. She sighed, probably eye-rolled, though I couldn't see it, and guided my body into a more comfortable pose. Relatively speaking. I could never fully relax when close to Rake. I felt…uncertain, stimulated, and on edge. There was a kind of electric current between us. I didn't know exactly what I wanted from her. Or what I felt. But whatever it was, I felt a lot of it.

After some more nervous fidgeting on my part, Rake finally said, "Oh my God, Amara, seriously, relax. Lean back. What do you think I'm going to do to you? We're up a tree. I just want to cuddle and watch the sunset. Chill out."

Strangely, this worked, and I settled into her embrace. Once I relaxed, it actually felt really good to feel her, solid and reassuring, behind me, her warm breath on my ear as we watched the brilliant colors of the setting sun. Another day ending in a brilliant burst of color that demanded appreciation and attention.

"I mean…if you begged me, I could probably find a way to—"

I laughed and punched her playfully on the bicep where her arms were wrapped tightly around me.

"What? I'm just saying, you *do* realize how many girls would die to be snuggling in a tree with me right now?"

Now it was my turn to roll my eyes. Rake was…popular with women. And I could hardly blame them. She was extraordinary. And made me feel extraordinary too. But…something always held me back. I mean, what if it didn't work out, and we ruined our friendship for nothing? I couldn't imagine my life without her. She'd always been there. Like my mom. Like the sunrise and sunset. I needed her.

Besides, she didn't always treat her girlfriends well. Never really seemed to fall for any of them. Said she was just having some fun and holding out for "the one." But why bother dating if her heart wasn't fully in it? And how would it magically change when the right person came along?

My mom always said, "People show you who they are." Rake had shown me more than enough times. She was not a good girlfriend.

Besides, I was sure she only flirted with me because she was a born flirt. It meant nothing.

We lapsed into a long, companionable silence, and I studied the sky. I couldn't help but imagine how I would sketch this scene. I scrutinized the shades of sunset, the tints of twilight, trying to feel the precise moment when time itself shifted from one state to another.

Rake's voice, uncharacteristically shaky, broke my contemplation. "I'm starting to forget what her face looks like."

I knew she meant her mother. More than anyone, I knew the secrets of Rake's heart. And maybe *that* was what I gave her. The space to be quiet and still enough to feel and reveal those secrets. She was always “on” with everyone else. Always performing, charming, hustling, laughing, the life of the party. But with me, she could be real. She could be sad. She could be boring or tired or bitter or whatever she really was in any given moment. She could be herself.

I didn’t say anything. I just took her hand, turned, and rested my head against hers, a little sound of empathy escaping my throat. We stayed like that as the subtle shift to night occurred. I offered what I could. Sitting with her, connected, in the sorrow of unspeakable loss.

I never imagined just how connected in loss we would become. Until my own mother disappeared the very next day.

CHAPTER TWO

Do Not Go Gentle

Was it better or worse to know how and why your mother abandoned you? I couldn't say what it felt like to have a parent up and disappear out of thin air with no warning and no clues. But I figured out what it felt like to wake expecting to find my mother making breakfast as usual and instead finding only a note. A note. A freaking note. That was what she left me. And a ton of money. And an even bigger ton of questions.

Nothing she said made sense. Nothing. Made. Sense.

I must have sat at the kitchen table and reread that note a dozen times before even a fraction of its import sank in. I was sinking in. The world was sinking in. My stomach, my heart, the universe as I understood it, everything felt like it was collapsing in on itself.

I fingered the money while my brain imploded. The bills' crisp, polymer edges poked my fingertips. They were Hydra bills. Citizens only ever used cyber-credits, but Hydra still produced physical currency, mostly for dealings with outsiders. Every once in a while, a family out here would come into a huge pile of it. The payoff for some son or daughter being deemed worthy of becoming a BabyDoll. Or a smaller but still substantial pile for some other relative desperate enough to become a Drudge. Like my mom had done to "give me a better life," according to the note.

I shivered violently, and some of the bills fell to the floor. I went to my knees and started gathering them, cleaning the mess in a mindless, habitual response. Once down there, though, I couldn't seem to force my body to get back up. I felt frozen. Stuck gathering the bills that my mother in some *un-fucking-believable* way had thought I would value more than her. I started to shake. I wanted to scream. But instead, I burst into overwhelmed tears and curled up on the floor, under the table, just sobbing and sobbing and not understanding at all.

I didn't know how long I was under there. It seemed an eternity. Like I had always lived under the table, its four legs the walls of a self-imposed prison cell. My thoughts became irrational, and I figured maybe I'd just stay right there forever. I traced the curves of the table legs idly, my mind a blissful blank. I'd stay right here. Right here was good. Everything was good. Everything was fine.

I touched a familiar scrawl, and I sat straight up, smashing my head in the process. I'd forgotten about this! How old were we when we'd taken a marker to the underside of the table, risking my mother's wrath to leave a secret message? Young enough that Rake had both her parents. And still wore dresses a lot. Without the combat boots that now accompanied them on the rare occasion that they made an appearance in her repertoire of outfits.

"R and A were heer. Dont tell A's mom."

Laughter burst out of my throat, unbidden and shocking. What an inane thing to write. Well, in our defense, we were, like, seven or something. Underneath the words, I'd drawn little stick figure girls in triangle skirts and pigtails, holding hands. Honestly, it was pretty amateur. Didn't bode well for my future as an artist at all.

The momentary laugh and levity ironically brought all the sadness back. Heaviness returned, and I lay back on the floor, dejected but more myself again. I forced myself to think. What did I know? My mother had left to give me a "better life." Had gone off to join the enclave in the only way she could as an older, New Blood woman. Had left me the business and the payoff and a note that sounded nothing like her.

Something was off. She would *never* do this. Sure, older people left to become Drudges all the time. They did it for their families. But my mom wasn't desperate. And she wasn't that old. We had the business. We were doing just fine. And she loved me to pieces. She wouldn't just up and leave with no warning. I knew it in my bones.

But then, where had the money come from? And the handwriting did *look* like hers; it just didn't *sound* like anything she would ever write or do. She was a caretaker, through and through. But what if this was some twisted idea of caretaking? I was set for life now, at least financially. A business and a nest egg. Few people in the Freelands had so much.

So much that meant so little. I wanted my mother. And the truth.

And I was going to find them, no matter the cost.

I got off the floor, my body as sore as my aching heart, and set out to find Rake.

❖

Rake freaked out when she heard about my mom, but she freaked out even more when I told her about my plan. Plan might have been an overstatement. It was more like a vaguely conceptualized idea of becoming a BabyDoll, somehow magically finding my mom, then stealthily evading Hydra security to bring her back home. When I told her about it, Rake blanched, then grabbed my arm and dragged me through the streets, never once loosening her death grip, telling me only that she was taking me to "someone who could help."

We ended up in some cute, dilapidated little place that smelled like cookies and cats. Rake didn't even knock. She just walked right in and dragged me unceremoniously into the middle of some stranger's living room. It contained such an odd assortment of incongruous people that I was momentarily stunned. I saw a pair of young street punks watering houseplants beside a middle-aged man working on some kind of electrical gadget under a giant lamp. There was also a little old lady crocheting from a comfy chair in the corner. And cats. More cats than people. And the cats, at least, were not impressed at our intrusion.

"We need to talk," Rake announced. And as though this was an ordinary occurrence, the people—all but the old lady and one particularly chill cat—left the room. "This is Amara. Maria Rodriguez's daughter. She…she needs your help."

The stranger left off her crochet work and looked sharply at Rake over her spectacles. "What did you tell her?"

"Nothing. Just that I knew someone who might be able to help."

The stranger continued to look sharply at Rake, who was more jittery and anxious than I'd ever seen her. The elderly woman took off her glasses and carefully placed them on a side table, a slight tremor in her gesture. "You can go for a walk. Come back in an hour," she directed at Rake.

"I'm good. I'd rather stay here," Rake replied, finally releasing her painful grip on my arm. She ran her hands nervously through her hair and adjusted her clothes unnecessarily.

"It wasn't a request, my dear." The woman's voice was sweet but also carried a kind of confident, no-nonsense authority I wouldn't have expected from someone who looked like her.

Rake glanced uneasily from me to her but didn't make a move. For a few seconds, we were all frozen in an awkward, silent standstill, until the one cat randomly decided to make its opinion known, meowed loudly, and trotted toward the front door.

"Templeton will show you out," the old woman said, a twinkle in her eye and the hint of a smile about her lips. It was so weird that I gave a little half laugh, and Rake visibly relaxed.

"I'll be back in an hour," she affirmed, making intense eye contact with me that she didn't break until I gave a little nod.

Then she left, and it was just me and the stranger.

"You can call me Nana," the stranger offered, getting up, grabbing a cane, and coming toward me. "Let's have some tea and chat, shall we?" She led me into the kitchen where fresh-baked cookies were cooling on a rack. I offered to help as she began fussing with a kettle, but she reminded me that I was a guest and bade me sit.

I tried to breathe out the sense of urgency I felt creeping up my spine. I pushed away thoughts of my mother and looked around. There were more plants, more crochet work, and more cats, a cozy little theme, it seemed. An aquarium stood on a counter, and I watched colorful fish swim by for a time. It was difficult not to get up and help. I was used to helping Mr. Hernandez.

I studied this strange woman out of the corner of my eyes. She had to be in her eighties. She was wearing a floral print top and a long, pleated blue skirt. Her hair was silver white, plaited, and looped in a simple updo. Why had Rake brought me here?

Nana finally settled at the table, her hostess role completed, the cookies on a pretty plate between us, and hot tea steaming in both our cups. They were the old-fashioned kind with tiny little handles and the saucers and everything. I wasn't sure if there was a special way I was supposed to hold it or something, so I watched her carefully for clues, then mimicked her gestures.

"How can I help you, Amara?" Her body might have been a little stooped and shaky, but her mind and eyes seemed sharp. She stared at me over the rim of her raised cup, expectant.

"I…I don't really know. Rake just said you might be able to."

"Tell me everything. What's going on?"

I told her. In a voice I barely recognized as my own. I just blurted it all out, ignoring my tea and spilling all my secrets to this stranger sitting across from me.

She was quiet for a long time when I finished. Then she got up, groaning slightly, and headed back to the cupboards. "We're going to need something stronger for this." She returned with a flask and poured a generous amount of what I could only assume was some kind of alcohol into her teacup. She motioned to mine, but I shook my head, and she hobbled back to the cupboard to replace the flask. I was shocked but also amused and impressed.

She lingered at the aquarium. Stared at it silently long enough that I thought maybe she had forgotten about both me and her newly spiked tea, but she started speaking, her eyes trained on the fish. "Did you know that the paradise fish…that's the electric blue and tangerine beauty here." She tapped the glass with a bony finger. "Did you know that it's one of very few fish that can change its colors? It's aggressive and hardy and can survive in almost any aquatic environment. A tenacious, scrappy survivor, this little guy."

I tried to be patient and follow her line of thought, but frustration began to creep in. What the hell did this have to do with anything? Why did Rake leave me with this doddering old woman going on about fish? My mother needed me. I needed a plan. I didn't need a lecture on marine life.

She turned her icy blue eyes on me and asked, "What do you know of the Defiance?"

That took me aback. "Um, not much," I admitted. "Just rumors. They're the resistance to Hydra. They're, like, terrorists or something."

Nana smiled and settled back down beside me, bringing her teacup to her lips and taking a generous swallow. "One man's terrorist is another man's freedom fighter," she pronounced almost merrily. "I'm the Barrio's Crone, Amara. I help organize and plan acts of resistance for the Defiance. We're scattered all over, small pockets, each led by a respected elder." She pulled down her shirt collar, exposing a tiny tattoo of a blue and orange fish. "It's one way some of us flag our connection to each other. Have you noticed your friend's?"

It took me a second to realize she meant Rake. *Wait. What?*

"She's been helping out for a few years now. A valued trader. Can charm most anyone into most anything. But you must know that." Her eyes twinkled mischievously.

I shouldn't have been surprised, but I was. How could my best friend have kept that big a secret from me? It felt like an unexpected punch in the gut. I didn't know anyone in my life anymore. Not really.

"I could help you," the Crone confirmed, offering the plate of cookies. "But it has to be mutual. A trade." The cookie plate wavered, and I took one quickly so she didn't have to keep holding it aloft.

I bit into it, tasting nothing, my mind racing. I swallowed with difficulty and offered everything I thought I had. "I have the money my mom left. And her food cart. It's an established business. Profitable. That's…everything I have." I swallowed some tea, trying to wash down the remains of the cookie as well as the choking feeling in my throat.

"What we need is more precious than money. We need information. And I have no doubt you could get it, with our assistance." The Crone reflected for a moment, then continued. "Leave the money and the food cart here for your friend. She'll need something to keep her going. Tell her you're entrusting her with it. That she needs to look after it for you until you get back. She won't be happy to see you go, but she'll manage." She tapped her shirt where the tattoo lay beneath. "Scrappy survivors," she said and winked.

I didn't know what to do with that. With any of this. But what could I do? Besides agree. "How?" It was the only question I could think of.

"We have people on the inside. We can get you into a high-level household. Divert you to the right doctor. One who won't actually sterilize you. We'll use our contacts to search for your mother, although she may come to you if she hears you're on the inside. Once we find her, we'll smooth your exit. Take you to a safehouse. You'll have to start over far from here, though."

I nodded.

"In return, you'll watch your proprietors. Watch their movements, their guests, their routines, their preferences, everything and anything that can be helpful. Watch for carelessness especially. They may accidentally leave things out that you can observe. Do you understand?"

I nodded again, then realized I didn't really understand. "But how would I communicate with you?"

"We've got that covered. What three personal items do you plan to take?"

I hadn't considered that. Hydra permitted newcomers to bring three items of sentimental value. Nothing else. I considered. "My sketchbook and pencils, then something from Rake and my mom, I guess."

"The pencils will count as an item. Do you have the sketchbook with you?"

I always had my sketchbook with me. I nodded and fished it out of my bag, reluctantly handing it over for her inspection. She flipped through the pages silently, and I noticed that the skin on her hands was a translucent peach color, even more thin and delicate than the pages of my book.

It was her turn to nod. "You've got a good eye. Quite talented."

My mother's note fell from the sketchbook to the floor with a quiet whoosh.

"Would you mind?"

I scrambled up, scooped the hated note from the floor, and handed it to her reluctantly. I didn't know why, but I almost resented her reading it. Between the sketchbook and the note, I felt oddly exposed.

"This is good," she muttered. My face must have done something strange because she explained, "I just mean that you should glue this in here. It provides a nice sentimental backstory for them when they inspect your belongings. But you'll have to draw one of these bubbles you're so fond of around it, or they'll notice the pattern is broken."

"No!" I didn't know why I shouted. My vehemence surprised even me.

"No?" The Crone looked at me, her eyes full of curiosity tinged with something else, perhaps a touch of amusement, a touch of annoyance, maybe a little sadness?

"Sorry. I don't know why I yelled like that. I just…I hate that note. It's not like my mother at all. I don't want it in my sketchbook. I don't want it all."

The Crone's eyes settled on annoyance. "You're about to enter the monster's den, and you're balking at this? We live in a war zone, my dear, whether you've acknowledged it or not. And you have to decide. Do you want to face the enemy empty-handed, or do you want to be a soldier, someone with access to weapons, tactics, and intel? It's up to you. You can go solo, or you can be part of a coordinated team. But soldiers take orders. And you'll be asked to do much more than this if you hope to get in and out alive."

A shiver of dread passed through me. She reached for my hand. I took hers instinctively, and she placed her other one on top, patting softly. Her hands were cold and incredibly soft, like a newborn's.

"The Old Bloods treat us like we're all mere babies, even withered old women like me, but you really are a mere babe, Amara. Such a sweet, young thing, fresh and full of hope. It's beautiful to see. And I don't want to take that from you. But innocence can't last. We all have to grow up and make impossible choices, fumbling along as best we can, learning to live with things we don't want at all." She let go and offered me back the sketchbook and the note. I tucked it inside for safekeeping, fear making my hands shake, mirroring the way hers did with the frailty of old age.

"Look, Amara, I know you don't care about the cause. It's obvious that you're not political. It's not about justice or any kind of lofty principle for you. You just want your mother back. That's why you're here, and that's why you just might agree to join us and do this thing. I get it. But do you? Don't you wonder what happened to Rake's mother? Or all the others who've gone missing? What do you think happens to them?"

I thought about the rumors. People said a lot of things. But how could I ever know what was real and what was just salacious gossip and scared conjecture? Half the things people said were too outrageous to be true.

"Haven't you thought about it?"

"Yes, of course, but…I don't know what to believe."

People disappeared a lot in the Freelands. It was a rough area. Anything could happen to anyone. But there were whispers. About the Farm, for example. Hydra didn't want virile New Blood men in the enclave—only young girls and twinky boys ever made it in as BabyDolls, while older men and women could work as Drudges, kept out of sight and doing the most dangerous, dirty, or labor-intensive jobs. Men were encouraged to volunteer for the Farm, supposedly doing manual labor in agriculture, but no one ever came back from the enclave, and some people said the Farm didn't exist. That it was just a way to siphon off the strongest members of the borderlands so we couldn't rise up against them. What happened to the volunteers was the subject of wild speculation. Some thought there really was a Farm, and they were worked to death on it. Others thought they were forced into some kind of peasant army. A few thought they were simply killed. Or experimented on. Lots of theories made their rounds, some too disturbing to give credence to, like the theory that so many older women disappeared because they were abducted and forced to be "Hot Tots," a revolting moniker for the disturbing idea that perhaps old age was a kind of erotic fetish for some in the enclave, now that it was rare in their world.

"I just don't know," I said.

"Well, we know for certain that increasing numbers of us are being trafficked. The question is why. Labor exploitation? Sexual exploitation? Scientific exploitation? All of the above?"

I could see she was getting worked up, and it reminded me of Rake. How she'd go off on rants against the powers that were. I'd usually tune out, but this time, for once, I tried to tune in.

"I lived to see gender parity in my lifetime. I'm not suffering anyone to call me any kind of 'baby' ever again. They make life out here so hard, have us so desperate, that we beg for the privilege of being chattel in there. Where you can either be infantilized and glorified or demonized and degraded, depending on your relative youth and beauty. Youth and beauty. That's the Old Blood wet dream. Eternal youth and beauty. Which they think means endless happiness. Though it doesn't." An orange tabby cat jumped up and settled on her lap. She began to stroke him thoughtfully.

"I'm eighty-two years old, Amara. I've earned every one of these wrinkles and the right to serve as Crone. I'm a veritable font of wisdom over here, isn't that right, Mr. Muffins?" The cat purred its assent, and she continued, seemingly buoyed by his vote of confidence. "So you can believe me, young lady, when I tell you that there are some things that we only learn through aging, through its struggles and gifts. They'd have us believe that we're useless past a certain age. No longer fuckable. No longer breed-able. No longer contributing to the economy. What's the point of the elderly? They can't be used. But that's the secret to our power. We belong only to ourselves, at last. Oh, I was young and foolish once. Worrying about others' opinions of me when I should have been worrying about *my* opinion of me. But eventually, I reached a certain age, and frankly, now I don't give a flying fuck what anyone thinks of me. That's real freedom. What a burden to lay down."

I laughed, charmed. It always amused me to hear older people swear and tell racy stories. She fed off my laughter and kept going.

"And so here I am, growing old as disgracefully as possible, teaching the younger generations methods of sabotage and espionage. Turns out, I'm very good at plotting. Who knew?" She cackled, and I found myself joining in, momentarily forgetting my problems and the immensity of the decisions I was facing. It felt good to let go of my worries and lose myself in the allure of another person's stories, if only for a moment.

I ate a cookie, suddenly ravenous, as she finished her second cup of tea, both of us comfortably silent and contemplative for a while.

"Okay, enough of my blathering. Follow me," she commanded, dumping the cat and getting to her feet. I handed her the cane and followed her back into the living room, which was full of cats once more. This time, they didn't scatter at my entrance but simply eyed me with varying degrees of curiosity and suspicion from an array of cozy spots and hiding places. The Crone took a hardcover book off a shelf. She faced me, stroking the book's cover as she spoke.

"You have a choice, Amara. You can go into this blind, give up the chance to bear your own biological children, hope you blunder your way into finding your mother, and then somehow miraculously manage to outwit Hydra surveillance to escape the clutches of corporate ownership and escape back to the Freelands. The odds aren't good. But you're young, determined, resourceful. It's not *utterly* impossible." Her eyes, like her words, didn't offer much hope. "Or you can take this." She held out the book. "Are you familiar with it?"

I glanced at the cover and read, *The Picture of Dorian Gray*, by someone named Oscar Wilde. I shook my head.

The Crone sighed. "Too bad. I hate when my humor is lost. Ah well, it is the plight of the clever to have their brilliance missed all too frequently. It's fine. You'll have plenty of time to become familiar with it on the inside, and I'm sure you'll figure out why I chose it. This will be your third personal item and your means of communication. You have to be very careful with it." Her eyes sharpened, and I instinctively stood more at attention. "Don't ever read it around others. Show little interest in it. Connect it in no way to your mother. Say your friend Rake gave it to you. Show more interest in your sketchbook."

I nodded, and she continued. "When you turn the pages, you must only ever touch the outer blank edges, never any of the writing. Like this." She demonstrated, and I nodded again, wondering why I needed to be told how to turn the pages of a book.

"It's made of special nano-paper," she said, answering my unspoken question. "The writing is wired to send signals to the Defiance. So to communicate, you will need to be patient and spell out the message using words from the story, tracing your fingertips over each word in sequence. Like this." She demonstrated once more but on the cover this time. "Do you understand?"

"Yes. I think so," I answered, though I was pretty sure I didn't, really.

"Unfortunately, it's a one-way form of communication, but we're confident that it will escape Hydra scrutiny." There was a pause, and she hobbled closer, bringing the book. "This is a gift of great value and great responsibility, Amara. We'll be investing significant resources into you. Your intel has to be worth it."

That made my heartbeat speed up. "What if it isn't?" I couldn't help but ask.

"We'll place you in a position to be successful, an Old Blood council member's home, if possible. They often have mini-labs in their homes, and who knows what else. I believe you can do it. You have the motivation, and we'll provide the means. Now it's just a matter of choice." She held out the book. "Let me be brutally clear, Amara. Your childhood ends here. You do this, you step into the ring, and there's no going back."

The book wavered slightly between us in her shaky hands.

But I didn't take it right away. I hesitated.

Then I thought of my mother's smile, its warm, tender acceptance of everything I was and might be, the exasperated, patient amusement that streamed from her eyes when she looked at me, her only child, her headstrong, sensitive, wayward daughter. The quiet one with her head in the clouds and her heart on her sleeve. Maria's girl.

I took the book.

"Welcome to the Defiance, my dear."

CHAPTER THREE

Promised Walks Never Taken

Sometimes, when my emotions got too big and threatened to overwhelm me, I managed this trick of hyperfocusing on something practical and just concentrated all my energy on doing it step by step. It helped me not to freak out. So when the Crone suggested I go home and get my things in order, I grasped the idea with a gratitude born of desperation. There was so much I was trying not to think about. The dangers. The whys. The hows. The what-ifs. It was a lot of anxiety to keep at bay. But I could get my house in order. I could make arrangements for the business. That would keep me occupied for a few hours, at least.

So I left Nana. And Rake too. The Crone said she needed to speak to her but would send her along shortly, and I didn't question it. The hyperfocus had already started, and I trusted Rake would show up. She always did.

I was rummaging through my mother's closet when I heard our door open, and her familiar tread made its way closer. She stood in the doorway, arms crossed tightly, and just stared at me, her face clearly upset.

She didn't say anything, so I started rambling nervously. "Rake, I need you to look after the food cart till we get back. You know what to do. I know you probably don't want to cook, but I'm sure Mrs. Garcia would be happy to do the day-to-day cooking. You can figure out a reasonable split of the profits."

Rake continued to lean in the doorway, unnervingly silent and staring. It made me ramble faster.

"And Mr. Hernandez. You can't forget about him. He doesn't have anyone to look after him. You know how my mom is. Oh, and the

Miller twins. Don't forget that they run errands in exchange for a meal on Sundays. Just make up anything for them to do."

Her eyes narrowed.

I rushed on, "I know you know all this. Sorry. I just…you will help, right?"

There was a long pause. It seemed like Rake was weighing what to say, which was totally unlike her. The gravity was totally unlike her. It was all very unsettling. "This is a terrible idea, Amara. I don't think you should do this."

For some reason, her words sparked anger in me. Perhaps because they touched on my own secret fears. Was this a terrible idea? "I need your help right now. I don't need you second-guessing me." I couldn't keep my voice from rising in volume and pitch.

Her voice rose to match mine. "Amara, think about it. There is so much you don't know. And so much that could go wrong."

"You and my mother…you never believe in me. You never give me any credit," I fumed, turning my back on her and pulling items furiously from the closet.

"That's not true."

"It is!" I was already surrounded by a mess of my mother's random belongings, but I kept delving through the contents of the closet, looking for nothing and everything, just wanting to feel close to her, to see what she'd held on to over the years. "Look, either help me or leave me alone. I can't handle this right now."

She scoffed. "You can never handle anything, but sure, go take on the entire Old Blood establishment. I'm sure that will work out well."

I didn't exactly mean to throw a shoe at her head.

But I threw a shoe at her head.

Evidently, she had good reflexes because she batted it away and laughed. "*Now* you're going to get all redhead-passionate on me?" It was an old joke of hers that I was the most dispassionate redhead she had ever met and didn't I know that there were stereotypes I was duty bound to uphold. I felt a pull to join her in the laughter, to let go of the rage and fall back into our usual, joking dynamic, but I just couldn't do it. I was too wound up. Her comment just proved my point.

"Look, Rake, I mean it. Help or leave. I need to focus."

She crossed the room, stepping carefully around my mother's things that lay scattered about the floor. Her proximity shook me up, stirred unbidden, unclear feelings I didn't want to feel, making it harder to remember my focus.

"And what about what I need, Amara?" Her voice was softer. I could smell her skin, she was so near to me. "It might be our last night together. Don't you care about that?"

I started to tremble and avoided looking at her. I turned back to the closet and redoubled my efforts to focus on the practical. There were things to accomplish. Things that had to be done. My hands shook as I fumbled around in there while trying not to think or feel. I could sense her waiting. And her body close behind me. "Of course I care. Of course I do. But…I…I just can't afford to think about that right now," I said without turning to face her.

A hard note creeped into her voice. "Now is all we have, Amara. Since you're set on doing this foolish thing. How long do you expect me to wait for you to think about it?"

Her tone irritated me, and I was almost grateful to have annoyance return and save me from more confusing feelings. I whipped around and let my annoyance show. "What are you even talking about?"

Rake seemed surprised but irritated too. She muttered, "Never mind," and started to leave the room, then changed her mind. "You are so unbelievably selfish, Amara. You know that, right? It's always about you. Maria and I bend over backward for you constantly."

"What? Leave my mom out of it, first of all. And second of all, what are you even saying? Bullshit. Like when?"

"Oh, I don't know," she said sarcastically, "maybe like always protecting you and making things easy for you. And avoiding upsetting you because you're 'sensitive.' Not to mention doing all the practical hard stuff because you're 'artsy' so you can't live in reality. We orbit you like you're the goddamn sun," she said, yelling outright by the end.

"Clearly not," I yelled right back. "My mom fucking left me!"

"She left *for* you, you fool. And you're throwing her sacrifice away."

The words were so big, so full of frightening possibility that we both stopped. It seemed like they echoed in the space between us, all but vibrating with tension, pain, fear and longing. I let the words in. Unwelcome guests in my mind. I considered them as objectively as I could manage.

"No," I said after a moment. "What child wants money more than their parents? Maybe abused ones, but not children with loving parents. And if Maria knew anything, it was how to love. You know it too. She wouldn't do this, Rake. Something is wrong here. Someone forced her, or she's being blackmailed, or she's keeping something from me, but she didn't do this willingly. I know it. I just know."

I started crying and buried my face in one of my mom's old sweaters. I felt Rake's hand, tentative on my arm, and I pushed her away. "No. Really. You have to decide. Either be here and help me or leave me alone. I can't have you here making me doubt myself. I'm fucking terrified," I said, bursting afresh into new sobs. "Maybe you're right, okay? Maybe I am selfish and foolish and can't handle things, but *I'm going to do this*. I have to. So I need you. I need you to help me believe in myself. That I can do this and that I'll see you and my mother again. That it's not all just a crazy gamble where I might just lose everything." I threw myself at her, hysterically repeating, "I'm freaking out. I'm freaking out, Rake! I'm freaking the fuck out."

She held me close and murmured reassurances while I spent my tears. She was taller and older and stronger, warm and familiar and comforting. I drew strength from her. Eventually, the panic subsided, and a weary semblance of calm replaced it.

"How can I help?" she asked.

"I don't know," I said, sniffling and wiping my face. "Can you stay here and look after our place too? I know I'm asking a lot…"

"No, it's nothing. Of course I can."

"I just don't want someone taking our things. The neighbors will watch out for a while, but if they think I'm not coming back…"

"Yep, I'm on it."

I looked around at the total disarray of the bedroom. "I wish I could bring something of hers."

"You can. You get to bring three personal items into the enclave."

"But the Crone gave me something to communicate with them, and that only leaves me two items. I can't live without my sketchbook and pencils."

"The pencils count as an item?"

"Yeah."

She considered for a minute. "Hmm…what if we create a new pencil case out of one of Maria's old scarves or something? You've got sewing supplies around here somewhere, right?"

My heart leapt, and I bounced with excitement, grabbing Rake and crushing her to me in a grateful embrace. "That's brilliant."

She laughed and disentangled herself. "Okay, you find me the supplies, and I'll make the pencil case while you whip us up something to eat, please. I'm starving. Aren't you?"

I realized I hadn't eaten all day, except those cookies at the Crone's place. No wonder I was so volatile. I was both physically ravenous and emotionally overwrought.

I threw something together for us, watching Rake from the corner of my eyes. She liked sewing. It seemed like an odd interest for someone who looked like her, but I knew it was because her mother had taught her. She could do all these complex embroidery techniques and everything. If anyone razzed her about it, she'd say something like, "I'm a complex, multidimensional person. Don't try to box me in," and wink playfully.

I paused and really looked at her for the first time today. She was standing by our rickety table, the one I'd had my mental breakdown under just this morning. She was standing and sort of swaying, humming to herself as she focused on sewing the seams of the pencil case. Her hair was tucked behind her ear. She was wearing a faded black band shirt with a man's formal gray vest over it, plus ripped black jeans and combat boots. Her tattoo was showing, and I couldn't stop myself from coming over and rolling up her shirt sleeve farther to inspect it. She looked at me curiously, paused mid-stitch.

She had a lot of tattoos, but this one was distinctive. Large and intricate and beautiful. A turquoise and tangerine paradise fish on her bicep, swimming amidst roses and skulls. "Why a fish?" I blurted without explaining what I meant.

"They eat hydra, dummy. Hydra don't have many natural enemies."

"Why didn't you tell me you were part of the Defiance?" It was hard to keep the hurt out of my voice.

"Well, it's not something I'm supposed to advertise. Besides, you have all of zero interest in politics. You zone out whenever I say anything even mildly political."

I couldn't argue with that. Though it did seem like a stupidly risky form of advertising to ink your resistance on a visible part of your body. Maybe Hydra didn't know the symbol. Did they even care what we did out here? What threat did the Defiance really pose? I had no clue. And yet, I'd thrown my lot in with them, hook, line and sinker.

Rake was looking at me strangely, almost smirking, and I was aware I had been running my fingers along her arm, stroking her tattoo. I blushed and backed away, returning to our meal preparation while all frazzled.

She had that effect on women, I reminded myself sternly. Her tattoos were all courtesy of an older woman she dallied with. The poor thing was mad for her. Would do anything for her. What did Rake do for her? The question bothered me. I knew she did odd jobs for her. Probably flattered her? Definitely flirted with her. Maybe more? It was hard to say.

I grabbed our plates and went to bring them to the table, then started as I turned to see Rake removing her shirt.

I was surprised I didn't drop the plates.

She was matter-of-fact. And thankfully, wearing an undershirt. A very tight undershirt.

"Um…uh…what are you doing?" I bumbled my way to the table.

"Continuing to be brilliant," she replied, taking the scissors to her shirt and carefully cutting out a piece. Intrigued, I came closer and saw that she was removing the word "Believe" from the band name: The Make-Believe Facts. "Now you can have a piece of me and a piece of Maria on your new pencil case," she declared triumphantly.

It was sweet. Resourceful and creative. I smiled and passed her a plate. She motioned for me to set it on the table and continued her work. I sat and ate, watching her. The new pencil case was made from brilliant scarlet material that used to be mother's favorite shirt. Rake was creating crazy, mismatched, different-sized stitches to affix the patch to the front of the case. She used various colors of thread, and the overall effect was sort of zany and imperfectly striking. It was really her. I loved it.

"You're literally giving me the shirt off your back," I teased.

"Anything for you," she retorted without missing a beat, and my food stuck in my throat as I realized how true this was. Everything she'd said to me in anger, everything about bending over backward, it was all true. She would give me anything. There was part of me that knew that. Had always known it. For the first time, I really acknowledged how there were all these women vying for any little piece of Rake that she might be willing to share, and meanwhile, here I was with all of her on offer, unwilling to accept it. Why? What was wrong with me?

I shook my head to dispel the thoughts. This wasn't the time to think about these things. It was complicated with Rake. Always had been. Besides, I reminded myself for the zillionth time, she made for a terrible girlfriend.

Or did she? She never made promises to anyone. They knew what they would get. Just some lighthearted, indulgent attention from a self-confessed free spirit. Right?

It didn't matter. I mean, how narcissistic and foolish would it be to think that things would "be different" if we were ever to cross over into something more? People didn't change. They were who they were. And Rake might have been a loyal friend, but she was also a relentless flirt.

I finished my meal and convinced myself to let it go. Rake wolfed down her food, then dragged me back to my mother's room. "Okay, so we could rip out an old zipper and sew it in, but that would just be losing the opportunity to sneak another souvenir into the enclave." She went for a box in the closet and held it out expectantly. I waited for an explanation. "You don't remember this box? You'll remember plenty when I open it," she promised, tearing off the lid dramatically, then reaching inside with a flourish to present…my old tap shoes.

"Oh my God," I squealed, grabbing them from her. "I loved these."

"I know. You drove the whole neighborhood crazy. Where did they even come from?"

"Some guy. I can't remember his name. He traded with Mom for something. I don't know the details. I just remember how happy I was to have clicky shoes."

"Clicky shoes." She laughed.

"I still like clicky shoes," I said. "Shoes that make noise when you walk. Like those red pumps Sophia wears." I turned the tiny shoes over in my hands, memories flooding in. "God. I made up so many dumb dance routines with these. I was such a dork. Why didn't you stop me?"

"It was cute. You amused everybody. I was thinking we could use one of the laces to tie the pencil case. It'll remind you of happier, dorkier days." She smiled and held my eyes with hers. Her eyes were a deep, dark brown color. I always felt funny when I looked into them too long, but today, I did. I smiled back, holding her gaze for once.

"That's perfect." For a few seconds, I forgot that I was sad and scared. "I wish they still fit."

"Oh, I can finagle you some tap shoes if you'll put on a show for me," she promised. I started to laugh and protest, but she was already digging through my mom's things. There was never any talking Rake out of a ridiculous idea once she got it in her head, and so fifteen minutes later, we were in my kitchen, and I had coins duct-taped to the bottom of my shoes. It worked surprisingly well, and with some teasing and cajoling, between bouts of laughter, I managed to remember and perform a few simple moves.

"Oh my God. Do you remember that routine you forced me to join you in?" She groaned.

"For Mrs. Flores? Yes." The memory made me burst out laughing, and I forced her to come stand beside me as we tried to recreate it all over again. We couldn't remember much besides the fact that she was supposed to stand next to me, all sad and forlorn in her regular, boring, non-clicky shoes, while I tap danced my little heart out with lively enthusiasm all around her. The straight man comedy to my clown. It was still hilarious, and we both cracked up heartily, back to our usual, easy connection.

She twirled me, and then we were dancing. Like, slow dancing. Her hand on the small of my back and my hand in hers, and the transition was both too abrupt and very smooth.

"What are you doing?" I asked, uneasily aware of her clunky belt pushing into my pelvis. The swell of her chest next to mine. The black bra strap poking out on her tanned shoulder.

She leaned in close to whisper, "I thought maybe we could dance like grown-ups now."

"I…I don't really know how," I admitted nervously.

"Funny. Because you're already doing it," she replied. "There's nothing special to it. Just keep on following my lead."

She was so smooth. I didn't know whether to roll my eyes or melt.

I let her lead me around the small kitchen, fighting the urge to run, fighting the urge to give in. She smelled…amazing. Warm and familiar but exciting at the same time. Her hair tickled my cheek. Her hips moved with mine. I felt hot, jittery, and light-headed. I wasn't sure I liked it.

Okay, I was totally sure I liked it, but I didn't *want* to like it. Not now, especially. I had to leave tomorrow, for God's sake. I broke away awkwardly.

"Okay, um, thanks," I mumbled, putting space between us. I could feel my face burning. "Aren't you cold? You look cold. You should put your shirt on."

It sounded inane the moment it came out of my mouth, but it was too late. To my mortification, Rake seemed to realize what was flustering me, and it only encouraged her. "Cold? That dancing's got me all hot and bothered. I should take more off. You should join me." She made to peel off her undershirt, and I ran from the kitchen to the sounds of her amused laughter. "I'm just teasing, Amara. Come back."

"That's all right. I'll…I'll just give you time to get decent," I sputtered.

"Relax, Amara. You're such a prude."

"I am not," I said indignantly, coming back into the kitchen just to prove myself.

"You are too. You run away at the slightest hint of anything sexy."

"I do not," I insisted, incensed. "I've listened to talk about sex a million times."

"I've *never* talked about sex with you. Not once. I know better. You can't even handle mild flirtation."

"I can too handle it. I…I just don't appreciate it." What? What was I saying?

"What do you mean?" she asked, eyes narrowed, a hint of hurt in her voice.

I rushed on, not thinking, angry at being painted a prude. "I just mean that maybe I don't want you to treat me like all the random girls you fool around with until you're bored and move on."

There was an awkward silence. A superlong silence. Like, a "please say anything," superlong, and awkward silence.

"I've never treated you like anything but a fucking princess, and you know it," she finally said. Clearly pissed.

There was more awkward silence, but it was shorter this time because my fuse was shorter than it had ever been in my entire life. I was clearly out of control and out of my mind. "Well, maybe I don't want to be your fucking princess."

I didn't know why I said it; it was the biggest lie of my life, and I knew it.

But she didn't.

She didn't say anything. Just stared at me a second, a quick succession of emotions crossing her face, then turned and walked away.

Let her go, I thought. I had to let her go. Maybe that was why I'd said it, after all. Because I needed to push her away if I was going to do this tomorrow. If I was going to walk away from her and everything I'd ever known here in the Barrio.

But the second I heard our front door close, I knew I'd fucked up. I didn't mean it. I ran to the door and shouted for her.

But if she heard me, she didn't come back.

I fell apart. Ended up sobbing in my mother's bed, surrounded by her things, wondering how I was ever going to find it in me to do this thing tomorrow.

Night fell. I heard the door creak open and sprang up in the bed, straining to hear the familiar footsteps. Rake lingered in the doorway to the bedroom, and my heart all but leapt out of my chest. I should have apologized right away, but the first, illogical words to blurt out of my mouth were, "I wasn't crying!" An obvious lie, as tears were clearly streaming down my face.

"I wasn't crying, either." She removed her boots and crawled into bed with me. There was nothing presumptuous about it. It felt sweet, like when we were little girls sleeping over. The scent of marijuana wafted toward me as she turned to face me, careful to keep her distance until I pulled her close, wrapping myself around her, trying to convince myself that she was really here. Her hair fell across her face, and I tucked it behind her ear, then noticed that her face was wet.

"You *were* crying! You never cry."

She smiled wryly. "Congratulations, Amara. You are officially the first girl to break my heart."

We lay looking at each other across the pillows, so much unsaid throbbing between us.

I didn't think. I leaned over and pressed my lips tentatively to hers. They were soft and perfect. It felt perfect. Like something precious received after a long and difficult wait.

She started a little at first, no doubt confused by my "go away, come here" vibes all night. But she quickly embraced the shift in energy and kissed me back with the utmost tenderness.

I thought all this time that us growing up together and being best friends meant that we shouldn't be together, that we risked ruining something by making it romantic. But maybe it was just the opposite. Maybe I was always meant to be with her. In some strange cosmic way, we felt promised to each other. So maybe not making it romantic risked losing something rare and special. Something most people only ever dreamed of having.

She shifted her body so that she was pretty much lying on top of me, and it felt nothing like little girls sleeping over. Her mouth grew hungrier and her hands more searching.

I grew more conflicted. Why was this always my response to her? I wanted to go there with her. I did, more than anything, but I wasn't as experienced as her, and I didn't want my first time to be…like this. Rushed. Mixed up in loss and fear. I might never see her again, though. That made me want to stop, and it made me want to keep going. I was muddled up again and started crying.

She backed off. "Sorry. Was that too much? I'm so sorry."

"No, I—" I cried harder, embarrassed and inarticulate.

"I don't want to pressure you into anything. I should have let you lead. I just got carried away. I'm so sorry," she continued.

"No, it's fine. I like kissing you. I'm just all mixed up. I don't know how to explain it."

She cracked a stunning smile, and her teasing manner returned. "Hmm…so…you like kissing me, huh?" She waggled her eyebrows ridiculously, and her triumphant smirk charmed me into stopping crying. It was part of Rake's magic that she could shift energies so effectively. Our banter always made me feel safe. It returned me to myself, and I was able to pull myself together enough to tease her back.

"Well, don't get too cocky about it," I warned. "I haven't kissed many people, so maybe it's just the novelty."

She laughed. Her eyes twinkled, and her smile grew even more stunning, if that was possible. I basked in its glow, happy for the way we always seemed to be able to pull each other back into connection.

She stroked my hair thoughtfully. "Listen, today was a big, crazy day with big, crazy feelings, and tomorrow's going to be more of the same. It makes sense to feel mixed up. What if tonight, I just stay here and hold you? No more funny business. We can just snuggle, and we'll be together until you have to leave tomorrow. Sound good?"

I hesitated. "I believe I mentioned that I like kissing you. Does kissing count as funny business? Because I want more of that."

Her eyes twinkled some more. "Woman, I will kiss you all night long if that's what you want."

I did want that.

And she kept her promise.

Chapter Four

Into the Next Room

I overslept. The sheer exhaustion of the past few days, the extreme sadness, the extreme happiness, it was all too much. I woke groggy and confused, with an unclear nagging sensation bothering me until…I remembered! My mom. Rake. The day ahead. I shot straight up in bed and looked around wildly for Rake, but she was nowhere to be seen. I jumped out of bed and ran around looking for her but couldn't find her.

Then I saw the note. *Another fucking note!* I wanted to scream, but I stumbled to the table instead, still not fully awake, and tried to focus my eyes enough to read what it said.

You're the one, stupid.
So don't die.
I'll be here waiting,
Rake

Then I did scream.

And ripped it up.

Then freaked out that I'd ripped it up.

My first and only love note, of sorts.

And so I found myself on my knees under the table again, trying to pull myself together, gathering torn bits of paper. Why the fuck was everyone I loved leaving me with only a note? What the hell was going on?

I placed the pieces on the table, then went rummaging through drawers for glue. I passed a mirror on the way and startled at my own reflection. I looked wrecked, alarmingly haggard with crazy bedhead. I had to get it together if I was going to pass inspection as a potential BabyDoll. I looked at the time, and panic rose inside. I had at least a three-hour bike ride to the right gate. I glanced out the window and saw that it was pouring rain.

"*Fuck*," I screamed, then grabbed a dish from the drying rack and threw it against the wall. It smashed with satisfying intensity, so I threw a few more, realizing I could really get into this whole passionate redhead thing.

Once there was a sufficiently impressive pile of broken shards, I felt the panic subside. I could think again. *Okay, focus. One step at a time. Write a list.* Lists always soothed me.

I found a scrap of paper and methodically wrote each step I needed to take today. I stared at the tidy list with relief. Nothing to it. Just cross each item off in order. That was how I would get through. Taking care of my physical needs first, I sat at the table to glue Rake's torn note into my sketchbook. I drew a bubble around it, adding a gleam of color around the words "the one." It was a waste of time. I mean, I could have done it later, but it felt like the act of closure I needed. Only afterward did I realize I couldn't risk taking it into the enclave, so I tore the page from my sketchbook and tucked it under my mattress.

But I needed to leave Rake a few words too. How did I get sucked into this horrible note-leaving business? I thought about leaving her with nothing. She'd come here, see the smashed plates, and read into how I felt about her note. But that wasn't the last feeling I wanted her to have from me. I knew she was terrible with good-byes. She probably couldn't handle it. That thought cheered me slightly, to think that were some things that even the uber-capable Rake couldn't handle. It pleased me even more that this thing had to do with her feelings for me.

I grabbed a slip of paper and stared at it blankly. What could I write? The words I wanted to say felt too big, too personal and intense to put on scrap of paper. She said I was "the one." Whenever I thought about that, I got warm inside and happy. I should have given her something similar. I wanted to leave her with that feeling. But I just couldn't bring myself to write out the words. It felt awkward and strange to think that she would read my deepest feelings when I wasn't even here to see and share in her reaction. In the end, I scribbled:

I'm coming back. Save me kisses.
Amara

It wasn't enough. But it would have to do.

Because I had a mission to complete.

❖

On a good day, the bike ride should have taken me three hours. But it was not a good day. My body was wrecked, it was pissing down rain, and the rickety bicycle that the Crone had given me was a complete piece of shit. I'd wrapped the two books I was carrying in plastic, tucked inside my handbag, but I was still totally paranoid that they'd be ruined by the time I arrived. I kept stopping and running under apartment stoops to check how they were holding up. *They* were fine. *I* wasn't. I was worried I was going to be too late for today's inspection. I'd gotten a late start, and though I vaguely knew where I was going, I was worried I'd take a wrong turn.

I should have been thanking my lucky stars for the rain. The rain kept folks inside. But when it let up, I was relieved. At least until I really looked around. The East End was rough. Everyone knew that. But it was one thing to hear about it and another thing to see it. While shivering and soaking wet on a bicycle, a piece-of-shit bicycle that nonetheless seemed to be attracting far too much attention. I pedaled harder and kept my eyes peeled, very much aware of the paper money stuffed in my bra, money the Crone had given me to buy my way out of trouble should it find me. I'd left my mom's money with Rake.

A man hung his head out a window and yelled something incomprehensible at me. I sped up.

Nestled into my bra with my left boob were Hydra bills, uncomfortably pokey. These were for *real* emergencies. Nestled into my bra with my right boob was an assortment of other, less valuable currencies. These were paper, worn and crumpled, meant for minor emergencies. A ton of currencies from the various post-Dissolution states circulated in the Freelands. We weren't picky. Desperate people took anything, and someone was always ready to make a deal.

A bunch of young guys hanging out on an apartment stoop stood and started approaching down the litter-strewn street. Typical street rats but of the dodgier, East End variety. "Hey. Hey, cutie. Slow down," one of them yelled.

"You're new," another said. "Stop and chat a second, why don't ya?"

They spread out, blocking the street. My heartbeat sped up, and I decided to veer to the right, trying to speed past them on the sidewalk, but one managed to grab the strap of my bag slung crossways over my body. I was forced to stop and forced to commit my first truly violent act. I mean, throwing shoes and tableware in frustration really didn't count in quite the same way as a vicious palm strike to the nose. Turns out that Mr. Brown, my old self-defense teacher, was right. It *was* an effective getaway move. The guy's nose exploded in blood, and I took off, freaked out equally by the blood splatter and the enraged gang of guys now screaming obscenities and chasing me. I quickly decided this was right-boob kind of trouble, reached into my bra, grabbed the bills, and threw them into the air. Turned out, Crone Nana was right too. The guys couldn't resist free money and stopped chasing me to chase the bills, giving me enough time to put some distance between us.

I was so freaked out and hyped up on adrenaline that I got all turned around. I knew I was getting more and more lost, but I couldn't bring myself to stop or even slow. The only thing that felt safe was speed.

Eventually, rationality returned, and I pulled into a side alley to catch my breath and get my bearings. I used my shirt to wipe the blood off my face and hands as best I could. The blood bothered me. Where was the rain now to wash it away?

I saw movement out of the corner of my eye and tensed. But it was just a shabby, middle-aged woman combing shamelessly through the trash strewn about. She looked at me shrewdly, evaluating. I held her gaze and waited, deciding her threat level too.

"Got anything you can spare?" she asked.

I felt unsettled looking at her. She was my mother's age. Reduced to begging and scavenging for survival. Did she have a family? Loved ones? What was her story? Did it matter? "I might," I said. "Can you tell me how to get to the East End gate?"

She nodded like my appearance here made sense now. "You're applying?"

I nodded back.

"You better hurry."

I wasn't sure if she was referring to the danger of the gate closing or to the people starting to come out after the rain. She tilted her chin up and to the left behind me. I turned. At the intersection, I could just make out the corner of a giant, weather-beaten billboard with a BabyDoll logo.

"Follow the signs. Straight on that road a few blocks, then take a right." She started to approach, and I stiffened. She froze in her tracks. Shame coursed through me for making my fear and revulsion so obvious. She was helping me. She wasn't going to hurt me or to try to take the bike.

At least, I didn't think so. But I couldn't afford to be wrong.

"Thanks," I said, turning to go. She must have thought I was scamming her, taking her help and giving nothing in return. I saw resignation on her face as she accepted yet another of life's disappointments.

I never got to see her expression when I threw all the left-boob bills behind me. But I liked to imagine it. Her surprise and joy at the unexpected windfall. Money like that was a life-changer, and I had to get rid of it before reaching the gate anyway.

Before I knew it, I was approaching the gate with its electric fence topped by barbed wire running along the edge of the street. I followed it and the vandalized billboards to an imposing concrete building. It was only a few stories high, but it was strikingly clean and neat. A perfect square with a recessed indent along the right-hand side where an impossibly tall black door stood, the only feature on a block of unblemished concrete. It looked like nothing in the Freelands. It was too perfect and orderly. Freakishly impersonal. Two guards clad in jungle green uniforms lounged around outside it. One was talking with a woman at the gate, and the other was watching.

I took a second to compose myself, knowing I was not at my best, sweaty and disheveled from the long ride, sporting an outrageously bloodstained shirt. I patted my hair down and arranged my clothes as best I could.

I'd honestly never cared much about how I looked. Perhaps that was weird for someone so attuned to beauty in the world, but it was the truth. I'd always just figured that I was passably good-looking. Though I loved to stare at the world around me, it made me uncomfortable to look at myself too long. My mom's friend used to chide me that I'd be a knockout if I just tried a little and owned it, but owned what? I never understood what she meant by that. Besides, I didn't want to knock anybody out. I wanted to be unnoticed so I could be the one noticing, undisturbed by other people's wants and expectations.

And now here I was, asking to be noticed. Noticed in a big way. A no-going-back kind of big way. This was it.

I ran through my options once more. I could go home and meet back up with Rake and try to live without my mother, never knowing what had happened to her or why she'd left or how she was doing. Just try to live around a giant, gaping question mark the way I'd watched Rake struggle to do.

Or I could "believe," as Rake's T-shirt patch urged. I could trust in myself and the Defiance. Use the information I had that Rake never did. Get in. Get the truth. Find my mom. Get out. Do a little light espionage while I was at it. No big deal, I lied to myself as I stepped toward the gate, leaving the bike behind.

The guard was laughing but not in a happy way. "How many times you gonna try to pull this, Jennica? You ain't got no teeth, for Christ's sake. No one's ever called you a doll in your whole pathetic life. Not even as a real baby. Now piss off."

The woman persisted. "That don't matter, mister. They fix up your teeth in there, I heard."

They noticed me, both looking up from their conversation. The woman was rough-looking indeed. Seemed drug-addled. What some folks called a "Pop Tart." Pop being the street name for one of the nastier drugs pushed these days. She stood no chance of passing inspection.

"Well, well. What do we have here?" the guard asked, perking up. He yelled over his shoulder, "Hey, Shirls, c'mere. Got a last-minute contender."

The woman in line before me glared while the guard openly ogled me. He was joined by a second guard, this one a woman. "Jesus, what happened to you?" she said, staring at my shirt.

"Sorry for the state of my clothes. I…I ran into trouble on the way." I didn't know how this interaction was supposed to go, so I figured I'd be polite, give minimal information, and just follow their lead.

"Bet you did. Bet you did. A pretty girl like yourself," the male guard replied.

My heart leapt at his words. It was a good sign that he'd called me "pretty."

"Whaddya think, Shirley?" he said. "A no-brainer, right?"

The female guard scrutinized me silently, then made me turn in a circle. She asked me to smile wide. I complied. "Yep. She'll clean up good," she finally concluded. She pressed a button on her shoulder lapel. "We got a candidate. Open up."

The woman beside me began to shake. "Aw, come on. Tell them you have two. Tell them you have two."

The male guard pulled a gun from his holster and warned her to leave.

"Aw, come on, mister. I could make it worth your while. Her too, if you like. I could make it worth both your whiles."

The guard fired in the air and spat some particularly insulting epithets her way. She finally backed up but not before shooting me a hateful glance, one full of spite and jealousy. I barely had to time to register it before the gate opened inward.

I stood rooted to the spot, awed. The gateway to Hydra itself was opening before me. Was it the maw of a monster? The path to the promised land? I'd grown up on a steady diet of rumors about this place. So much was imagined about the enclave and so little was known. Now I would know.

"Whaddya, just gonna stand there and stare all day? It's already late. Let's go," one of the guards chided, but I barely registered their words. The giant black door to the concrete block was opening too. Outward. And it didn't run the full length of the building. That was an illusion. I mean, it was still an impressively large door but not designed for giants, as in my first wild thoughts about it. I stumbled forward, guided roughly by a hand on my arm.

Inside, there wasn't much to see. Just tables and scanners. A full body scanner to look for weapons and who knew what else. Thankfully, I'd given away all my cash, so there was nothing to find. There was a vein scanner to begin the process of registering my biometrics for the official ID, the first of my life. They asked me some basic questions—name, age, where I came from—then inspected my belongings. I held my breath as they leafed through the book, but it was just a lot of words to them, and they threw it, disinterested, into yet another scanner. Nothing beeped, to my great relief. The woman flipped through my sketchbook, being nosy more than anything, while the guy emptied the contents of my pencil case onto a table.

The guy literally said, "Aha!" as he picked out the small metal sharpener mixed in with the assorted pencil crayons. I hadn't been trying to hide it, so I just stared back at him. What good were they without a sharpener?

"You fig this counts as a fourth item, Shirls?" he inquired of his partner.

She barely glanced up, seeming quite intrigued by my drawings. She made a dismissive sound and muttered, "Don't be a prick."

"What? I'm not being a prick. Just following regulations. Besides, she might use it as a weapon."

The woman snorted, slammed the sketchbook shut, and threw it into the scanner. "Really, Garrett? What's she gonna do? Sharpen some poor guy's dick off? You worried because yours is that small?" She waggled her pinkie finger at him derisively, and he threw the sharpener at her head, along with a few choice words. Next thing I knew, they were scuffling, fighting for the stupid sharpener, and all I could do was awkwardly stand there and wait it out. This was *not* how I imagined my entry to Hydra would go.

A set of opaque glass doors slid open, and a doctor, a ridiculously handsome doctor in an impeccable white lab coat, stepped into the room. The guards froze mid-scuffle. He raised an eyebrow, and they sort of slunk into the corner like dogs who'd been caught misbehaving by their owner.

"I assume you two buffoons managed the bare minimum of competence and passed her through initial inspection and registration?" They nodded, and he turned to me. "Okay, then, grab your things, and let's get you ready for the next steps." He waited while I nervously rushed about gathering the pencil crayons and sharpener that had scattered all over the floor. Neither the doctor nor the guards exchanged a word. The contempt and resentment in the room was uncomfortably palpable. I rushed to the doctor, dazzled by his good lucks and brilliant white coat. Nothing was really pure white in the Barrio. It gave him an aura of authority and filled me with a kind of unsettled awe.

As we passed through the automated doors, he said, seemingly loud enough for the guards to hear: "Don't mind Tweedledum and Tweedledumber. They're perfectly likeable in small doses. The trick is to limit your exposure so their stupidity remains charmingly quaint."

I couldn't stop myself from glancing back toward the guards to gauge their reaction, and though the door was closing, I could just catch a glimpse of the male guard performing a particularly lewd gesture in the doctor's direction with great gusto. I had to stifle a laugh.

We entered a new room, and the first thing I noticed was a young man standing attentively near the entry. It must have been the doctor's assistant, for the doctor didn't greet him, just gave him orders and passed him something.

"Go tell Elder Sister this one came too late for pickup. I'll drive her over myself. You can go too. I've got this."

The assistant gave me a strange, inscrutable look and quickly departed.

The doctor handed me a gown and told me to throw my old clothes in the garbage. He also told me to shower, put on the gown, then lie on the table, put my feet in the stirrups, and we'd get started.

I'd only ever read about stirrups in books about horses, so I was looking for leather straps by the table to help me get up, wondering why I couldn't just use the little footstool by the bed.

"Just step on the stool and get up," he explained, a note of exasperation creeping into his voice. Great. Now I was going to be considered Tweedledumbest. I complied and lay down, anxiously wondering what the "next steps" were.

He patted the metal wings near the bottom of the table. "Feet in the stirrups."

I started to panic. Did he not know that I was with the Defiance? Was I at the wrong gate? Was this the wrong doctor?

"I…I'm Greek. Did you know that?" I blurted, not weaving the code word into conversation in any kind of subtle way.

"Yes, I heard that we'd be receiving a Greek girl with red hair. Most unusual." He smirked. "We can talk openly. Thankfully, as you're about as subtle as a sledgehammer." He patted the stirrups again. "I still need your feet in the stirrups so I can administer birth control. An old-fashioned IUD. Completely reversible."

"No," I replied. "I don't need birth control. I'm not going to sleep with anyone."

The doctor's scant patience grew thinner. "Yes, you do. You might change your mind, and I'm not risking being exposed for failing at my job of sterilizing incoming girls. Let's get this over with, shall we?"

"No. I…I like girls, anyway. And I'm not going to have sex with anyone."

The doctor lost his patience. "You might not have a choice."

The words were harsh and the idea horrifying. He must have seen the fear on my face because he immediately softened. As much as this guy seemed to soften.

"Look, I don't think you need to worry about that. If they went to all the trouble of getting you here, I'm certain your friends will pull strings to get you in a good house. A safe house. Now come on…" He patted the stirrups yet again, and I reluctantly placed my feet in them. The position was so humiliating and exposed that my legs shook. I tried to focus on breathing steadily, and it helped calm the trembling.

He chattered on while preparing, but it completely undid any sense of calm he had momentarily inspired with his earlier, softened tone.

"It's harsh but better to face realities and know what you're getting into. All these young people come in here all starry-eyed about being BabyDolls, and they don't realize how vulnerable they'll become. You're corporate property now. Your owners can do what they like with you. I could do whatever I like with you."

I stiffened, and he laughed.

"Don't worry. You're safe with me. I'm far too pretty to be straight."

I laughed too, mostly out of surprise and relief. I didn't know how I felt about this guy. He was kind of a dick, but at the same time, he was helping me. Why?

I was about to ask when he said, "It's a good thing for you that folks don't realize I'm gay. They all assume I'm taking advantage of you right now, and that plays into our hand."

The assistant's inscrutable look became much more scrutable.

"Okay, here, we go. This might…Wait. Are you a virgin?"

My face burned, and I mumbled a yes.

"Hmm…and here I thought all the Freeland girls were…well, free."

Okay, now I *did* know how I felt about this guy, even if he was helping me.

"It's okay, I have a smaller speculum around here somewhere."

After fifteen minutes of shocking pain and utter embarrassment, I was all fixed up.

"All right, you lie here and rest for a few minutes while I go fudge some data. I won't be long." He left to the efficient whooshing sound of another automatic door. I listened to his footsteps fade until I couldn't hear them anymore.

Alone with my thoughts, I reviewed the day's events. So many crazy things had happened to me in the last two days. Thinking about it, I started to laugh. It wasn't really funny, but it was that or cry. So I laughed. All by myself in this strange room in a strange place where I knew no one and nothing. What the fuck was I thinking? How was I going to get through this? I felt a cramp and clutched my abdomen. Then I started to stroke my lower belly softly, the way my mom used to do when I was younger and first getting used to period cramps, using my hands to create a soothing rhythm over the place that hurt. Being gentle with my pain. Things my mother taught me.

My mother. All of this was for her. Was she really even here? Would I find her? Could I pull this off, or was it all a colossal mistake?

I stared up at the impersonal ceiling and tried to recall her voice once more. The way she laughed with her customers each day. The slight Spanish accent that made her words bouncier than they needed to be in English. The amused compassion that often colored her words.

My mom used to say that we came into this world alone, and we left it alone. But in between, we could do some good for others. She did so much good for others. She was a good person, through and through. And she wouldn't just abandon me like this.

I looked around the doctor's tidy office and felt my determination grow. I was scared. And there was a lot I didn't yet understand. But I believed. I had to.

So the enclave? It was just another world. And I might have been entering it alone, but I'd be damned if I would leave it alone.

CHAPTER FIVE

Places Where I Fear to Go

Dr. Ahmed—he had finally deigned to tell me his name—seemed in a rush to get me to the training center. Before I knew it, I was on my feet and shuffling through a seemingly endless hallway while clad only in a gray, polka-dot medical gown with thin, disposable booties as footwear. The hallway was like nothing I'd seen before. It was a long tunnel of gray concrete, but it had thin ceiling windows that let in slats of light in a disorienting pattern that made it seem as though the space was tilting.

"Dazzling architecture, isn't it?" Dr. Ahmed said.

"More like confusing and nauseating," I replied.

He scowled, no doubt dismissing my opinion as that of a hopeless philistine. But I was usually into beauty in all its forms, and in another circumstance, I might have been able to appreciate the construction. It was just strange that something that looked so much like an overly simplistic box on the outside could contain such a puzzling use of light on the inside.

Besides, my belly was tender, and fear was making me cranky. I had to walk through alternating stripes of light and shadow, and I was just thinking that I was feeling a bit woozy, when I abruptly vomited.

All over the doctor's shoes.

"I'm so sorry," I squeaked before turning away to lean my head against the cool of the concrete, trying to steady myself.

"It's fine," I heard him say, not without strain. "They pay me the big bucks to deal with people's fluids and meat. It's *fine*."

It did not sound fine.

"So glad you managed to miss your disposable booties and hit my designer shoes instead," he grumbled.

"I'm really sorry," I repeated, already feeling slightly better.

I wasn't sure if was nerves, an aftereffect of the procedure or the architecture, but something had thrown my stomach for a loop.

I glanced up to see him arranging a neat pile of tissues over the vomit. He drew a few more from his bag and gave his shoes one last, disgusted swipe before adding them to the pile. He asked how I was feeling. He was clearly anxious to get going, so I told him I was feeling better. He advised me to look where I wanted to go and ignore the light patterns. It did help, and we managed to make it to his car.

His car. No one had a car in the Freelands. Okay, gang leaders and foreigners might, on a super rare occasion, roll through at their own risk, but almost no one had the means for such a luxury. Who would fix it if something went wrong? How could anyone make sure the electricity would stay on long enough to charge it? How would they keep people from stripping it? I stood staring, probably embarrassingly open-mouthed, until I heard him laugh.

"Red not your color?" he said. "Sybil, change external color to…" He paused, waiting for me to offer a color. When I didn't, he finished off with, "Gold." The car changed color.

I couldn't help getting excited. I'd never been this close to anything so cool. "Purple. *Deep* purple," I clarified, breathlessly expectant.

Sibyl obeyed, and the car was now a wondrous, royal purple.

"Digi-paint. Pretty cool, huh?" he asked as the doors opened, and he slipped inside. He was clearly loving showing off his plaything, but I didn't care. I was loving seeing it. It was…out of this world.

"All the bells and whistles on this beaut," Dr. Ahmed said. He went on for a bit about different things, but I could barely take it in. We were reclining, facing each other as the car drove itself to Dr. Ahmed's destination, the Rosemont Academy. I hoped it was a long ride, as I just wanted to soak in this strange new experience.

I tuned back into his words as an odd smell filled the car.

"Full scent-ual immersion, they call it. What does it remind you of?"

I couldn't place it. There was a whooshing sound and some kind of bird calling. The scent was…clean, fresh, subtly calming and rejuvenating.

"Ocean," he said. "My go-to, end of the day pick-me-up."

I smiled and inhaled deeply. I'd read about the ocean. So this was what it smelled like.

"What's your favorite smell? Maybe I have it. I have over sixty programmed scent profiles. Whole sensory scenes or just one-offs. Pick one. Let's see if I have it." His eyes were sparkling like a little boy's, all excited about his toy.

I gave the question some thought. "Um…maybe fresh coffee?" Though I preferred tea, I associated the smell with my mother, for she never failed to begin her day with a fresh cup.

I could tell I hit on a winner because his eyes lit up. It went on like this for some time. Him demonstrating all the cool features. The vibrating massage. The holo screen. The flashier digi-paint options. It was overwhelming. After a while, I had to turn away and just look out the window. Reorient myself to reality. My new reality anyway. My stomach roiled once more.

"How long until we arrive?" I asked, a resurgence of anxiety starting to course through me. I felt vulnerable once more. Painfully aware of the fact that I was wearing next to nothing, stuck in close proximity with a stranger, heading to God knew what at some kind of corporate cult headquarters.

That last bit was Rake's voice in my head. Maybe a little cynical. But I needed a touch of her cynicism right now in order to prepare myself.

"Shouldn't be long. Maybe fifteen minutes."

We both fell silent, and I continued to stare out the window, trying to ignore the fact that he was staring at me.

He broke the silence. "A little advice…" I reluctantly tore my gaze from the passing scenery. "I don't know why you're here, and I doubt even *you* fully know why you're here, but it doesn't matter." He waved his hand dismissively. "What does matter is…there will come a moment where you have to decide." He held my gaze, and I found myself tuning in to his words despite wanting to resist. "When that moment comes…*be selfish*."

I waited for him to continue, but that seemed to be his full message. I couldn't keep my face from registering my disdain.

"You think you're the first girl they've sent through me? I'm telling you. For your own good. In a war, you don't pick sides. You *play* sides. You *pick* yourself. That's the key to living well through anything," he said, caressing the leather of his car lovingly.

I scoffed. I couldn't stop myself.

"And you better learn to control your face," he added.

It was true, but it annoyed me all the same. Were all Old Bloods such selfish dicks? And why was he betraying his side to help us anyway? Money, I supposed. "So that's what you're doing helping me?

You're playing sides? Betraying the other Old Bloods so you can buy more toys?"

"Old Bloods? I'm no Old Blood, honey, or I wouldn't have to slum it here." He gestured vaguely outside, and I was confused. I looked outside again, just to be sure, but everything was as neat and orderly as I had seen it since leaving the gate.

"What? What do you mean?" I asked.

"I'm a New Blood like you. Just a useful one with a needed skill set. So they let me live here, in the inskirts."

"Wait…this isn't the enclave? This isn't Hydra?"

"No, it's the second buffer zone. God, don't you know anything?"

I struggled to keep up. And to keep my temper from flaring. "What do you mean the second buffer zone? What's the first buffer zone?"

He looked at me like I was hopelessly screwed.

I had to repeat the question. "What's the first buffer zone?"

"The Freelands, you fool."

I just stared at him. Blinking. Foolishly.

"The Outskirts. The second buffer between Hydra and all the other states. What? You think you're really free?"

I continued to stare. To blink and to realize how utterly foolish I really was.

"How naive can you be? Who do you think instigates all the chaos that keeps you from organizing your own governance?" He got on a roll, building energy as he ranted. "I mean, really…Who do you think pays for your shitty, unreliable hydro, keeping you just barely functioning? Who sends out pop pushers to the streets to fuck up the next generation? Haven't you ever wondered about these things?"

He started laughing, and I wanted to punch him in his stupid, arrogant face. Hot tears of frustration and humiliation fell from my eyes. I'd never listened when Rake ranted. I'd never paid attention to anything political. I didn't see how it applied to me. Now, I wished I had listened.

Dr. Ahmed's eyes narrowed. "I don't get it. Why in the world would they send *you* when you don't even understand the most basic facts about how things work?"

Flustered and upset, I sputtered the first thing that entered my head, "Maybe I understand how *other* things work." It was a bluff. I understood precisely diddly fucking squat.

"I hope so," he murmured and turned away, flicking on a holo screen and leaving me to my tears.

I wiped the tears away furiously. I had to pull myself together. Make a good impression at the Academy. My mind cast about for some calming thought. It landed on a memory of Mrs. Flores. Another time I was crying and feeling stupid, albeit with much lower stakes. I didn't remember what I'd been trying to do. Some impossibly complicated math question, probably, since that was always a source of frustration for me. Everything else she taught had come so easily to me. I barely had to try. But for some reason, math had always tripped me up. Everyone else had seemed to get it and run with it, and I would be three steps behind, still trying to wrap my mind around the basic idea, let alone all the variations, applications, and extensions others were getting into. I was mad at myself for being so dumb. Mad at math for existing.

Mrs. Flores had seen my frustration and had kept me after class. I didn't remember exactly what she said. More her calm energy. Her understanding eyes. She'd told me about her own early struggles with spelling. In typically obscure Mrs. Flores style, she'd told me about the Socratic paradox too. The seeming contradiction that wisdom valued ignorance. That all knowledge began with and required it. She'd made struggle and not knowing seem perfectly human, perfectly fine, even good.

I took a deep breath and tried to hold on to that lesson. There was clearly a lot I didn't know. Now I knew I didn't know it. And that was the first step to wisdom. It was perfectly fine. Perfectly human. Maybe even paradoxically good.

"Arriving at your destination," Sibyl announced as the car came to a gentle stop.

Dr. Ahmed grabbed my arm, startling me. "Remember what I said in the hallway. Look where you want to go. The rest is a distraction."

He held my gaze with surprising earnestness. I wasn't sure how to react. What had the good doctor shown me of himself? That he was arrogant, insulting, dismissive, self-centered, and opportunistic, a fine specimen of a man overall. And yet, he was trying to help me in his own strange way. So I nodded and thanked him as sincerely as I could.

He dropped my arm, rearranged his face, and stepped out of the car. I took a breath, then followed suit, stepping into the next, great unknown.

Before us stood a sleek building, all gray brick and glass. Coming down the entrance steps was a woman in a striking hot pink business jacket. "Dr. Ahmed, a pleasure to see you again. Thank you for taking a personal interest in this girl." Her tone bore the slightest suggestion of implying something more, but I couldn't be sure.

The doctor turned his smile up a few notches. "She came so late, and I didn't want to hold up the entire group. I know how you like to run a tight ship."

The woman said nothing, though her eyes seemed to say a lot. She inclined her head slightly, then turned her gaze on me. Her eyes were dark like her hair. They seemed bottomless and rather mesmerizing. The word "fathomless" popped into my mind. "I'm Elder Sister Dara. What was your name?"

Startled by the use of the past tense and the mystery of her eyes, I stumbled in my reply. "My…oh…my name's Amara. Amara Rodriguez."

"We'll shorten it to Amy. Follow me, Amy." She nodded to the doctor. "Good-bye, Dr. Ahmed." She started up the stairs, and I just watched her, too shocked by my abrupt and absurd renaming to get my feet to work. As she approached the door, I got ahold of myself and rushed up the steps.

She ushered me into an imposing entryway and through a side hall into a kind of clothing storeroom where she assessed me silently, then collected various sizes of different articles of clothing.

"This should do," she said, handing me a neat package. "You may change behind one of the curtained stalls along the back. Hurry, please. The rest of the new candidates are waiting."

I was so eager to get into real clothing again that I nearly tripped over myself on the way to the stall. My hands shook just holding the little bundle. It was all so new and fresh and clean. Perfect. Untouched. Although it didn't have much to recommend it in terms of style—it was just a pale pink sweatshirt and matching sweatpants—it was my first entirely new outfit. I almost cried as I slipped the white cotton undies up my legs. I had been so uncomfortably aware of being naked under the gown the entire ride. It made me feel so vulnerable. I felt more myself now. More than my usual self, in fact. I marveled at my attire. A white sports bra. White socks. White tennis shoes. Real white. Unblemished. Pure. I stared at my feet in awe.

"Do let me know if any of the sizing needs adjustment," Dara called, and it reminded me that I was supposed to be hurrying. I gathered the medical gown and booties and rushed out to greet her again, feeling strangely elated by the new apparel.

She had me dispose of the medical gear and handed me a bag for my three personal items. There were several changes of clothing inside and what looked like pajamas. We rushed into another room and out some glass doors to a small courtyard where several other people were gathered: six other girls, dressed exactly like me. There were also two women dressed like Dara. They stood in front of a weird, abstract sculpture of a tree. Or that was what I thought it was at first. I was distracted by it throughout the other Elder Sister's speech, and it took me a solid five minutes to realize it was supposed to be a hydra, not a tree. That those were tentacles, not branches. I couldn't suppress a shudder. I didn't know why but their wobbly, gelatinous bodies always creeped me out.

The short one was speaking. I was vaguely aware of her previous words: welcoming us to the Rosemont Academy, talking about what an honor it was to be selected, how they had high expectations of us, etc. Now she introduced her companions.

"This is Elder Sister Portia. She's our Head of Social Graces." An elegant, aging blond woman stepped forward. "Sister Portia will instruct you in etiquette and deportment such that you will be ready and able to work in our most elite households. Now, who remembers the Rosemont motto?"

I hadn't been paying attention and had no clue, but the girl beside me raised her hand high and was literally vibrating with eagerness. When called upon, she answered proudly, "Service with civility."

The short woman smiled approvingly. "Exactly. Sister Portia is our civility expert."

I snuck a look at the girl next to me. She was a fair-skinned South Asian girl with a decidedly smug look on her face. She was clearly here to win and wanted all of us to know it. It irritated me. I had always been competitive in Mrs. Flores's classes. I was determined to pay attention and excel right then and there.

"Tomorrow, after the orientation and makeover sessions, you'll begin your first classes. Each instructor offers extracurriculars after dinner. I'm sure Sister Portia would be delighted to have some of you join either her Bible study or floral arrangement club."

I thought I heard someone make a small snort of derision to my right, but I couldn't be sure, and when I looked over, everyone was staring ahead with a straight face.

We were formally introduced to Dara next. Evidently, she was in charge of Household Management. I had no idea what that meant, and the short woman's explanation that she focused on "protocol and pragmatics" gave me no further insight. All I got was that she represented the "service" side of the Academy's motto and offered fitness boot camp and chess club as her extracurriculars.

Dara thanked Eldest Sister Mallory, whose name I had missed earlier. Mallory told us that though we passed inspection at our respective gates, graduation would be hard-won here, and we were in for a rigorous training program.

"All right. Let's have a closer look at you and see what the gates have brought us this time," she said as she came before us. We all straightened as she made her way along the line of girls. My heartbeat sped up, and I struggled to look calm and collected.

"Turn around," she said, and we obeyed. "Smile."

I wasn't sure whether to show teeth or not and wanted to see what the other girls did but didn't dare turn my head. It was awkward to hold the smile as she took her time walking the line, inspecting each of our faces.

"Now, curtsy."

Only the brown girl and I knew what to do. I'd read about it in a book. I put one foot in front of the other and bent slightly at the knee with my head bowed. I wasn't sure what to do with my hands since I wasn't wearing a skirt, so I just held them out like I was holding the folds of an imaginary gown. I wasn't sure if that was foolish or the right call. I peeked out the side of my eyes to check the placement of my competition's hands. She'd kept her hands folded primly in front of her, and my heart sank, knowing that was probably wiser.

Sister Mallory tutted. "Pitiful. Sister Portia will have her hands full with the lot of you. Kudos to the two girls out of six who knew the most basic form of courtesy. What are your names?"

"My name is Ida," the girl to my left quickly shared.

I almost called myself Amara but remembered at the last second. "I'm…my name is Amy."

"Excellent. We'll expect good things from you two. From all of you." She returned to her companions, whispered something to them, and then announced, "That's it for this evening. You'll be led to your dormitories now. Have a pleasant evening and sleep well. We start bright and early tomorrow."

I risked a glance at Ida and saw that she was sizing me up too, the fire of competition burning in her eyes. That fire just sparked my own.

We were taken to our dorms in a separate, but equally striking, gray brick building. I was the last to be shown her room. "Your roommate's name is Bree. She should be back shortly from her extracurriculars," Dara explained, ushering me into the room. "We don't normally encourage snacking between meals, but I wasn't sure you had eaten, so I arranged for a little snack just in case."

I could have cried when I saw the tiny plate of fruit, cheese, and crackers. I was famished. I hadn't eaten since breakfast, and it had been yet another insane whirlwind of a day. All I could think about was stuffing every item on that little plate into my mouth at once. I waited impatiently for Dara to finish, and the moment she closed the door, I wolfed down the food in a most "uncivilized" fashion. It amused me to imagine Elder Sister Portia's reaction to my table manners. The food wasn't enough, but it took the edge off my hunger. I could make it to morning now.

My hunger sated, I looked around the room. I was just thinking that there wasn't much to it when the door burst open, and a girl rushed in. She saw me, started, and blurted out, "Who the hell are you?"

"Sorry. I didn't mean to scare you. I'm your new roommate. Amara," I said, holding out my hand, then awkwardly realizing I was probably being too formal.

She ignored my hand and kicked off her shoes. "They let you keep that name?" she asked dubiously. This was going well. This chick had barely looked at me, busy disentangling her hair from a ponytail.

"No. Sorry. I'm…I'm not used to it yet. They want me to go by Amy."

"Well, hello, Amy. I'm Bree. And that's my actual name. Glad it passed muster because I don't think I could have gotten used to a new name on top of everything else." She threw herself on the bed and sprawled there a minute before turning on her side to scrutinize me.

I did the same. She was pretty. Everyone here was, I supposed. She had light, copper-colored hair, fair skin, and hazel eyes. There was a cute little sprinkling of freckles across her nose.

"Wait." She sprang up on the bed. "You're a redhead too?" She laughed and seemed to instantly warm to me. This girl was all-off or all-on, it seemed. "What were they thinking? We're going to get up to so much trouble together. Ginger Gang. Whaddya say?"

I felt no particular affinity for other redheaded individuals, and she could barely pass as a ginger, leaning more to the strawberry-blond side, but I could have really used a friend in here. So, of course, I laughed right back, and said, "Hell yeah," cementing an alliance based on a ludicrously random commonality.

Bree did not shut up after that. Not that I was complaining. She'd been here a while and knew things. I could see this connection being helpful. But I was exhausted from a long day and losing the thread of the conversation, which mostly focused on her missing boys, gossiping about the other girls, and complaining about how stupid the classes were.

There was a tinkling bell tone, and the lights flashed.

"Ten-minute warning to lights-out," Bree explained.

I was relieved. I just needed to stop and let go.

Bree jumped up, started to take off her sweatshirt, then stopped. "Wait. You don't care if I change here, do you? You're not a prude or a lez or anything?"

I blushed and didn't know how to answer since I was honestly probably both. "I don't mind," I squeaked.

"Then hurry up and change too so I don't feel weird about it," she said, stripping off her shirt as she talked. I blushed and hurried to keep up. The pajamas were soft and inviting. I didn't think I had ever been so ready for a good night's sleep.

Eventually, the bell rang again, and the lights went out. I snuggled into my little bed and tried not to think about all the events of today or all the events that lay before me tomorrow. Just rest, just let go, I told myself.

"Good night, Amy."

It took me a second to realize she was talking to me. "Good night, Bree."

I closed my eyes, and flashes of my day started coming, but I tried not to give them any attention. If I started thinking about my day, I'd never fall asleep, no matter how exhausted I felt. I did let my mind wander to last night, though. Was it only last night? It felt like a lifetime ago that Rake was holding me, caressing me, kissing me to slumber. I felt her energy with me still and let myself fall into it. *Let everything else go...Let it go.*

I woke after what felt like five minutes with a little choking cry. It was just a dream, I tried to reassure myself, patting my face anxiously. Not that it helped relieve me, for in my dream, I'd been back in the tree with Rake, snuggling cozily until our tree lurched, and I fell, tumbling and tumbling. Where the ground should have been, a huge hole opened up, and I tumbled farther and farther down. I just fell and fell, scrambling to grab on to anything, dreading the impact whenever I finally hit the bottom. But when I hit it, instead of smashing into pieces, I transformed into a cartoon character and just bounced back up. When I landed again with a jolting thud, all my features rearranged. I screamed, but it didn't sound like me, and the horror of that feeling woke me up.

"Please tell me this is just first-day jitters," croaked a voice.

I was even more alarmed, forgetting where I was and what was going on. It came back quickly, and I felt my face go hot. "I'm so sorry." I didn't know what else to say.

"It's fine. You've been tossing and turning for a solid half hour, but it's almost lights-on anyway." Bree yawned and looked at me with a smile. "Ready for an exhilarating day of learning how to fold napkins?"

I laughed. More than her joke required, nervousness and relief all mixed up in me.

But I *was* ready. I'd made it through the gate unscathed. I'd already impressed my teachers, and I had a worthy adversary to compete against in the annoying keener, Ida.

Not to mention that I was part of a kick-ass ginger girl gang.

I could do this.

Chapter Six

In Search for Teachers True

The next evening found me up on the rooftop of our dorm after lights-out, drinking stolen brandy with my roommate's friends. Bree was a bad influence of the best sort, and I had always been a sucker for a charming rebel. She reminded me of Rake as she cajoled me into trying the swiped liquor.

"I'll take full responsibility if we get caught," she said. "I'll say I held you down and forced it down your throat." She held out the bottle. Very much aware that Zen and I were the only new girls here, I reached for the bottle, accepting this stupid act of rebellion—which I knew was really the most cliched kind of conformity—as the price of fitting in.

Her friends laughed at the face I made after sipping. I'd never had brandy, and it was different from what I'd expected. I didn't exactly dislike the taste, but it surprised me.

Zen needed no encouragement. She grabbed the bottle and swigged enthusiastically, much to our new friends' approval. "How'd you get this?" she asked, passing the bottle along.

Bree smirked. "Eldest Sister Mallory likes a nightcap." She looked around mischievously. "And I'm an excellent thief."

A girl I didn't know piped up, "Lucky we're in House Ashbury and not House Thorncliff. Sister Dara misses nothing. You'd never be able to pull this off with her."

I watched, amused as Bree bristled at the suggestion that her pilfering skills might be subpar. I thought she might get bitchy about it, but she burst out laughing. "Sounds like a challenge. I'm in, if anyone wants to join me." She looked around, eyes twinkling. "In fact, let's sweeten the deal." She reached up and unhooked the silver chain about her neck. "This necklace will be our prize. Whoever pinches the best item gets it." She placed the necklace on the roof between us. It was just a short simple chain with a cheap heart pendant, sterling silver at best, but I could feel the envy radiating from the other girls. Jewelry was rare. We weren't even allowed to wear it once we graduated, except during off-hours. It must have been one of Bree's three personal items. Why would she sacrifice it?

Her friends must have been thinking the same thing, for one of them asked, "Isn't it…special to you? Did your mom give it to you or something?"

Bree snorted. "Naw, I told you. I'm an excellent thief." When she saw we were smiling, she elaborated. "Took it off this slag back in East Side who stole my man. Only seemed right to steal something back." She chugged from the bottle. "Trust me, she got the shittier deal. Dale sucked in bed."

A few girls sniggered.

Zen squinted at her. "But it's yours. What do you get if you win?"

Bree considered. "I get whatever you lift and…"

"The glory of corrupting young girls into a life of thievery," one of her friends interrupted, holding aloft the bottle in a toast.

"Sure," Bree replied, laughing. "Honestly, I'm sure I can steal another one the next time someone is dumb enough to flash jewelry around me." A few girls' eyes widened, and she rushed to add, "Obviously, not you guys. I wouldn't steal from my sisters."

"Who you gonna target, Jane?" one girl asked another.

"I don't know," Jane answered, bored, picking at her nails. "Maybe Sister Portia. She seems clueless."

I had no intention of joining this challenge, but it intrigued me enough to wonder what would become of it.

There was a brief silence, then Zen burst out, "I'm taking something from Mallory." There was a surprisingly intense edge to her voice. "That bitch is racist. Y'all heard her today."

A ripple of discomfort ran through the group. The girls looked at each other warily, and I became more aware of the fact that almost everyone in the academy was white. I could only think of three girls of color in the entire school. Strange that it hadn't occurred to me until now, since I grew up in the Barrio, where white people were the minority. But it meant I knew enough to believe Zen when she said that. And thinking back, they had made a pretty big fuss about the difficulty of her hair during our makeovers.

Bree made a defensive gesture with her shoulders and said, "They don't get many…people of color here, I guess. It's not their fault."

"And why don't they get many?" Zen pushed. "Because they don't think we're attractive, so they don't let us past the gate."

"Or they don't think you're docile enough," I added, trying to show I was on her side, though I worried that she'd hear that wrong. I rushed to add, "You know, I mean, the whole racist, 'angry black woman' thing." Zen glared at me, angry indeed, and I stumbled on awkwardly. "I'm trying to say that I think you're right. Most of the Old Bloods are white. It's their world we're entering. They choose who gets to enter, and it just makes sense that some racist ideas would exist in a mostly white enclave."

"There are quite a few Asians too, I hear," one girl added.

"Lucky for them," Zen said.

Bree bristled, and several girls were looking around uncomfortably.

Zen looked at me hard, then seemed to accept me at my words and went on, directing her comments to me alone. "It's like my name. Why the hell can't I keep my own name? It's short and easy to say. It's not like I'm even asking them to use my full name."

"Zen's short for something?" one of the girls asked.

"Yes, Zenobia," she replied without looking at her. "No, Zen's too 'exotic,' so they gotta give me the whitest name possible. *Ruth*." She said it with such exaggeration and disdain that it was hardly recognizable.

"I already had the whitest name of all time, so I got to keep mine," Jane drawled. "But they picked Ruth because it's biblical. Haven't you noticed how many of the new names are biblical? This place is like a weird, old-fashioned, wannabe convent or something."

"Do you know the story of Ruth?" I asked Zen.

"Yeah, she was the loyal and obedient handmaid who said, 'Whither thou goest, I will go.'" Zen rolled her eyes.

"Guess they're hoping you'll live up to your namesake," someone said.

"Oh, I will. Zenobia was a kick-ass queen," Zen replied, grabbing the bottle and swigging hard. We laughed, and the mood shifted back to a more relaxed vibe.

❖

These girls might have been wrapped up in their silly stealing competition, but I had my own competition going on: trying to outperform that annoying kiss-ass Ida. She gave me a run for my money in Sister Dara's household management classes, but in Sister Portia's lessons in social graces, I had a definite advantage, thanks to my time under Mrs. Flores's tutelage. Turned out that the "classic" education Rake had found so "useless" actually had its uses. Mostly for rubbing right answers in my current rival's face. All that reading really came in handy when Sister Portia went on one of her meandering lectures about the importance of how we spoke to our proprietors, about learning to use polite phrasing. How to ask delicate questions. To show deference.

The girls hated her classes and mocked her viciously behind her back. I think she knew, and it hurt her. What did she expect? Teaching elocution and etiquette to girls raised in the streets? It demanded ridicule. Her curriculum included such critical soft skills as personal grooming, posture, and "impression management." Not to mention discretion, good manners, and forms of address. Plus, everyone's perennial favorite: best practices for how to enter and exit a room.

Bree was the worst. She baited her constantly. "Excuse me, Miss Portia?"

"It's Elder Sister Portia. Proper forms of address are important."

"Yeah, right, sorry 'bout that. Elder Sister Portia, I have a question."

"That's not how to apologize. We've covered this. What should Bree have said? What's an appropriate way to present an apology to one's superior?"

Ida's hand shot up, and I let her take this one, not wanting to contradict my friend, who I knew full well was just messing with Sister Portia.

Sister Portia nodded at Ida, and she said, "It would depend on the severity of the misstep and the station of the potentially offended party, but direct, sincere simplicity is best. I would have said, 'My apologies. Thank you for the reminder. I won't forget again.'"

"Excellent. Thank you, Ida." Sister Portia turned to Bree, who was scowling. "Now, Bree, you had a question?"

Bree perked up. "Yes, I do. You've been teaching us all about proper words and whatnot, and I'm really listening hard because I sure don't want to offend anybody with my rough street words, so I was just wondering, when I'm doing laundry, and I gotta clean my mistress's gitch, what's the fancy word for that?"

A few girls sniggered, and Elder Sister Portia looked confused. "I'm…I'm not familiar with that term."

"Gitch. You know. The thing you wear to cover your arse and

cooch. I just wanna know the fancy 'appropriate' name for it so I don't offend no one." Bree's eyes glittered mischievously, and the girls around her were all predictably enthralled by her daring. She didn't even really speak like that. But it was satisfying to throw it back in Sister Portia's face. The way she thought we were all uncouth heathens who spoke like Neanderthals.

Sister Portia's face reddened slightly, but she seemed to take the question at face value and tried to be matter of fact. "You refer to them as undergarments. Brassieres cover one's bosom, and undergarments cover one's buttocks and…" She wavered uncertainly, and the class collectively held its breath. We would return to this moment many times on the rooftop, finishing her sentence each time with a different explosively crass euphemism for female genitalia. It was pure comedy gold. "It covers the rest," she finally finished.

"Yes, Miss…I mean, Sister Portia, but what about—" Bree began.

Sister Portia cut her off though. "I think it's best if you write down any questions you have, and I will be happy to answer them privately." She no doubt thought this would quell the issue, but Bree's eyes lit up, and she began madly scribbling, no doubt writing down every nasty, crude word she had ever heard in her life.

It was amusing, but there was a part of me that felt for Sister Portia. She struck me as a sad woman. As an only child, I had grown up connecting more with adults than with other kids, and I liked to watch people. When I really scrutinized Sister Portia, I sensed that there was something fearful and timid behind all this focus on civility and deportment. She wanted to do things right. To please. To fit some ideal in her mind. Sadly, it seemed like she worried that she—and the whole world—didn't quite make the grade.

I looked at her more closely. It was strange. She had all the trappings of conventional beauty—fair skin, blond hair, blue eyes—but wasn't quite beautiful. She was aging and anxious about it, for sure, but it wasn't that exactly. I had the feeling she had this defensive, "trying too hard" energy that took away from her looks no matter her age. I could see on her face that she knew she had lost this class's respect and that no one cared about the things she seemed to care so very much about.

I felt sorry for her. Maybe that was why I stayed after class to offer to join her Bible study. I wasn't particularly religious, but my mom was, and I figured saying the prayers might help me to feel connected to her.

Portia seemed elated. “I’m so delighted to meet another fan of the good book.”

“I’m a fan of pretty much all books,” I admitted.

“I figured,” she replied, gathering her things. “Your vocabulary is superb, and your general knowledge seems extensive. That comes of good reading habits, which is a credit to both your parents and yourself.” Her items gathered and organized, she paused, seemingly lost in thought. “When I first came to Hydra, all three of my personal items were books.”

It took me aback realizing she had once been in my position. It made me look at her differently.

“The Bible, obviously, was my first choice, to keep me on the right path.” She looked up at me, something surprisingly playful in her eyes. “Can you guess the other two?”

I smiled, warmed by the intimacy of the invitation. Book lovers bonded in the strangest of circumstances. I paused and reflected, thinking of all she’d revealed about herself in the few classes I’d had with her.

“I’ll give you three tries. If you can guess at least one of them, you can borrow my books. I’ve amassed a decent library at this point. Eldest Sister Mallory doesn’t mind. They’re teaching tools, after all. Not so strictly speaking.” She actually winked, and I thoroughly warmed to her, wishing the other girls could know her like this.

The thought of being able to peruse her books and choose titles to read at my leisure was extremely compelling. I weighed several possibilities. “Do I need to guess the exact title, or will the right author be enough?”

“I’m a generous teacher. The author will suffice.”

“Then one of Jane Austen’s novels.”

She laughed heartily and clapped, thoroughly pleased. “Am I that transparent?”

“I’m just that good,” I said immodestly.

“All right, I have to make it both harder and more rewarding. If you can guess the final book, then you may have one of my books for your very own. Any but my Bible. It’s a family heirloom.”

“Three new guesses?”

“You already spent one guess. So, no, two attempts.”

“I thought you were a generous teacher,” I teased.

“I am,” she said. “Four personal items will require explanation and string pulling.”

"Fine. But the author rule still applies, right?"

"That's correct."

I narrowed my eyes as though that would help me. I'd been fairly confident about my first guess. I mean, she was a Southern lady through and through, and it seemed predictable that she'd be into classic romances that centered on issues of love and class. What else? Her name was Portia. Was that a *Merchant of Venice* reference? "Shakespeare. One of his plays."

"I'm afraid not. I admit, I find his writing rather challenging. That leaves you with one guess."

"Can I think about it?" I figured she'd reveal more about herself in the weeks to come, and I could ask vaguely helpful questions if she gave me time.

"Certainly. You've already earned the right to borrow books. I'm busy this evening, but come by House Summerfell tomorrow after extracurriculars, and I'll be happy to show you my library. Now, you best get going. I've kept you most of break."

I hardly had time to meet up with my peers before the afternoon's classes began, this time with Elder Sister Dara. Her classes didn't inspire the same level of ridicule from the girls, though it was hard to say why. Some of them were just as ludicrous. We really did learn rules for napkin folding. But somehow, we didn't dare make fun of Sister Dara. She was brusque and no-nonsense. If she taught a skill, there was a pragmatic rationale behind it. Even now, while showing us the best way to pack and unpack a suitcase, when someone dared to ask why this was necessary, Sister Dara answered plainly, "Because your proprietors will have bespoke, designer outfits that cost more than entire generations of your family will earn in their lifetimes. You don't want to be the one to ruin those outfits. Trust me."

And we did.

I was distracted, mulling over options for Sister Portia's third book as I absentmindedly folded and placed articles of clothing. That was when I noticed Sister's Dara pen, set aside with her black notebook on a table next to my suitcase. She was the only sister who didn't use a datapad, preferring old-fashioned pen and paper. She had her back turned, helping another student, and I grabbed and pocketed the pen, my heart racing wildly. A girl saw me do it and gave me a strange look. She wasn't in our social circle, so she wouldn't know about the competition.

The competition. The stupid competition that I had had zero

interest in participating in but was now risking expulsion for like a complete fool. My mouth was dry, and I started coughing. I tried to repress the coughs, but the more I tried, the worse they got. My face was flushed, and people were starting to look at me, which only made it worse. Eventually, Sister Dara directed me to get a glass of water, and I fled from the room, feeling as though my heart would beat out of my chest.

Why had I done that? To impress some stupid girls who really didn't matter in the end? Rake was depending on me. My mother was depending on me. The Defiance too. I couldn't get wrapped up in the silly games of these girls. It was too risky.

I was so busy berating myself that I didn't hear Sister Dara enter the room, and I squealed and started when I turned and saw her just a foot away from me. "Are you all right? Did the water help?"

"Yes," I said, awkwardly shielding my right pocket where the stolen pen lay.

Elder Sister Dara scrutinized my face, and I could feel my color rise and my armpits start to sweat. I was the world's worst rebel. I just stood there, no doubt giving everything away with my obvious fear.

"I believe you have something of mine." She held out her hand, and it was a command I knew better than to disobey. I placed the pen in her outstretched palm, avoiding her eyes. The fear was making my whole body shake. How could I have been so foolish? I had risked everything for a fucking pen?

"You're a terrible thief, Amy. Let's see if you're a terrible liar too. Why did you take it?" She lifted my chin in a surprisingly gentle manner. Her eyes were searching. I saw no anger or reproach. Just a strange, intense curiosity.

"It was foolish and wrong of me, and I'm really sorry. I…I don't know what came over me. It won't happen again," I said in a breathy rush. "Please don't kick me out."

"That's good to know. But it doesn't answer my question," she insisted.

I squirmed, not wanting to rat out my friends.

She just let me squirm. Waiting.

Eventually, I said, "A couple of girls have a silly competition going. To see who can swipe the best thing. Don't ask me who, I won't tell you." I raised my chin stubbornly.

She surprised me by smiling. "Well, while I can hardly approve of such actions, it's a timeworn tradition for the help to skim a little extra off the top." I could have sworn that her eyes twinkled. I could hardly believe what I was hearing. "You won't last long if that's your attempt to be sneaky." She turned and began heading for the door. I didn't know if she was going to report me or not and was about to ask, panicky, when she turned. "You have one week to improve. Steal something from me without my noticing. If you can accomplish this, I won't bring the story of your poor judgment to Eldest Sister Mallory."

I stuttered, taken aback. "Wha...you...I don't understand. You want me to steal from you?"

Her fathomless eyes looked unaccountably sad and strangely excited at the same time. I could never figure her out. "I want you to excel at everything you do. That's the Rosemont way," she said in a strange tone and turned on her heel.

I didn't know if she was joking or bored or crazy or what, but I knew I had just been given a second chance. I didn't intend to squander it.

The next three days were like some kind of cruel joke. I kept trying to catch Sister Daras unaware and botched every single attempt. I'd enlisted Bree's help and had become much more adept at sleight of hand and diversion but was at a significant disadvantage because my target knew my intentions. Bree and I had tried to break into her room, but she'd stationed a girl we didn't know outside her door, and no matter what we said or promised or threatened or offered, that girl was immovable.

On the third night, the Ginger Girl Gang—not so aptly named since only two of us were actual redheads—was brainstorming ideas on the rooftop when Zen showed up late, brimming with excitement. "Look!"

She held out a datapad. They were strictly off-limits for us, as the school didn't want us being "distracted" by news of the outside world.

"Holy shit! Where'd you get that?" Bree asked, wide-eyed.

"Mallory. She has two in her office. This is her old one. She hardly ever uses it. Bet she won't even notice it's gone."

"We could get in a lot of trouble for this," Jane warned, but Bree was already embracing Zen and removing her necklace.

"Nobody's gonna top this, let's be real. This is fucking amazing. Isn't it locked?"

Zen laughed. "No, that's the crazy thing. I don't know if she's so old that she can't remember passwords or feels so safe that she thinks she doesn't need one, but whatever the reason, we've got access to the Eldest Sister's files. Who knows what's on here?"

A hush passed over the group as we considered the possibilities.

Never one to miss the opportunity to prove her boy-craziness, Bree said, "Screw that, we have access to the net and holos. Let's watch some big dick porn."

Everyone jostled around Zen, yelling out suggestions for sites to visit, when a red news alert flashed. Zen tapped it, and a news anchor holo shimmered from the screen.

"We have breaking news tonight of a horrific double murder in Hydra. Authorities have confirmed that two Old Blood council members, the Honorable Dr. James Hall and his wife, Mrs. Lynn Hall, were found mutilated and murdered in their Westwood home. One of their own servants, a BabyDoll by the name of Molly, has claimed responsibility, as well as membership in the terrorist organization popularly known as the Defiance. Stay tuned to Hydra Prime for more details as they arise."

"Click the red thread," Jane urged, and we skimmed the comments pouring in.

"Oh my God. They're saying she carved wrinkles into their faces with a paring knife. That's fucking sick."

"Bullshit. What BabyDoll could do something like that?"

"She wasn't just a BabyDoll. She was a terrorist."

The girls all talked over one another excitedly. "Does it say what academy she went through? Where was she from?"

"Why would anyone do that?"

"Can you imagine if she was from here?"

I couldn't take it all in. A girl named Molly. A BabyDoll. Defiant. Like me. But…I wasn't like that. That wasn't something I would ever do. And not something I could imagine a Crone like Nana asking anyone to do. It was cruel and unnecessary. Vindictive. Was that the kind of movement I had joined?

But then again, was this girl really Defiance? Had she even done it? Or had the authorities just made that up? Was this propaganda?

I felt bile rise in my throat while thinking of that couple being carved with the trappings of time that they'd thought they had escaped. Sure, the Old Bloods were selfish and privileged, but I understood why they wanted to keep the Remedy to themselves. The planet couldn't sustain the entire human population living indefinitely. From everything I'd seen and read, it seemed like human nature to hoard something precious for yourself and your loved ones. But revenge was human nature too. Keep a people down and they tended to rise up, hungry for revolution. Whether they were fighting to stay on top or to get there, there was a lot that was secretly dark and ugly in people that was bound to come out in the end.

I shivered while watching the girls gossip excitedly about the lurid news.

All I could think was…what had I gotten myself into?

And how the hell would I ever get out of it?

CHAPTER SEVEN

A Quaint and Curious Volume

News of this double homicide stirred things up at the school. The girls started playfully guessing who here might turn out to be a murderous psychopath or a secret terrorist, little knowing that I was one if not the other. I hardly felt like either. The news had shaken me too, and I began reading the book the Crone had given me to try to suss out the nature of the people I had agreed to work with. I needed to understand their intentions and minds better. Who were these people? Rake trusted them, but did I? The book was my only link to their way of thinking, so I delved into the story and looked for clues. Nana said she'd chosen it on purpose and seemed disappointed that I didn't get the point of its selection.

I got the point now. It was genuinely clever. I'd never read anything by Oscar Wilde before, though I'd heard of him. A witty dandy arrested for being gay back in the late 1800s. Mrs. Flores had a collection of his plays, but I'd never gotten around to reading them, though she'd recommended them to me.

The Picture of Dorian Gray was a creepy story of a man who sold his soul to stay young and beautiful forever. His portrait grew old and ugly while he lived a frivolous life of hedonistic pleasure and privilege. The cover art was appropriately unnerving, showing an elegant, stunningly gorgeous young man with half his face rotting away. It wasn't hard to read into this as the Defiance's metaphor for the Old Bloods and their selfish, immoral choice to hoard the Remedy while the rest of the world aged and suffered. Dorian ruined anyone foolish enough to fall for his charms. A warning.

I was impressed. It was a telling choice. Reading it put my mind at ease about my allegiances. While I knew little of the Defiance, if it trusted elderly, cookie-baking, crazy cat ladies to plot rebellion, it probably wasn't the bastion of evil that Hydra made it out to be. That Molly story was suspect, I decided, and my conscience settled.

The girls weren't the only ones stirred up by the double homicide. The teachers were decidedly on edge. I wondered if the academies were under increased scrutiny now. After all, the murderer had evidently graduated from one. There was much more speechifying from all the sisters about the great privilege we were granted as BabyDolls, about our position of sacrosanct trust and responsibility within the sanctuary of Old Blood homes.

Eldest Sister Mallory was most affected. The smallest infraction was severely punished now, and things eventually came to a head with her and Zen. It was an utter nightmare watching her pick on Zen while not being in a position to do anything about it. Mallory hated her, and it was increasingly obvious that it was totally a racist thing, just as Zen had claimed.

When our crisp new BabyDoll outfits arrived and we were being fitted, Mallory made a huge deal about how they fit on her. Zen was curvier than most of us, and the head of the school didn't lose the opportunity to berate and shame her about it in front of everyone. It was awful to witness, but what was I supposed to do? Stand up to the headmistress in front of everyone? Call her out for racism and body-shaming? I'd just get myself kicked out.

So I just stood there and listened as she said horrible things. "Look at your figure. Just look at you. You don't fit properly into any size." Sister Mallory was tugging on her shirt, trying to adjust it. Zen was shaking but silent. "Your behind and your bust are too big. What are we supposed to do with this?" She gestured to Portia, who seemed sympathetically concerned. Dara's face was inscrutable, as was often the case. The girls shifted uncomfortably.

"She looks like a slut. I'll say it. She looks like a slut who would only tempt the household into inappropriate relations."

Zen stood ramrod straight, looking away, her eyes hardening and her breathing coming fast. I could see she was trying not to cry or explode. Her fists clenched at her side.

I snuck a glance at Bree, but she seemed amused to have heard a dirty word come out of the headmistress's mouth. I felt the sting of disappointment in my roommate and looked to see if I was the only one suffering alongside Zen. I wasn't but didn't see the sympathy I expected, and my disappointment only sharpened.

I resolved to become Zen's best friend, to support her however I could through the rest of our time here, but Zen disappeared after that with no warning or explanation.

When I stayed after class the next day to ask Elder Sister Portia what happened to her, she only replied, "Ruth was deemed unfit for service."

"But where is she? What happened to her? What happens to us if we fail out?"

Sister Portia smiled benignly and said, "Don't you worry about that. It's not going to happen to you."

I guess it never occurred to them that some of us might have cared about more than just ourselves.

After that, it was harder for me to connect with the girls and my teachers. I'd come here on a mission, yes, but was also genuinely open to making new relationships and learning. Now it all felt tainted. Zen was a strong, amazing person. I didn't deserve to be here any more than she did. It upset me that everyone just went on like nothing had happened. I started to withdraw and keep to myself. I sketched Zenobia swigging that bottle of brandy and sat in my feelings.

It wasn't like I was surprised that life wasn't fair. No one who grew up in the Freelands had the luxury of being that stupid. But there was a small part of me that hoped that things might be different in the enclave. That if I worked hard and played by the rules, things would work out. Life was supposed to be better here. Wasn't that the dream that all of us stuck outside the gate believed? That maybe here we'd find order and beauty and an inkling of justice, things in short supply in the Freelands. But what wasn't in short supply in the Freelands? Here, with that abundance of wealth and time, why wouldn't things be perfect? Or as near to it as possible. It was embarrassing to realize that although I was here to rescue my mom and had joined a terrorist organization, I still harbored childish illusions about the place.

I started overthinking. Or maybe finally thinking the right amount. I'd never been one to consider the big picture. My mom and Rake could get into heated, political discussions, but I always tuned out. I was rooted in the present and in people, not ideas, not systems. But now I was starting to see how the two ways of thinking could be connected.

I liked Elder Sister Portia as a person. We bonded over books and our love of beautiful words. She was helping me. But she wasn't my friend, and she wasn't on my side. Not truly. She was part of the system that crushed people like Zen. Eldest Sister Mallory's bigotry was more overt and ugly, but Sister Portia supported it. She thought that way too. Which I found out for sure when she finally told me her third book choice after one last incorrect guess on my part.

It was *Gone with the Wind* by Margaret Mitchell. Of course. The classic tale that exulted the lost beauty of the idealized Old South, a world where men were gallant gentlemen and women were ladies fair. A world where everyone knew their place. Black people most of all. The book where all the kind, chivalrous gentlemen turned out to be Ku Klux Klan members in the end, but that wasn't presented as a detraction from their supposed nobility. Mrs. Flores had had a few of us read it alongside *Uncle Tom's Cabin* by Harriet Beecher Stowe as a study in contrasting depictions of slavery by Southern, white, female authors.

When Sister Portia told me, I was both surprised and not at the same time. It made sense that this was the society of refined deportment that she yearned to be part of. And I couldn't pretend that the book hadn't held a confusing kind of appeal for me. I'd loved to hate the feisty, spoiled character of Scarlett. But there was no part of that world of genteel cruelty that I wanted to return to. Okay, perhaps the pretty clothes. The gowns sounded spectacular. And I was sure Sister Portia would have delighted to have us all decked out in some old-fashioned maid's uniform, but since we actually had to do a lot of physical labor, skirts got in the way. Plus, they were too provocative to proprietors—so the rumor went—even when lengthy.

So simple black slacks and a fitted, hot pink golf shirt constituted this year's uniform. One sleeve of the shirt was black, and the other sleeve had two thin black stripes on it, creating an asymmetrical sense of balance. It had a black zipper that traveled partway down the front. It was rather sweet and sporty, actually, with a pert, upturned collar. It was so much more striking and attractive than our formless, pale pink sweats. Everyone was excited to be fitted. And while redheads weren't supposed to wear pink, according to popular wisdom, it actually looked fine on me. The only annoying thing was that a standardized hairdo was part of the prescribed look, so we all had to get our hair chopped into this mid-length bob that flipped up on the ends into a cutesy curl. Evidently, there was a huge competition each year in Hydra to design that year's BabyDoll outfit. It was broadcast on the holos, and citizens voted for their choice. It was a whole big thing. Sister Portia had been excited to announce the year's winner to us, but since most of us had already seen the outfit on Mallory's datapad or had heard it described through gossip, its big reveal was a bit of letdown.

Which was how I won the stealing challenge Elder Sister Dara had set for me. All the academy had gathered to witness the reveal of this year's winning outfit before our fittings, and when the girls didn't react as expected, the teachers seemed confused. It was oddly satisfying to know my actions led directly to their disappointment. When I informed Sister Dara afterward that I had succeeded in stealing something from her, she'd been intrigued.

"What did you steal?" she asked.

"Your thunder." I went on to explain, omitting some key details, how the girls had managed to see the new outfit ahead of time.

Dara smiled and seemed impressed. I had always been a sucker for a teacher's approval, so it gave me my first good feeling since Zen had disappeared. "Well played," she said. "I think you should join my chess club."

"No thanks. It seems boring."

"Well, if reading scripture is more riveting…"

Was she jealous of me choosing Sister Portia's extracurricular over hers? That seemed ridiculous. But maybe teachers had their rivalries too. I tried to explain. "Sorry, but I just don't get the point of chess. You sit in silence forever just randomly moving little pieces around a board trying to corner each other. Seems like a stupid way to prove you're smart."

Sister Mallory laughed. "Firstly, it's not random. It's very strategic and revealing, that's why I like it. It shows you how someone thinks."

"Why would I care about that?"

"Why wouldn't you?"

"Because I'm just a glorified slave, and it doesn't matter what I think?" I didn't know what made me risk honesty. It just seemed like Sister Dara could handle some truth. She was pretty real with her students.

"Are you? Is that all you are, Amara?"

Her using my real name made me feel strange. I shifted uncomfortably.

"Maybe that's what the powers that be think of you, but their ideas don't totally define you, do they, Amy?" She placed a strange emphasis on my assigned name. "They confine you within certain parameters. It's not unlike a chess game. But you have certain moves you can make. You can take advantage of the possibilities granted to you by your station. A bishop can move diagonally. A knight can move in an

L shape. There's order and possibility. Patterns. Life is really just a big chess game if you think about it."

"Seems like a perfectly apt metaphor. Since I don't know how to play chess."

We both smiled at that.

"I can teach you. It's actually really fascinating. Just sixty-four squares but a million possible outcomes arise from them. The game develops patience, planning, discernment, and adaptation."

Why was she telling me all this?

As if she read my mind, she added, "You have a good mind, Amy. You should develop it. I can see you love to read and draw, and that's great that you're creative. But maybe you should balance it out. Try something new. If not chess, then boot camp."

"So you can yell at me like a drill sergeant?" I asked skeptically.

"Best part of my day," she said, and her eyes twinkled.

I wanted to be drawn in by this burgeoning intimacy between us, but the whole thing with Zen still had me distrustful and on edge. "Why are you being nice to me?"

"Why wouldn't I be?" she countered. "I want all you girls to be strong, mentally and physically. Your position is…challenging. You have what it takes to be a steward, given time. That would be a good position for you. Safe. Relatively respected."

I was surprised. The steward was the head servant in a home. "You'd recommend me?"

"Depends if you try to broaden your horizons."

"So this is a 'tit for tat' thing?" I said, annoyance clear in my voice.

"Stewards are leaders. Leaders embrace opportunities to build their skills sets."

My anger flared. "You're manipulating me."

She only smiled. "That's a pretty harsh word to describe the way I'm trying to set you up to succeed. It usually doesn't require this much effort to help someone advance, just so you know."

"Why?" I insisted. "Seriously. Ida's just as good as me. In *your* classes, at least."

"Ida doesn't have what it takes. I think you do." She paused, then added slyly, "Besides, I don't know if you've noticed, but she's an annoying kiss-ass."

That made me laugh. I couldn't help it.

Sister Dara made to leave but turned to say, "Boot camp starts at six a.m. by the hydra statue. Expect to be miserable."

As she was leaving, I yelled, "Fine. I'll join your stupid chess club, but you're not making me sweat before I'm even fully awake."

She didn't acknowledge my reply as she left the room.

After that, I relaxed with my teachers again. It was hard not to enjoy them, despite everything. I loved learning and had always been drawn to teachers, seeing them as people much more than my peers seemed to. Maybe it was an only child trait. In any case, later that week, they called me in for a "chat." It was in a part of the school I'd never seen before, and all three of my teachers were there. Just seeing them together, expecting me in a room, made me sweat. What did they want? What was this about?

After some niceties, Eldest Sister Mallory took charge of the conversation. "Your teachers have only very positive things to say about you, Amy. It seems you may be graduating soon." She paused, and I rushed to reply.

"That would be an honor. I've…I've tried my best to live up to the Rosemont standards." Ugh. Who was the annoying kiss-ass now?

"We'll be placing you in an elite household and recommending you for stewardship training. This is a great privilege, Amy," she said, peering over her glasses. "We expect you to make us proud."

I felt my cheeks flush. The Defiance had come through with pulling strings. Or Sister Portia or perhaps Dara had used their influence. Then again, maybe I'd earned this on my own merit. Whatever the case, the plan was working. I was going to a high-level home. Somewhere I would hopefully have access to information useful to the cause. Information I would trade for help finding and escaping with my mom. It was all coming together.

Mallory cleared her throat. Pointedly. I was taking too long to reply. "Sorry, I'm…I'm just overwhelmed with gratitude. Thank you for this opportunity. I won't let you down. I promise."

"We trust you won't," Sister Mallory said. "Now, there are some girls here who don't demonstrate the same attitude or aptitude. Given everything that's happened recently…" She gestured vaguely, but I knew she was referring to the double homicide, which we weren't supposed to know about but obviously did. "Given all that…we think it's important to engage in some housekeeping."

I was confused, and Sister Mallory looked to Sister Dara, who got straight to the point. "Your roommate, Bree. What do you think of her? Is she Rosemont material?"

I just stared, frightened by where this was going.

Sister Portia jumped in. "I'm sure you can understand that we can't have girls graduating who might damage our reputation, so we're just asking a few questions of all the girls to ensure the cream of the crop is representing us in Hydra. Don't be afraid. You can be honest. Please tell Eldest Sister Mallory what you think of Bree."

"Why are you asking *me* about Bree?" I said, uncertain how to play this.

"You're her roommate, silly," Sister Portia scolded. "You know her best. What do you two talk about? How do you think she's adjusting?"

My heart started racing. I knew Sister Portia disliked her. Were they doing this to all the girls? Would they call Bree in to ask about me? A wild and unlikely thought crossed my mind that maybe all the rooms were bugged, and this was a test of my loyalty. To see if I'd tell the truth. Would they take away my promised post if I messed this up? I could feel my face burning. How could I wiggle my way out of this while being truthful enough but not throwing Bree under the bus?

Sister Dara tapped her pen rhythmically on the table, the way she sometimes did while she was teaching me chess, and it made me focus. I was cornered. I didn't want to sacrifice myself or my friend. What was the best move?

I looked at Portia, and inspiration struck. "I can't tell a lie," I said at last. "Bree is what people used to call 'high-spirited.'" I used this word on purpose, making careful eye contact with Portia while I said it, willing her to understand the reference. Melanie Wilkes, the very definition of Christian, feminine piety, defended Scarlett in *Gone with the Wind* with that very phrase.

I saw the understanding dawn in Sister Portia's eyes and went on, encouraged by her comprehension. "Bree can be a little too lively and needs a strong hand, one I know you can provide." I made eye contact with Sister Mallory, then Sister Dara. I could tell Sister Mallory liked the implied compliment. "Bree can be a handful at first, for sure, but she's hardworking and loyal to the core. She'll make an excellent BabyDoll given more time and training, plus the right set of proprietors. Some probably appreciate a little personality in their servants, I presume?"

The teachers exchanged glances, and relief flooded my system as I deciphered their looks. My move had been the right one.

Still, the whole interaction left me feeling unsettled. I had been asked to spy for the Defiance, and now, it seemed I was being asked to spy for the teachers too. Or perhaps they had been spying on us and were just confirming what they already knew? It was confusing. But whatever the case, I knew my true allegiances.

I was going to graduate soon. I would be entering Hydra proper, not just the inskirts. And I would see an ageless Old Blood for the first time. What would the family be like? How would I fit in with the other BabyDolls? I couldn't stop myself from wondering about these things, even though they didn't really matter. All that really mattered was that I would be one step closer to finding my mother.

That night, as I said my prayers, a strange new habit I'd picked up here, I ended by speaking directly to her in my mind, telling her, "I'm coming for you, Mom. Hold on. I have a lot of yelling at you to do." I could imagine the upraised eyebrow and lovingly exasperated facial expression that would have greeted these words if I had been able to speak to her in person.

Hold on. I'm coming for you. I love you. I'm on my way.

It felt like things were truly coming together. Like I could do this impossible thing. After all, what was it that playing chess with Dara had taught me?

Sometimes a well-placed pawn could be more powerful than a queen.

Chapter Eight

Into the Darkness They Go

I was leaving. This was it. Graduation day.

As my roommate, Bree had been given special permission to miss her morning classes and see me off. We'd spent most of the night whispering across the small space between our beds, too excited to fall asleep. I knew I'd pay for that later, but I was too full of adrenaline to feel tired yet.

At lights-on, Elder Sister Dara showed up at our dormitory door with my new uniform, presented in an elegant black box wrapped with a bright fuchsia bow.

"Congratulations, Amy," she said. "Get dressed, eat some breakfast, and say your good-byes to everyone. We leave at nine fifteen sharp. Be in the entry hall."

Breakfast was an unusually rowdy ordeal as everyone vied to say their good-byes both to me and to Ida, who was also graduating early. She wasn't being recommended for stewardship but didn't seem fazed by losing out to me, and I wondered if perhaps the competition had been one-sided all along. I was relieved when everyone had to scurry off to morning classes, as I didn't really know what to do with all the attention, envy, and sheer noise of the group good-bye. I'd hardly eaten a bite and now forced myself to put something in my belly before departure.

I was grateful to have Bree by my side, the closest thing to a real friend that I had in here. Last night, hanging out for the last time, I had drawn her portrait in my sketchbook because I didn't want to forget her face, and who knew if we'd ever cross paths again? She'd loved posing and was only slightly annoying in the way she kept breaking her pose to try to see the sketch as I worked on it. She said she wanted to be sure I was making her "look good." When it was done, she loved it so much that she made me draw it all over again on another page and rip that page out to give to her. I happily complied.

I was less happy to comply with Bree's insistence on returning the favor and drawing my portrait right back. I didn't want to waste precious space in my sketchbook, but she said, "I can't give you anything you can take with you. Let me give you this," and her eyes had been so soft and imploring that I'd had to give in.

Her "portrait" was atrocious. It took up an entire page and was one step up from a child's stick drawing. My lips were literally just a curved pink line and my red flippy hairdo was as big as the rest of my body. I didn't know whether to laugh or cry, then I read the writing below it and snorted in a combination of indignation and embarrassment. In cutesy bubble letters with ridiculous hearts dotting the I's, she'd written a bunch of nice things then capped it off with, "p.s. Sometimes you fart in your sleep, but I still liked being your roommate."

"Oh my God, Bree. I'm scratching that out. What the fuck?"

Bree cracked up and grabbed my pencil case, keeping it from me. We struggled over it for a minute before I gave up, my face burning.

"Do I really?" I asked in a little voice, horrified.

Bree hesitated a moment, making me sweat. "No," she admitted at last, a sly expression on her face. "But I thought it would make you laugh when you look at it. Help you remember me and how much fun I was."

Her face was strangely vulnerable, and I realized how little I knew her but also how much I appreciated the little she felt she could show me. Bree didn't like to open up. I could see how all the humor was just a way to invite people into a connection while still keeping them at arm's length. I found myself saying a little prayer for her, for this lively, fun-loving girl, that she might not have her spirit crushed by this new world we were getting ready to enter. I pulled her roughly to me in an awkward hug, unsure how to express everything I was feeling for her. And in the hug, I felt her own inarticulate reciprocation of my feelings.

Because that whole interaction with the sisters had spooked me, I tried to warn her to be careful, to be more compliant and respectful to our elders, but she just laughed it off. Watching her later, eating a banana and talking with her mouth full, the same sense of worry came over me. How would she fare in this world if she didn't learn to temper her wilder impulses? But she'd survived here before me, I reminded myself. And besides, if she was anything, it was a wily survivor.

I'd probably never see her again. The thought made my heart sink. It was strange how quickly we'd bonded. I wished we could somehow end up in the same household before remembering that was only going to be temporary anyway. The truth was, there was nothing else I could do for Bree. We were on our own in here.

I tuned out of my own thoughts and into what Bree was blathering on about. She almost never shut up, and if I was being honest, I was looking forward to having a new living arrangement where I would hopefully have some solitude.

"Here's hoping your proprietor is a smoking hot beast of a man," Bree declared, raising her orange juice in a toast. When I didn't raise mine in response, she asked, "What? You know half these rich guys are gonna wanna bang the help. Let's at least hope they're good-looking if we gotta deal with that."

"It's not that," I said, disturbed by her casual acceptance of the sexual peril of our station. "It's just…" I hesitated. But now that I was leaving, I couldn't see any reason not to tell her. "It's just that I'm not really into men. I prefer women."

Bree, who had seemed impatient waiting for me to "cheers" her, had begun drinking her orange juice. She choked now, and some of it flew out back into her glass.

I just laughed at her reaction, trusting it was simply surprise and nothing unaccepting. She wiped her face and the spray on the table with a napkin, then turned to me. "Are you telling me you were lezzing out on me all this time?"

"No, I'm telling you I prefer women to men."

"So you weren't lezzing out on me all this time? What the fuck? Why not? I'm gorgeous."

I laughed again. "Yes, but you're my friend. And besides…" I hesitated, but the need to talk about Rake felt overwhelming. I'd most likely be seeing her again in a few hours. Graduation meant final good-byes and the exchange of credits. "Well…there's someone back home," I said shyly.

"You have a girlfriend?" Bree asked, her eyes practically popping out of her head.

"No," I said quickly. Then fumbled. "Well, I mean, sort of. I don't know. It's complicated."

Bree was looking at me like I was a whole different person, but her eyes were soft, sort of amused and also with a trace of something like compassion, at least as close as Bree ever got to that. "So, basically, you're saying that labels are tricky, but you care about some girl back home?"

"Yes," I said, my eyes brimming with tears.

"Is she gonna be there?"

"I think so. There's no one else to collect the credits."

Bree nodded thoughtfully. "You ready to face her? You can't cry, you know. If you show too much emotion, they'll say you're not ready. They'll bring you back here, and you'll have to start all over again."

"I know," I said, but even as I said it, I felt the tears spill over when thinking of seeing Rake again.

Whack! Something hit my face hard, and I just about fell off my chair. I realized with a start that Bree had just smacked me right across the face. I stared at her in open-mouthed shock.

"You…you hit me," I stammered.

"Yeah, and I'll hit you harder if you don't control yourself and wind up back here. You take those feelings and you bury them deep. You didn't come all this way and endure all this bullshit just to wind up back where you started. And why? Because you have butterflies for some stupid girl? You gonna let Ida win? You gonna deny the people you left behind the credits they need? Because you're a crybaby? No. You start to feel like you're gonna cry, you remember, I'll fucking beat your ass if you end up back here. I mean it."

She was red in the face and breathing hard. I realized she was trying to help me in her own messed-up way. It crossed my mind that she was talking to herself too, that she must also fear failing graduation when standing across from the family she left behind, the ones she sacrificed her own future to save. She'd told me enough to know that she didn't want to be here. She did it for the money. For her little siblings, who didn't have enough to eat.

My cheek stung, and we sat there staring at each other in a kind of anguished silence. It wasn't the good-bye I would have chosen. But it was probably exactly what I needed. I'd avoided thinking too much about seeing Rake because I was afraid of what I'd feel. But I needed to face it. To prepare myself.

Bree glanced at the clock, and my eyes followed hers. It was time to go.

We both stood and pushed in our chairs.

I wasn't sure what to say. I went to hug her, "Bree, I…"

But she stepped back as I stepped forward. Her eyes went hard.

"Go pass this last test, Amara. I don't ever wanna see your face again." And with that, she turned abruptly and stalked out of the dining hall.

It felt like a piece of me was being torn away as she left. I wanted to yell her name, ask her to come back, tell her I loved her, wish her well, say I understood why she'd hit me, all those things. But she already knew. I knew she did. This was just how it had to be. Practice. For a much worse good-bye to come.

I watched her walk away and buried my feelings like she had advised me. I would feel them later. I could cry later. Right now, I had one last test to pass. And she was right. I wasn't going to fuck it up just because of I couldn't control myself. I owed everyone more than that.

I composed my face, smoothed my clothes, and picked up my meager belongings. A little thrill of trepidation ran through me. One step at a time, I reminded myself, then breathed out a long breath and made for the entry hall.

Sister Dara said some things to me. I hardly took in her words. Then the van arrived, and I was shuttled off with Ida and a bunch of other graduates from nearby academies. There were boys who wore outfits almost identical to ours but in black and robin's egg blue. They were all young and handsome but effeminate. Unthreatening and compliant. The kind of young men who would be proud to be called a BabyDoll of Hydra. We tried not to stare at one another as we each wrestled with our feelings in silence during the seemingly endless ride to the gate.

Eventually, the van stopped, and we were herded through that same austere building with the giant door that I'd traversed with Dr. Ahmed. I looked for him but saw no familiar faces anywhere. An Elder Sister and Brother who I didn't know shepherded us to a makeshift platform erected before the gate. While the Elders and a bunch of official-looking people conferred, I took my first look out at the crowd amassed beyond the gate.

It was shocking to see the ugliness of poverty again. Had I really lost touch so quickly? I was horrified and embarrassed by the wave of shame that flooded me as I scanned the shabby people with desperate faces behind the fence. The dirty torn clothing on the kids upset me. Sadder still, I saw signs that folks had made a real effort to look their best. Old women wore faded, ill-fitting dresses. There were shiny, too-big shoes on feet with mismatched socks. Homemade jewelry. Scrubbed faces. This pride in doing their best to show up looking decent for the gatekeepers shook me more than the poverty itself.

I felt Ida stir and followed her gaze to a family in the crowd. A mother, father, and two younger brothers. They stared up at her with such evident pride. The mom kept wiping her eyes, and the father was patting her shoulder, comforting her while the boys pointed and yelled to everyone, "That's my big sister!"

Ida was beaming. She was trembling but seemed to have herself under control. I looked back to the family and watched as the dad took the youngest child up on his shoulders so he could see better. He was waving so wildly, I worried he'd fall off his father's frail shoulders. They were all thin and clearly in need of the credits their eldest daughter would provide for them today. Another wave of shame flooded me. Why the hell had I been competing with this girl? She was just trying to help her family. We had everything in common, but I'd decided not to like her just because she was as capable of success as I was. What a superficial fool I'd been.

I scanned the crowd for Rake's face, full of both fear and yearning. I couldn't see her in the throng. There were only seven graduates today but tons of people. The academy held graduation at noon on the first day of each month, and folks just had to show up and hope their loved one had made it. Some families must have shown up month after month, I realized. Hydra didn't care that it was stressful and inconvenient for poor people to make the trek here each and every month. If they wanted a shot at the credits and to claim their kin, they would manage it.

The crowd started to mutter and shift as people realized their children were not among the graduates. I watched as a dignified, older black woman's face registered resignation after scanning the platform. She closed her eyes and murmured something to herself, then turned to go. I wondered if she was Zenobia's mother. She had the same way of carrying herself that reminded me of Zen. She stood strong and tall, as if the hardships of life hadn't diminished her at all. But, no, Zen would have been dropped back off at the gate after flunking out, right? Unless they'd kept her for a Drudge. But she seemed far too young and pretty for that. A niggling fear that something worse had happened to her unsettled my mind again, but I shook it away. It really bothered me to not know what had become of my friend, to have no idea what happened to folks who never managed to graduate. But there was nothing I could do about that. I redoubled my efforts to find Rake in the crowd.

The Elders approached the podium and began making a speech, and still, I couldn't find her. I started to fear she wouldn't show up.

Hadn't she skipped out on our last good-bye? Rake was an avoider when things got too real. I felt myself becoming angry, feeling abandoned.

Then, there she was.

Being pushed forward by someone. There she was.

I choked back something between a laugh and a sob. She looked so good and so bad at the same time. It was a lot to take in. She'd dressed up. Was wearing plaid gray dress pants, a skinny black tie, and a white button-up. I remembered when she'd found it. It had a big grease stain on it, but she'd liked the way it fit and just cut a couple of squares of gray and black from something else and sewed them in an overlapping diamond pattern over the stain, making it seem like a feature of the shirt. She was always resourceful like that. Making something cool out of nothing special.

But damn, she looked bad. She'd lost weight, her hair was faded, and she hadn't bothered to re-dye it. It seemed like she was growing it out too. Or maybe just hadn't cared enough to cut it. She was too pale and seemed like a sorry shadow of herself. It freaked me out.

With sudden, startling insight, I realized that maybe she needed me more than I realized. Rake had always seemed so powerful, so carefree and capable that I hadn't really worried too much about her being left behind and what it might do to her. Guilt coursed through me. I had barely spared a thought about how she was doing. I'd just assumed she'd be okay. I'd watched her weather plenty of disappointments and losses. But maybe this was too much. Her dad. Her mom. Her surrogate mom and now me. It was a lot. How could I not have realized that? We were all the family she had left.

I heard my name over the microphone and startled, pulled back into the moment.

"Please step forward, Amy. I repeat, Amy, née Amara Rodriguez. Does anyone claim this girl?"

I moved forward woodenly, everything feeling unreal.

The woman with Rake elbowed her, then grabbed her arm and raised it for her.

"Thank you for coming," the Elder Sister said from the podium. "Amy has earned a place among the Old Bloods. She is a credit to you. You have two minutes to say your farewells."

I was ushered to the fence, preoccupied with controlling my face and feelings, but not too much to notice that the older woman with Rake was holding her hand. Trying to comfort her, no doubt. Right?

Wasn't she the one who'd done Rake's tattoos? Irene something? I tried to focus. Two minutes to say everything. What could I possibly say?

Rake was holding herself rigid, as if she would fall apart if she relaxed for even a moment. It was strange and unnerving. Where was the sassy, playful, cocky girl I knew? I approached the fence, uncertain. I scanned her face as she scanned mine. Her gaze lingered at my lips, and heat rushed through me. Our fingers found each other between the links in the fence, and I moved closer.

How many times had I looked into her eyes, and how many things had I seen there? Mischief, sorrow, joy, shame, fear, desire, the gamut of human emotion: I knew how they all played out in Rake's familiar face, how they shifted her features and the depth of color in her warm brown eyes. I couldn't pinpoint her look now; there was too much in play. Like me, she seemed to have a myriad of roiling emotions underneath the surface of her strained expression.

Still, just being close to her once more. In her presence. It was such a comfort. I wanted to feel her arms around me, to inhale her scent and have her play with my hair. I closed my eyes and choked down a wave of emotion.

"Time's up," an official said by my side. "Amy, go join your peers."

Panic rose up in me. We hadn't said a thing. Not one damn word.

The official began speaking to Rake, telling her where to go to access the credits.

"I believe in you," Rake said to me, ignoring him. I could see she was waiting for a reply, but I didn't trust my voice, and I didn't know what to say. The official began to usher me away, and I saw the panic rise in Rake too.

"Amara. Say something. Say anything," she begged.

What could I say? They were listening. Rake spoke half-assed Spanish like I did, but plenty of people here spoke Spanish. I didn't want them to understand whatever I might have to say to her. It was ours.

The official had his hand on the small of my back and was pushing me forward, but I turned and blurted out, "Iay illway omecay ackbay. Iay romisepay."

The official halted, his expression confused, but Rake's face lit up.

It was Pig Latin, a silly language game we used to play when we were little and wanted to speak in front of the grown-ups without them understanding. Rake's dad had taught it to us, and we'd gotten so good at speaking it super quickly that even he couldn't keep up once we got on a roll.

Rake started laughing, even as tears spilled from her eyes. "Iay ovelay ouyay," she said.

"Emay ootay," I replied before the official steered me aggressively away.

I started laughing in almost hysterical relief. The Elder Sister raised her eyebrows at me, seemingly unimpressed at my lack of decorum but not displeased enough to halt my graduation. I stifled the laughter but couldn't stop myself from smiling. It was too ridiculous. The first time I'd ever told someone I loved them, and it had been in Pig Latin? But everything that was happening was bizarre.

I couldn't see Rake from my new position beside my fellow graduates, but I was flying high on the feelings she'd left me with. She'd said she loved me. And I'd said it back. I'd never said that to anyone but my mom. And it was so like us to do it in such a weird, cute, roundabout way.

Doubt wiggled in beside the elation after a while. What did it even mean to say that? Did I know? Did she? Did she only say it because I was leaving? Because of the intensity of the moment? There was something oddly intimate in the way she'd interacted with Irene or whatever her name was. Were they lovers? Had she turned to her for comfort? Maybe Rake just meant it in a best friend kind of way. Like how I'd wanted to tell Bree that I cared about her before we left.

I stood with the other graduates and tried not to laugh or cry or feel anything. But I felt it all. I thought back to the way Rake had held me on our last night together. The way she'd whispered my name and the warmth in my heart had told me she meant it. For real. She did. She loved me. And I loved her too.

So I meant both things I said. I *would* come back to her. One way or another. Because love meant never giving up. It meant risking everything. Even heading into the maw of the monster.

For here we were, lined up in our blue and pink wrappers like so many cute little bonbons about to be swallowed up by Hydra's greedy hunger.

I shivered and braced myself.

Down the hatch we go.

CHAPTER NINE

Though I Be Among the Dead

I learned the true import of several familiar words on my first day in Hydra proper, starting with "stupefied." I was stupefied by the sheer, obscene wealth and splendor. I was dumbstruck that such homes existed, that people could casually claim such privilege. I had to consciously keep my jaw closed as a BabyDoll named Ivy led me on a tour.

The estate was imposing and enormous, with elaborate grounds, perched atop a dune before the ocean. I'd never seen the ocean, had only read about it in books, and its immensity and power awed me deeply. I couldn't take everything in. I wanted to stop every few minutes and capture what I saw in my sketchbook, but that wasn't possible, so I was overflowing with the bombardment of potent impressions with no outlet to process them. It left me shaking and discombobulated.

I didn't think I'd made a very good impression with the steward of the house, a self-important pretty boy named Huxley. I was to shadow him in all aspects of household management so that one day, I might move up the ladder and become steward of a similar home. But Huxley had no interest in having a shadow, and he seemed to have doubts about my fitness for the post that he made all too clear with a haughty once-over when I first arrived. Just my luck to get a bitchy gay guy for a boss.

My real boss, though, my legal proprietor, was Dr. Rebecca Keenan, an Old Blood council member and one of the FirstGen originators of the Remedy. I was relieved to hear the household was headed by a woman. All my fear of a looming sexual threat dissipated. She might still be threatening in other ways, though. She was famous, on the team who pioneered the cure. I was dying with curiosity to meet her, but our initial meeting was brief and curt. She was an important person, and even as a steward-in-training, I was no one special.

Still, there had been curiosity in her eyes in the few brief moments we exchanged greetings. Her eyes seemed to lay me bare. She was tall, thin, and severe. Everything about her suggested an intensity of purpose that found me—and anything else that took her from her work—to be a complete waste of time. She fit her home. It was stark and cold and minimalistic. Undeniably elegant but the kind of elegance that repelled and judged. It was not a place to relax or feel comfortable. It demanded to know what you were doing in it and said, hadn't you better make yourself useful?

Still, she was fascinating. She looked to be in her forties but as one of the FirstGen, she had to be into her second century of life. She was older than Nana, older than anyone I had ever met. A real Old Blood. In the flesh. Flesh that still looked youthful and vibrant. What had she seen in her time? She should have been dead several times over. It was a creepy thought. Her parents, her siblings, her childhood friends, had they all passed on? Or had they managed to secure a priceless spot in Hydra too?

I tried not to betray my curiosity, but it was difficult to hide. What kind of brilliant mind had created the cure? What kind of heart had agreed to hoard it for a precious few? Dr. Keenan was a fascinating mystery.

And I was here to unravel her.

At least partially. I was really here for my mother, but houses like this did not keep Drudges. They might be hired in for a specific, difficult, or dirty job, but they were not kept as help. There were eight BabyDolls in total, excluding myself, who kept the household running efficiently. I hardly seemed needed, and yet, here I was. I supposed it was a status symbol to own so many servants. We had our own quarters close by in a tidy beach house not far from the main estate. My roommate was a sullen brunette named Claudia who seemed to resent my intrusion on her privacy. I tried to be friendly and accommodating, but my efforts just seemed to annoy her more, so I stopped interacting with her. No one seemed to want me there, which felt awkward.

Huxley kept passing me off to other BabyDolls, ostensibly to learn how Dr. Keenan liked things done, as each person had their own responsibilities, but I think it was mostly to get me out of his hair. I spent time learning Dr. Keenan's preferences for how to make a bed and set the table and such, but I was mostly left to my own devices. I wandered the house and grounds, being nosy, an excuse at the ready should I be questioned, but no one seemed to care much what I did as long as I wasn't in their way. That suited me just fine and boded well for my espionage mission.

The place was unimaginably clean, excessively large, and disturbingly empty. So much wasted space almost physically hurt me. Entire families could live in these closets. The place held a mesmerizing kind of pull for me. While I was repulsed and angry about the excess, I was undeniably moved by the seductive beauty. It was severe and repellent yet awing and striking all at once.

Like the giant hydra holo projection that served as art atop one of the grand staircases. I could stare and stare at its immense, unnerving form for long stretches of time. It was so freaky that I wanted to turn from it, yet in some eerie way, it was also hauntingly compelling and kept me rooted to the spot. Hydra came in different colors, but were most often shown in their vibrant, alien-green shade. This holo showed the purplish-white variety. It was uncanny to watch how the hydra, cousin to the jellyfish, looked like a beautiful woman dancing in a form fitting gown. It had a soft, gelatinous, translucent body topped with a crown of slender tentacles that undulated like a woman's flowing tresses. I tried to figure out if this was a live feed of a fish tank or a loop but I always lost that purpose and just stared at the subtly luminous figure drifting in a dark tank like some kind of otherworldly creature adrift in the cosmos. Sometimes I felt a strange, nonsensical kinship with it, even as the thought weirded me out. But what was I if not adrift? I always pulled away from the holo with a bizarre mixture of regret and relief.

There were plenty of other, less unsettling things to capture my attention. Like the west wing of the house with Dr. Keenan's bedroom on the second floor and her home lab beneath. Only Huxley had access to the west wing, which seemed closed off and forbidding, unlike the open concept of the rest of the house. There were giant floor to ceiling windows and retractable doors in most of the house, but not that wing. That only made it all the more intriguing, and I figured that whatever the Defiance was looking for, I was most likely to find it there.

I began ingratiating myself with Huxley, hoping he'd give in and take me under his wing. But he was prickly and standoffish, so I knew it would take some time to wiggle my way into his confidence. But I was determined. I lay awake at night, thinking of ways to win him over. Finding out I was also Team Rainbow might buy me a few points.

Mostly at night, I thought of the women I'd left behind. Rake and Bree and all the girls at the academy. I worried about them and wondered what they were doing. It was odd, but sometimes, I snuggled with my pencil case at night, just to feel my mother and Rake close to me. My mother. She was close. Somewhere nearby.

What were her days like as a Drudge? I didn't know much about that role and began asking the other servants, but they didn't know much either. They were called Greenies sometimes because of their green uniforms. I supposed there was irony in that. Drudges were typically older New Bloods who were still considered "green" to the ageless Old Bloods. I hadn't seen one yet, just an image on Eldest Sister Mallory's stolen datapad. Their uniforms were formless unisex jumpsuits in a dull grayish-green shade that made me think of dreary November drizzle and sleet on moss. They looked like prison uniforms.

I sent messages to the Defiance whenever I found out anything that seemed useful. It was thrilling to finally use the book, although the lack of response was a letdown. How did I know it was even working? Nonetheless, I looked through the book and easily found the words "left the," then bemoaned the likelihood of finding "academy" until I realized this was an old-fashioned book about a painter and lucked out in the very first chapter.

It became sort of fun, looking for words that might be useful. I was supposed to watch Dr. Keenan's comings and goings, but she wasn't easy to pin down. Her morning routine was predictable, but no one could ever say when she'd be home, and when she did get home, she had food sent to her suite. She hardly ever deigned to walk through the house, let alone enjoy it. It seemed almost offensive to have access to so much luxury and to pay so little attention to it. She never had visitors and seemed to do nothing but work.

The only interesting break in the pattern came when she caught a cold and worked from home. The entire household was in a flutter of consternation at the disruption of routine. Huxley was unbearably bossy and anxious. But in attempting to cater to her every possible need, he requested my help, and I was permitted to come with him to the west wing. I carried a tray with honeyed tea while he brought extra linens and small comforts.

"Don't say a word. Just put the tea on her desk and leave quietly," he said as he submitted his right hand for a biometric scan.

I'd seen vein scanners at the gateway, but it seemed strange to have in the door to a bedroom. Although it really was a suite. There was a freaking grand piano looking out at the ocean. A shiny, white, full-sized freaking piano. In her bedroom. Either the place was soundproofed, or she never played and it was all for show. In any case, three walls were austere white like the rest of the house, then the fourth wall was the only window in the whole west wing. There was a sitting area, a bed, and a desk. All in one massive room with an ensuite. She didn't even need the rest of the house.

I deposited the tea silently on her desk, sparing a moment to glance at her things, trying to suss out what she was working on, but her datapad was off, and she was blowing her nose by her bedside. There was nothing much to see. Still, it was an odd thrill to enter the inner sanctum, a place where anything could be happening. Who knew what scientific breakthroughs she might have been working on at this very moment? Perhaps she should have been working on a cure for the common cold that seemed to be kicking her ass despite all her brilliance.

For the rest of the day, I was kept busy helping everyone. When I got back to my quarters that night, I was anxious to send a message but would have to wait for a solitary moment, as my roommate was taciturnly sulking across from me as usual.

The next day, I snuck away to peruse the book. I found the word "laburnum," which was evidently some kind of flower, but I wasn't sure my finger could be sufficiently precise to transmit just the first three letters. After some perusing, I managed to find a useful sentence about how one of the characters had spent a great deal of time at Cambridge University "working in the laboratory," but how to tell them about the biometric scanners? That wasn't going to make an appearance in a novel this old.

I spent an inordinate amount of time skimming and reskimming the book. At last, I found the line where Dorian locked away his hideously aging portrait: "There was no other place in the house so secure from prying eyes as this. He had the key, and no one else could enter it." Once I found the words "veins" and "are" and "the keys," scattered about in different chapters, I closed the book, smugly satisfied that I was not, in fact, a completely useless informant.

The next big uproar in the household occurred when Magnus arrived. Magnus was a cat. An insanely expensive designer breed called a Royal Ashera, evidently a cross between a regular domesticated house cat, an Asian leopard, and an African wildcat called a serval. The help was all abuzz about how this cat cost as much as a modest house. He was a handsome specimen, with a tan, spotted coat and a long, lean body. I liked animals, and caring for Magnus seemed to fall naturally to me as I had no clear role anyway. I gathered from all the gossip that the last cat in the house had been an ill-tempered sphinx named Cato, who'd hated everyone except his owner. No one wanted anything to do with his replacement, but Dr. Keenan was eager to have him leash-trained for no apparent reason. She never walked the grounds, and besides a daily hello and good-bye, she hardly seemed to pay the cat any mind, so I couldn't understand why training him to walk on a leash mattered, but it was my job to follow orders, not question them, so I dutifully set about to get the little guy to go for walks with me.

I didn't anticipate how difficult this task would prove.

I knew cats were independent and stubborn, and so I should have predicted that this would be a nightmare, but Magnus was easygoing and took to the harness quickly, so I thought it would be smooth sailing. He did well indoors, though he was mostly leading me around. Evidently, taking a cat for a walk was really more like the cat taking me for a walk. We'd explored the front grounds a few times with relative success, and I thought he might be ready to explore the dunes and the beach.

At first, he just sat and stared out at the ocean, his ears attentive, his whole body alert. Then he made for the wooden stairs that led down the dunes. He stopped on a step to chew on the beach grass. I tried to urge him forward, but he didn't seem to understand that stairs were a means to a destination, not a place to stop. He made himself comfortable on the sunny step, stretching out and occasionally chewing a stray strand of grass. I sighed and settled in beside him.

The ocean amazed me. It was a living thing, so much louder and more dynamic than I had ever been able to picture. I watched the waves surge and recede, surge and recede, a lulling rhythm that made me want to curl up on a sandy step just like Magnus and take a luxurious nap in the sunshine. Maybe cats had it right. They listened to nothing but their own whims and valued nothing above their own sensual delight and self-sovereignty. I could respect that.

A butterfly winged by, and Magnus went on alert, vibrating with predatory instincts. He chased the butterfly down a few steps, and I rushed to follow. He jumped on the handrail and sprinted gracefully before lunging for the insect. He caught it and ate it proudly, chomping with grotesque satisfaction. I looked away, repulsed.

Then I heard her.

A sweet peal of laughter carried over the surging waves. I turned to the sound and finally understood the true meaning of another word: breathtaking. A blond goddess of a girl dressed in a semi-sheer white sundress splashed through the waves, her face lit up with delight.

I blinked. Dumbstruck. The sunshine in her hair made a golden halo about her head, and it shone through the dress where it did not hug her curves, showing her silhouette in a natural, innocently sensual way. She looked at me, her eyes still aglow with joy, and I felt rooted to the spot with something I didn't know how to describe.

Then Huxley appeared beside her, his BabyDoll pants rolled above the knees so he could wade through the waves alongside her. He saw me and blanched. It occurred to me that he might not be gay after all. That she might be his girlfriend. The thought repulsed me more than the insect chomping, but I didn't have time to think it through because something burned across my hand. I looked down and realized Magnus had taken off, sprinting across the dunes, running free with the leash dragging behind him. I yelled after him and began running.

"Don't lose him," Huxley screamed behind me.

I sprinted up the steps, sick at the thought of how many credits I'd owe Dr. Keenan if he escaped. I could see him, a brown blur in the sand, causing commotion amongst the tufts of grass. He ran toward the servants' quarters. My heart was pounding. I feared he'd just keep running until he was out of sight, but he scampered up a tree by the building, and the awful fear in my stomach loosened some of its grip.

Huxley and the girl weren't far behind. I could feel the barely contained rage emanating from Huxley as he made his way to the tree. He'd always thought I was useless, and I'd just proven him right. I bent and tied my shoes carefully, ignoring him and preparing to climb the tree.

"I'm going to get a plate of tuna," he said while panting, before taking off for the main house.

Then it was just me and the girl. I couldn't look at her. She must have thought me a complete idiot. I put all my focus into getting this goddamn cat out of the tree. I talked calmly and quietly to Magnus for my whole climb up. The leash had snagged, and he was stuck and panicking, pulling, thrashing his head this way and that. I got close enough to grab the end of the leash and disentangle it.

Now how to coax him down without getting my eyes scratched out? I remembered the treats in my pocket and began placing them on a branch within reach, one he could jump to without getting even more tangled.

I didn't try to get any closer. My position was precarious enough. I just laid out the treats and started humming. He seemed to like it. He watched me, wary but curious. Though part of me was painfully aware that the most stunning human I'd ever met was watching and listening below, another part of me was more aware that I absolutely had to catch this cat, or else… I didn't even know what. I swallowed my pride and began singing softly, careful not to make too much eye contact with Magnus, feigning disinterest, as if I'd often spent my afternoons serenading creatures stuck in trees.

I took a treat and nudged it. He didn't budge, so I pretended to eat one. He bristled and jumped to the branch to claim them. It took everything in me not to grab him. I held the leash close and let him finish. When he was done and looked at me for more, I gently scooped him up and started to make my way down. He barely squirmed, and when my feet hit the ground, I dumped a decidedly unhealthy mound of treats on the ground for him.

I closed my eyes and held my hand over my chest, willing my heart to calm down. When I opened my eyes, she was beaming at me.

"Where did you learn how to climb trees?" she asked in a breathless voice dripping with admiration.

I was sweaty and disheveled, a nobody from nowhere standing before a girl so beautiful, I couldn't even handle it. I might have been cute enough to merit being a BabyDoll, but she was dazzlingly gorgeous in a way I'd thought only existed in movies and books. I should have been intimidated into awkward silence, but something about the way she looked at me made me feel…strangely bold. This girl was sheltered. Probably hadn't done or seen half the things I had. The thought made me feel oddly powerful.

"I learned a lot of strange tricks in the Freelands," I said vaguely, fighting the urge to straighten my clothes and pat down my hair. I held her gaze, and she blushed. I didn't know why that pleased me so much.

"I'm Stella," she offered, extending her hand shyly.

"I'm Amar…Amy," I answered, taking her hand. My stomach fluttered at her touch.

"I like your voice, Amy. What song were you singing?"

I wasn't actually sure of the title, so I just said, "Something my mom used to sing around the house sometimes."

"My mom never sings. I can't even imagine it." She laughed and gazed up at the estate.

I started, alarmed. "Is…is Dr. Keenan your mom?"

"Yes. I take it you're a new BabyDoll?"

"Yeah. I mean, yes, ma'am," I stammered, realizing I should be treating her with more formality.

Laughter tinkled out of her lovely throat. "Please don't change how you speak to me. We're around the same age, hardly old enough to be called ma'am. That's one of the reasons Hux and I get along so well. He's never treated me like a proprietor. Which I'm not, by the way. I don't even live here. When my dad left, I went with him. I'm just back to help plan the Juvenalia."

Huxley reappeared, sweating and red-faced, with an unneeded plate of tuna. Magnus stretched his full length and began feasting on the tuna right out of Huxley's hands before he could set the plate down.

"We were…working…just so you know," he said between labored breaths. "Collecting seashells…for the Juvenalia celebration." He looked defensive, but I couldn't care less if he was goofing off. I spent most of my days goofing off too.

"Hux, you never told me Mom had a new BabyDoll. Amy here just climbed this huge tree to get Magnus back. You wouldn't believe how high she was, and she didn't even seem scared. She sang to him and tricked him with some treats and saved the day," she said, petting Magnus along his outstretched back.

"It's hardly saving the day if she caused the problem," he grumbled.

"Don't be petty, Hux. She's a hero if I say so, and I do. We're going to be great friends. I can already tell."

Huxley glared at me, making it clear that he had no wish to share his friendship with Stella with me. But I hardly registered his jealousy because she had taken my arm and was leading me back to the house, Magnus trotting along behind us, sated and inexplicably obedient as any dog. Her body swayed next to mine, and she chattered on about nothing in particular in the most charming possible way.

All I wanted to do was look at and listen to her. To draw her and be near her. To bask in the glow of her. I tried not to think too hard about what that meant. I just let her lead me along, my heart fluttering like a wild thing in my chest.

Chapter Ten

And If Thou Wilt, Remember, and If Thou Wilt, Forget

In the days that followed, I forgot myself. Or at least, I forgot the me I'd always assumed I was. Now I was Amy, a BabyDoll in Hydra. A pretty girl from the streets with an edgy backstory. That was how Stella saw me, and I liked the me we created together.

In her eyes, I was brave and knowing and strong. A girl who grew up in the ghetto and understood how to survive in dangerous places. With her, I felt bold and suave and capable. I wasn't just Maria's girl or Rake's shadow but whoever I chose to be. She knew nothing of me except what I told her. So I told her that I broke a thug's nose on the way here. Which was probably true. But even if it wasn't, who hadn't exaggerated a tale to impress a beautiful woman?

In a way, I both lost and found myself in her. I really was all those things, after all. I just hadn't seemed them when set in a different background.

I was supposed to be spying for the Defiance and trying to track down my mother, but I spent most of my time trying to make this stunning woman laugh. I loved her laughter. The way joy flowed from her lips. I had counted five distinct laughs, my favorite being the cute one where she'd wrinkle her nose and giggle, though I was partial to the wide-eyed, full-bellied one too, the one Huxley often elicited with his shockingly inappropriate comments. I loved her sounds. Her movements. Everything.

I was utterly captivated. And once again, I found myself thinking about the true meaning of words. I was besotted and enthralled but happily so. And maybe this feeling was a stupid kind of bondage, but wouldn't it have been stupider to resist it? I'd met hundreds of people in my time on this planet, and none of them had inspired this feeling before now.

Which was where the guilt came in. Because there was Rake. There had always been Rake. And we had just begun to tiptoe around being "Rake and Amara" in a whole new exciting way. I loved her. No part of me doubted that. But it was confusing to compare my feelings for Rake with these new feelings for Stella. They were nothing alike.

Things with Rake had always been unclear and intense. She scared me. Maybe because I wasn't sure what I felt for her. Or maybe because I did, but I didn't want to risk losing her since she was one of the most consistently loving people in my life. I'd always felt ambivalent about her charm and uncertain about her in-your-face sexiness. She'd always been more at ease in her body than me, though I'd felt that shifting lately. The bigger issue was that I'd never known if she meant it when she flirted with me because she flirted with everyone. Then, I'd come to realize that she had meant it, and I'd relaxed into it, but then I'd had to leave. And now she was there, and I was here, and where did that leave us? Was she messing around with that Irene woman, or was Irene just taking care of her in a way that I should have been grateful for? A way that she clearly needed in my absence. Did it matter? What had we promised each other? Nothing explicit. Everything implicit. So I was torn.

But how could I not have had my head turned by Stella? I'd spent my whole life chasing beauty, and she was so…pristine. So impossibly gorgeous. I had never had access to anything really, truly, utterly beautiful before. In the Freelands, I'd immortalized small fragments of tattered beauty in my sketchbook, grateful for scraps of loveliness. I'd never encountered impeccable beauty. Unblemished. Radiant. Pure. It made me realize just how shabby life really was on the outside. I felt ashamed of that life and ashamed of my shame about it all at the same time.

But Stella and I were more alike than anyone might have imagined too, given the vast gulf between our life experiences. We shared the language of aesthetics. She was studying to become a fashion designer, much to her mother's disdain. We spent hours poring over her sketchbook, which was filled with ideas for everything from elaborate ballgowns to smart BabyDoll outfits.

She had the world at her fingertips, and maybe that should have led me to resent or envy or despise her, but it actually reminded me of what mattered. Because despite all the vulgar wealth she took for granted, she was also fundamentally sad, yearning for the approval of a mother who was only ever disappointed in her. I could feel the loneliness behind her easy banter with Huxley. She was an only child and LastGen to boot.

There would be no new generations in Hydra, the original Old Blood enclave. Mrs. Flores had taught us about the controversy over the reproduction ban and how it had led some Old Bloods to migrate elsewhere and start new enclaves all over the world. Places without access to the Remedy but where they could have the freedom to continue to become parents. What kind of life would that be, though? They'd just watch their offspring grow old and die as they lived on and on after them. Looking younger than their grandchildren? It gave me the shivers.

I watched Stella flip through her sketchbook, looking for designs to show me, and it struck me as logically inevitable that the Old Bloods would have to limit reproduction at some point if they hoped to stay in comfortable luxury, but it also struck me as unthinkable and unnatural. A place without children? How cold. How quickly that society would become stale and rigid. Her mother was FirstGen, one of the revered pioneers of the Remedy, those who held the most sway in Hydra, but her daughter was LastGen, the famous and forever infantilized final generation of Old Bloods.

Everything with Stella was so much clearer. Our roles. Our mutual desire. It was exciting and risk free. She looked at me like I was strong and exotic, and I liked feeling that way. Being the street punk to her sheltered princess. It was hot. I wanted her, and the feeling didn't scare me anymore. I was still reserved and cautious by nature…until I wasn't. Once I made up my mind on something, I was all the way in. And it felt good.

"Can I tell you a secret?" she asked, slamming the book closed, her eyes twinkling with adorable mischief.

"Seems like you've made up your mind to."

"I'm thinking of getting a tattoo."

She announced it like it was something scandalous. I tried not to laugh, but she must have read my poorly hidden amusement because she added, "What? Do you have one? I guess they must be pretty common in the Freelands."

"They are. But I've never gotten one. Too afraid of both needles and permanence."

"You never seem afraid of anything."

"Seeming and being are very different things. Only a fool is never afraid of anything."

"True. Do you think I'd look good with a tattoo? I'd have to leave the enclave to get one. Can you imagine my mother's face?" She laughed her laugh number two, the one where she'd tip her head back slightly as joy tinkled merrily from her throat. Maybe that was my favorite.

"Nobody gets tattoos here, I take it?"

"No. Oh my gosh. Only ruffians like you unsavory street rats sport tattoos." She was kidding, but I bristled a little at the phrase, having never heard it applied to me.

I shook it off, understanding her intent to tease. "Yeah, well, I guess it would be hard to pick an image you'd like to have on your body for centuries."

"I don't know. Some things about us don't change. I can think of images that would be meaningful forever, can't you?"

I shook my head slowly, unable to think of anything.

"Hmm." She got up from the little love seat we were perched on and wandered to the writing desk by the window. Stella's room was very different from the rest of the house. It was cozy and inviting. Her aesthetic was old-fashioned and refined, but there were soft feminine touches everywhere that blended into an overall feeling of gracious warmth and well-being that permeated everything. It was all gold and dusty pastels, unlike the harsh whites of the rest of the house.

She picked up an abstract figurine of a chickadee by the window. "I'd choose something pretty and free and strong in its own way. A bird, perhaps." She leaned against the window frame, facing me, stroking the figurine's head and eyeing me strangely. I couldn't say why or what shifted, but I felt the moment ripen.

She wore her hair in a face-framing French braid along the crown of her head. It was no exaggeration to say it made her look like a storybook princess.

Time to be a prince, I thought, and made my way to her desk. I picked up an old-fashioned ink pen from beside some pages filled with her handwriting and calligraphy practice. I brought my body purposefully close and watched her breath quicken.

"Turn around and I'll give you a tattoo," I offered, along with a wry smile.

The corners of her mouth twitched, and she blushed but turned her back to me, obediently facing the window. I came closer, almost touching her. I paused, savoring the delicious tension.

"Do you trust me?" I whispered.

She trembled and nodded.

I carefully gathered her hair and moved it over one shoulder, exposing the tender nape of her neck. It took everything in me not to kiss her there. Instead, I traced lightly down it before starting to unzip her dress. She stiffened.

"I need a canvas to work on," I reminded her, and she exhaled. She nodded again, and I continued the zipper's descent. Down, down, all the way to the dip of her lower back, just before the swell of her bottom. I could see the pale pink lace of her panties, the matching sheen of her bra running across her back. It must have clasped in front because it was nothing but a strip of pale fabric. I wanted so badly to reach inside the vee of her dress back, unclasp the bra, and caress all of her, feel all that perfect, tantalizing flesh in my achingly eager hands, but I forced myself to focus.

I ruined her pretty pink bra. Just drew right over it. I could have moved it to the side but took some kind of perverse thrill in marking it up. I used her figurine for inspiration, working in electric silence. When I was done, there was a chickadee on a curving cherry blossom branch on her right shoulder. It was delicate and sweet and natural, just like Stella. Again, I fought the urge to kiss her neck and instead zipped up the dress.

"I gotta get to work," I whispered. "Don't look at it until tonight when you undress." I stepped back, and she turned. She looked delectable, trembling, seeming full of fear and yearning. I held out the pen. "If you like it, let me know, and I'll mark you up again."

She took the pen, face flushed, and I walked away, knowing I had her right where I wanted her: wanting me. It was a perfect kind of excruciating.

It didn't take long for her to come to me after that day. To shyly hold out the pen and tell me she'd liked it. Her confession emboldened me. Magnus was taking me for a walk again, and Stella had found us by the very tree that I had climbed less than a week ago. So much had shifted since then. I took the pen and pushed her slowly but firmly up against the tree, careful not to let go of Magnus's leash again, lest I have to prove my feline rescue skills once more.

"Stay like this," I said, then tied Magnus's leash to the trunk of a smaller, nearby tree.

I liked the way she waited for me. The way she listened. So eager to please. To see what I would do next.

Honestly, I didn't know what to do next. This was all new to me, and yet, it didn't feel strange. It felt…fun. A queer kind of relief. To be bold for once. To be bossy and in charge. I liked the way her feminine softness brought out something cocky and masculine in me.

She waited. Cheeks flushed. Eyes bright. Breathing shallow.

"You liked it?" I repeated.

"Yes," she admitted.

"Should I give you another one?"

"Yes, please."

The ocean was choppy and loud. Its waves punished the shoreline, and the wind shook the leaves in the trees. I took a breath and stepped closer. She startled slightly, then laughed at herself.

"You good?"

"Yes, sorry. Just…excited to see what you're going to do…to draw," she added quickly, as though she'd revealed too much.

I smiled and came even closer, up against her. I traced the pen, lid still on, along the top of her shirt where flesh met fabric, my face inches from hers so that our breath mingled. I popped off the cap and tugged down her shirt to reveal more of her cleavage. Her breath caught, and I made eye contact, asking her silently. She inclined her head, and I continued, drawing a simple swirling pattern of birds in flight across her shoulder and down into the swell of her chest. I didn't spare this bra either. She could buy more. And I liked marking up her intimate garments; it felt like marking my territory.

I brought my mouth close to hers and felt her strain toward my lips, but I pulled back abruptly, amused by the way I was toying with her, curious to see just how much I could torture us both. I was having fun being a bit of an asshole, but Stella seemed done with my games and pulled me to her hungrily.

I liked that she insisted. I liked how she came to me. I liked the way she tasted as the wind whipped our hair about our faces.

We were unstoppable after that. Indiscreet and reckless.

I particularly savored being her servant, then turning the tables. Attending to her needs, then insisting she attend to mine. One memorable day, she told me she wanted tea served to her that afternoon with cucumber sandwiches, just like in a book she had read. I told her she better dress the part of a fancy lady. The whole time I was preparing her refreshments, all I could think about was where I might draw on her next. How bold I might get and what she'd let me get away with.

When I entered the sitting room a short while later, she was perched daintily on the sofa in a gauzy, light blue dress that I knew she'd designed herself. The color made her eyes pop, while the flouncy cut accentuated her slight curves. I couldn't help but appreciate her affinity for semi-sheer fabric.

I served her tea and asked, "Will there be anything else, ma'am?" purposefully using the form of address she most despised.

"Yes. Sit and share tea with me."

"That would be most inappropriate, I'm afraid."

"Oh, I can think of much more inappropriate things." Her eyes twinkled as she patted the sofa beside her. We ate and drank and talked silly, flirty nonsense for a time until she noticed the pen displayed prominently on the serving tray and picked it up. She held it out and raised an eyebrow.

That was all the invitation I needed. I knelt before her. Her legs were crossed primly, one foot dangling before my face. It was encased in a satin, baby-blue ballerina flat with ribbons that laced up the length of her slender calves. She reminded me of Cinderella in that pose and dress, and somehow, it made me even more aware of the fact that this couldn't last. That what we were doing was just fairy-tale, fantasy fun. Eventually, midnight would strike, and I would go back to sweeping the proverbial cinders while she married a real prince or as close to it as Hydra Old Bloods went. It didn't upset me, though. It was part of what I liked about all of this. With Rake, I'd held back because I had everything to lose. With Stella, I had nothing to lose. So I dove right in, running my hands up the smooth skin of her legs made even smoother by the silkiness of the ribbons.

I simply had to untie them. I liked disheveling her. She often wore her hair in a loose bun held up with a pretty assortment of hair sticks. I loved removing them and watching her hair tumble about her face. Sometimes, I'd walk by her, wink, and randomly pull loose one of the many laces and bows she liked on her shirts and dresses. I didn't care if the other servants saw.

I didn't care now. I unwrapped the laces and removed the shoe. She laughed and said, "Are you going to give me a foot massage?"

"Your wish is my command," I replied.

She wiggled her other foot in my face. I removed that shoe as well, after some strictly unnecessary caressing of her leg. I massaged her feet one at a time, amused at how tiny and cute they were. It took a lot of restraint not to let my eyes wander to the shadows of her skirt.

She began to make little sounds of pleasure, and it was too much to bear. I dropped her foot and picked up the pen I had abandoned on the floor. I tore the cap off with my mouth and kept it there. I made eye contact and parted her legs suggestively. Her right thigh was exposed, and I began to mark it up, pushing up the flounces of her skirt to a decidedly risqué level.

I didn't look at her face, but I could feel the heat coming off her. She was trembling, so I used my one hand to steady her leg in a reassuring grip, then focused all my energy and creativity on designing something beautiful in this deliciously intimate space. I didn't have any grand plan, just followed my whims, and somehow, a design full of flowers and hummingbirds emerged. I was working on the finer details in one of the bird's wings when a voice made me jump.

"What's going on here?"

Reckless. Indiscreet. Foolish. Those words might have crossed my mind in the seconds it took me to place the voice. Huxley. Not Rebecca.

Relief flooded through me, and Stella's sparkling laughter helped my heart calm down. I turned to face Huxley, shifting quickly from mortification to defiance. "It's lesbian kink. You wouldn't understand," I said.

More sparkling laughter burst from Stella.

Huxley's eyebrows arched. "Well, in that case, carry on, and I'll run interference. Dr. Keenan's back from the office, but far be it for me to get in the way of queer carnal pleasures."

He left, and Stella threw herself on top of me as we burst into huge belly laughs. We were quite literally rolling on the floor laughing until she bit my shoulder unexpectedly. Something flared inside me, and then we were rolling around on the floor, groping each other fiercely.

"...think Stella's in her bedroom," I heard Huxley say far too loudly and anxiously.

I didn't have to look up to know I was screwed. All the life and joy was sucked out of the room in an instant. We began disentangling ourselves.

"Oh. Oh, look, there she is," Huxley said from the doorway.

I added to the bad acting of the scene by saying, "I...I spilled some tea." It was the first thing that popped in my head. I grabbed a napkin and began blotting an invisible stain on Dr. Keenan's very expensive imported carpet.

"Mom, you were looking for me?" Stella asked, settling on the sofa and composing herself much more convincingly than either Huxley or I.

Rebecca's silence was brutal, so I risked looking and immediately regretted it. It was clear that she knew everything and was not impressed.

I mumbled something about getting cleaning supplies and rushed from the room. When I returned, mother and daughter were seated together, calmly discussing the upcoming Juvenalia festival plans. I pretended to clean the carpet, then interrupted their conversation to show Dr. Keenan the dirty rag. I thought I was clever because I'd poured tea on it in the kitchen to make my lie seem more plausible.

But her face showed nothing but repulsion and scorn. "You don't have to show me the filth. Just clean it quietly and leave."

Sister Dara would have been so disappointed in my dereliction of duty.

I left them and spent the rest of the afternoon worrying and trying to catch Stella alone. Before I could see her again, Dr. Keenan summoned me to the sitting room through Ivy, who couldn't stop herself from helpfully reminding me, "I told you that you were playing with fire."

I stood before Dr. Keenan with my hands clasped behind my back and my heart thumping out of my chest. What the hell was she going to say? Just how bad was this? "You wanted to see me, ma'am?"

She made a sound of irritation. "I've asked you not call me that. It makes me feel old. Call me doctor."

Fuck, I was forgetting everything from the Academy. "My apologies, Dr. Keenan. You wanted to see me?"

"Let's not insult each other with lies. You like my daughter, and she likes you. For now, at least."

Well. That hurt more than I'd expected.

"What you don't know about my daughter is that she's silly and frivolous and doesn't think things through." Dr. Keenan began to pace, and I watched her carefully. "She likes to make friends with the help. She doesn't know her place, and she has no discretion. That's fine. I have no expectations of her. I gave up on my expectations for her long ago."

An uncomfortable mixture of anger and sadness started to burn in my chest as I listened to her speak about her daughter that way. How could she have been so blind to Stella's worth? Even if they were very different, wasn't it natural for a mother to feel pride in her children?

She stepped uncomfortably close to me. "I do, however, have

expectations for my help. I expect you to know your place and to have discretion." Her eyes bored into me, and my discomfort grew. "Do you understand?"

This was not a woman to mess around with. There was nothing overtly threatening in what she was saying, but everything about her was so intentional and precise, driven and unrelenting, that I didn't want to imagine how frightening it would be to get on her bad side.

"I can assure you, I understand, Dr. Keenan. I apologize for my behavior. It was unbecoming of a graduate of Rosemont Academy, and it won't happen again."

She didn't say anything, so I racked my brain to think of what else I should say.

"Your daughter is…"

She clucked her tongue and made a dismissive gesture, so I turned to go and clumsily knocked into a side table, almost overturning a vase of flowers. I righted them at the last second and threw her a sheepish grin.

She offered me a death glare.

Sister Portia had been right: I really did need to practice how to enter and exit rooms with grace.

Chapter Eleven

The Peanut-Crunching Crowd Shoves In to See

Stella didn't seem upset that her mother knew of our connection, and I realized it was part of the thrill for her that her mother disapproved. I didn't know why, but that irked me. Ever since Rebecca had said, "for now, anyways," I'd been bothered by the pointless, time-limited nature of our relationship. I mean, where could this possibly go? Was she going to fall madly in love with me, propose, and then insist that her mommy give me the cure so I could become an Old Blood too? Were we going to live happily ever after in Hydra? Maybe she'd even help me find my mother, the Drudge, and gift her with virtual immortality too. Oh, and I couldn't forget Rake. Surely, my new girlfriend wouldn't object to me bringing my old girlfriend into the Old Blood fold. True love made people do crazy things, right? So maybe I could even convince her to share the Remedy with all of humankind so everyone could live happily ever after in comfort.

No. The truth was that Stella was dallying with me. Slumming it and rubbing it in her difficult mother's face. She was using me. But I was using her too, I guess, maybe, so…whatever. It didn't matter.

Except…was I? Was she? There was nothing deceptive or conniving about Stella. And though I knew better than to harbor secret fantasies of us lasting a lifetime, I couldn't say my intentions toward her were anything untoward. I was genuinely enamored. And I was pretty sure she was too. It was just a lucky bonus of happenstance that our connection pissed off her mother.

I wasn't able to see Stella much when the entire house was in upheaval preparing for the Juvenalia festival, the annual celebration of the discovery of the Remedy. Evidently, it was a great honor to host the festivities, and though Dr. Keenan was none too keen on planning a massive party, she seemed clever enough to understand the social weight of the opportunity. She seemed pleased to have finally found a use for her "frivolous" daughter, for she left Stella in charge of everything. That was why Stella had moved back home, to take on all the details, leaning heavily on Huxley's eager assistance.

Stella was in her element. She and Huxley were inseparable and seemed of one mind as they handled detail after detail of this momentous social event, both of them luminous with excitement, as if they'd lived their entire lives for this very moment. Huxley was in such a good mood that it even appeared like he had warmed to my relationship with Stella, although that could have been wishful thinking. In any case, time with Stella became difficult to come by, and I slid into taking care of Huxley's usual responsibilities since I was training to be a steward anyway, though Dr. Keenan still insisted on being served exclusively by Huxley in the west wing, a privilege he made sure we all understood that he suffered with the patience of a martyr.

When I did manage to get Stella alone, she wanted only to talk about the event. It was frustrating, but I figured it would pass and feigned interest in the preparations, even though all I really wanted to do was shut up her nattering with some kind of witty flirtation before I threw her down on the closest piece of furniture. A girl could dream, after all.

It was honestly cute to watch her get all excited about her plans for the party. She was telling me about how she got to design the outfits for the new hires, and my heart leapt at the realization that our estate would be welcoming not only a bunch of honored Old Blood guests but also a bunch of New Blood workers to serve them.

My mind went to Bree and Ida. Would Bree have graduated yet? Would Ida make an appearance? Would there be Drudges? Would I find my mom?

Stella laughed when I asked if she had a list of which BabyDolls were coming. "BabyDolls are for every day. This is a celebration. We use hirelings."

My heart fell. "Hirelings?"

"Older New Bloods we hire for parties," she answered, continuing to flip through her sketchbook, oblivious.

"You mean Drudges?" I asked, trying to sound casual.

"Well, yes, technically, I guess most of them are Drudges."

My heart sped up again at the possibility of crossing paths with my mom.

"They're like entertainment." She looked up, a spark of mischief and desire clear in her eyes. "BabyDolls aren't entertainment. *You* are not entertainment."

She hadn't looked at me that way for days, and I was not about to miss the invitation. So though I should have asked follow-up questions to try to suss out info that could help me with my mother, I got sidetracked into a sexy back and forth about how I was, in fact, very good at "entertaining" her.

I tried my luck later with Huxley, who didn't have irresistible feminine wiles to distract me. But when I asked if I could see the list of hirelings, he fixed a hard stare on me and said, "Let that go."

I tried to pretend to misunderstand, but he wouldn't have it.

"You want to see if there's someone from the outside who you know on the list."

I thought about denying it, but there was no other reason for me to ask, so I just held my ground under his disapproving stare.

"Amy, forget all that. Honestly. It's not worth it. Life is good here, and it just makes it hard if you reconnect with someone from the outside. Trust me."

"I still want to know," I said after a pause, weirdly shaken up by the conversation.

He rolled his eyes and grabbed his datapad. "Fine. If you want to be a masochist about it…here's the list."

My hands were shaking as I scanned the names and images. I had to read it three times to be sure I hadn't missed anything. Huxley stood there impatiently the whole time, huffing occasionally so I'd know just how much I was disappointing him.

She wasn't on the list.

I couldn't stop my eyes from brimming with tears. I held tightly to the datapad, willing my tears to go away. I couldn't face Huxley's smug flippancy right now. I just couldn't.

But he surprised me by putting a hand gently on my shoulder. I looked up in pure surprise.

"This is our life now," he said, and his eyes were actually kind. "As long as you don't look back, it's a pretty sweet one." He pried the datapad from my hands and left me to my thoughts.

The day before the party, everyone was rushing about the estate. I only saw Stella once when she grabbed my arm to pull me aside and tell me, "Look for a surprise outside your room tomorrow morning." She winked and took off before I could say anything.

The BabyDolls were under strict instructions to stay in our quarters. Only Huxley was permitted to mingle amongst the guests and direct the hirelings. He even got to wear a special outfit for the evening. He looked very dapper in his white dinner jacket and black, satin-striped trousers. I had intended to join the other BabyDolls in sulking about our exclusion while trying to sneak peeks at the festivities, but when I woke that morning, it was to the sound of Ivy banging on my door. When I opened it to keep my roommate from murdering me for disrupting her sleep, Ivy thrust a gift bag in my hand and announced, "You're a bitch, and I hate you."

"Good morning to you too," I mumbled, still half-asleep.

"Open it. Open it," she urged, barging into our room, flipping on the lights, and throwing herself down on my rumpled bedsheets.

"What the hell?" Claudia complained, rubbing sleep from her eyes.

"She got a gift from Stella," Ivy explained. "I think I know what it is. Open it."

The bag was huge and silver with a thick ribbon for a handle. There were a bunch of boxes inside. I pulled out the largest, thinnest box, then lifted the lid and pushed aside layers of tissue paper to find a black silk dress inside.

"I knew it. You bitch," Ivy wailed.

"What is it?" Claudia asked, clambering out of bed to look.

"Hold it up, stupid. I want to see it," Ivy insisted.

I held it up. It was gorgeous. A sleek, form-fitting, floor-length gown with a draped bodice and a cowl back. Vintage Hollywood glamor. Exactly the sort of thing Stella would choose.

"Wow. I hate you even more now," Claudia said, eyeing the delicate fabric longingly.

"I know, right?" Ivy said, though there didn't seem to be any real malice in her envy. "What else is in there?"

I pulled out another box and found some dress shoes in my size, plus a hat, a cute little felt number with a black lace veil. When I put it on, the veil fell across my eyes to the tip of my lips and gave me an alluringly mysterious vibe. I laughed, overwhelmed.

"Oh, I almost forgot, there was a note on top," Ivy said, grabbing the envelope she had carelessly tossed among my strewn covers.

I tore open the envelope, very much aware of my two curious onlookers. It was a handwritten note from Stella telling me that although BabyDoll Amy was forbidden to leave her quarters, she still hoped that her girlfriend Amy might show up.

"Come find me," she'd written, then ended the note with a lipstick kiss. The paper even smelled like her, and I wondered if she had spritzed her perfume on it.

"You're going to the party, aren't you?" Ivy asked. "That's why the hat has a veil, right?"

"I guess so."

"Lucky you," Claudia mumbled, making no attempt to hide the bitterness in her voice.

"You have to tell us everything," Ivy said. "We want details. What everyone's wearing, what they're eating, who flirts with who, who gets too drunk, everything."

"I don't know these people."

"That doesn't matter. Just describe them and give us the dirt. We're going to be stuck in here all bored while you get to have fun out there. At least take pity on us and tell us stories afterward."

"Fine. Fine. I'll fill you in," I said, hoping to get them to leave me alone so I could think this all through. It would be a good opportunity to learn more about the Old Bloods. My eyes wandered to the book the Defiance had given me. Maybe I'd have something to tell them after tonight. Who knew what I might learn as the champagne flowed?

Eventually, Ivy left to spread the gossip, and I was left alone with Claudia, who ignored me in icy silence as she gathered her things for the shower. When I was finally alone, I looked again at the note and noticed there was writing on the back side too.

"P.S. I noticed you needed new pencil crayons, so I got you some. Enjoy!"

Confused, I started looking amongst the boxes for something I'd missed. Indeed, at the bottom of the silver bag, under some tissue paper, was a brand-new set of high-end pencil crayons in a wooden box with gold writing on it. I lifted the lid. There were twenty-four perfect specimens inside, the body of each pencil the same dark shade of wood as the box, with only the pre-sharpened tip and a little stripe of color at the bottom to indicate their hue.

I lost it. I didn't know why, but the perfect pencils set me off in ways I couldn't explain.

I started pacing, crying and unaccountably angry. I tried to calm myself down enough to figure out why I was so upset. It took a while to piece it all together.

The dress, the shoes, the hat, those were things I'd expected from Stella. She wanted me to join the party, and the only way I could do so was if I had something appropriate to wear. Fashion was her thing, so it made sense that she'd surprise me with a beautiful outfit. I was grateful for the chance, and I was excited—if anxious—about wearing something so beautiful and undoubtedly expensive. But I'd honestly never cared much about clothes or parties, so maybe this gift would have meant a lot more to someone like Ivy, someone who daydreamed about getting to be the pretty princess at the ball.

I understood the value of the gift on an intellectual level, and I wasn't entirely unexcited, but it wasn't the fairy-tale romantic gesture I'd dreamed of my entire girlhood or anything.

But the pencils as a casual afterthought? That slayed me.

I crouched near my bed and grabbed my pencil case, the one Rake had sewed for me from the shirt off her back and my missing mother's scarf and my childhood tap shoelaces. I dumped out the pencils.

They were ugly. There was no denying it. They were mostly mismatched stumps. Some chewed. Some half-broken.

But at the same time, they were precious. They were *real* gifts, hard-won and meaningful.

Rake would hide them somewhere in the apartment, and I would just stumble across them in random places. Poking out of a potted plant. On top of the mirror. It was a game. I'd casually mention the next time I saw her that I'd found a pencil crayon inside my favorite shoes.

"Weird."

"Very weird."

We'd never acknowledged that she'd given them to me. That she was probably trading and cajoling and needling and charming her way into them. Because she loved me. And she knew what they'd mean to me. When I lived out there.

But in here, my most precious possessions were nothing. They had cost Stella almost nothing, and it meant almost nothing. Which just made me sad and angry.

What the hell was I doing? I'd thought I was discovering new parts of myself in here, but maybe I was just forgetting who I was and where I'd come from.

I put on the dress. But I used one of my pencil crayons from home to affix my hair in an updo under the hat. That pencil was imperfect but valuable in ways Old Bloods would never understand. Its presence comforted me as I stood awkwardly before the other girls who came to see me off in my fancy new outfit. I felt odd. I could see in the mirror that I looked…well, frankly stunning, but I didn't recognize myself in that tall, elegant stranger.

I drifted toward the party, following the noise. There were mesmerizing skydancers in the shapes of purple and white hydra, fabric tubes dancing in a flailing motion to the air currents of the fans beneath. I could hear live music and laughter. I slipped among the guests, anxious about being discovered and determined to find out something useful to the cause. I kept Stella far from my mind as I wandered among dozens of well-heeled Old Bloods sipping champagne and enjoying exotic hors d'oeuvres served by New Blood hirelings. But there was no escaping Stella. She had orchestrated every detail of this evening. Details I had been stupid enough not to understand.

Stella liked old-fashioned things, so when she'd said there would be a 1930's theme and had blathered on about vintage this and art deco that, I'd just nodded. When she'd told me the theme and had showed me her sketches of the hireling outfits, I'd found them charming, adorable even. I hadn't pieced together that they'd be worn by elderly people.

Now I watched a woman older than Nana offer shrimp skewers to guests with a shaking hand, the flab of flesh under her arm wobbling with the effort. I took it all in, detail by detail, like it was a scene in a movie, a series of sequential close-ups: Sparse white hair wrangled into the world's saddest pigtails. Pastel pink floral dress with cutesy smocking on the front accentuating her sagging breasts. Delicate mother of pearl buttons down the back straining, ill-fitting, leading to a large pink satin sash drawing attention to her lack of a waist. Skirt too short. Varicose veins standing out on her exposed legs. Ruffled bobby socks and strappy, shiny Mary Jane shoes appropriate only on a toddler.

I felt bile rise in my throat even before remembering our conversation: "Did you know women used to make dresses out of flour sacks during the Great Depression? That's where the idea came from."

I thought she'd been admiring their resourcefulness. I thought she'd found inspiration in their ingenuity. But she was laughing at them. They were "entertainment."

I wanted to throw up. I wanted to grab that woman's hand and take her away from here. But there were dozens just like her. Old men dressed up like newsboys with plaid caps and sweater vests or suspenders and socks up to their knees. The one taking people's coats was stooped with age and balding but trying to hide it with a side swoop of the few long, straggly pieces of hair. An Old Blood tossed his coat at him carelessly, but the elderly man already had his hands full, and the weight of the coat almost knocked him over. The coat fell to the ground, and the Old Blood began berating him loudly. I had to walk away, tears and the veil obscuring my vision.

"Hirelings." The word echoed "underlings." This was more than just not giving a shit about us. This was humiliating and scoffing at all New Bloods. Infantilizing our elders and ridiculing them as if there was something funny about their frailty, about the vulnerability the elite had escaped with the Remedy.

How could someone as good as Stella be a part of this?

I stumbled into a tent set up as a giant fighting ring. The other BabyDolls had prepared me for this. Evidently, it got boring living so long in the lap of luxury. Sometimes, an Old Blood had to get the juices flowing again with a little controlled danger, a harmless outlet for centuries of pent-up rage. They paid to fight New Bloods. Some liked winning. Some liked losing. But all yearned for the wild thrill of sanctioned violence.

Two seemingly young men stood in the ring. The only way I could tell who was who was by the tattoos. Only New Bloods wore them. The New Blood was winning. Smirking as he bloodied the Old Blood's face a little more before the referee called the round. It was mostly men in this tent. Far drunker than I'd yet seen. Their unrestrained animal anger frightened me.

I went to leave but was drawn to the sound of hooting and hollering. An old lady had entered the ring. My stomach dropped. She had a kerchief about her head and was swinging a large purse. The crowd howled with laughter as she yelled threats in a quavering but feisty voice. She was inviting someone to test her wrath. A cocky-looking guy stepped into the ring to much applause from his pals. He removed his dinner jacket and rolled up his shirt sleeves, then stood with his arms folded, looking doubtfully at the old lady. She walloped him with her purse, spitting curses. He just laughed and took it, looking back to his buddies to assure himself of their amusement.

Enough. I wandered out of the tent and back into the cool night air.

We were a joke to them. Nothing but sad little clowns that existed to serve and amuse them on their thrones. How had I fallen for one of them? I was disgusted with myself.

Huxley appeared by my side, grabbing my arm and urgently whispering, "I need you to cover for me."

"What? Why?" I wondered how he'd recognized me, then realized he was probably in on Stella's surprise.

"You're not the only one capable of attracting some Old Blood attention." He gestured behind him, and I saw an impossibly gorgeous young man looking our way. "Come on, I ran interference for you and Stella."

"Yeah, and we still got caught."

"Whatever. I've been nice to you lately. You owe me." He thrust his datapad in my hands.

I rolled my eyes. "Fine. Go for it. Just be safe."

"Safe is a boring illusion, darling," he said in his most dramatically gay voice before scampering off with the young stud.

I couldn't help but agree. I'd been playing it safe. Okay, it was probably more accurate to say I'd been playing it distracted. By Stella. But now I was here, and I was unsupervised, and I had no intention of leaving this party without getting some kind of useful information for the Defiance. I spent the next few hours lurking in shadows and eavesdropping on conversations. While I heard and saw plenty of juicy things that were sure to amuse Ivy and the other BabyDolls, nothing very useful crossed my path.

There was a lot of talk of the gala event down at an invite-only tent by the beach. Those who hadn't been able to secure a ticket were seething with jealousy. I figured it was worth checking out and made my way to the dune steps. There was a ton of security there, though. Armed men surrounded the tent, and folks had to line up and show some kind of translucent plastic key to gain entry. I loitered near the top of the steps and pondered how to sneak in.

I decided to approach from the back. I took off my shoes and walked carefully down the dune, sliding in places and snagging my dress on prickly grasses. Once at the bottom, I put my shoes back on, composed myself, and walked confidently in the direction of the armed guard posted at the rear of the tent.

"Stop. Identify yourself," the guard said, seeming startled by my sudden appearance out of the darkness.

"I'm BabyDoll Amy, steward of Dr. Keenan's estate," I said brusquely. "Dr. Keenan has requested your presence at the entrance to the main building. She says it's a delicate matter and to come directly."

The guard squinted. "Why me? What's going on?"

"Dr. Keenan is a council member and the hostess of this event. I don't question her orders. I follow them. I suggest you do the same."

I stared him down coldly, hoping I looked official with my datapad and haughty air.

I expected more questions, but he harrumphed and stomped off. I didn't waste a second. The moment he was out of sight, I got down on my belly and wiggled under the tent. So much for being a vintage Hollywood glamor queen.

I lucked out and ended up behind giant speakers that hid me as I got up and dusted sand from my dress as best I could. I stuck to the shadows but watched warily as couples entered and mingled. A smug air of superiority permeated the space as they congratulated each other on securing an invitation. Men slapped each other on the back as women side-eyed other women.

A host took to the microphone and bellowed out a welcome. I shrank into the shadows, my curiosity piqued. I looked for Stella and Rebecca. I didn't have to look hard. Dr. Keenan was invited to the microphone to say a few words as the hostess and a founding member of the Asenescence Corporation. I tried to listen to her speech, but Stella distracted me as usual.

She was stunning, an unearthly beauty in a glimmering rose-gold dress with a slight train and an open back that exposed the dip of her lower torso. Her hair was smoothed into a tight bun, with sparkling floral barrettes accentuating the crown of her head. Diamonds dripped from her ears, neck, and wrists. I wasn't the only one noticing. Men noticed. Women noticed. But Stella only had eyes for her mother.

I followed her gaze. Listened as Dr. Keenan said something about raising funds for a worthy cause. She introduced a head researcher of some kind and made her way back to Stella's side, acknowledging greetings, congratulations, and thanks along the way. Stella was beaming at her mother. It was hard to watch the way she was so proud of her. The way she wanted her love. All this effort she'd put into the Juvenalia, and it was really just another bid for her mother's approval. Watching her look at her mother so longingly, I felt ashamed and confused about my reaction to the evening. Was Stella really to blame for all this? This was how she was raised. It was all she knew. She was fundamentally a good person but one raised and trapped in a bad system, so of course she'd be led astray sometimes.

I was focusing on these thoughts and only half listening to the researcher, so I was startled when I looked toward the stage once more and saw a very elderly man slumped in a wheelchair. His face was heavily lined, his bald head covered in liver spots, and tremors shook his emaciated frame. Pity flooded me, and I looked to the researcher, finally tuning in to his words.

"Senescence, or biological aging, was once considered an inevitability. Thanks to your generous donations, we've been able to continue our work, disproving this theory and besting Mother Nature. Tonight, your donations will help stop suffering like this. Let's take a close look at this man's genetic deterioration." The researcher swiped his datapad, and a huge holo of the man's medical chart shimmered in the air before the audience. He walked the onlookers through the way time had taken its toll on the various systems of the poor man, now drooling in the wheelchair before us. People listened, spellbound, their champagne and hors d'oeuvres forgotten.

Perhaps because it was getting too dry and depressing, the host jumped onto the mic and joked with the audience. He pointed to a handsome man in the crowd who looked not a day over thirty. "Hey, Artie, you're two-hundred and two. Imagine how frail your bones would be if not for Asenescence." It broke the nervous tension, and the room let out a collective sigh of relief. I imagined it was uncanny, even horrifying, for Old Bloods, seeing the reality of the decrepit body they'd narrowly avoided.

The host began taking bids from the crowd. Stella and Rebecca watched with pleasure as the bids climbed higher and higher. Eventually, it came to a head between two gentlemen, one red-faced with drink and one pinched with competitive anger. Both their wives seemed alarmed at the number of credits being bandied about. The whole tent watched their pissing match with bated breath. Eventually, the drunk man's wife hit him with her fur stole and yanked him away from the crowd, much to everyone's delight. The pinched-face man was declared the highest bidder, and murmurs of appreciation ran around the room at the impressive figure the bids had ended upon. I snuck a glance at Dr. Keenan, and she seemed as pleased as she ever deigned to be.

"Congratulations, Thomas, you stubborn old goat. Jeffery should have known better than to bet against you." The host wiggled his finger, and the crowd laughed heartily, clearly familiar with the two gentlemen in question.

Once the laughter died down, the host took on a solemn air. He cleared his throat, straightened his tuxedo jacket, and looked out at the crowd gravely. "You've earned the right to end this man's suffering, Mr. Livingstone. Choose your method."

A hush fell over the crowd, and I looked at the stage just in time to see the host remove a cloth covering from a table set near the wheelchair.

On it was a syringe and a gun.

Chapter Twelve

With Vilest Worms to Dwell

Like everyone, I wanted to believe that I would be the hero in a critical moment. That I would make the right choice. Would do the right thing. Stand up. Be decisive and save the day. But I just stood there, paralyzed with dawning horror, as the pinched-face man picked up the gun, aimed, smiled, and shot the old man dead.

It happened so quickly and seemed so surreal that I just kept thinking, *What is happening? What is happening?* I looked at the crowd, hoping they could answer what my brain was asking. Their faces confirmed my worst fears. Actually, their expressions deepened my worst fears. I saw every emotion imaginable. Satisfaction. Envy. Bloodthirst. Rage. Shock. Fear. Revulsion. Excitement. Pity. Sorrow. Boredom. Amusement. Everything except the panic I felt rising in my own body.

With dread, I forced myself to look at Stella and her mother. Dr. Keenan looked utterly unperturbed. Her head was slightly cocked as though she was analyzing something. Stella was clasping her hands tightly and staring at the man. She glanced at her mother and quickly brushed a tear away.

The host solemnly draped the dead body with the same cloth that had covered the instruments of death. This seemed some kind of signal. Everything shifted. The spectacle over, the crowd began to come back to life, talking in hushed whispers, interspersed with nervous laughter. But before long, they began picking up the volume, picking up their drinks, and heading outside toward the main party.

I stumbled after them, still disbelieving, hearing ragged snippets of conversation.

"Should have known Thomas would choose the gun. What would you choose?"

"Ugh. There's blood on my dress."

"That's brain matter, Brigit."

"Ew."

"They should vary the choices. It's always the same thing."

"I'd kill myself before I'd end up drooling and pissing myself like that."

"Let's go fuck up some New Bloods in the rings. C'mon."

I put one foot in front of the other and walked into the fresh oceanside air. I just kept putting one foot in front of the other, trying to get as far from the tent as possible.

I didn't want to be here. I didn't want to be here.

Not in Hydra. Not in a world where people paid for the privilege of watching someone be murdered. Someone vulnerable who needed help and compassion. Who was that man? What was his life story? Did he have children and grandchildren? Would they ever know what had happened to him? One foot in front of the other, I marched along the beach, the crash of the waves somehow comforting, reflecting my own swelling and crashing emotions.

How had I ended up here? What was I doing? This wasn't me. I kicked off my right shoe, and it went flying into the dune. I bent and picked up the left and threw it into the ocean, screaming out some of my fury as I did. It felt good to scream. It felt needed. I ripped the stupid hat off my head and started tearing the lace veil apart.

"Amy? Amy."

I finally acknowledged that I'd heard her yelling my name for some time now.

"What are you doing?" Stella's eyes were huge with alarm. "That lace is from Paris. It's really expensive."

"Good," I said, eyes blazing. I tore it up deliberately, crumpled the hat and threw it at her.

She just stared, blinking her stupid, beautiful doe eyes. "What's wrong with you? What's going on?" she asked.

"What's wrong with *me*? What's wrong with you? With *you people*?" I wanted to scream at her, but sobs burst out of me without warning. Huge, racking ones that had me bent over double and struggling to catch my breath. I was so angry and so sad and so overwhelmed. I couldn't…I just couldn't. I couldn't breathe.

"You just stood around…and watched…someone murder someone," I finally wheezed.

I stood around and watched someone murder someone, I thought, burning up with shame.

"You're looking at it all wrong." I glared at her but she went on anyway. "I know it's hard to watch, Amy, but he was going to die anyway. We choose someone who's terminal and suffering. We ended his suffering and raised millions of credits by doing it this way. It's tradition."

I gave a harsh laugh. "It's tradition to auction murder to the highest bidder?"

"It's tradition at the Juvenalia to raise money for further research into ways to keep people from suffering like he was. The money raised tonight could save countless people from degenerating like that."

"Yeah, except you Old Bloods aren't so good at sharing your discoveries, are you?" Part of me wanted to hear her, to listen and understand and forgive her. To see her point of view. But another, better part of me knew this was just plain wrong no matter how she spun it.

The wind off the water was blowing her golden hair out of her tight bun despite the sparkly barrettes. I fought the urge to come closer. To smooth her hair out of her face and bring her lips close to mine. Damn it, why did she have to be freaking alluring all the time?

She looked at me like she was thinking hard about her next words. When she spoke, she spoke carefully, "Not everyone can live forever. It's not fair, but it's the truth. We paid for the research. It belongs to us." When I didn't react, she went on, and I saw Rebecca in her when she added, "It's a simple matter of math and logic, really."

I turned from her and screamed in sheer frustration. Fucking math and logic? Murdering the elderly for entertainment was a matter of math and logic? I started stomping into the ocean. I didn't know why. I just wanted to get away from her and her dazzling beauty and wicked reasoning. I wanted the fury of the waves to just wash everything away.

She started yelling after me, "Amy? Amy. What are you doing? You're ruining your dress."

I whirled around. "I don't give a fuck about this dress. Who gives a shit about a dress? It's a thing. It doesn't have feelings. It doesn't have a family. That man did." I paused, realizing I wasn't actually sure about that. "Presumably," I added lamely before rallying. "I care about people, Stella. People. Not things. I've never had things. I had people. People I care about still, but you don't know that because you don't know anything about me."

"I do," Stella insisted, stepping closer to the water, seemingly wary of it ruining her shoes. "Amy, I do. I know you."

I laughed. Bitterly. Looking to the stars for patience. Praying for some kind of peace to rescue me from this excruciating turmoil. "That's not even my name, Stella. You don't even know my name."

She looked surprised and struck by this.

"Just go back to the party and enjoy your night, Stella. We're from different worlds, and this couldn't last. We both know it. Forget about me and our silly little fling. None of it was real anyway." I turned and dove into the water. The dress was an annoying encumbrance as I kicked, but it felt good to immerse myself in the cold embrace of the sea, to leave Stella and her gorgeous, perfect, awful world behind for the dark reality of the ocean's watery depths. I surfaced and let the waves buffet me, enjoying their predictable, rhythmic forcefulness.

I heard a squeal and looked toward the beach to see Stella struggling toward me in the water. She looked scared and cold and wild-eyed. A large wave knocked her off her feet. She shrieked and sputtered and struggled to right herself. I thought about just watching her work for it, then remembered she'd told me that she was not a particularly strong swimmer and that the ocean frightened her. It was a big deal that she was braving her fear to get to me. I softened and went to help her.

Her teeth were chattering, and she gripped me as if worried she was going to drown. Her nails pierced my flesh mercilessly. "It was real. It was. For me, anyway." Her wet hair clung to her face and neck. "Were you just pretending?" Her eyes filled with tears, and her chin wobbled, and I had to look away.

"I wasn't pretending," I managed after a minute. "But it's hard for anything to be really real when I can't be myself here."

"But you can be yourself. Tell me your name. Talk to me. I want to know you." She brought herself close and tried to catch my eyes, but I kept looking away.

"You don't understand. They took away my name when I came here. There's no room for my truth here. There's no space for the real me."

"I'll make space," she pleaded. "Please, trust me. I'm sorry I didn't know that Amy wasn't your real name. There are a lot of things I don't know. But I want to know. I do."

I couldn't keep from scoffing. "You think you can just 'make space' because you think you can do anything. Fix anything. Have anything.

That's just your Old Blood arrogance. You don't get it because you've never really suffered. You've never really come up against your own powerlessness."

Anger flared in her face. "I know I haven't gone through the things you've gone through, things I can't even imagine, but it's not like I've had a perfect life, despite appearances. I do know what it's like to come up against my own powerlessness. I didn't even have a choice as to whether I wanted to be an Old Blood or not. Do you know what I really want to be more than anything?"

I started to reply, but she interrupted me.

"It's not a designer. It's a mother. I want children. I want a whole pack of little humans to love and nurture and raise and give all the love I never felt from my own mother. That's what I really want. But they took that choice from me. And I just have to live with it. For centuries."

I met her gaze and held it. She was more than I was giving her credit for. She wasn't just a beautiful, spoiled princess, sheltered and oblivious. She was strong and smart and hurting and yearning in her own ways too.

She didn't choose this life. But it did seem she was choosing me.

I kissed her. Fully aware that perhaps I was being foolish. Blind. Too forgiving. I kissed her anyway. Because she felt right curled into me. Because we were both pieces in a game we had little control over. And because she was the most precious spark of splendor I'd ever had the good fortune to encounter.

And she wanted me.

I kissed her under impassive stars, immersed in a roiling ocean.

"My name's Amara," I whispered.

"Amara." She tried my name out on her tongue. I liked the way it sounded coming out of her mouth and showed my appreciation with several more impassioned kisses.

"Nice to meet you," I said at last, stepping back and holding out my hand for a formal handshake. It made us both laugh and shifted the energy, creating levity, however brief.

"You're shivering. Let's get you warm," I offered.

We made the trek up the dune, back to my quarters, with some difficulty. Stella struggled on the shifting sands of the ascent and was clearly miserably cold. We were greeted by a number of BabyDolls hanging out behind the servants' quarters, engaged in a party of their own. On spying Stella, they tried to hide the bottles of no doubt pilfered alcohol and rushed to her aid.

“Oh my God, what happened to you, Miss Stella?”

“I’m f…f…fine. Just cold. Does anyone have a blanket or a sweater?”

Stella was quickly wrapped in a blanket, and I hurried her inside my room, ignoring all their enquiring stares. Claudia was unimpressed as usual but went out of her way to attend to Stella’s needs, offering to go to the main house to get her some hot tea.

“No. I’ll be fine. Just need to warm up a bit,” she answered.

I was freezing myself and would have enjoyed a cup of hot tea. I thought about manipulating the situation to get some, then realized there were bigger things I needed to work out. “Claudia, would you mind spending the night in Stella’s room? We have things to talk about and would appreciate some privacy.”

Claudia’s face clearly registered her disbelief that there’d be much “talk” going on. I hoped Stella wasn’t also reading this as a prelude to physical intimacy because it wasn’t. I mean, I’d fantasized many times about what I’d do with her if I ever got her alone in my room, but there was no way in hell we were having sex for the first time tonight. Things weren’t all magically fixed between us. I was still too shaken up about the murder and her defense of it. There really was a lot to talk about. But I wanted her close as we worked through it. If we could work through it.

“I don’t want to get in trouble—” Claudia began.

“You won’t,” Stella interrupted. “No one will even notice. You can always blame me. Say I demanded it. My room has a stocked mini-fridge and a full holo library. Help yourself.”

Claudia needed no further convincing. She gathered her things and took off, a rare smile teasing the corners of her normally downturned lips.

I grabbed a clean set of pajamas and held them out to Stella. She took them, smiling shyly. She was making eyes at me. *Fuck, she does think we’re going to fool around.*

“Stella, listen, I meant what I said. We have a lot to talk about. I’m happy to have you stay the night but—”

She interrupted, dropping the blanket, turning her back to me and saying, “Unzip me.”

Her flesh was all goose-pimply. Her bun was messy, and wet strands had fallen loose and were sticking to her neck. I looked at her zipper, and the thought of removing her dress sent a shot of desire straight through me. What was she wearing under there? It would be wet. Probably see-through. *Stop thinking about that.*

"Stella…" I couldn't get my voice or my hands to work. I didn't know what to say or do. Or I did, actually, but I wanted two very different things at the same time. Both to resist and to give in.

She wiggled closer, and anger flared in me rather than desire, winning out. She couldn't just seduce her way into avoiding this conversation. Of course I wanted her. I would always want her, looking the way she did, but did I respect her? Could I trust her? I had to know these things if our connection was going to grow into something really real. I held her away from me, and she turned, looking confused and somewhat hurt.

"No funny business tonight," I asserted. "We have big things to work out." She blinked at me, and I continued, "You can stay the night, but I just want to talk. I mean it. Don't make it harder than it needs to be. I'm asking you to respect my wishes."

She nodded, looking annoyingly cute, like a child chastised. "I really do need help getting out of my dress," she said. "Just undo the clasp and start the zipper, and I can do the rest."

I approached the task with a brusque efficiency to make Rosemont Academy proud. Nothing sexy here. Just undressing the most beautiful woman I'd ever set eyes upon. No big deal.

"Turn around and face the wall so I can change too."

I removed my own torn and soiled dress. I'd truly ruined the fine silk and felt a pang of sadness for such waste, but the clean comfort of pajamas was a blessing after being all dressed up. I burrowed under my covers and invited Stella to join me. We lay for a time, just warming up, relieved to be alone together and cozy. A strange elation came over me to look across my pillow and see her lying next to me. I hadn't seen her from this intimate angle before. Tête-à-tête. Somehow, she didn't seem quite so inhumanly untouchably superior while snuggled up across from me in my tiny bed. She was a girl. I was a girl. We were both trying to find our way. I reached for her hand and held it as I sorted through the things I wanted to ask.

"Do you ever think about what life is like for us? For New Bloods?" I started.

She flushed and took a moment to answer. "Honestly, no. I guess…I don't know. You just accept things are the way they are. In school, we learned about stuff outside the enclave, and I mean, I don't like to see anyone suffer, but I sort of just…accepted that that was how things are, you know? That might be stupid and selfish, but it's the truth."

It was the truth. That was how things were for most people. Including me. I'd been stupid and selfish and willfully blind before, just like her. I hadn't listened when Rake had gone on her rants about politics. I hadn't seen the point. The world was what the world was. It wasn't like I could do anything about it, and complaining just made folks angrier, it seemed to me. So I knew where Stella was coming from in not really getting worked up about the state of the world. I could understand that.

But the hireling outfits. She'd purposefully, cruelly mocked our elders. I couldn't understand that. There was nothing mean-spirited in Stella, at least, not that I'd seen so far. "What about tonight? At the party. The hireling outfits. How could you humiliate them like that?"

"Who? The hirelings? That's just tradition. Besides, they volunteer. No one forces them to do it."

I bit back an angry response and tried to get her to see past this excuse. "But think about it, Stella. Why would they volunteer?"

"I…I don't know. Maybe they like it. Or maybe it's the bonus."

"Would you like humiliating yourself for money?"

"No."

"Then?"

"For the money?"

"For the money."

What could Stella understand of the kind of desperation that would drive a person to willingly demean themselves? When had she ever had to sacrifice anything to get what she needed? I wanted to let go of her hand and turn away and go to sleep and leave all this behind. It was too hard to show someone how privileged and entitled their life was. But at the same time, she was here and listening and wanting to love me. She might be privileged and entitled, but she wasn't clueless or blasé about it. She wanted to learn. So show her, I thought.

I sat up and grabbed my sketchbook. I'd looked at her sketchbooks a zillion times, but I'd never shown her mine. She knew I could draw, of course, and that I liked it. But I hadn't wanted her to know me and my world the way she would once she saw my sketches. It was like revealing my soul to someone, and I just hadn't trusted her enough before now. But she had battled her fear to meet me in the water and ask me to be real with her. So I could battle my fear too and give her a glimpse into my world.

"This is Mr. Hernandez," I said, flipping to the first page. "He lives in my neighborhood, and ever since his wife died, my mom and I have been sort of unofficially taking care of him."

Stella scooted close to look. I wasn't sure how she'd respond. Maybe that was even why I started with this one. I'd drawn him in his ramshackle living room, a hoarder's paradise that was basically just a chaotic mess of broken furniture, assorted knickknacks, and random piles of everything imaginable. He was holding up an antique compass, a goofy, proud, partially-toothed grin spreading across his wrinkly face. There was a cheap, child-sized birthday hat perched precariously on his balding head because we'd given him the secondhand compass for his eighty-second birthday, a lucky barter we'd managed to finagle. He'd been so delighted with it. I could hear his wheezing laughter even now. We'd eaten cake, sung songs together, and listened to stories of his youth. It had been a special kind of magical. A gift to both him and to us, to spend time together and be in simple joy with each other. That was what I saw when I looked at this sketch.

Did she see that? Or could she only see ugliness? Imperfection. Poverty. Decrepitude. I was scared to look. What if her face registered disgust? These were my people. The Barrio was my big, extended family. We cared and looked out for each other. I just knew that if she couldn't see what was beautiful in spite of the ugliness in this image, then there was no way of moving forward for us.

I looked. It was hard to read her face; there seemed like a lot of emotions in play. But her eyes were full of tears and she said, "Tell me more about him."

My heart swelled with relief, and I poured out story after story. We spent the night flipping through odd pages and then getting sidetracked with long stories of people back home and how things were in the Freelands and what exactly was happening in this or that sketch.

It was late when I happened to flip to a sketch of my mother. It hurt to look at the image, and I made a small sound in my throat and went to skip the page, but Stella stopped me.

"Who is this?"

I forced myself to really look. My mother hated being sketched, so there was a strange mixture of tension and amusement in her face. She was wearing that characteristic look that screamed, "I am just indulging you because I love you, you mildly irritating little weirdo of a daughter." She was resting against the food cart, looking directly at me while people around her looked to her, Mama Maria, who always had the best tamales and good-natured gossip. She looked good for her age, her lush black hair still unmarked with gray, her skin still tan and smooth.

"It's my mom," I said simply.

"Oh. I didn't know you were adopted."

I gave her a weird look. "I'm not."

She gave me a weird look back. There was a strained silence as I tried to figure out why the hell she'd say something so rude.

"So…in the Freelands, you do have schools, right?" Stella asked awkwardly.

Was she trying to insult me? "Not exactly, but we have people who teach us stuff. We're not totally ignorant," I replied, bristling. "I had a teacher named Mrs. Flores. Why?"

"But…like…did you study biology?" Stella's face was strangely concerned, and I grew uneasy.

"It wasn't exactly Mrs. Flores's specialty. She was more an artsy-fartsy person. Why?" I asked again.

Stella hesitated. "Amara, I'm so sorry…but…there's no way this woman is your biological mother."

Chapter Thirteen

Fair Creature of an Hour

There was one sketch in my sketchbook that was unfinished: Rake's mom. After she disappeared, I tried to gift Rake with a sketch of her from memory, but I couldn't quite get her face right. It irritated me no end that I couldn't really recall the details and contours of her face. How was that possible when I'd seen her most of my life? But no matter how often I'd tried, something was always off in the sketch, and I couldn't give it to Rake until it was right. So I had never given it. The page was a palimpsest of imperfection, recording not her image but erasure after erasure, a record of my defeat, until the paper itself around the outline of her face had become indented, rubbed away by frustration and time.

I ran my fingers along the slight indent in the page now, thinking of my own mother and her equally mysterious disappearance and identity.

Who was my mother? My real mother? Who was I if I was not Maria's girl? How could I have been so ignorant? Of course I knew that I looked nothing like my mother, but I'd assumed my father had been a ginger. I didn't know anything about the complexities of biology or what a "recessive gene" was all about.

When she'd seen how upset I was, Stella had tried to soften her statement, explaining how redheaded-ness worked, how it was technically possible, just surprising, for Maria to be my birth mother, since redheadedness had to be carried on both sides for it to express itself, and that Latinos weren't exactly known for carrying the gene.

She'd asked about my birth father and about my mom's extended family, if any of them were redheaded, but I knew nothing about either. My mom had hated to talk of her past, and I'd never pushed. Maybe it seems strange, but it had never really bothered me that I didn't know my dad or my aunts and uncles. In the Freelands, chosen family was everything, and I was blessed to have a huge extended family of people who cared for me. So it just didn't seem important to pry into my mother's private pain to satisfy my own selfish curiosity.

The few times I *had* tried to ask questions, her face had shown how unwelcome and hurtful the questions were, and so I'd quickly backed down. People died, people fought, people did terrible things to get by. That was life. People disappeared. They left in search of a better life. Family wasn't the stable, rosy thing in the outskirts that it might have been in the inskirts and the enclave. So I had just accepted what I'd been told…and not told.

But now, there was this seed of doubt. What if I was just another stray taken in by Maria? Taken in more fully, perhaps, but really no different from Mr. Hernandez or the Miller twins. Just another person in need who Maria provided for. Did it matter? Did it change anything? My whole life, my mom had taught me to care for others like family and that family was more than blood.

She used to say, "Family is who shows up." She took in Rake to the extent that Rake wanted it when she was left abandoned. Was I just an earlier version of this same impulse to nurture an orphan? Did it mean she loved me any less? Was that why it had been so easy for her to leave me?

The thought sent an arrow of pain through my chest, and I slammed the sketchbook shut. I got up and paced my bedroom.

It didn't matter. Nothing had changed. Those were fearful, insecure thoughts unworthy of real consideration. I knew my mother. I did. Even if I didn't know all the details of her story and how mine intertwined with it, I knew Maria Rodriguez's heart. I had grown up in the generous glow of it. I knew she loved me. And I knew I loved her, and I was going to find her, and we would figure out whatever needed figuring.

I was startled by a knock at my door. I figured it was Stella, come to draw me away from my brooding, so I opened it without much thought.

It was Dr. Keenan. I panicked. I was still in my pajamas, though I was supposed to be working.

"Dr. Keenan. My apologies," I spluttered. "I…I haven't been feeling well." I could feel the telltale blush rising in my cheeks, something that happened whenever I told a lie I wasn't prepared for. I tried to calm my breathing and get ahold of myself.

She just stared at me, perceptive as a hawk. "May I come in?"

"Certainly. Excuse the mess," I said, keeping my eyes from wandering to the Defiance book sitting by my bedside.

Thankfully, it was really only the unmade bed that was messy.

Both Claudia and I were neat by nature. The room was minimalistic in its furnishings, but I rushed to offer her the chair by the desk. She shook her head slightly, and I lingered nervously by the desk while she looked around our room, her face inscrutable.

Why was she here? Was I in trouble? Was she on to me? I didn't know what to say or do, so I just waited and tried to calm myself enough to focus on getting through this interaction unscathed. Oddly, in the back of my mind, I flashed back to playing chess with Elder Sister Dara. I could hear the echo of her pen tapping the table. It was strangely soothing. *Play this right*, I thought. *Think things through*. I waited for Rebecca to make her move.

"I'm sorry to hear you're not feeling well. I'll have Ivy bring you some things when I return to the house," she said, still not looking at me but peering about the room.

I thanked her and continued to wait.

She walked toward my bed, and all I could hear was my heart thundering in my chest. I was sure she was going to pick up the Defiance book, call me out, and arrest me for being a terrorist or something, but she grabbed my sketchbook instead. "Do you mind?"

I did but could hardly say so. I nodded, working hard to control my face.

She flipped through it rather thoughtfully. I hated seeing it in her hands. Hated imagining what she was thinking as she looked at the precious pieces of my life on the outside. It was hard enough with Stella. But at least with Stella, there was something genuinely good and caring and sweet in her to help her see through the shabbiness of hardship I'd captured to the kind of flawed beauty that could flourish on the streets. I could only imagine how it looked to a haughty FirstGen council member like Dr. Keenan.

"You have a unique perspective," she said at last, still flipping. "A strangely compelling way of highlighting the possibility in struggle."

I thanked her and resisted the urge to wrench the sketchbook from her hands.

"Why bubbles? A commentary on the fleeting nature of things?"

I was taken aback. But she was smart. I knew that. Of course she'd "get" my sketches intellectually. Not that that was really the way I wanted them to be understood. "Yes. I suppose." Then, out of a stubborn sense of pride, I added, "It's about the ephemeral nature of beauty, actually."

For some reason, I needed her to know I knew big words too. That

I wasn't just some stupid street rat turned mindless BabyDoll servant. I might not be a world-renowned genius like her, but I wasn't a fool either.

She smiled. A slow, satisfied smile that unnerved me even more than her unexplained presence here. She turned back to the book. "Who's this example of 'ephemeral beauty'?"

It was a sketch of Rake sitting on a graffitied apartment stoop, smoking a joint and looking wistfully into the distance. She looked super dykey with her fresh fade, tats, white tank top and combat boots.

"Just a friend," I answered vaguely.

"Pretty erotic focus for friend," Rebecca replied.

It irritated and alarmed me, and I struggled to compose myself. Had she noticed the fish tattoo, recognized its meaning and realized I was affiliated with the Defiance, or was she just worried about my connection to her daughter and fishing for insights into my romantic intentions?

While I struggled to fashion a reply, she went on, "I could sell some of these at auction for you. I bet I could get two, three, maybe even five thousand credits for one of these, if we present them wisely." She turned the sketchbook toward me. "This one. With the child and dog, for instance. It's really quite touching."

Anger and confusion flared in me. "They're not for sale."

"You don't want to make credits?"

"No."

"No? There's no one on the outside who could use some? Your 'just a friend,' for example?" She smiled again, and I could see that she was enjoying flustering me.

It pissed me off, and I answered more heatedly than I should have. "No. They're private. I'm not comfortable sharing them."

"Okay. I just thought you might want to use your skills to benefit others if not yourself."

Bitch. I didn't miss the dig in that. She turned, and I thought with relief that she was going to put the sketchbook back where she'd found it, but she turned back, holding out a particular drawing. "And who is this?"

It was my mom. That was why she was here. I could feel it in the air. This was why she'd come. She knew something. We stared at each other, calculating. I figured she already suspected the answer, or she wouldn't be asking this way, so I told the truth.

"It's my mother."

Rebecca nodded. Probably pleased that I hadn't hidden it. What was she playing at? What did she know? And what did she really want? "And you left her behind?"

"No. She left me behind. On the outside. She's here. Working as a Drudge. There's a note…" I trailed off, not really wanting her to read the hated note, even if it did corroborate my story.

She closed the sketchbook and held it against her chest, looking intently at me like she was studying my reactions. "And why did you decide to follow her here to Hydra?"

Careful. Think.

"I wanted a better life."

"Hmm." She raised her eyebrows doubtfully. "But she came to the enclave before you, so she must have left you some credits. If that was her food stall, then you couldn't have been hurting too badly, financially speaking. And then there's sexy Ms. Just Friends. Not to mention the surprising fact that you just turned down a chance to make credits for selling a mere scribble." She took a step closer, her eyes boring into me. "I'll ask you again. Why. Are. You. Here?" She enunciated each word carefully, and that answered the question of why *she* was here. She suspected me of some ulterior motive in coming to Hydra, to her home.

The gloves were off. She didn't trust me. Because of my relationship with her daughter? Because she'd somehow figured out I was with the Defiance? Because I wouldn't jump at the opportunity to make a few credits like the desperate New Blood she'd thought me?

In a voice dripping with obvious sarcasm, I said, "Well, Dr. Keenan, I just believe so very deeply in service with civility." The Rosemont Academy motto. I didn't know why I'd said it except I couldn't think of a better answer, her whole demeanor had upset me, and I'd never been very good at hiding my feelings.

Her face twitched. "And?"

"And…" I weighed my options. It seemed safest to assume she just didn't understand my intentions toward her daughter or why money didn't tempt me. I had to give her a motive she could understand that wouldn't suggest any affiliation with the Defiance. "And I want to find my mother."

"Why?"

"Why?"

"Yes, why?"

"What do you mean why? You're a mother. You know."

"I don't, actually. Explain."

I stared, trying to figure out if she was playing dumb or actually oblivious. "She's my mom. I love her. I want to see her again and make sure she's all right."

"You don't trust she'd be well treated here?"

"No, it's that I don't trust *her*. I mean, I don't trust that she's doing okay. That she understood how hard this would be. She needs people. She needs me. I just don't understand why she left." I hadn't meant to say that part, but that was the problem with telling some of the truth; more of the truth often popped out.

"Oh, but it's all right here," Dr. Keenan drawled, turning to the page with my mother's letter. She knew which page to turn to, so she must have noted it earlier. Perhaps even before today? Had she gone through my things? "She wanted a better life for you. She sacrificed herself for you. And you just threw it all away." She threw the sketchbook on the bed in an uncharacteristically dramatic gesture, stepping closer. "Isn't that right, Amy? That's what happened. You gave up the money. You gave up the business. You gave up the girl who you insist isn't your girlfriend. And you gave up the chance to be a mother one day." She cocked her head. "Seems you don't value motherhood that much after all."

"I love my mother," I insisted. "That doesn't mean I want to be one myself." I waited to see if she'd buy this. She looked skeptical, so I continued, "Kids are noisy and gross. There are too many brats running around the streets where I come from to be sentimental about motherhood."

"Well, here we can agree, at least. Children are overrated."

My heart sank for Stella. Dr. Keenan really didn't love her own child. How was that possible? It was so unnatural.

She was close now, so uncomfortably in my personal space that I had to crane my neck to look up at her. She was tall and using it to intimidate me. She peered down, her face frankly disbelieving. "Even so, you gave all these precious things up. So that…what? What's your endgame, Amy? You find her and run away back to the Freelands? Steal a Drudge back from Hydra and live as corporate fugitives the rest of your lives? That hardly seems a well-thought-out plan."

I felt the familiar pull of anger at the way she called out the stupidity of my admittedly rather vague plan. But there were pieces of it that she didn't seem to have guessed. I wasn't alone. I remembered Dr. Ahmed's advice to learn to control my face.

I gave an ingratiating smile as fake as hers. "No, it's not. I guess I just hoped my proprietors would be kind enough to let me see her from time to time."

"You know that's not allowed."

"Not allowed and never happens are two very different things," I said, not breaking eye contact.

She liked that. I could see the corner of her mouth twitch in approval. "You're not wrong there." She finally took a seat on the chair I had offered earlier. Something was shifting. I sat on the bed and waited for her next move. We were closing in. "Is that why you seduced my daughter? To curry favor with me? Because that could really backfire as a strategy, you know." She perused the meagre possessions on the desk, both Claudia's and mine.

"No. Stella was a sweet surprise. I really care for her. I'm not using her, I swear." For some reason, I needed her to believe this. I wasn't sure why because I couldn't even say for certain that her mother really cared deeply one way or the other. Part of me suspected she just wanted to understand the score.

She glanced at me briefly and went on. "But it is convenient. Is that why you want to transfer homes?"

I blinked. "What are you talking about?"

She seemed to lose her patience and stood. I stood too, alarmed at her sudden shift in energy. "Amy, I'm two hundred and seven years old. I was one of the founders of the Remedy. I sit on the Old Blood council. You don't get to be those things without having the ability to tell when someone is lying." My back was to the wall, and she was too close again. I could feel her breath on my face. I tried not let her frighten me, but I was honestly freaked out. "Trust me when I tell you that I am not someone you want to cross. So decide. Either stop insulting me by making up more plausible lies, or be smart and play it straight with me."

I had no idea where this vicious turnabout had come from. I scrambled mentally to think back to what I could have said wrong or how I'd played my hand incorrectly. It was something about transferring houses. "Dr. Keenan, I assure you, I have no idea what you're talking about…I—" Her eyes narrowed, and I thought fast. "Stella mentioned wanting me to come back to her dad's place with her. Is that what you mean?" I could see by her face that it was and hurried on. "I didn't think she really meant it or that it was possible. Of course, I'd love to go with her, naturally, but I'm happy to stay on here and serve out my contract. I'm sorry. I didn't actually expect she'd go through with a formal request."

"It seems my daughter doesn't want to part with you."

"I'd prefer not to part with her either," I risked.

She made a little grunt of begrudging acknowledgment and walked a few steps away, straightening her blouse. I pulled my sticky pajama top from my chest. I was sweaty and discombobulated. How long was this stupid chess game going to last? Hadn't I given her what she wanted? I was just a girl in love with her daughter looking to find and occasionally check on her mother. Nothing too dangerous in that. *Don't look any further.*

"I could help you find your mother. You'd have to tell me about her, though. Name. Age. Gate of entry."

"You'd do that?" I asked suspiciously.

"Well, I am your girlfriend's mother, am I not? Wouldn't it just be natural for me to help you out when I can?"

That made me all the more suspicious, and it must have shown on my terribly transparent face because she laughed lightly. "I need to understand your family situation. It's important if we might be connected for some time. I could...promote her to some more respectable role, something more fitting for the mother of my daughter's current sweetheart."

The word "current" pissed me off, but the suggestion of assistance in finding and helping my mother piqued my interest all the same. Was she for real? Why wouldn't she be, though?

As though reading my mind, she went on, "It's one thing for my typically rebellious LastGen daughter to be dating a BabyDoll, but it's quite another thing for her would-be mother-in-law to be a common Drudge. I don't think we need to feed the gossip mill that particular piece of juicy scandal."

So she was trying to shield her reputation. It had nothing to do with helping me or even Stella. That made more sense to me.

I told her my mother's details.

"When your mother left, Amy, did it come as a surprise? Had she been acting strangely? Were there any new visitors to your home or the food stall?"

"No. Nothing unusual. That's part of what I don't understand. It came out of nowhere."

Dr. Keenan breathed deeply, and I sensed our meeting coming to a close. "Okay. I'll approve the transfer of houses, and you can spend more time with my daughter and ex-husband. I'll begin to search for your mother through official channels, but if she should contact you through more informal networks, I ask that you inform me right away. I need to stay ahead of this information leaking, you understand?"

I nodded, and she went on.

"I'll provide a datapad with a direct line to me. Don't hesitate to contact me the moment you connect with your mother."

I nodded again.

"One thing more. I'll indulge this request, and I'll help you find your mother, but in return, I ask that you treat my daughter well. Stella is…silly. She's emotional and always follows her heart, and that means she's easily hurt. I might not be the world's best mother—it's difficult to be the outstanding at *everything* you do—but I don't want my child toyed with. I would not take kindly to that. Do you understand me?" She held my gaze, and I felt the truth in her words.

Okay, so maybe in her own sadly insufficient way, Rebecca really did love her daughter. I reconsidered. Was I being too hard on her? If Rebecca was a man, would I have been so judgmental of her distant relationship with her child? She was a bona fide scientific genius who had achieved the impossible. Was it really so surprising that she had poor social skills? Wasn't that part of the genius stereotype, perhaps for a reason? Maybe she didn't know how to show love. I mean, she loved her cat Magnus and barely interacted with him.

It was unsettling to think that maybe mothering didn't come naturally for all women. My own mother had maternal instincts in excess; she mothered everyone who needed it in an effortless, generous way that brought her genuine joy. But maybe Rebecca was one of those people who shouldn't have had kids. Maybe Stella had been an accident. It seemed like Stella disappointed her somehow, but nonetheless, here she was, protecting her and trying to make her happy, even if her choices were embarrassing or upsetting.

There was more to Dr. Keenan than I could unravel in this moment, but I was conscious of my own perhaps sexist bias. I felt willing to give her the benefit of the doubt. Besides, her request to be good to her daughter was hardly a difficult thing to agree to, and I eagerly consented.

Dr. Keenan summed up as though concluding a business meeting: "So we understand each other. I approve this transfer, and you'll treat my daughter well. You'll do your best to make her happy for as long as this thing lasts. I'll try to find your mother through all the means at my disposal. But if I can't find her, you'll seek her out through more informal means and keep me informed using the datapad. I'll promote your mother to a better position, and everyone will be satisfied. Yes?"

"Yes."

It seemed straightforward. It seemed like a good deal. So why did I have a niggling sense of doubt?

She turned the door handle. "I hope you feel better soon. I'll send Ivy with some soup and such." She closed the door, and I was left bewildered by yet another frustratingly enigmatic mother figure.

Chapter Fourteen

Repressed Their Noble Rage

A few days later, I found myself at the house of Stella's father, Dr. Henry Keenan. His house was just as spectacular as his ex-wife's but had a very different feel to it, due in part to the fact that Stella was methodically redecorating it from the ground up. As a consequence, it was much warmer and more comfortable than Rebecca's home, full of wood and antiques and furniture that actually invited use.

The second Dr. Keenan was surprisingly older in appearance. He had gray hairs about his temples that he didn't bother to dye, and I wondered how that affected how he was perceived in Hydra, signaling as it did that he was a FirstGen who had taken the Remedy later in life. It certainly made him stand out amongst Old Bloods, not that he'd probably notice, for he was as oblivious and as obsessed with his work as his ex-wife, though he seemed more balanced in the sense that he always made time for Stella. He kept crazy hours but made a point of having dinner with her. And me. For I was treated not as a BabyDoll but as a valued guest. I was even given regular clothes and a guest room, much to his other BabyDolls' envy and curiosity.

Henry was often distracted and lost in thought. But I liked him right away. He had this adorable habit of sort of patting Stella every time he was near her. An awkward, loving little tap on the shoulder or knee or the top of her head. I found it endearing. And he seemed to accept her for exactly who she was, with none of the disappointment her mother showed. He showed me all around the house when I first arrived, proudly showing off the rooms his daughter had transformed.

"Of course, I know nothing of interior decorating," he explained. "I just told Stella, 'Make it nice,' and she's got such an eye for these things that it's just right," he said as he pat, pat, patted her on the arm.

No wonder Stella chose to live with her dad over her mother. She bloomed in his presence, at ease and eager to please, always looking for little ways to attend to his comfort. He was a soft-spoken man, quiet and easygoing with a dry sense of humor. Though he was very different from Rebecca, I could see how they fit together, and I wondered what had driven them apart.

Stella was delighted to have me all to herself without my regular BabyDoll duties, and we found many frivolous, fun ways to fill the hours. If her father disapproved of our connection, he never let on. I hadn't forgotten my mission, though. I'd updated the Defiance after the Juvenalia and my "chess game" with Rebecca. I'd informed them of the house switch, though I'd assumed they would somehow be keeping tabs on me, even without the book's secret message. I wasted no time in trying to get Stella's dad to help me find my mother. He seemed like the kind of person who would genuinely want to help, not out of self-interest like his ex, but out of an authentic desire to make his child's beloved happy.

But it seemed he already knew about my conversation with Rebecca, that they were still in communication. Perhaps they were still close? "Rebecca told me. We searched the official records, but there's no mention of a Maria Rodriguez. She's looking through each file manually, trying to make a match based on your sketch and information, but it's time-consuming, and I'm afraid it doesn't appear promising."

My heart sank. Stella reached across the dinner table and took my hand.

One of his BabyDolls was bringing in the second course. It felt strange to be served, but I played my new part dutifully, accepting her offerings with good manners. I hardly felt like eating, though, despite the deliciousness before me.

"There's still hope," he went on, seemingly registering my reaction. "I just think we have to prepare ourselves to look for her in more…unsavory locales."

I looked to Stella, and she seemed as lost as I was.

He took a bite of his steak and chewed thoughtfully. I waited, burning with questions.

Stella was the one to ask. "What do you mean?"

"I mean…" He paused to wash down the steak with a sip of red wine. "That if she's not here officially, there are only two places I can think of where an undocumented person might be eking by through unofficial channels."

We both just blinked at him, and he seemed to realize we were clueless. “The fighting rings or the…” He hesitated. “Well, let’s try the fighting rings first.”

Stella made a sound of disgust. “Ugh. I don’t understand why we allow those places. They’re barbaric.”

“I don’t disagree, but barbarism is surprisingly popular. And very lucrative. If a respected council member were to pop by and speak to the management privately, I bet we could persuade them into providing some information about an undocumented person of interest.”

Stella looked at me and squeezed my hand. My mind was racing. Did he mean that my mother was fighting? That seemed so unthinkable that I laughed, and they both stared at me.

“Sorry, I don’t mean to laugh, but I just…I just can’t picture my middle-aged mother in a fighting ring.” I started laughing again as an image popped in my head, the image of Maria spitting Spanish curses at her opponents, then performing the dreaded Latina “chancla,” kicking off her flip-flop and using it as a weapon against her stunned opponent, pummeling them over and over with her shoe. It was ludicrous.

“You’re laughing because it’s a funny image, a middle-aged woman fighting, but that’s a big part of what the rings are about. Half the fighters are there for comedic relief, the other half for real brawling. Honestly, it’s not as unthinkable as you might assume. It’s worth checking out.”

Well, that made me uneasy. I thought back to the fights I’d witnessed at the Juvenalia and realized the truth of what he was saying. It was a show that was part joke and part bloodlust. Was my mom playing the clown for their amusement? The thought was horrifying. I still couldn’t make it fit with anything I knew of her, but I also recognized that we had to leave no stone unturned.

“Okay, that sounds like a promising lead. When should we go?” Stella said.

“You won’t be coming,” her dad replied, and the conversation just got awkward from there. It took us both some time to come around to Dr. Keenan’s position that it would be best if he and I went alone. He was delicate in how he presented it, but it became clear eventually that he thought it would be helpful if the management thought he was there having a sordid affair with the help.

“I recognize that’s an uncomfortable position for all of us to be in, but it would strike the right balance of intimidation and relatability that I need to influence Tony into giving me information on his more illicit dealings.” Both our faces must have shown our discomfort. “I know

Tony's sort. He needs to understand why I'd be helping a BabyDoll find her mom. Low minds think low. He'll believe it if he thinks we're... together."

So that was how I found myself a few days later, sporting a far-too-tight little black dress, on a fake date with my girlfriend's dad. Talk about awkward. Though I had no idea just how much more awkward things were about to become.

Henry went out of his way to be kind and to make it as easy as possible for me, saying, "This whole experience is going to be distasteful. Let's just get through it with as much grace as we can muster, keeping our purpose in mind. Then we'll go back home to our real lives and comfort, okay?"

How could I help but warm to a man like him?

Henry had a driver take us, a pretty boy like Huxley. I couldn't fathom why he'd need a driver when all cars were self-driving, but it seemed like the rich always needed to conspicuously use and waste unneeded things. I was full of both dread and excitement as we pulled up and made our way into the crowd and toward the entrance of a building. Security seemed to be scanning some folks and waving others through, but when they spotted Dr. Keenan, they visibly started and began loudly instructing everyone to line up in an orderly fashion to be scanned. I hadn't realized Henry was that well-known, though on reflection, it made sense.

Henry just sauntered up the security guard and said, "Don't worry. I'm sure you don't need to scan everyone to know which riffraff to let in and which to keep out." Then he winked and sauntered right on in, past the line and scanner, pulling me along with him. It was like the crowd gave a collective sigh of relief and went back to its former unruliness.

The ring wasn't as big as I had expected, but it was well lit and surrounded by raised concrete bleachers. Loud music poured from speakers, and we were jostled as we made our way to some seats. I looked around. It was mostly men, though there were a few women too. The place was filling quickly.

A scantily clad woman paused before us and opened what looked like a briefcase slung on a strap around her neck, rather like an old-fashioned cigarette girl from a holofilm I'd once watched.

"Stims?" she drawled, looking bored.

Inside, I saw small vials, bottles, and canisters, all lined up neatly.

"Laughing gas? Dextros? Caffeine? Mystery fun?" The woman

looked at me for a reply, and I shook my head in surprise. The couple next to us motioned her over and partook.

"Is that legal?" I asked Henry, motioning to the stimulant pusher.

"Hmm?" Henry seemed distracted. I drew his attention to our neighbor, who was downing some mystery liquid. "Oh, yes, well, it's not well looked upon, but it's not illegal."

Whatever was in the bottle, it worked fast. The man's eyes went large, and he sort of flopped to the ground, laughing. "Woo! I fucking love water slides. Look out below." He was writhing on the ground like he was taking the twists and turns of a real slide. I looked to Henry, alarmed.

"Probably salvia. A fast-acting hallucinogen, related to the mint plant. It's been used by the Mazatec Indians for centuries. The trip won't last long, and it's mostly harmless." I kept looking at him, still alarmed and now surprised. He shrugged. "When you let a people live for hundreds of years, you have to permit them their little outlets." He looked at the man with a combination of pity and distaste. "Believe it or not, existence can become a little dull once you've had, seen, and done it all. People will risk a lot for a little stimulation. That's what this place preys upon."

An announcer came on then and riled up the crowd. Another scantily clad woman stopped before us, but this one was ancient. She was wearing the same outfit: fishnets, short shorts, a studded bra and glitter paint. Her hair was even in identical space buns. But she was old and overweight, and the outfit made her look pathetic and ridiculous. It reminded me of the hirelings and filled me with embarrassment and anger.

"Popcorn? Licorice? Chocolate?" she asked with the gravelly voice of a lifelong smoker. I shook my head, and she waddled past us to the next potential customers. The first act was beginning. I thought it an act because it was hardly a fight at all. It seemed more like theatre, featuring a shabby old man in a dirty wifebeater using a cane to beat up a rich-looking businessman.

I turned to Henry and asked, "Are these staged?"

"I don't know. I think the actual fights are real. The final showdown I do believe is authentic, but I'm sure these smaller, comedic warm-ups are at least partially scripted. But I don't honestly know. This isn't my usual cup of tea."

It wasn't mine either. The next act seemed a legitimate fight. It was bloody and awful, and I had to look away. The people in front of us kept jumping up to shout obscenities and encouragement, but I was grateful that they blocked my view most of the time. Humans were vile. I looked around, and it was revolting to see how the crowd cheered for violence and humiliation. Maybe some of the cheering was for actual fighting skill, but that wasn't a skill I felt compelled to cheer for. I scanned the crowd, looking for workers with dark hair like my mother, but saw no one who looked like her. The fights went on, and I grew restless.

The fighters had stupid over-the-top names and did outlandish, flamboyant signature moves that made the crowd grow rowdier than ever. There was a lot of call-and-response between the announcer and the crowd and just a lot of hooting and hollering and general idiocy. The last act before the intermission involved a girl called "The Emasculator." It made me laugh despite myself. In the flashes of her that I could see between the shifting bulk of the people, she had tattoos and tanned skin and hair plaited back tightly into dark brown and ombre blue cornrows. I was a little irritated with the folks in front of me now because I was actually curious to see a New Blood girl my age beating up Old Blood assholes. The crowd loved her. Her fight seemed a mixture of actual scrapping and pure, self-aware spectacle. The crowd was screaming in satisfaction. It was contagious, and I gave in to my curiosity and stood, trying to peer around my neighbors, but it was too late. She'd already won the match and was pretending to perform a lewd act on the man, earning her moniker. I went to look away, disturbed, but something called me to look more closely.

I knew those tattoos. Holy shit. I knew *her*. Rake.

She was pulling him around the ring by his hair in a victory lap to much appreciative applause, then she dumped him in a corner, made an obscene gesture, gave the crowd the double finger, and swaggered out of the ring.

I started laughing, and I couldn't stop. For a solid two minutes, I thought it was the funniest thing I've ever seen in my existence.

Then I started crying, and I couldn't stop. Henry was trying to catch my attention, but I couldn't even register what he was saying.

The crowd was starting to jostle us as people mingled and made their way to the washrooms during the break.

"Amara, what's going on? Are you okay?" I finally registered Henry asking.

"That's a friend from home," I managed. "I…I didn't expect to see her here."

He nodded. "Look, why don't we head to the backstage area now, rather than staying for the whole performance? I'm all blood-lusted out if you are."

I nodded weakly, still reeling from the unexpected sight of someone from home. Henry led me carefully down to the backstage area, where a security guard went to hold us up until a man in a very loud shirt waved security away.

"Councillor Keenan," he said. "I didn't know you enjoyed the rings." His mouth smiled, but his eyes darted around the backstage area warily, as though looking for anything a council member might find questionable.

Henry smiled back. "Well, Tony, sometimes people develop surprising new tastes as they age." He looked meaningfully at me, and I blushed.

"Aha. I see. I see." Tony leered. "You gonna step into the ring and impress your girl? Never had a council member fight, but we could market the shit outta that. Sure to fill the place. I could pick a girl that would go easy on you. Or maybe you like it rough?" He leered some more.

Henry laughed. "No thanks. I just escaped decades of brawling with my ex-wife. You don't have a fighter here that could compare. I barely escaped with my manhood intact."

Tony threw his head back and laughed loud and long. He waggled his finger at Henry. "She is a hellcat, that one. You can tell. You can always tell. Even from afar."

"I'm actually looking for someone." Henry gestured to me, and I passed him my sketchbook. "She'd be undocumented. In her forties. Latina. Might go by Maria. Looks like this. Any chance you've crossed paths? Unofficially?"

Tony stiffened and narrowed his eyes. "I run a clean joint, Mr. Councillor," he replied carefully.

"As do I, of course. But we're two businessmen, right? We both know the score. So…unofficially…have you seen her?"

I held my breath as Tony hesitated. "Why?" he asked at last.

"I don't ask too many questions about your business, and you don't ask too many questions about mine." The two men locked eyes and seemed to size each other up.

Tony broke away first, looking to a door close by. "How about if we talk in my office?" When he noticed Henry glance at me, he added, "Your girl will be fine here. My fellas will look out for her."

Security gave me a tight smile, and I gave one back, then began wandering the room under their mildly watchful eyes. Not watchful enough, for less than minute after I was left alone, I was pulled roughly into the shadows and all but thrown against the wall.

Rake pinned me, her arms on either side of my face, her lips achingly close to mine. She looked sexy as all hell in her little sports bra and boxing shorts, all sweaty and intense with emotion, muscles taut. I could feel my body respond as she stared at me in the shadows. I had to explain, but there was no time for that. Her mouth was on mine before I could protest, hungry and searching. I didn't want to betray Stella, I didn't, but I found myself kissing Rake back, just as hungry, just as elated to be returned to her touch, rough and tender and uniquely her own.

She gripped my face fiercely like she would never let me go. And I didn't want her to, even as I did. I started to choke on emotion, confused and overwhelmed. She growled, bit my lower lip, and pulled away.

"What are you doing here? Who was that guy? Where'd you get this dress? I like it. It's not like you at all." Her last question was accompanied by very wandering hands, and I had to struggle to focus as her groping left warm trails of desire all over me.

"That's my proprietor. He's trustworthy. He's helping me look for Maria."

She stopped feeling me up, her hands lingering on my hips. "Why would he do that?"

I couldn't exactly say, "Because I'm dating his daughter," so I just said, "It's complicated. What are *you* doing here?"

She grinned cheekily. "Isn't it obvious? I'm making a name for myself." She gestured to the embroidered moniker on her boxing shorts. I glared until her she offered a serious answer. "Okay, I got bored of sitting at home waiting for you, and a friend mentioned I could make some money and have some fun fighting in the rings in Hydra, and I thought, why not? I figured I could keep an eye open for our mutual friends and make some extra cash. I don't know. It was something to do."

I cocked an eyebrow, skeptical. "Beating people up for applause is something to do?"

"Yeah, and it pays really well."

"You could get hurt."

She just laughed. "I'm fine. Besides, I was already hurting sitting around at home." A vulnerable note creeped into her voice, and I thought back to the last time I'd seen her. She'd looked really bad. Lost and not at all herself. She was certainly back to herself now, stronger and more confident than ever. Though I didn't really like the part of her that needed the ego boost of an appreciative audience, I could see that it did something for her. Even if I didn't like the fact that she was fighting in these preposterous rings, I couldn't deny that it had helped her get her mojo back. That was plain to see. She had needed something to inspire her to keep going, and if this was the thing that would lift her spirits and bring her back to herself, then I could hardly resent it.

She went on, "It's just a six-month contract, Amara. It's no big deal. I made sure it was mostly on the light side. I'm good at entertaining people. It's easy money."

"Six months? Did you read the contract carefully?" I asked, worried.

She rolled her eyes. "You really think I'm an idiot, don't you?"

I started to protest, but there was an awkward cough, and we pulled apart to see Henry standing close by.

"Amara, we'll be heading back now. We can talk in the car."

I looked at Rake, trying to memorize her face, knowing we wouldn't see each other for a long time, though I could probably talk Henry into taking me to the rings occasionally.

He spoke up again. "Ms.…er…Emasculator, you're coming with us. I've bought out your contract."

"What?" we both yelled.

"Gather your things, please. I'd like to head home now."

A huge grin lit up Rake's face, and she sped off to grab her belongings while I raced to understand the implications of what had just happened.

"What…what did you do that for?" I stammered.

He looked at me, seemingly perplexed. "She's your friend. I thought you'd want her away from a place like this. You seemed upset seeing her fight. Was I wrong?"

I couldn't exactly tell him that Rake was my ex who thought she wasn't my ex. What the fuck? This was all about to explode in my face.

He put on his coat. "She can stay in the other guest room. I'm sure Stella would be delighted to meet a friend of yours from home."

I'm sure.

Fuck.

CHAPTER FIFTEEN

Don't Go to Someone Else

"I need to talk to you," I managed to whisper to Rake as we made our way to the car.

But there was no privacy for me to even begin the difficult conversation we needed to have. Dr. Keenan's car was open concept, like Dr. Ahmed's, and we were all lounging together for the entire ride home, an interminable, torturous ride in which Rake never once shut her mouth. She was loud and excited, going on and on about the car and the scenery and telling us all about how she got into the rings.

I just sat beside her, mute and miserable, sweating and sweating about how to disentangle this mess. Rake didn't belong here. Not just in the sense that it was interfering with my plans and tearing my already uncertain heart in two but in the sense that she just didn't fit in Hydra at all with her booming voice, edgy look, and larger-than-life personality.

Henry was observing her with amused fascination, as if she was some kind of foreign species. I couldn't even begin to imagine how Stella would see her.

Why did she have to show up now? Looking so good too. She'd jumped in the shower super quick before returning to me and Henry, and she smelled fresh and enticing and familiar while brushing up next to me in the car. She'd always been fit, but she was ripped now. I couldn't keep my eyes off her biceps. What the hell was wrong with me? Would this ride never end? And yet, I didn't want it to end because what the fuck was I going to do?

I hadn't even talked to Stella about Rake. Not once. I just couldn't. I couldn't say a single thing about her without gushing out the whole, complicated truth. It was too raw and real. I was afraid that I'd say too much, and Stella would see that it wasn't really over between Rake and me, that I wasn't sure about my connection with her, that Rake had this irresistible pull. I couldn't risk that, so I'd pretended Rake had never existed. It was easier that way. To compartmentalize things. There was Amy, and there was Amara, and they were different people with different love stories.

How had I turned into such a two-timing asshole? I hadn't broken up with Rake. The last thing I'd told her was that I loved her. But in my defense, there had been no way to communicate with her, and I'd meant it when I said it. I still meant it.

But…I cared for Stella too. At first, I'd thought it was just a silly fling, a way to pass the time and explore my sexuality and identity without all the pressure and worry I felt in my connection with Rake. It was supposed to be temporary, superficial fun. But it had morphed into more than that, and now my worlds were about to collide, and no one was prepared, and I didn't know what to do.

When we pulled up in front of the estate, Rake let out a low whistle of appreciation. I followed Henry inside woodenly, making eye contact with no one, full of dread. Stella greeted us at the entrance, looking as sweet and gorgeous as ever.

"You're back. How did it go? Was it awful? Did you find any leads?" She kissed me on the lips, briefly and casually, before moving to hug her father. I couldn't see Rake, but I could feel a massive energy shift, like all the air had been sucked out of the room. Stella seemed to notice I was stiff and silent. "What's wrong? Did you…Oh." She looked over my shoulder, then, and her eyes were enormous.

She looked at me expectantly, as did her father, but I couldn't find my voice, and eventually, Henry broke the uneasy silence. "This is a friend of Amara's from the outside. I…I'm sorry, but I didn't learn your real name."

"It's Rake." Her voice was tight and choked, and my heart squeezed painfully. This was unbearable. How was this even happening?

"Rake, well, welcome to our home. This is my daughter, Stella." Henry passed his coat to a waiting BabyDoll and began to make his way to the living room. "That was quite the evening. I could use a nightcap. Anyone else?"

We followed him, each of us seemingly lost in her own thoughts. I wondered vaguely if Henry was oblivious to the tension or if he was well aware. I often found him to be distracted, but he was perceptive at the same time, so it was hard to say. He poured himself some whiskey and offered some to us as well. Stella declined, but I was eager for anything to ease the pain of this encounter, and Rake seemed the same.

Henry plopped onto an easy chair and sipped his drink. "I'm sorry our evening didn't turn up anything about your mother, Amara, but at least it's ended with a reunion of friends." He looked at us, and we both gave weak smiles. Stella's face registered confusion, but I was pretty sure that Henry was clueing in that something was off.

"Have you and Amara been friends a long time, Rake?" Stella asked uncertainly. She no doubt assumed Rake couldn't be very important to me since I had never mentioned her.

Rake put her feet up on the coffee table like an uncouth heathen and glared at me. "I don't know. Would you say we're close, Amara?"

"We've known each other our entire lives," I answered quickly, both replying and avoiding at the same time.

"Did you know Amara's mother?" Henry asked.

"Yeah, we were close. She was like a surrogate mom to me. I was probably closer to her than Amara, in fact."

Was she trying to hurt me? I could hardly blame her. And it was probably true. They clicked, their connection uncomplicated by a real parent-child dynamic. They got each other as individuals, something that had always sort of unnerved and irked me and which had probably contributed to my hesitance to be with Rake in the first place. My mother would be overjoyed to see us together. So I'd always resisted out of both stubbornness and a fear of letting them both down.

I snuck a peek at Stella. She was staring wide-eyed at Rake, like she'd never seen anyone like this in her entire life, like an honest-to-God, green-fleshed, tentacled alien was sitting in her living room making tense small talk while drinking her dad's whiskey. So much for my cool street punk persona. Rake was blowing all my credibility. She was so much tougher than I was, but so tough that Stella seemed genuinely frightened.

Henry had a strange focused expression that reminded me of Rebecca. It was the look she got when she was measuring a person or calculating a move. It weirded me out to see it on Henry's face, especially since it was directed at Rake. "You were close to Maria, Rake. Would it surprise you to learn that she's not listed as a Drudge in the official Hydra records?"

What was he probing for? Rake seemed to be measuring him right back. She took a long swig of whiskey, then looked him straight in the eye and said, "Not really."

Wait. What? "What are you talking about? What do you mean you aren't really surprised?"

"I mean, people don't always tell everyone the whole truth, now, do they?" She said it bitingly, intending to subtly call me out, but my whole body went cold, and I didn't feel the sting of the accusation at all.

"Rake, what are you saying? Did…did you know my mom was going to leave? Do you know where she is?" It felt like the whole world condensed down to the three feet between us. Nothing else existed or mattered. Had she betrayed me? Was no one who I'd thought they were? What the fuck was happening? I waited for her answer, tense.

She sat and stared, defiant and silent.

"Do you know where she is?" I yelled.

"No."

Relief flooded me. I relaxed enough to become aware of Stella and Henry once more, her bewildered, him attentive. "Did you know she was leaving?"

"Yes."

Anger flooded me now. I slammed down my glass and got up in Rake's face. "Why? Why didn't you tell me?"

"Because she asked me not to." She went to sip her whiskey.

I lost my temper and smacked the glass from her hand. It went flying and smashed impressively loudly on the floor. I heard Stella's little exclamation of surprise and fear, but I had no space to deal with her. "What's going on? Why did she leave? Where did she go? Why aren't you telling me the truth?"

"Maria is with the Defiance, isn't she?" Henry asked.

We all turned, frozen. He waved to the BabyDoll lingering by the entrance. She rushed to clean our mess.

"The fuck you talking about, old man?" Rake replied, menace clear in her voice.

My mind was whirling. There was too much to take in.

Henry got up and refilled his glass while the BabyDoll scurried from the room, no doubt dying of curiosity. I held my breath and waited to see what he would say. I figured it was best to say nothing until I understood what was really happening here.

"Ladies, there are layers upon layers of intrigue happening here, and I think the moment has come to take a leap of faith and tell the truth. I know I certainly need to understand the whole truth if I'm going to help you."

Neither Rake nor I said anything, both of us just listening.

"With respect, I know more about Maria Rodriguez than either of you. Everyone in Hydra is looking for her. If you want to find her before the authorities do—and trust me, you do if you care about her well-being—then we need to clear the air and trust each other."

I was barely wrapping my brain around the idea that Henry Keenan knew my mother when Rake burst out, "And why would we trust you? Why would you help us? If what you're saying is true and Amara's mother is with the Defiance—*which she isn't*—that would make her a terrorist. If we knew about that—*which we don't*—we'd be abetting a terrorist. You're an Old Blood council member. Don't fucking stand there and pretend you'd be willing to turn against your own people. To free a suspected revolutionary when you represent everything the Defiance is fighting. That's complete bullshit. And it's insulting that you think we'd be stupid enough to believe you."

Henry smiled a surprisingly sad smile. "I understand your distrust and hostility. You think it's your people versus my people, New Bloods versus Old Bloods, but that's a false division imposed on us by the powers that be. People—"

"You're the powers that be," Rake interrupted.

"In a way. But ultimately, you need access to power in order to make real change, so you'd be wise to listen."

She narrowed her eyes and folded her arms across her chest, but it shut her up.

"I'm not saying the divisions aren't real. These 'sides' are powerfully impactful in our lives in tangible ways, it's true. But in the end, people are just people. We have more in common than we are led to believe. That's how people fall in love across these divisions." He gestured to Stella and me, and I couldn't help but grow warm at the tender smile that lit up Stella's face. "And that's why sometimes, they change sides. Like Maria did."

Well, that got my attention.

"Maria is an Old Blood, Amara."

"What?" For the second time tonight, Rake and I were echoes of each other.

"Well, technically, Maria isn't her real name. Her name is Valentina Lopez, and she lived in Hydra for many years before leaving for the Freelands."

Rake and I looked at each other. I was utterly shaken, our recent animosity completely wiped away by alarm. What. The. Actual. Fuck.

"You're lying. Why are you saying this?" Rake said the words, but her face said something entirely different. She was spooked, and I could see her wheels turning as desperately as my own. My mom, an Old Blood? That didn't make any sense.

Henry perched delicately on the arm of the sofa. "I'll tell you what I know of your mother, Amara. Believe me, I wanted to from the moment I met you and saw the way my daughter looks at you. There's nothing I wouldn't do for someone Stella cares for." It was a sweet thing to say, but I cringed inwardly at the fact that he'd said it in front of Rake.

Henry put his hand lightly on my arm. "But I think you can understand why I might be hesitant to help. I'm sure you'd agree that it's only reasonable to want to be reassured that assisting you won't result in anything harmful for my so-called 'side.' If your mother's mission is terribly violent, well…I can't in good conscience help you, can I?"

Frustration flooded through me, and I blurted, "I don't know her mission. I didn't even know she was affiliated with the Defiance."

"As you are?"

I looked at Rake and didn't say anything.

"Rebecca suspected you of being a spy. We knew you were Maria's daughter and hoped she'd come looking for you, which is why we placed you in a council member's home as bait. But of course, she never materialized. No one knows why she's back or how she disappeared. We assumed something might happen at the Juvenalia."

"Back up a second," Rake said. "Let's say we were with the Defiance—*which we aren't*—I still don't understand why you'd help us. Just because your daughter has a crush on Amara?"

Henry smiled that same sad smile, got up, and paced the room. He took his time before speaking. "Do you know that I'm the second oldest person in existence?" He gave a strange little laugh. "Just think of that. What a bizarre accomplishment. I've been around so long that my annual existential crisis has turned into a perpetual crisis of faith. I helped build this enclave, just as I helped pioneer the cure." He looked out the window, his back to us. In the slight pause, I struggled to gather my thoughts and feelings, but there was just too much going on for me to process.

"You can't always predict or control where some discoveries will lead." Henry turned to us again. "My ex-wife is a brilliant woman. She has the most genuinely astonishing mind I've ever encountered. But… not that I want to slight her in her daughter's presence, but…it's only true to say that she is ruthless and obsessive in her intellectual pursuits. Something *more* is happening in her research right now. I don't know what because it's been granted the highest security protocol possible, and I've been given the cold shoulder since our split, but I have my suspicions, and they're…not good. Not for either of our sides. I suspect Maria's return might have something to do with it or that she might know something useful. But it's just a hunch."

"Some people think folks in the Freelands are being abducted for medical research," I said. "Is that possible?"

"Definitely. We need test subjects, and if Rebecca is working on somehow improving upon the Remedy, as I suspect, they would have to be New Bloods."

"Let me get this straight, you're willing to help us find Maria because you want to mess up your ex-wife's research out of jealousy?" Rake asked. Her eyebrow was raised skeptically, but I could see she was softening to him.

He laughed. "Perhaps. I'd like to think I just want to be a good dad and spare the world yet another dangerous scientific breakthrough, but maybe you're right. Maybe it's partly that I'm a spiteful ex-husband dying to know what my brilliant ex is up to. Perhaps I'm just bored of my second century of life and want to take a risk and feel alive and do something reckless. Who can say? Human motivation is complex and difficult to pinpoint."

I could feel Rake relax. She looked at me questioningly.

It was up to me. I tried to listen to my gut, but the pressure was too high to get a clear intuitive signal.

I looked at Stella. "Should I trust him?"

I could feel waves of resentment coming off Rake for that. Stella was pale and frightened. In a way, it was funny that I was asking her. The real question was probably whether she should trust me after all she had learned tonight. But Stella was nothing if not pure of heart. I felt certain I could trust her judgment.

She cleared her throat nervously. "I hardly know what to think. I'm not really sure I fully understand everything that's happening. But if you're asking if you can trust my father…" She looked at him, and he gazed at her steadily until she broke away to return to me. "He would never betray me. And by extension, you. My mother, on the other hand, well…you've met her."

I nodded. Henry knew things I didn't. He was powerfully connected. He'd never given me any reason to doubt him. I'd watched him do uncomfortable, unsavory things to help me. And he loved his daughter with everything in him. That was obvious.

"Tell me about my mother," I said softly.

He did. He told me all about how her father had used all the extreme wealth of his commercial empire in Mexico to purchase one exorbitantly priced dose of the Remedy, back in the early days, when it was still possible to purchase it outright. He'd given up everything to get it for his only child. Even his life. To make sure she took it and didn't look back, he killed himself and his wife, placing his beloved child in Hydra's care.

No wonder she didn't like to talk about her past. My poor mother. How had she lived through something so unthinkable and come out the other side so strong? An obscure pain racked my body at the mere thought.

"She lived an uneventful life here until the reproduction ban. Then she decided she was ready to have a child. Perhaps the trauma of her past kept her from having one earlier. I can only guess. In any case, it was too late. The ban passed. But there was a special exception given to a select group of women who would be given a child to adopt in exchange for service to the state."

"What service?" Rake didn't hesitate to ask.

"Fifteen years of surveillance in the Freelands. Then they could come home. Bring the child with them. Or not. They were given food carts outfitted with special equipment."

"Oh my God. The fucking food cart was bugged?" Rake burst out.

"Yes."

"I bitched about Hydra a zillion times hanging out there. What the fuck? But wait, she…she was just pretending to be Defiance or…oh my God, I took her to the meetings. It was me. I got her involved. And she was betraying us or…"

"We think she had a change of heart. Became a double agent. Perhaps you led her to the Defiance, but she never reported anything useful. So that confirms it. She switched teams. What do you know about her mission?"

Rake paced around now, no longer hiding anything, it seemed. "Nothing. I knew nothing except that it was important for her to go right away. There was something about the timing. Holy shit, I can't believe Maria is an Old Blood. No wonder she looks so good for her age."

"It's been over fifteen years, so she could easily return via any gate. But she must have had help on the inside because she disappeared once she was initially processed. That's what has everyone spooked. Not all council members were on board with the surveillance project to begin with. Too much risk of them 'going native' and becoming a blood traitor, which Maria's case only demonstrates as a plausible danger." He mused to himself more than to us. "I suppose it's hard to live out there, see all you see, and maintain an allegiance to the state that's keeping everyone in such dire straits."

"You don't say?" Rake replied sarcastically.

"So…I was 'given' to Maria in exchange for her service?" I asked in a small voice.

"Yes. I don't remember anything about your background, but I could look. Most of the children were orphans. Typically of addicts who'd overdosed. I'm sorry, Amara."

I nodded thoughtfully. It was a lot to take in. I felt tiny and bereft.

"What do we do now, Dad? How can we help?" Stella asked.

"We need to find Maria and get answers. We've exhausted our own stores of knowledge. Unfortunately, the only other place I can think of that an undocumented person could be hiding is a place called Hot Tots." He said the name with some distaste.

"What's that?" Stella asked.

"It's a…brothel, to be frank. But a front for all kinds of illicit activity, I suspect. Let me think on how we could manage to uncover the goings-on there. We're all exhausted, and I, for one, could use some sleep."

He said his good nights, distracted as always, and left us.

I was the furthest from sleep, though. My mind and heart were racing with all this new information, but I bid him good night absentmindedly before realizing his absence left me alone with only Stella and Rake, both of whom were looking at me with complicated expressions.

"Would you mind giving me some time to talk to Rake?" I asked Stella. "I'll come up and say good night later if you're still awake, okay?"

She nodded and came and gave me a hug, shaky, no doubt with emotion and uncertainty. I avoided Rake's eyes and returned the hug awkwardly.

Then it was just Rake and I.

"I don't suppose Richie Rich has any pot hidden away somewhere?" Rake asked.

"It's illegal here."

"Mmm." She made her way to the bar and poured herself some more whiskey.

"Can I have some too?"

"Sure. Would you like one finger or two?" She stuck up her middle finger for the first option and made a lewd sexual gesture for the second.

I ignored the insult—and invitation?—and simply answered, "One."

"Sounds about right. You never could handle very much."

"I've handled quite a lot since coming here," I said, getting up and swiping my glass from her, feeling my cheeks flush with anger.

She cocked her eyebrow, and I got flustered. Did she think I was talking about sex?

"This hasn't exactly been a cake walk."

"No. Not at all. I mean, look around you," Rake replied sarcastically. She sipped her whiskey without breaking eye contact over the rim. "Okay, Amara. This is the moment where you tell me that this thing with Miss Prissy Rich Girl is all an act, a difficult sacrifice you just had to make to find your mother. So go ahead. Tell me that's what's really going on." Her eyes were hard but also pathetically pleading, and I had to turn away.

"Listen, Rake. I didn't mean for this to happen, and I had no way to talk to you and tell you. It was just supposed to be a meaningless, flirty thing, and then…I don't know…I sort of fell for her." I cringed, waiting for Rake's reaction.

"You 'I don't know, sort of fell for her,' " she repeated icily.

My mind whirled for an excuse, guilt eating me up. I landed on the last time I'd seen Rake and the weird way she'd been interacting with that Irene woman. It was easier to be angry and accusatory than to feel what I was feeling. I knew I was deflecting, but I couldn't stop myself. "What? I'm supposed to believe you were an angel the whole time I was gone? What about that woman who was with you at my graduation? You seemed pretty close to her."

"Irene? Are you kidding me?" Rake exploded. "Did I want to lose myself in the comfort of someone else's arms? Of course I did, *but I didn't*. Irene helped me. She was there for me. She was kind and sweet and—"

"Sounds like you should have slept with her," I interrupted, illogically jealous.

"Maybe I should have," she said back, seething.

We stared at each other in a livid standoff for a few minutes.

She gave a mirthless little laugh. "Could you have picked someone more different from me, Amara? My whole life, I've wondered if you were attracted to me. If you could be into someone like me or if maybe I was nothing like your type, and that was the problem. I couldn't figure out what you wanted, but maybe that was because you never wanted anything our life out there in the streets could give. You wanted some prissy, perfect, Barbie doll princess."

"Don't insult her," I said. "She's done nothing to you."

"No. She just stole the girl I've spent my whole life loving," she said, choking on the final words.

Fuck.

I tried to think of what to say to make it better, to explain. "Maybe I picked her precisely because she's nothing like you, but that's not necessarily a bad thing. I could be someone new and different with her. I could explore other parts of myself. It was easier. There was no baggage, no history."

"I'm baggage and history?"

"No, Rake, that's not what I mean. I—"

She interrupted, loudly and angrily. "You do understand that I literally have girls throwing themselves at me every night in the rings? Like, I don't need to work this hard with anyone else. I don't know why I'm so fixated on you. Why I want someone so badly who has shown me over and over again that she doesn't want me back."

I wanted to say, "But I do. I do. I want you." But I was very much aware of Stella waiting for me anxiously upstairs and that the awful truth was that my heart was torn. I cared for them both in different ways, but that was impossible and wrong.

Rake looked at me in a way I cringed to see. A look bursting with hurt and disappointment, fury and disgust. I was trying to think of what to say to fix us when she blurted out, "Go tuck in your girlfriend, Amara. And go fuck yourself while you're at it." She stomped away without looking back.

I started bawling. I couldn't hold it in. Rake. My mom. My mom? Stella. Everything. It was too much.

She didn't come back, though I was sure she heard me. I didn't deserve to have her come back. I didn't deserve either of these women.

I stumbled to the bar and poured myself a veritable fist of whiskey, chugged it down between choking sobs, and lurched up the stairs to Stella.

She wanted to talk. She wanted to snuggle. She wanted reassurance. But I couldn't give her any of it. I couldn't do anything but flop down on her bed and fall asleep in a sloppy, miserable, wasted stupor.

CHAPTER SIXTEEN

Dead Men Naked

I woke the next day in an agony of heart and body.

"I don't suppose your scientific genius of a father knows some miracle cure for a hangover?" I mumbled, returning to bed from Stella's ensuite, my head pounding with every step.

"I'm afraid he's working on more pressing problems," she replied, holding open the covers for me. "But get in and relax, and I'll be back with a few things that might help. You're mostly dehydrated, so expect me to push liquids on you all day."

"Sounds good," I said, snuggling into the covers as she took off.

Stella stayed with me all that day as I hid in her room, as much to avoid seeing Rake as out of necessity, given my sorry physical condition. I didn't want to *see* Rake, but I did want to know what she was doing, so Stella checked in with the BabyDolls, who reported that Rake was hanging out on the beach and had ordered a huge picnic from them. She was drinking and had invited several of them to goof off and join her, which they had respectfully declined.

"Sounds about right," I said. Rake would make sure she took advantage of this rare opportunity for luxurious self-indulgence. She was going to ensure she had some fun. But it didn't mean she wasn't hurting.

Stella asked me about her eventually. I knew she would. We must have made the strangest impression last night. I wanted to avoid and plead that I was too ill to talk, but honestly, I just wanted the conversation over with too.

"So…your relationship with Rake seems intense," she began.

I told her everything. There was nothing to hide now. She knew I was working with the Defiance, for God's sake. If that didn't push her away, she could handle knowing about Rake.

All she said at first was, "Oh, well, that explains a lot."

She asked me about the Defiance, but I didn't have much to share. My connection to them was less involved than Rake or my mother's connection had been. Mostly, she just stayed with me and snuggled and reminded me to eat and drink from time to time.

"Do you like being read to? My nanny used to read to me when I was sick."

Though I knew she was super rich, it was still weird to hear words like that come out of her mouth. "You had a nanny?"

"You think my mom stayed home and took care of me when I was sick?"

We both smiled at the thought. "Guess that's not a job that exists in Hydra anymore, eh?" I asked.

"No. Like everything else associated with children."

"It must have been weird growing up as part of the last generation." We stared at each other across our pillows.

"For sure. We were sort of famous, I guess you could say. The news reported on us all the time. Recorded all the lasts. The last kindergarten graduation. The last night of trick-or-treating. The last lone believer in Santa Claus…"

I wasn't sure if she was joking about the last one.

"We were pretty spoiled but also under this weird pressure, like, it's hard to describe, but it was almost like a self-aware nostalgia for something that wasn't yet lost. I don't know if that makes sense."

"Sure. I bet Old Bloods were mourning the end of an era through watching you grow up. I'm sure there was a lot of grief, even if they did vote for the ban."

"I guess…" She seemed lost in thought, then brightened. "What's it like in the Freelands? I mean with kids. What are they really like? I remember being one, obviously, but I don't know what children are like to have around as an adult."

It struck me again how strange it was to live in a child-free society. I considered, then answered sarcastically, thinking only of my pounding headache. "They're loud."

Stella seemed disappointed, so I tried again, remembering how she longed to be a mother, a dream that had been taken from her. "Okay, well, yes, they're loud and messy and chaotic little creatures, but they're also really pure and magical and the sweetest things in existence. It's both. They're exhausting to be around and rejuvenating to be around too. Some people thrive around them, and some lose their minds. That's what I've seen, anyway."

"Do you like children? Do you think you'll have your own one day?" Her eyes showed far too much interest in the question and a hint of pain.

"I honestly don't know. I haven't thought about it. That's way in the future." I was tired of this conversation and tried to change the subject. "Didn't this start out with an offer to read to me?"

She perked up. "Yes, anything in particular you'd like? My go-to when I'm sick is poetry. I can't always follow a fictional plot, but with poetry, you can kind of drift in and out, and it's perfectly fine."

"I could get behind that."

Stella brought an old-fashioned paper book to the bed. "This is my favorite. e. e. cummings is perfect when you're sick. It's all beautiful nonsense, so you don't have to work too hard to focus. Just enjoy and let it wash over you."

She read to me for what felt like ages. She stroked my hair occasionally but otherwise seemed perfectly content to get lost in voicing the lovely, rhythmic words aloud. My mind wandered. I couldn't help but think of Rake. I hoped she would forgive me. She was fiery and passionate but not one to hold a grudge. Her emotions were big, but they settled. She was a peaceful, happy-go-lucky person at the core. She'd be okay, and we'd find our way back to something like before. I had to trust in that.

I dozed, and when I woke, Stella was at her desk doing something on her datapad. "You're up. Good. My dad wants to talk to you."

Henry came to share his plan for checking out Hot Tots the next night. He wanted to go alone, but I protested. Of course he didn't want to expose me to the place and the "ugly" things he'd have to do to get some information, but I had this strong feeling that I needed to be there. It didn't hurt that it would give me another chance to avoid Rake.

I supposed that there was an element of curiosity driving me too. I'd read about "houses of ill repute" in books. What were they like in real life? Living in the Freelands, I knew plenty of people who worked the streets to make ends meet, but I'd never seen a genuine brothel. It was oddly thrilling to think about. I wanted to see one for myself. It took some work, but I managed to convince Henry that I could be useful, that we could use the same charade of me being his lover. He still hesitated until I pointed out that I wasn't just some innocent young girl, that I'd lived on the streets where there was a sex worker on every corner and that I was a spy for the Defiance. I could handle a little blackmail in a whorehouse. That had shocked him into agreement.

And so, the next evening, feeling significantly more myself, I once again left the Keenan estate on a fake date with my girlfriend's father, sporting yet another uncomfortably revealing dress. To add to the drama, Stella and Rake both saw us off. I suspected Stella had let Rake know and that she was working behind the scenes to try to reconcile our friendship. I couldn't imagine how that conversation went, if indeed it had happened, but I could imagine Stella trying to soothe Rake and play the peacemaker. She was a hard person to hate, so maybe she could do some good. In any case, they both went to the door to wish us well. Rake just about choked when she saw my outfit. I was pretty sure I'd heard her mutter, "You really are trying to torture me," but she didn't storm off, as I half expected.

There was no driver this time, unsurprisingly. We spent the ride reviewing our plan. Evidently, the owner of the brothel was a woman named Anastasia Morozov. Henry knew little about her, other than the fact that she was from a powerful Russian family, secretive and paranoid. Tony, the owner of the fighting rings, was exactly what he seemed, a somewhat slimy but fairly benign criminal whose seedier side interests included minor drug trafficking, gambling, and animal fights. Anastasia, however, had no known seedy side interests. She might have been a mere peddler of flesh, but the nature of the industry made this suspect. Henry warned me that nothing would be as it seemed. There would be no vein scanners, for example, which put clients at ease, thinking their visit would be untracked. But Henry thought that unlikely. Rather, we had to assume we would be registered, tracked, and recorded in every interaction.

The car pulled up, and a valet in a smart uniform rushed to welcome us. He motioned us to two "ushers," huge, menacing guys who looked more like special ops soldiers than bouncers. They walked us inside a surprisingly nondescript building. There were more "ushers" everywhere. I supposed it made clients feel both protected and on edge, serving as a reminder that they were safe to indulge their illicit desires but also that house rules would be enforced.

Greeters welcomed us at a front desk. They were dressed like sexy secretaries, took our coats and offered us a welcome drink. We declined. I was buzzing with a strange, foreign excitement. "Have you visited before?" one greeter asked.

"Yes," Henry answered.

"Which floor?" one of them asked, pointing to the directory on the wall. Each floor had a name that suggested something of its offerings. I scanned it, burning with curiosity, trying to figure out what pleasures were promised by each name.

"The Vineyard."

"Excellent choice. And which package?" She gestured to a plaque on the wall.

"Gold is fine."

"Wonderful. The lady will be accompanying you?"

"Yes."

"Great. That will be one thousand credits, sir."

Henry pulled out actual Hydra bills, something I hadn't seen him use before, but it made sense that most people would pay in cash here.

"Since you're a fan of the Vineyard, I should let you know that next Friday, we'll be having a Toga Party in the great room. You won't want to miss it."

Henry nodded and took the key cards she offered.

"Enjoy," she said, waving us toward the elevator where yet another usher awaited us.

We walked to the elevator. The usher joined us in the small space, and we stood in uncomfortable silence the whole ride up. When the elevator finally stopped at our floor, the usher led us to the main room and watched as we used our key cards to open its doors. It had been silent in the hall, so I was surprised when music and laughter poured out of the room with the opening of the doors. Henry took my arm, gave me a tight smile, and led me inside.

I was taken aback by the sheer size of the room. In the middle of it was a sort of giant sunken square lined on three sides with a plush scarlet couch. The fourth side, the one closest to the door, featured stairs that led down to the lounge area. Each corner of the room had a Roman style column, and there was greenery everywhere, like we were in some garden villa in Tuscany. There were chaise lounges and embroidered pillows. The floor was a mosaic of tiles, and the walls were painted with idyllic pastoral and mythological scenes. There were busts and sculptures and bits of pottery everywhere. It was gorgeous. Right away, I wished Stella were here to see it. Then I realized where I was and looked closer.

There were easily over two dozen people in the room. Drinking, talking, flirting, and lounging. The wine was flowing liberally. The men were all typical Old Bloods, white, young-looking and rich. The women, though, they weren't what I expected, not the nubile young things I assumed I'd find. They ranged from mature to outright old. I watched a pretty, gray-haired woman in a floral print dress laughing with a young-looking guy. The top few buttons on her dress were undone, revealing her weathered cleavage, something the gentleman in question kept eyeing between laughter and sips of wine. The woman had striking blue eyes and a free and easy manner. She seemed to be having a merry old time. Was that an illusion too? She had to be in her mid-sixties. But maybe her client was too. Actually, he was probably even older. Was that why it was called Hot Tots? Was advanced age a popular sexual fetish for Old Bloods? Were these women I'd call old mere children to them? What a strange thought. I realized that was probably what the floor's moniker implied. That the women on offer here would be aged like a fine wine. Of various delicious vintages. I looked at the women more closely, and they were all beautiful in their own way. Truly. It was odd and refreshing and slightly unnerving to see mature women embracing their age and refusing to shrivel up and hide their continued sexiness and lust for life and all its pleasures.

A woman joined us and interrupted my musings. "Henry, darling, I haven't seen you here since Councillor Austin's bachelor party," Henry blushed at this, and I realized with discomfort that he might not have been lying when he'd said he'd been here before. "Come, sit. Sit." She motioned to a nearby alcove, and we dutifully sat. She snapped her fingers at a shirtless man. "Max. Wine." Henry tried to decline, but she wouldn't hear of it. "Nonsense. Who stays sober at a cathouse? You're insulting my hospitality. Now drink up."

I realized with a start that she was in charge here. Did that mean she was Anastasia? Or just the madam in charge of this floor? She didn't look Russian. Whatever that meant.

Once we'd both obediently drunk of her offering, she looked at me pointedly, no doubt at my telltale hairdo, and said, "Dr. Keenan, I do believe you're getting stereotypical in your old age. Banging the help? What a cliché."

"Yes, well, stereotypes spring from kernels of truth, I suppose. It's been lonely since my split with the missus."

"Aw, yes, I was sorry to hear. Well, we can certainly help ease some of that loneliness." She arched her eyebrow meaningfully. "Anything in particular you're looking for?"

"I like them bitchy, as you can imagine, having met my ex."

The woman laughed heartily, and I couldn't repress a smile.

"Who's that?" Henry asked, nodding toward a woman talking with another working girl. I recognized her right away. Henry had shown me an image of the target.

"Helena. She's elegant and discerning in terms of who she entertains. Probably right up your alley. Should I introduce you?"

"No need." He rose, and I went to go with him. "Stay here," he commanded and glanced at the madam. "Drink. Relax. I'll be back with a treat for us both."

I smiled awkwardly at the madam and just people-watched. It was all rather fascinating. I was surprised at how relaxed and jovial the atmosphere seemed. It was definitely sexually charged, but I don't know, I guess I had somehow expected something dingier, darker and more shame-soaked for a den of iniquity. My literary learning had clearly led me astray.

Fifteen minutes later, we were leaving the main room for a private one, just the three of us. My heart was beating like mad. Henry was making suggestive comments. How awkward was this going to get? But not long after we got in the room, Henry's speech grew slurred, and he seemed unsteady on his feet. How could he possibly be so drunk so quickly? I gave him a quizzical look. His face registered alarm, and then out of nowhere, he collapsed on the bed.

"Henry?" I ran to check him when the door to our room burst open.

And my mother walked in.

Just appeared. *Poof.* Like magical wish fulfillment after all this time.

"Mom!"

She threw herself at me, and we embraced, both of us shaking and crying. *My mom. My mom. She is right here with me again. Everything is going to be okay.* I knew I had to come here with Henry. I felt it. I fucking knew it.

"Amara." She said my name like no one else. A distinctive trick of pronunciation with her lilting accent. I hadn't heard my name said properly in months. She felt and smelled and sounded like home.

I couldn't forget Stella's father, though, and disentangled myself long enough to ask if he'd be all right.

"A mild sedative. He'll be out for a few hours, then he'll be fine." She swore in Spanish. "What are you doing here? How did you get here?"

"What are *you* doing here? And don't give me any of the bullshit you wrote in that note. I know about the Defiance."

Her eyes widened, and she motioned for Helena to close the door. She touched my hair and rattled off questions, not stopping long enough to give me a chance to answer. "You're a BabyDoll? Is Councillor Keenan your proprietor? Are you having an affair with him? Amara, you can't have babies now. What were you thinking? Why are you here? Where's Rake? Who's looking after the business and all the people? You need to get out of here."

"I'm fine. Rake's fine. Everything is taken care of on the outside. Dr. Keenan is my proprietor, but he's helping me. He's a good guy."

My mom raised her eyebrows.

"No, seriously. Mom, we have to get you out of here."

She clucked her tongue like she always did when she thought I was being stupid.

"Mom, listen. The Defiance helped me get in. They didn't sterilize me. There's still plenty of opportunity for you to be a grandma…" I rolled my eyes, but her face lost some of its worry. "We need to get you away from here. Why are you even in a brothel? What are you doing here? No…wait, do I want to know?"

She gave a brief laugh, then hardened. "Amara, I'm where I'm supposed to be. You're the one who didn't stay where she was supposed to. You're the one who needs to leave. If the Defiance got you in, they can get you out. Go back to the Freelands. Rake will take care of you. Just—"

"Rake is here. At Dr. Keenan's house."

"What? Why? What do you mean?"

"It's a long story, but we're here trying to get you out. We all need to talk. To make a plan."

"I didn't ask to get out. I have things I need to do."

"Mom, stop being stubborn. I risked a lot to get here." I felt heat rise to my face.

She took my face in her hands. "Amara, there are things you don't know."

"Like that you're an Old Blood?"

She started, and her eyes darted to Helena, who pretended poorly that she hadn't heard.

"Mom, Dr. Keenan knows all about you. He told me everything. He just wants to help."

"And why would an Old Blood council member want to help the Defiance? Amara, he's playing you, and you led him straight to me."

"It's not like that."

She exhaled deeply, showing her mounting frustration. "Baby, it's time for you to go home. There are things happening here that are way beyond you."

I lost my temper. "Mom, stop treating me like a child." It would have helped my cause more if I hadn't stamped my foot like a toddler having a temper tantrum, an act that wasn't missed by my mother, who looked at me with exasperation. I pushed on, trying to make up for that misstep:

"All of Hydra is looking for you, and *I* found you. *Me*. I had to break a guy's nose just to get to the gate. Then spend weeks learning to excel at stupid fucking shit like floral arrangement at the BabyDoll academy, all to be able to get into a council member's home so I could spy on her. Not that I saw much. She turned out to be a psycho genius, and I honestly spent most of my time learning to walk her goddamn luxury cat…" I realized I was rambling, and frustration made me burst into tears, which also didn't help my cause. For reasons I couldn't understand, I blurted, "And did I mention that I watched someone get murdered?" My voice cracked. "I stood there and watched, and I didn't do anything."

Her expression darkened, and I rushed to say something more positive so she wouldn't worry too much about me:

"But I met a girl, and I fell in love, and Dr. Keenan is her dad, and he's helping us. He is. I've made powerful allies. You need to trust me. I can freaking handle things. You need to tell me your mission. I can help." What a disastrous attempt at persuasion. I gave up and just looked at her.

My mom stared at me in silence for what felt like a long time. "You've become a real potty mouth, Amara."

I don't know why, but that made us both laugh. A needed break from the tension.

She looked to Helena, who nodded and slipped from the room. "All I'm going to tell you is that there's an important negotiation happening between the President of the Confederacy and the Asenescence Corporation. The Defiance needed an Old Blood to learn more about the nature of the negotiations. That's why I'm here. It couldn't be anyone else. Now tell me more about him." She gestured to Henry, still passed out, drooling onto the bedcovers. "And his daughter." Her eyebrows rose somewhat teasingly, and I blushed.

"Henry Keenan is a councillor. A pioneer of the Remedy."

"I know who he is. I just don't understand the nature of your relationship or why you trust him."

I explained about the fake affair and how I'd come to live with him instead of his ex-wife. I tried to explain about Stella but faltered, feeling some obscure negativity emanating from my mother when I mentioned her. She was probably disappointed about me not choosing Rake. Or maybe she didn't want me getting involved with an Old Blood? I wasn't sure, but it wasn't the focus in this moment. I rushed on, explaining why Henry was trustworthy, why he wanted to help. I could tell she was both intrigued and wary of working with him.

She paced the room. "He would have access to the main Asenescence labs?"

"Yes, all but the highest security ones where Rebecca's latest project is housed, but he thinks we might be able to find a way in."

"Do you have a way to communicate with the Crone? Does she approve this step?"

"My communication is one-sided. I have no clue. What about you?"

"Same." She sighed. "I've already completed the first part of the mission, and the second part is iffy at best. If Henry is playing us and turns me in, well, I don't think they really have much on me besides returning and going AWOL. I already accomplished the most important part. We know more now about what's happening with these negotiations, what they're about, and when further meetings will go down. But if Henry is really on our side, if we could actually get inside and see what's going on in these secret labs, that could be a huge win for the cause. It's a gamble…" She trailed off, clearly thinking.

"We have to lay everything on the table to decide. If he's playing us, which I really don't think he is, then we're in a bit more trouble than that. Rake and I have basically admitted we're with the Defiance. If he turned on us, the Defiance would have to help us out."

"Or cut ties. We might be a lost cause in that case. Rake told him? She must trust him too." I nodded. "Rake's a good judge of character," she mused aloud.

I swallowed my irritation at the fact that she trusted Rake's judgment more than mine.

She came close and held my face again, a familiar gesture that always made me feel safe. “What do you think, my girl?” One of her pet endearments. But it rang strangely this time, and I saw her feel it at the same moment. She was probably wondering if I knew. Compassion for all the awful truths I learned about her past flooded through me.

“I know you adopted me. Dr. Keenan told me about the surveillance project. He told me everything he knew about your past, actually. I’m… I’m sorry about your parents.”

Her eyes filled with tears, and her body tensed. She seemed to be struggling to speak. I just waited. Giving her time to collect herself to say whatever she needed to say. “Like I said, what do you think, my girl?”

This time it didn’t ring strange. It was true. I was her girl.

We both smiled.

“I think we’re both very good at beating the odds. So I think it’s time to go all in.”

Chapter Seventeen

Those That I Fight I Do Not Hate

We returned to Dr. Keenan's house late. I was concerned about the servants seeing my mother, but Henry insisted they were all trustworthy, and they wouldn't recognize my mom anyway.

"Are you certain none of them are in Rebecca's pockets?" my mom asked.

"Loyalty and love run deeper than greed. I'd vouch for any of them. They enjoy many freedoms and kindnesses they'd get nowhere else, and I know each of them personally. They won't betray me."

What could we do but trust? There were an awful lot of leaps of faith going on. I only hoped none of them ended in regret.

My mom's reunion with Rake was touching. And unnerving. They had this whole, intense, silent conversation where subtle shifts in expression seemed to convey everything required. I was jealous of the way they got each other all the time. Mom put her hands on Rake's face the way she did to me in moments of hurt, and I had to look away because it made me terribly sad to know she was comforting Rake for the pain I'd caused her.

My mom met Stella too. Everyone had stayed up. I wasn't sure what to expect, but they were both polite, curious, and eager to like each other. My mom didn't hide her surprise. Was she shocked that I'd landed a girl as stunning as Stella? Probably. I was still pretty shocked about it too. Not that I wasn't pretty, but Stella was a whole other level of gorgeous.

Though the hour was late, no one thought of sleep, not even Henry, who claimed he felt extra alert despite the drugging, a fact he didn't seem to hold against my mother. Stella fetched a pot of strong coffee, and we all settled in for a night of intense revelation and planning.

The first order of business was to understand my mother's

mission. She hadn't gone into detail, and I was dying of curiosity. She hesitated, but after another silent conversation with Rake, she went on. "The Defiance had intel that there were negotiations happening at the highest level of security between the Asenescence Corporation and the President of the Confederacy."

Henry's eyes widened, and he couldn't sit still. He got up and started pacing but didn't interrupt. I tried to think what this could mean. Since the disbanding of the United States, the Confederacy had emerged as one of the biggest and most powerful post-Dissolution nation-states, comprised of what had previously been Southern states in America. The president was an outspoken Texan with big ambitions and a "tough on crime" platform. He was super young to be president and rather handsome. That was all I knew of him.

"They knew he'd be in Hydra for negotiations. They were fairly certain, given his past actions, that he'd make a stop at Hot Tots before leaving. They needed someone to bug him."

"So it was a covert monitoring mission? How did you evade bug sweeping?" Henry asked.

"I don't know the technical stuff. I just knew I had to place this little thingamabob in his burner. President Johnson is obsessed with his ivory e-cig burner. Real elephant tusk. Hard to come by. Illegal in most nations, if not the Confederacy."

"That explains the timing, but why you?" Rake asked. "Anybody could have placed the listening device."

"Bugging him was step one, and the only part of the plan that had any chance of succeeding, in my opinion. But step two was trying to develop a relationship with him, to seduce him and try to convince him to take me into the council district after hours, where we had a friendly on the inside. They needed an Old Blood to get past the bloodwall."

I couldn't quite focus on the last part, though I knew it was important. My mind had imploded at the word "seduce."

Stella returned and poured the coffee. I would've been amused to see her doing the work of a BabyDoll and could have offered her some tips on protocol if my mind wasn't trying to reassemble itself post-implosion.

"What's a bloodwall?" Rake asked.

Henry said, "The council district hosts both the Asenescence labs and the council chambers. It's the heart of Hydra. Just to get in, you have to pass a blood test. Old Bloods like myself can bypass it because the gatekeepers know us by sight, but it's meant to keep all but the most necessary New Bloods out. That's one of the vulnerabilities of Hydra. We need New Bloods even in our most high-security sites to do the drudge work. They're carefully vetted but—"

"That's the wrong question," I said. "Back up. What do you mean by 'seduce him'?"

I knew I'd phrased the question wrong the moment it came out, but Rake and my mom exchanged a tickled look, and I had to just deal with their amusement at my expense.

I tried to clarify. "Okay, I know what the word means. I meant to ask…like…you didn't…"

Okay, so much for clarifying.

My mom smiled. "Feel free to erase all of this from your memory, my girl, but, yes, I slept with the president. He was surprisingly good—"

She said more, but I didn't hear it because I'd shrieked and covered my ears with my hands. I could see that everyone was laughing, but I didn't take my hands away until Stella scooted next to me and gently took my hands.

My mom and Rake were not ones to let a good laugh go, especially not when it would make me squirm, so I should have known better than to let Stella pry my hands from my ears.

"Babygirl, you've always been so conservative," my mom tutted.

"You're Catholic," I protested.

"Yes, but it's mostly cultural, and I know enough to take it with a grain of salt. I mean, the average life expectancy was thirty-something when the Bible was written. It's not so hard to be a saint when you die before your sexual peak."

Rake was killing herself laughing, and I turned to glare at her. "What? People are willing to die for a cause. What's so bad about getting laid for a cause?"

"He's a good-looking man," my mom added.

"Ew. Stop. You're, like, twice his age."

"Am I?" She eyed me over her steaming mug, and I realized with a start that I didn't actually know how old she was.

"How old are you, Maria?" Rake asked, seeming to read my mind.

"Biologically? Twenty-four. Experientially? One hundred and eighty-seven."

I was glad I wasn't holding my mug. I would have dropped it and spilled hot coffee all over myself.

Rake cracked up even more. "You're a cradle robber, Maria."

Maria shrugged. "I was his type, and I could get past the bloodwall.

The fifteen years of my surveillance contract were up, so I'd be easy to get inside. It just fit."

Dr. Keenan cleared his throat. He seemed to want to get back on track, and I was certainly more than happy to move on from this topic. "So you fulfilled the first part of the mission. What did the surveillance reveal?"

The energy in the room shifted. Maria's face hardened. "They're negotiating a contract for prisoners. Asenescence is offering him one dose of the Remedy in exchange for felony criminals from the Confederacy being transferred to Hydra for their discretionary use."

Henry made a scoffing sound, and we all looked at him. "They need a steady, reliable supply of test subjects for whatever they're working on. This isn't good."

"Well, the negotiations have been difficult. Mostly because Johnson wants four doses, one for his wife and two kids too. They got him down to three but are trying to get him down to two. Trying to convince him to pick his favorite kid. He's not too fond of his wife, I guess. He should be back on the twenty-second for another round of discussions, likely the last. He's getting anxious about sealing the deal on his virtual immortality." She said the last two words with a hint of sarcasm, but it wasn't too far from the truth. No one really knew yet just how long Old Bloods could last. So far, none had died of old age, only accidents, foul play, and diseases they hadn't yet found a way to cure.

"What about the second part of your mission?" Henry asked.

"I don't know. It always seemed far-fetched to me. They did some kind of psychological profile on the guy. I guess he was rejected by some Latina girl when he was a teen, and he never got over it. Chose a WASP for a wife but keeps chasing these haughty Hispanic women who want nothing to do with him. It's an easy role to play, and he's eaten it up, but I don't know, I just don't think I've got him wrapped around my finger enough to get him to take me into the council district after hours. I was thinking I'd pretend not to believe him, to question his story. He's pretty arrogant and defensive about his own importance, so it might be enough to push him into doing something dumb, but I'm not sure."

"Sounds like a vague and stupid plan," Rake pronounced.

"Agreed," Maria said.

"Yeah, but my plan was vague and stupid, and it's got us all this far," I countered. That gave them all pause.

"You have a friendly on the inside?" Henry asked.

"Yes, a Drudge on the night shift."

"It won't be enough," Henry said. "I have some of the highest clearance in Hydra, and I can't get to where we need to go to find out what's really going on. This is big. If the president of the Confederacy is involved, it's potentially huge, in fact. We need a way to get into Rebecca's labs." He wandered the room for a bit, seemingly lost in thought and randomly fidgeting with various things. We were all quiet for a while, but I couldn't really think of any way to help.

"Should I get us a little something to eat?" Stella offered. We agreed, and she slipped from the room while we all still brooded on the situation.

Stella returned with some nibbles, but none of us had broken the silence. I was just munching on a cookie when Henry said, "Rebecca used to go on about the need for an alternate. An alternate ID. It would allow her to come and go as she pleased at the lab without being tracked. It seemed improbable. I mean, how would she bypass the liveness detection of the vein scanners? But if anyone can do it, it's her…"

He paused, and Stella pushed some nourishment on him. He ate mechanically, but it was clear that his wheels were turning. "If Rebecca did pursue this…if she somehow managed to create an alternate fake ID for the system, it's probably in her home lab. That would be the safest place to keep it when it's not in use. I used to have access, but I'm sure she's deleted me since the divorce."

"I have access," Stella said. "Mom still clings to hope that I'll take an interest in science and assist her in the labs again. Some of my silly school projects are still in there. I could do it."

Henry looked at her uncertainly.

"I can. I can do it. Mom would never suspect me of being capable of anything clever or sneaky. I could get in and look around when she's sleeping. Huxley will let me in, and he won't ask questions. I know he won't."

Henry let out a long breath. "It's worth a shot. Maria, you said President Johnson returns on the twenty-second? I assume he'll be in a town a few days?" She nodded. "Then we should plan for the twenty-second. Not that we need him, except as a fall guy. That gives us two days to think this through."

We looked around to each other, confirming. Relief and nerves battled it out inside me.

"Sounds like a plan," my mom concluded.

Rake let out a huge yawn. "Thank God. Devising plots is

exhausting work. I'll see you fellow co-conspirators in the morning." She went to give my mom a hug, then pulled away just before embracing her. "Wait, do you want us to call you Valentina now? That's your real name, right?"

"I always hated that name. I chose Maria. I like who I've become since using it."

"Then I'm glad to see you again, Maria. Sleep well." They hugged, and I looked away to say my own good night to Stella. I wasn't sure if she'd expect me to spend the night with her, but there was no way I was leaving my mom's side now that I finally had her back. We were sharing a bed. I didn't care if I was too old for it.

Stella seemed to understand perfectly. She kissed me sweetly and said, "Go reconnect with your mom. I'm so happy for you, Amara."

My mom didn't think it was weird at all that I wanted to spend the night together. It was like I was a little kid all over again, jumping in my mom's bed because the thunder had freaked me out. Maria was always willing to give affection and comfort, and now was no different. She smoothed my hair from my face as we gazed at each other, quietly content in the Keenans' giant guest bed.

"You've grown up. You look different," she said. "Not just the haircut. You hold yourself differently. More confident in your own skin, I think."

"Thanks."

She looked exactly the same. And now that I scrutinized her closer, I wondered how I had ever thought she was middle-aged. She dressed sort of frumpily. Was that a disguise? There was still so much I didn't know about her. But she was here. Here with me, the safe and reassuring presence I needed. She said I looked more mature, but I felt like a lost little kid who just wanted her mom.

She looked at me in silence, and though it was comfortable at first, after a moment, I realized I had some explaining to do. My mom wouldn't ask, and she wouldn't say what she thought. She'd wait. I knew this trick.

I sighed and ripped off the proverbial Band-Aid. "I know you're disappointed about things with Rake." She continued to just look, so I bumbled on. "I know you were hoping that we'd end up together."

"I did," she said. "But that's because I know Rake. I don't know Stella. If you love her, she must be extraordinary."

"She is."

"I'm sure. I look forward to getting to know her." Her words sounded too formal, and my heart sank.

I picked at the quilted cover, avoiding eye contact. "Why Rake? Like, of everyone in the Barrio that I could be with, why her?"

My mom seemed surprised at the question but didn't hesitate to answer. "She's loyal and a survivor. She'd protect you."

"I can protect myself."

My mom nodded. "I can see that now." She lifted my chin to look at me properly. "Amara, she adores you. How could I not love someone who thinks you're as great as I do?" That made me smile. "Besides, Rake's funny. She doesn't take life too seriously. You need that. But honestly, Amara, all I really want in this world is for my only child to be happy and to be good. That's it. If Stella makes you happy—"

"She does."

"Okay, then I'm glad. I'm sure I'll grow to love her too. But we just met. And Rake has been a part of our lives forever. You have to give me time to adjust."

"Okay," I said somewhat sulkily, feeling somehow let down.

"Okay."

I still felt something was off. I could see she was thinking, and I suspected she was considering whether or not to say something. "What? What is it?"

She sighed. "I don't know, Amara. It's just...what's the plan here? How do you think this thing ends?"

The questions made my heart speed up. I could feel the blood rush to my face. "I don't know. I...I haven't thought that far. We're just enjoying the moment. Not everything has to be planned out." There was a squeaky, defensive tone in my voice that I hadn't intended.

"Okay."

The word hung in the air for a while, bothering me because I knew, just like her previous "okay," that it was really just faux agreement masking more that she wanted to say.

"What? Say what you want to say," I practically shouted, sitting up and adjusting my pillows, all flustered.

She sat up too. "I'm not trying to rain on your parade. I know you're young, and young people jump into things and..."

I shot her a death glare, and she held up both her hands in a gesture of surrender.

"I'm just saying, Amara, you have to be practical. Do you think you'll stay here with her when this is all over? How long will this last when you begin to age, and she doesn't?"

I crossed my arms protectively around my chest. I hadn't ever thought of that.

"Do you think she'll use her connections to get you the Remedy? Do you want that?"

"I don't know," I said. "Both her folks are really important people. I'm sure they could if they wanted to, and you've already seen how far Henry will go for his daughter."

"Okay. So you become an Old Blood. What about Rake?"

"What about her?"

It was my mom's turn to give me a death glare. In her mind, she would consider it abandoning Rake to live here, but that wasn't fair. I didn't owe Rake anything.

"Rake's a 'survivor.' You said so yourself. She'd be fine. She'd continue to fight in the rings and have a zillion fans to stroke her ego every night, or she'd go back home and find a new girl to obsess over or…"

My mom had this look she gave me when I disappointed her, and every time she gave it to me, my eyes would instantly fill with tears. Just like now.

I'm not her keeper. She's not my sister. She's not even my girlfriend anymore, if she ever was. She's just someone I grew up with. But I knew those were lies of the most selfish and deluded kind. My mother had raised me better than that. I was ashamed to even think them, but my anger often overwhelmed my good sense.

I'd never secure two doses. God, the president of the Confederacy could barely negotiate two doses, and he was offering a lucrative international prisoner exchange contract. Staying here and trying my luck with Stella did mean abandoning Rake to her own devices. Letting her age and die while I lived on and on in the lap of luxury. But that wasn't my fault. I had to look out for myself.

Even as I thought it, guilt gnawed at my stomach. Could I do it? Abandon not just Rake but everyone still stuck on the outside? But they'd jump at the chance if they were in my shoes. Most people would anyway.

Somehow, I just couldn't picture Rake doing it.

As though sensing my thoughts, my mom asked, "Is that really what you want? To live here?"

"Why wouldn't I? It's clean and beautiful and easy."

She tutted. "I told you I wanted you to be good."

I bristled. "Okay, so this disastrous love triangle hasn't been my most shining moment, but you know I'm a good person. Stella brings it out more in me and—"

"And *doing* good is part of *being* good," she said. "What good can you do here?"

It was a strange question. It startled me into silence.

"It's your life, Amara. I left here for you, but you're an adult now, and you can make your own choices. I don't know what choices we'll actually have when this is all said and done, but if we're free to decide, I choose to be out there where I can help people, where I can do some good with the blessing of this extended life I've been granted. My parents died to gift me this. I have an obligation to use it for some legacy beyond self-indulgence."

"That's easy to say when you've had over a century to just enjoy everything," I muttered petulantly, hurt at her implicit accusations.

"That's true."

"I'm sure your parents didn't die so you'd waste your life living in the slums selling tacos."

That was too far. She tensed, and when she spoke, her voice was tinged with real anger. "My parents died so I'd have choice. That's what money brings. Money and the Remedy are the two most powerful providers of choice in this life, and my parents gave me both. They sacrificed themselves so I could have a long, happy, meaningful life. It's not about selling tacos, Amara. I can't believe you just—" She seemed too mad to continue, and I went to apologize, but she cut me off. "I choose to help people. That's what makes me happy. And it's a legacy my dead parents and I can both be proud of."

I felt miserable, wanting to fix things but still stubbornly defensive. I reached for her hand. She didn't pull away, but she felt unnaturally stiff. "Mom, I'm sorry. I didn't mean that. I've seen all the good you do. I'm sorry. I'm just…I'm not sure I want to be a saint like you."

There was a long pause, then I felt her relax a little. "I'm no saint. I whored myself for the cause, remember?"

I whipped my head around to face her, and her eyes were twinkling. "Mom. No. Those words. Erase. Erase." I waved my hand in front of her mouth like I was brushing away the obscene idea.

This made her laugh, and something shifted between us. It wasn't exactly easy between us again, but a lot of the tension had dissipated. We sat in silence for a while, each processing. I picked at the covers some more.

"I could draw and paint and create beautiful art that makes people happy. I could do portraits. Capture people's loved ones. That's something good."

"You'd be great at that. And it would be a real gift to others," she agreed as if trying to reconcile with me. But I felt the qualification she didn't voice. It wasn't good enough. I felt it even if she didn't say it.

"Mom, it doesn't make me a bad person because I like nice things and want my life to be a bit easier."

She pulled me in for a hug and whispered into my hair, "It doesn't, my girl. It doesn't at all."

When she let go, I rested on her shoulder, taking comfort from her proximity, feeling exhaustion start to pull me adrift.

"I'm just asking you to think it through, babygirl. Who do you want to be in this one, short life you've been granted? What do you value? How do you want to spend your precious time?"

I began to drift off thinking about how time was more precious than money for us New Bloods. Who did I want to *be*, and who did I want to *be with*? They were big questions for such a weary brain, and I left them to simmer in my subconscious as I slipped into slumber, safe at last in my mother's arms.

Chapter Eighteen

In a Kingdom by the Sea

I woke the next morning from the strangest dream. I woke with a start, flailing about trying to get imaginary bubble gum off me. In the dream, Rake had been walking toward me, dressed in all black athletic gear. She was binding her hands with dusky boxing wraps, intent on the action. I could hear a crowd roaring in the background. I wanted Rake to look at me, but she seemed oblivious to my presence.

Then she was Stella, still walking toward me but dressed all in white, a silk blouse, leather pants, and stilettos. Cameras were flashing, and she only had eyes for them. I felt the same sense of jealous longing for her attention.

It was back to Rake again. Then Stella. Back and forth in an increasing pace until the two images sort of superimposed, and they became this weird, blurry, yin-yang shape. The noise of the crowd and the flash of the cameras reached a crescendo, and I was looking at myself.

I was under huge spotlights, so I couldn't make out my surroundings. I was sporting these huge pink boxing gloves that felt ludicrously heavy. I couldn't even lift my arms. I kept wondering how I was supposed to fight. Was I supposed to fight with them? Or was I supposed to model them? What was going on? The gloves miraculously started to get lighter, and I was just starting to think they could be useful when I realized they were becoming insubstantial. They morphed into these glossy pink bubble gum bubbles that just kept growing bigger and bigger until finally they exploded in my face, leaving me covered in wet pink goo. Which was when I woke, thrashing, and just about punched my sleeping mother in the face.

Thankfully, she was a deep sleeper and likely to snooze for a few more hours. I couldn't get back to sleep, though. The dream was too unsettling. Like, what the hell was my mind even trying to tell me? Were dreams just nonsense, or did they have some kind of deep, secret meaning? I didn't know, but I didn't like the way that one left me feeling. I decided to sneak downstairs and make a cup of tea to enjoy outside before everyone else woke.

I had the tea and was headed to the sliding glass doors when I almost stepped on Rake, who was sprawled on the floor, staring up at me with a goofy grin.

"Oh my God, Rake, you scared the shit out of me. What are you doing on the floor?"

"Do you remember Lego?"

"Not the answer I was expecting, but okay. Yes. Your old dog, right?"

"Right."

"Okay. Why?"

"He used to like to sit in sunbeams. He was always cold, poor little runt. And sometimes, I'd just plop down on the floor with him and see the world from his perspective." She patted the ground.

I sat gingerly beside her but refused to lie down. I had a hot tea to drink. That was the only reason I stayed sitting up, I swear.

She sighed. "Now it's just something I do sometimes. When I need a change of perspective."

I sipped my tea, listening, trying to bury unwanted feelings that were stirring.

"Or when I feel defeated and need a breather. Whatever."

I tensed, knowing this was directed at me, that this conversation probably wasn't going to be pleasant. She had her head resting on her clasped hands, her arms folded behind her head, and she was staring at the ceiling. She'd taken out the cornrows, and her hair spilled haphazardly about her face. I hadn't seen her hair that long in years. She was in pajamas, black shorts that showed off her tanned thighs, and an ancient, ratty old band T-shirt that she'd cut the sleeves off of. On anyone else, it would have looked like shit. But she wore it well. It accentuated her shoulders and the taut lines of her arms. It struck me then that in her own way, Rake cared about fashion as much as Stella. She just had to be a hell of a lot more inventive about it, given how little we had in the Freelands. It felt odd to realize this. Maybe it was just the dream that had me seeing their commonalities. How they were so different and yet also surprisingly not dissimilar.

Rake interrupted my musing, her voice soft and pensive. "I think, when you really love someone, you want them to be happy. No matter what. I wish you would be happy with me…" She paused, and guilt pressed down on me like a tangible thing. "But…it wasn't really fair of me to expect you to follow this love story that I guess I made up in my head."

I wanted to say something, to contradict her, to comfort her, but my voice stuck in my throat.

"I just…I always thought we were meant to be, that we'd spend our lives together. And I was always just sort of waiting for you to catch up to my understanding of what seemed like an obvious fact." She gave a weak little laugh and turned toward me. "But I guess I was delusional."

I could see in her eyes that she wanted me to interrupt, to tell her she hadn't made it all up in her head. And I wanted to. There was a physical ache in my body urging me to do it. To say something. Say anything comforting. But was that wise? She seemed to be coming around to the idea of Stella and me. To be starting to accept things. I shouldn't mess with that. So I kept silent despite the pleading of her eyes and the ache in my own heart.

She sat up, leaned against the door, then looked away. "You didn't make me any promises. You were far away, and in a crazy, dangerous, exciting situation, and you just…you met someone else. And she's… beautiful. And nice. And sweet."

I could see her struggle. Each compliment seemed painfully forced. The effort she was making made me tear up. I could see what it was costing her, how deeply she felt it all, and it made me admire and want her, and that was confusing, so I looked away too, studying the far wall, as if it held the answers to our impossible situation.

"And if that's what you want, then I'll find a way to be happy for you. Even if I don't honestly feel it in this moment…I trust I will." I had to meet her gaze. Her expression was strained, her eyes full of pain and tenderness. "Because I've always loved you, Amara. And that means I want to see you happy," she repeated as though trying to convince herself.

My insides were all mixed up. This was the most open she'd ever been about her feelings, and they were so real and powerful and pure; it wasn't at all the superficial, meaningless, flirty thing she seemed to feel for me before. I had massively misunderstood and undervalued her. It embarrassed and confused me to realize how much she had always felt for me, how very deeply I had misrepresented her character. Why was

I realizing this now, in the very moment when she was moving on, as I wanted. That was what I wanted. Right?

She looked at me with her messy morning bedhead and her crumpled pajamas and her vulnerable face, and it seemed so intimate, so compelling, that I had to resist an urge to throw myself at her, straddle her, grab her face, and tell her I'd made a huge mistake.

Had I? Everything my mom had said last night came back to me. How long could this thing with Stella really last? What kind of future did we have together? Could I really just abandon Rake for her?

Just when I felt I was going to explode with emotion, Rake kicked me playfully and said, "Okay, enough serious talk. Whatcha got in that mug? Give it here." She held out her hand, and I passed over the mug, grateful for the shift in tone. She took a swig and grimaced. "Tea? Ugh. Why don't you just drink coffee like a real grown-up?" She handed the mug back and offered a slight smile.

I knew what she was doing. She'd always done this for me. And I was turning my back on her. What was wrong with me?

I struggled with my emotions some more, and she pretended not to notice, probably wondering if I was ever going to say anything. But I didn't know what to say. I was so deeply conflicted. A few moments passed, and when I glanced at Rake next, she had her cheekiest grin going on.

"What?" I asked, warily.

She shrugged. "I'm just thinking…now that I'm not trying to woo you, I guess I don't have to keep certain secrets from you anymore."

I narrowed my eyes, gratefully catching the playful spirit. This was what we were best at together, this banter. It had sustained us both through years of struggle. "What are you talking about?"

She cleared her throat dramatically. "It is with great sorrow and regret that I am now obliged to inform you that I was the reason Mr. Snuffles disappeared."

"What?" I set aside my tea, worried about spilling it.

"In my defense, I was trying to get him restuffed. I took him to the tailor, Mrs. Gomez, but then she up and died, and her family came and took all her things. Including your stuffie."

"You asshole." I swatted at her arm, shocked she'd kept it from me all these years.

"I'm not an asshole. My intentions were good."

"I don't care about your bloody intentions. I was distraught for weeks. He was my favorite stuffie. I'd had him ever since I could remember."

"I know," she said. "That's why I was trying to fix him."

"I didn't want him fixed," I protested, indignant.

She made a face. "Yeah, but he was all scraggly and scrawny and sad."

"I liked him scraggly and scrawny and sad."

"Wouldn't you have loved him even more if he was chubby and fluffy and cute again?"

"No, I loved him just the way he was. Oh my God, Rake. I blamed my mom for losing him. I yelled at her."

She made a strange face, like she was trying not to laugh.

"What?" I smacked her some more, and she burst out laughing. "She knew it was you?" She laughed all the more, and I knew it was true. "She knew it was you, and she took the blame?"

She shrugged. "Maria and I are tight."

"She just let me yell at her?"

"She was protecting her other daughter," Rake said, making an angel face.

"Argh, you two are ridiculous," I said, kicking her for good measure. It felt good to slip back into this normalcy with her. We both basked in it for a few moments, sneaking glances at each other, clearly both relieved that we could still do this, still be in this easy, familiar dynamic.

After a bit, Rake said, "Maria and I were thinking of making a day of it together down by the beach. You don't mind, do you?"

All the good feelings I had vanished. She was telling me she wanted me to leave her alone. To give her time to reconnect with my mom like I'd done last night. And of course, I understood. I'd needed it too. But it was hard to know they didn't want me around. That they needed to talk privately. That they'd be talking about me. Most likely about the hurt I'd caused. About how I'd disappointed them.

I swallowed nervously. "Sure."

"Great. I'm gonna go see if Kelly can make us a picnic. See ya later."

It shouldn't have been so hard to watch her walk away. But I let her walk away. So I had to make it worth it.

I threw myself back into Stella, looking to her to soothe my pain, to convince me I'd made the right choice. Though part of me was sad and distracted about the little rendezvous by the beach, I resolved to make the best of it and get Stella to spend some quality time with me by the pool.

It wasn't long before I found myself standing in Stella's insanely huge walk-in closet, listening to her squeal about how she had the perfect bathing suit for me. "It never fit me quite right, but you're tall. I think it will look amazing on you."

While she pillaged through a marble-topped set of drawers, I looked around in wonder. The closet was all glossy white, with a sparkly silver chandelier and a big round pouf sofa in the middle. I sat and let my eyes wander along the walls and walls of clothes and shoes and accessories, all beautifully arranged like works of art. There was a vanity table against one wall with the little theatre lights all around the glass, and a huge, full-length mirror in an ornate silver frame on another. Everything was all brightly lit and organized and unspeakably satisfying to look at.

"Here, try this," she said, handing me a white bathing suit with cutouts. "Ooh, and I have the perfect cover-up to go with it. Go change and come right back."

I did as she requested and was pleased to see how the bathing suit accentuated the lean length of my body. It had a strap on the left shoulder but not the right and sort of swooped down my right side, exposing the curve of flesh on my left torso. It was far sexier and more glamorous than anything I was used to. I walked nervously back into the closet, but Stella's enthusiastic clapping relieved any uncertainty I had about sporting such a swimsuit. She gave me silver aviator sunglasses and a white cover-up with metallic threads subtly shining through its fabric. For herself, she had put on a cute little peach bikini with a ruched bandeau top and bottoms with a ludicrously oversized satin bow on the right hip. She looked adorably delectable, as always.

"Will your bikini bottoms fall off if I pull this?" I asked, giving the bow a slight, suggestive tug.

"I'm afraid not," she answered, pulling me into a sweet embrace.

"Tease," I whispered between kisses. I bit her lip slightly and pulled away to look at us in the mirror.

"Oh, let's get a holosnap. We look so cute. Wait, I have to grab my accessories."

She grabbed a giant floppy hat and a cover-up, then her datapad. She wrapped an arm around me and posed. We took a bunch of shots, laughing all the while.

"I wish I could grow out my hair," I complained. I didn't have to wear it in that stupid up-curl anymore, but I still kept it standard-length, just in case.

"Go ahead if you want to," Stella replied, rifling through a drawer of sunglasses, looking for the perfect match for her outfit.

"Really? But what if your mom stops by? Or…I don't know… someone official from Hydra?"

"I'll just say I gave you permission," she said, inspecting herself in the mirror with a pair of clunky, square sunglasses.

I gave you permission. I repeated the phrase, feeling deflated. She'd said it so casually. I wasn't even *her* BabyDoll. I was her father's, and yet she felt she had the right to permit or not permit me things. And I guess that was the harsh truth. I was her father's legal property, and as quickly as I had been granted access to all this privilege, I could just as quickly have it taken away.

"Look at this one. It's perfect," Stella said, projecting one of the holosnaps after flipping off the lights.

I watched the projection make strange shadows on Stella's face and wondered if our love was like that holo, a shimmering illusion that was beautiful but fundamentally insubstantial. Didn't she ever think about where this could go? Had she given any thought yet to freeing me from corporate bondage? Would she even try to get me the Remedy?

But these were crazy thoughts. We were young. Who the hell thought about who they wanted to be with forever at this age? She loved me. It was obvious in every smile and look and touch. She probably hadn't thought of these things because she wasn't a thinker. It was just my mom planting these seeds of doubt in my head. I shook off the worry, and we headed outside to the pool.

It was just what I needed. I loved the way Stella clung to me so naturally in the refreshing waters of the infinity pool. She wrapped her legs around me, and I swirled her about while we talked and kissed and laughed. It was easy and sexy and comfortable. Just the feeling we'd been missing. I had forgotten how much I liked the way she made me feel strong. Some of the old boldness returned as we flirted back and forth. She was so dazzlingly feminine that she brought out something confident in me. Perhaps it was the way she looked at me, a simple kind of trust and patient desire, like she looked to me to lead. And I liked it.

Her nipples were poking through the thin fabric of the bikini top, and I had to bury my face in her neck and suppress the urge to unclasp it. I made a growling sound, frustrated, and whispered, "I really just want to take you upstairs and do fun things with you."

She pulled my head up to look at her, and her eyes were shining. "Really? So what's stopping you?"

I sighed and disentangled myself from her. I couldn't exactly tell her that I was having doubts about our future and that I was still attracted to Rake too, so I just stated the obvious reason. "Bit of a buzzkill to have our parents here."

"And your ex-girlfriend," Stella added.

I was surprised she'd called her that, but I nodded.

"That's okay," she said, coming close to smooth my hair from my face. "We have plenty of time."

Did we? Wasn't that the question?

Stella got out of the pool and made her way to one of the lounge chairs. I joined her, and we lay in the sun, drying off in silence. I tried not to think of Rake and my mom down by the beach and what they might be doing. What they might be saying. I tried to be present here. To think about how this could be my life. Just lying around doing nothing all day. Doing whatever I felt like. It sounded heavenly.

Out of nowhere, it crossed my mind that Stella didn't have a job. Her parents worked, but what was her plan? Did she need to work? "Stella, do you plan to get a job one day?" The words felt awkward, and I wasn't sure if the question would offend her.

"I have my own business."

"You do?" It seemed odd that she hadn't told me this before and that I hadn't once seen her do a lick of labor.

"Yes, silly. Didn't I tell you? I design custom couture. Like the dress I made you for the Juvenalia."

I cringed, thinking of how I'd well and truly destroyed her gown.

"It's not a steady flow of orders, sort of a seasonal thing. But I can pick and choose what I want to take on, and it brings in a modest income. Enough that I'm saving to buy a house. Dad doesn't mind me being here till then. There's no rush."

I guessed not. She literally had all the time in the world for everything she ever wanted. I wondered what that felt like. It was the pinnacle of privilege.

She eyed me with mock annoyance. "Did you think I got the hireling outfit contract just because my mom was hosting the party?"

"What? No. I don't know."

"Lots of folks in Hydra like my designs. And people pay a lot for custom work. One day, maybe I'll enter the competition to design the BabyDoll outfits. It's not my usual specialty, but you never know. It's good publicity."

I nodded and asked if she'd mind if I moved the umbrella closer now that we were dry. Both of us had fair skin that burned easily. She nodded, and I set about getting us some shade while thinking about her life and its bizarre ease. She only worked when she felt like it. What a fucking dream for most of the world.

But she was going to work for us tomorrow, trying to steal her mom's alt ID so we could use it to sneak into the Asenescence labs later that night.

I lay down, reapplied my sunscreen, and looked over. "Are you feeling nervous about tomorrow?"

She lifted her sunglasses to really look at me. "A little bit. I'm not worried about getting into Mom's lab or anything, but I'm nervous about what will happen if I do find it, if you guys go to the big lab. Like, what if something goes wrong?"

Henry had already explained the plan and how he'd take the blame if anything went awry. I hadn't really liked that, but he'd made me promise that I'd pretend I knew nothing and was just accompanying him as ordered. He said he couldn't risk my future. That he was well connected and could wiggle his way out of anything that came of it—which I didn't doubt—but it still didn't sit well with me. Not until he made me understand that I'd be agreeing to it to spare Stella worry about me.

I could see she was worried, though she tried to hide it. "Even if Dad does get caught, I know my mom, and she'll just lie and say he had her permission or something. To protect him from the other council members. I'm sure she'll rip him apart in private." I looked at her doubtfully, and she rushed on. "No, really. I trust my mom. I mean I know she's difficult and prickly, but she's not evil or anything. And she still loves my dad. She wouldn't want anything bad to happen to him. She was devastated when he left."

My face must have still looked doubtful.

"Mom is brilliant, Amara. Like truly an honest-to-God genius. Dad openly admits that she was the driving force behind the discovery of the Remedy. I know she's kind of hard to love, but she means well, and she cares. She wants to solve aging and disease. Think of how much heartache she's already spared us."

I bit my tongue and reacted negatively only internally to the telling use of "us." Rebecca's discovery had only spared some of us, and for others of us, its hoarding had caused widespread chaos and harm. But I wasn't about to criticize Stella's mother in front of her. Besides, today was supposed to be about reconnecting.

I decided to change the subject. "Can you put sunscreen on my back?"

Stella cheerfully complied. She rubbed it in carefully at first, then her touch slowly morphed into something else. She traced the contours of my suit ever so lightly. Her nails trailed across my skin. A feather touch brushed my exposed flesh, giving me goose pimples and little shivers of delight. It was wonderful, and I just enjoyed it for quite some time, hoping she wouldn't ever stop.

Of course, at some point, she popped back over to her own lounger, though not before planting a lingering kiss on my eager lips. I sighed, wonderfully relaxed. "Did you know there's a name for that?"

"For what?"

"To touch so lightly and softly that it almost tickles. Vellicate. That's the verb for it," I said, drowsy and content.

Stella laughed. "Did you read the dictionary for fun growing up?"

I stirred, roused by her teasing. "Yes. Yes, I did, actually. What's so weird about that?" She laughed some more. It was one of her more winning laughs, one that had a rhythmic quality, coming out in a little trill of merriment. Not my very favorite but still a joy to hear.

It inspired me to go on. "What? If someone likes horses and they read up on horses, that's okay, but if you like words and you read up on words, that's the definition of nerdy?"

"You're so strange."

I would have gone on defending myself, but a BabyDoll came by with the margaritas we had asked for earlier.

I took one and went to sip it, when Stella said, "Oh. There's no salt on the rim. Can you redo them?"

The BabyDoll apologized and went to take my glass back.

"No, it's fine. We don't need the salt rim," I said, embarrassed.

"Yes, we do," Stella said. "That's a standard part of a margarita. We want it right. Go refresh them, Kelly."

Kelly apologized again and quickly headed back into the house to fix her mistake. I was mortified. Who gave a shit about the salt rim? Obviously, Stella did. But it had embarrassed the BabyDoll Kelly and me to point out the mistake and refuse them. I snuck a glance at Stella, but she was oblivious.

Did she not realize that it was already super awkward to be served by a fellow BabyDoll? I mean, what did they even think of me? Were they resentful? Jealous? Inspired? Did it just make them roll their eyes? Did it give them hope that they could improve their station? What were their lives really like here? Henry had mentioned that he gave them exceptional kindnesses. What did that mean?

Kelly was the same one who'd made a picnic lunch for my mom and Rake. With a pang of discomfort, I realized that I hadn't even known her name before. Rake had been here for no time, and she already seemed to know all the help. Was probably flirting with half of them, I thought with surprising venom. Why hadn't I bothered to try to get to know them?

Maybe I was more like Stella than I wanted to admit. Oblivious in my own way.

Maybe I belonged here with Stella by the staid luxury of the pool, just as my mother and Rake belonged down there, no doubt at one with the wild nature of the ocean.

But did I really belong here with Stella?

I sighed. I was always overthinking. So Stella and I would have this little class thing between us. So what? We would find our way. But where? Here? How long would Stella be happy with me if we stayed in Hydra? I'd age, and she wouldn't. Plus, if we stayed here, we could never have kids. She wanted them, and I could have them. But only on the outside. I tried to imagine Stella in the Freelands. It was so far-fetched that it was depressing.

It made me wonder, though. How much of who we were was a product of our class? Like, who would Stella be if she had suffered the hardships of poverty? Would she be stingy? Hard? Bitter? Cruel? We'd never know, but it was possible that her sweetness and simplicity were to some degree a by-product of her economic privilege. Who might she become even now if she had to go without everything that made her life comfortable? Would she be the same Stella in the outskirts with me?

But then again, maybe privilege would have shifted us too. Like, would Rake be so generous, compassionate, and funny if she had always had everything given to her? That resourcefulness and creativity that I admired so much in her, would I ever have glimpsed it if she had grown up here? So if I stayed here, would I change for the worse?

I wasn't sure. But Rake and Stella had both been in situations that had tested their mettle in different ways, and they were both good people. Fundamentally, they were. They were different in their goodness, but they were both truly good. No wonder I felt so torn.

You're not supposed to love more than one person at a time.

But I did.

It was awful and painful and confusing and wrong.

But in my heart, I knew it.

I did.

Chapter Nineteen

Our Little Systems Have Their Day

I was glad we'd all enjoyed a day of idle relaxation because the next one was tense. We were all anxious and handling it in different ways as we counted down the hours, waiting for go time. The hours dragged on interminably until Stella finally got confirmation from Huxley that her mom was settled for the night. Stella left to rummage through her lab for the alt ID, and we were left to wait and deal with our worries.

What if she got caught? Was she a good liar? I didn't know. But that wasn't the part that scared me anyway. It was what happened next if she did find what we were looking for. Breaking into top secret Asenescence labs was a whole other level of danger.

I reviewed the plan in my mind: Henry and I would head to the lab with Rebecca's alt ID. Mom would stay behind since everyone in Hydra was looking for her. Stella and Rake were supposed to stay behind too, but they wouldn't hear of it.

Henry had argued, "I don't want you anywhere near this, Stella. They know I keep strange hours, and I'll just pretend I had a sudden flash of inspiration in the wee hours. I've done it before. It's not out of character. This ruse of having an affair with the staff is helpful. They'll just assume Amara's there to keep me company. But how would I explain the two of you? I wouldn't bring my child to the lab in the middle of the night."

"Dad, I know you want to protect me, but I should be there. What if something goes wrong and you need me…us?"

"If something goes wrong, the last person I need involved is my only child."

"No, but Dad, I'm explicable too. I could pretend I was coming to get you, that I was worried about you working too much."

"And I could kick ass if need be," Rake said.

Henry scowled. "There will be no kicking of ass, Rake. This is a quick in-and-out surveillance mission. We just want to see what's going on. We need to maintain our cover."

"You still don't want to leave behind the one person who can actually fight," Rake said.

"It's not going to come down to violence," he replied, his voice tight.

"No offense, Old Blood, but it always comes down to violence. You really think there's no chance of fighting? That we're going to waltz into a lab that's so top secret and high-security that not even a FirstGen council member who helped pioneer the goddamn cure can access it?"

I could see from Henry's face that he knew damn well that violence was possible, but he was trying to make it seem otherwise for his daughter, who now looked really concerned.

I intervened to joke, "You can take the girl out of the ring but not the ring out of the girl."

In the end, we decided that Stella and Rake would follow us an hour later in a separate car into the council district. They'd wait for a coded message on Stella's datapad. If we didn't return in two hours, they would come asking about us, using Stella's idea as an excuse and pretending that Rake was Stella's girlfriend. Their faces when Henry suggested this last part were hilarious.

Now I paced outside by the shimmering nighttime lighting of the pool. I'd been agonizing about my decision not to update the Defiance about our plan. On the one hand, it felt foolhardy to do this without alerting the wider network of resistance, but on the other, I wasn't sure they'd be on board with us trusting an Old Blood.

My mom poked her head outside, a welcome distraction from the heaviness of worry. "Come watch me butcher Rake's hair."

I followed her into one of the guest bathrooms with a mixture of amusement and concern. My mom didn't know how to cut hair. Not that that was going to stop either of them. This was typical. They were in high spirits, like two kids in cahoots, no doubt energized by the uncertainty before us.

I watched warily as my mom picked up some scissors. "Okay, time for a change. What shall we do?"

Rake seemed unconcerned. "Whatever. I trust you."

I couldn't keep quiet. "You do know she's never cut hair before, right?"

"I lived lifetimes before you were even born, babygirl. Maybe I was a hairdresser in one of them."

"Were you?" I asked doubtfully.

"Nope," she replied, snipping off one of the blue ends of Rake's hair. They both laughed, and I felt my heartbeat speed up, even though it wasn't my hair.

"Relax, Amara. It's just hair. It grows back." My mom was snipping in what seemed like an alarmingly random fashion.

I couldn't help but get agitated. "You're not worried what you'll look like?" I asked, peering at Rake's reflection in the mirror.

My mom gave me a weird look. Like I should know something that I clearly didn't. But what? Rake changed her appearance a lot. It was a playful thing but also an indicator of her moods, so maybe that was it. Maybe she needed a change, a new her, because she was trying to move on from me. But did that mean she didn't care what she looked like?

"It's not that I don't care," Rake said. "I'll fucking rock whatever Maria does to my head. I could wear a garbage bag and pick up chicks, Amara. You should take notes."

A little charge of discomfort made its way through the room. I bristled but controlled myself from replying that I didn't need to take notes since I'd already bagged the most gorgeous girl in the world. Even I wasn't oblivious enough to be that insensitive.

Other than that tense moment, the haircut was really fun to watch. They laughed and teased and nattered on, and it felt like home. Comfortable and familiar.

Henry stopped by and lingered for a while around the door, a dissonant reminder that this wasn't home. His presence recalled my own uncertainty about where I belonged. Watching my mom and Rake interact in their fun-loving, connected way, that was my past. Was it my future? Or did my future belong somewhere else?

In the end, my mom did a surprisingly decent job of cutting Rake's hair into a rough, shaggy, shorter look. Henry offered his clippers, and they finished with an undercut. All the blue was gone, and she was left with her natural brown.

I hated that she was right. She was hot enough to pull anything off. The 'do was choppy and messy and boyish but somehow worked. I imagined running my hand along the freshly shaved nape of her neck, then grabbing what was left of her hair to pull her mouth close to mine… Argh, why couldn't I stop thinking of her that way?

The fantasy made me wonder, though. How would she respond if I behaved with her the way I did with Stella? Rake had thrown me up against the wall backstage of the rings, but what if I wanted to throw her up against a wall or two? Would she like that? Or did she see being bold as her role?

No. The moment I asked the question, I realized the answer. Rake had no ego invested in anything other than being her playful adventurous self. She'd probably be happy to embrace any way I showed her my sexuality. Stella was the rigid one. She was so utterly deeply girlie that I had a hard time imagining us having more flexible interactions. She would always be the princess. Not that I minded.

Rake mussed her hair and posed unselfconsciously in the mirror. She looked too good. Desire and guilt shot through me, and I had to walk away.

Just in time. Stella came home, flushed and triumphant. She'd found it. She'd fucking found it. Holy shit. I tried to listen to her explain about the safe and guessing Rebecca's password, but all I could think was how we were really doing this. I glanced at my mom and could see she was scared and distracted too.

I made an effort to tune into the conversation.

"…cameras?"

"She hates cameras. Is too paranoid about them being hacked," Stella said.

I finally looked at the thing Stella held and jumped. It looked like a human hand. No, on closer inspection, it was more like a super realistic human hand glove. What the hell?

Henry took it gingerly with a look of unabashed wonder. He turned it over, shaking his head and inspecting it from all angles. "That woman's a bona fide genius," he whispered to no one in particular.

I got the lowdown on the glove on the ride to the district, and I was grateful, given how nervous I felt. I kept flashing back to everyone's good-byes. They'd felt too real, too full of import, as we'd all hugged and wished each other luck. My mom had had genuine fear in her eyes, as much as she had tried to hide it. Was this a crazy idea? Probably. But this was our shot, and we had to take it. There was no going back now.

I listened as Henry explained the glove. "We've been using biometric authentication since Hydra began as a form of ID and access control, for banking, for everything. Depending on the nature of the security required, it runs the gamut from fingerprints, iris scans, you name it, but vascular biometrics are the gold standard."

My face must have registered confusion.

"Vascular means related to the veins." Despite all my reading and education, as Stella had shown me, my knowledge of biology was pretty lacking.

"Oh, yes, okay. Rebecca had a vein scanner in the west wing."

"Yes. A palm vein scan is a powerful, highly accurate biometric that uses the internal vein pattern of your palm to identify you. Similar to fingerprints, each person's palm vein pattern is unique. But more importantly, they're stable, unlike fingerprints, which are susceptible to wear and tear since they're exposed to the elements. Most importantly of all, they're internal. Unlike your fingerprints, your iris, or your face, your palm vein pattern is not easily visible, which makes it much harder to steal or spoof."

"Spoof?"

"The industry term for faking biometric identifiers to impersonate legitimate users."

"Like Rebecca's been doing?"

"Yes. Though she's made up a fake user."

"Why did she do that? Isn't this project her baby? Wouldn't her own vein pattern work?"

"Yes, but Rebecca's paranoid. She always has been. For years, she's gone on about wanting an alternate ID, something that would allow her to come and go as she pleases without being tracked. She doesn't like being watched. That's part of why she hates cameras. My guess is that she used this glove to concoct a supposed shadow partner in the project. Who knows? There may be more to it. Her mind is difficult to follow. What's so incredible about this, Amara, what you may not understand, is just how difficult vein scanners are to fool. They're the best security in existence. They're two-hundred and sixty times more accurate than facial recognition. They have the lowest false acceptance and rejection rate of any biometric, and that's because there are just so many ways they're superior."

He was excited, and it was pulling me out of my nervousness and into amusement. He grabbed my hand. "Look at your palm. It has a much larger surface area than, say, a finger or an iris. That means we can capture a much larger number of data points. Typically, over five million for a single palm. Think about that. A palm vein scanner uses infrared light to map your vein structure, taking these five million data points and converting them into a unique encrypted code that becomes your biometric signature. They're incredibly accurate."

"Okay," I said, removing my hand from his grasp, aware of how sweaty my palms were. "But then how did Rebecca bypass this?"

Henry laughed as though delighted. I thought he really was. I could see how these two had been married. They both found so much joy in their intellectual pursuits. "That's what's so ingenious. Truly. Amara, you have no idea. We thought our liveness certification protocols would prevent this, but somehow, she found a way to deceive them."

"English, please," I said. "I don't know what you're talking about."

"Sorry. Liveness detection. It means…well, you need to understand that a palm vein scanner captures blood flow in your veins, so it has a kind of built-in, active detection, liveness test that is part of what makes it super secure. So if a spoofer somehow got ahold of your palm vein pattern, no easy feat in itself, they would still not be able to fool a scanner into perceiving live blood flowing through the veins. Or something that passed as live blood."

He squinted at the glove and muttered, "Maybe if there's time, I can perform a few quick tests to see how she's simulating the refraction sparkle of red blood cells…"

He was lost, then, speculating on who knew what science-y stuff. I stared out the window and tried to keep calm as we approached the council district. It wasn't long before we arrived at a gate. I stuck to the plan to let Henry do all the talking. The gatekeeper recognized him and waved him through, sparing me the briefest of glances. It didn't strike me as particularly tight security, but Henry was one of the trusted elite.

The car stopped at Henry's designated parking spot outside the lab. The building was white and imposing. I counted seven floors. Henry instructed me to put on the glove, and it gave me the creeps, but I shoved my hand inside and tried not to shiver at the weird, warm, pulsing sensation.

"Remember, Amara. Just follow my lead and say nothing."

I nodded. We got out of the car and made our way to the front entrance. I expected it to be quiet inside, but the moment we entered, I was hit with a blast of sound. Cheering and yelling. I struggled to orient myself, then realized the sound was coming from the front desk, some kind of sports holo that the night guard was projecting.

Spotting us, he rushed to flip it off. "Dr. Keenan. Welcome." He stood and fiddled with his uniform.

"Justin. Good to see you. What was the score?"

Justin flushed a little. "Tigers just tied it up. DiSantos is on fire."

"Man's a legend," Henry replied, casually placing his datapad on the scanning belt. He motioned for me to do the same with the thermos and journals I was carrying.

Justin looked at me curiously.

"She'll be assisting me tonight," Henry said. "It's late, but you know how it is. Gotta strike while the iron's hot."

I could see his eyes linger on my hairdo, which I'd purposefully done in this year's signature BabyDoll fashion. I hadn't worn my uniform. Henry had figured that this would signal the illicit nature of our supposed relationship, the leeway I was being granted due to our amorous connection. Justin seemed to take it all in. No doubt everyone would know of the Keenans' split. I watched him put the pieces together.

But he kept staring, and I got nervous. Don't look at my right hand, I kept thinking. Don't look at it.

I blurted, "Gotta keep him caffeinated. I think it will be a long night." I gestured to the thermos, and that seemed to jerk Justin back into reality. He fired up the scanner, and our items slowly moved away from us.

"Please," he said, gesturing to the full body scanners. I took a deep breath and walked toward it, praying that Rebecca's glove wouldn't set it off.

It didn't. I felt muscles relax that I hadn't realized I was clenching.

Our items were returned to us, and Henry led me toward the elevators. He turned back at the last moment and yelled, "I'll expect an update on the score when I'm done."

Justin smiled. "No problem, sir."

Henry ushered me into the elevator and pushed the button for the second floor. The door closed, and I let out a sigh of relief.

"I'm sweating. Are you sweating?"

When the elevator stopped at the second floor, I went to get out, but he pulled me back. "No. We're going down. I just wanted him to think I was going up to my office on the top floor. Hopefully, he'll be too distracted with his game to see the elevator is now heading down." He jabbed at a button labelled "S."

"S?" I asked.

"Secure," he replied, and I could sense his tension in the pitch of his voice. He grabbed my arm. "No more blathering, Amara. If you get nervous, just let it pass. Seriously. If you say the wrong thing here, we're in trouble. There will be a guard, and he'll know I don't have access to this floor. This is the riskiest part. Just be quiet and do what I say."

I nodded, fear flooding my system into an eerie alertness.

The door opened into a small entryway of sorts. There was a vein scanner in the wall by the door, but before that, there was a desk with a dataport and a guard. A guard who was very much asleep, his feet up on the desk and his head lolling back in contented slumber.

Henry's eyes were wide with surprise. He looked at me and smiled. He put his finger to his lips and motioned me to the vein scanner. I slipped my gloved hand into it and held my breath. Its light turned green, and there was a soft clicking sound as the doorway unlocked. We tiptoed through and closed it softly behind us. What insane luck. Maybe this was going to turn out all right.

For an underground lab, this place was lit up super bright. Maybe it was just because everything was white. White and surgical steel. I realized where Rebecca's home got its aesthetic from; it subtly recalled the cold sterility of a laboratory. This would make her feel at home, I supposed.

"No offense, but I think Hot Tots had better security," I whispered.

"Perhaps we've become lax and over-reliant on the cutting-edge nature of our tech." He rushed to a counter and began looking through everything, documenting it with his datapad.

I had no idea how to be helpful. None of this stuff meant anything to me. It was all typical stuff I'd expected to see. Machines and vials and instruments and dataports. I wandered to a set of vials containing a luminous green liquid. They were the most colorful thing in the lab, so they drew my attention. I stared at them curiously for a second before asking, "What are these?"

Henry glanced over, distracted, busy looking through the contents of a cupboard. "That's the Remedy. I think she's trying to build on it somehow. But why would she need this?" His attention was gone, fixated again on something else.

The Remedy. Twelve vials. Just sitting here. The most valuable substance known to man. The elixir of immortality. Something so precious that even obscene amounts of money could no longer buy it. Everyone had to negotiate with the Old Blood council, offer them something so valuable that even the elite of the elite did not have it.

I watched Henry carefully out of the side of my eye and snatched three vials. Quickly. Casually. Obscuring his sight line from the action, just as Bree had taught me. She would have been so proud.

I went to stuff them in the pockets of my pants, then realized I had no goddamn pockets. Fucking women's clothing. I panicked and put them in my bra, praying that Henry wouldn't notice my boobs had become strangely pokey in places. He was still intent on his inventory of the cupboards. I turned and tried to shift the Remedy into a better hiding position, annoyed that this stupid bra didn't even have padding to help disguise their shape. I reassured myself that Henry was always somewhat distracted and unlikely to be checking out his daughter's girlfriend's chest. I thought about trying to snag more, but Henry was already turning to me.

"Let's go," he said, heading toward the door to the next room. He pulled up short. "Damnit."

There was a simple number pad lock in the wall beside it. We'd come all this way, evading the highest security tech on the planet, and we were going to be stopped by a stupid four-digit number pad? Part of me was relieved. I had the Remedy. Three doses. That was enough for Rake and I to take one if we wanted, whatever happened between us and wherever we ended up. Plus, there would be one left for the Defiance to study and reverse engineer or whatever. What else mattered? Did I really care what Rebecca was up to behind that door? That was Henry's concern. I'd done more than enough for the Defiance. I had my mom and a decent amount of intel for the cause.

"We should head back," I said.

Henry shook his head. His eyes were closed as if he was concentrating.

"Henry. You're not going to guess the combination. We should cut our losses and get out of here before the guard wakes up."

"No. I know Rebecca. I can figure it out." But he was sweating.

I looked back at the nine doses of the Remedy still sitting on the counter. Was he distracted enough to risk taking more? He made a little sound of frustration, and I realized there was no way he was going to give up after getting this close. He was going to punch in numbers until we got in or got locked out, so I might as well hurry up the process.

"It's four digits, right? It's probably Stella's birthday."

He scoffed. "If she was your average woman, maybe. It won't be anything personal. All the codes I've ever known her to use have been dates of scientific significance."

"Okay, what about the day you discovered the Remedy? That's personal and of scientific significance."

He smiled and punched in the digits. There was a little beep, and a red light blinked.

His smile faded.

"Would she use the month and day or the year?"

"Oh, maybe it is the year." He went to punch in the numbers, but his hand shook, and he hesitated. "We probably only have three tries."

"It'll be something to do with the Remedy, right? You said yourself that she's trying to improve on it somehow. To take it further."

"Yes, but maybe the Juvenalia date is too obvious."

"Henry, we need to go. Just try it."

He punched in the numbers.

Same sound. Same red light.

"Damnit!" He punched the wall beside the number pad.

I looked toward the other door. What if the guard woke up? "Henry…"

"Shh. Just give me a second to think."

My eyes wandered back to the vials. I glanced at my boobs to see how well-hidden the pilfered ones appeared. Unless someone was being pervy and really looking at my chest, they probably wouldn't notice the lumps. I looked back at the door. Then at Henry.

His eyes were closed, and he was talking to himself in a low voice. I couldn't make out his words over the sound of my own heart pounding. I wanted to reach past him and just punch any random numbers into the damn pad so we would have no choice but to sneak back out the way we came.

His eyes flew open. "The Martinez study. 1998. The year scientists discovered hydra were biologically immortal, that asenescence was possible. It has to be that." His fingers flew over the pad.

Same sound. Then a click. And a green light this time.

Chapter Twenty

Somebody's Baby Will Waken No More

The smell struck me first. An odd chlorine-like odor but reminiscent of mold too. I followed Henry, wrinkling my nose in distaste. A bad feeling took root in my gut, but still, I followed him into the dimly lit space.

It was huge. A huge room full of glowing green pools. The water was lit up and casting eerie, wavering shadows over the walls. A walkway down the center of the room led to a workstation full of machines with blinking lights.

"Amara, I think you should stay here. Just wait. I won't be long." He started down the walkway but paused to inspect a pool.

I realized there were shadows in the pools and edged closer.

They weren't shadows. They were people. People floating naked and hooked up to some kind of breathing apparatus. "Henry, what is this?" I whispered, the hairs on my arms standing on end.

"She's really doing it…" he whispered, more to himself than to me.

"Doing what? What is this?"

He didn't seem to register my presence even as he answered my question. "Regeneration. She talked about it, but I thought it was impossible. I don't know how she…how many biovats are there?" He walked away, seemingly wrapped up in his own shock.

I didn't want to look at the people. Why did my head turn to look at the people?

In the biovat to my right floated a scrawny, white, middle-aged man. He had a giant tattoo of a dragon across his chest. I felt panic rising in my own chest. "Henry," I yelled, and my voice echoed with the strange, watery acoustics. It sounded too loud, and I looked to the door, uneasily. Henry hurried back. "Who are these people?"

"The unlucky. Come. Let's get you to a chair."

He went to grab my arm, but I pulled away. "We have to help them. Can't you unhook them or something?"

"And what? Help them walk out of here?"

I started to shake, and tears sprang to my eyes. Rows and rows of people. Rows and rows of them.

"Amara, I need to understand what's going on. Come to the workstation with me." I shook my head, and he sighed. "I'll be right over there, then. Stay here." He crossed the walkway to the far end of the room with its strange glimmering machines.

What did he mean by regeneration? What was Dr. Keenan doing to these poor people? I didn't want to look, but I couldn't stop myself. I looked to my left. Another man. This one black and muscular. Also tattooed. Probably another New Blood. How had he ended up here? He seemed to have a tumor or growth coming out of the side of his head. I bent to look closer. Several floppy lumps crowded around his right ear. No…several…ears.

I stumbled back and slipped, falling to my knees by another pool. A woman this time. Dark-skinned too. I scanned her body quickly, dread coursing through my veins. Fingers. Too many fingers. It felt like someone had kicked me in the gut, and a weird strangled sound of pain squeaked out of my throat. I crawled to the next vat. A man. One foot. Though several more were floating in the water beside him. And one seemed attached to his thigh.

I threw up. Sweating and shaking on my hands and knees, I retched and retched until there was nothing left in me.

I wanted out of here. I wanted my mom. What was this place? Why was I even here?

Henry pat-pat-patted me on the shoulder.

"Don't fucking touch me." I wanted it to come out angry, but it had come out weak and pathetic. That incensed me. I didn't want to be weak and pathetic. I had nothing left to spew but my rage, so I screamed, "What the fuck is wrong with you people?" My words echoed uncannily.

Henry was looking away. Staring at the door. Worried about his own ass. "Shh. We don't have time for this, Amara."

I started to laugh, losing it. I didn't care anymore. He tried to put his hand over my mouth, but I swatted him away.

He stood and stared at me, his face unreadable in the spooky lights of the pools. "I'm giving you space. I'll be right over there," he said at last, heading back to his investigations.

I didn't know why I found it so funny. An Old Blood saying he didn't have time. Wasn't that exactly what he had? Weren't people like this sacrificed to give him all the time in the world? Was this the ugly underbelly of Stella's life of oblivious luxury?

How was he just carrying on? I felt like the world's worst spy. I needed to pull myself together but how? Surrounded by the mutilated bodies of my people, I had to have time to react. There had to be time to feel. Otherwise, who was I?

Still, I had to document this. I had to get up. But every time I tried to get off my knees, an intense fear of tripping and falling into the vats made me woozy. I kept picturing it in my head: falling into that fluorescent dismemberment soup. Getting tangled in the tubing and drowning amongst bits of body parts.

I flashed back to the Crone, her words: "We live in a warzone, my dear, whether you've acknowledged it or not."

I acknowledged it now. I thought of the nameless man whose murder had been auctioned off to the highest bidder. I thought of the public spectacles of humiliation endured by the hirelings and the New Bloods clowning in the rings. Of Drudges and Hot Tots and Pop Tarts. Of the girls who didn't make it through BabyDoll training. The men who volunteered to be part of the Farm. The women who disappeared off the streets. Did they all end up here? Was this where Rake's mother had wound up?

The thought made me retch again, but I felt something shift in me too, the outrage crystallizing into something powerfully determined.

I had gotten here. Me. A young girl from the streets who wasn't particularly good at anything except drawing. I'd made it here. I'd passed all the tests. I'd outplayed everyone. I'd followed my heart and my gut, and even if I didn't always control my face and my feelings, my choices had landed me here. In the innermost sanctum of Hydra. In the nightmare of its hideous truth.

I wasn't going to waste this.

"*Look where you want to go.*" Dr. Ahmed's advice echoed inside my head, and I focused on the workstation. I rose, unsteady as a newborn foal. I could hear Henry calling my name while fiddling with something in a refrigeration unit. I put one foot in front of the other. Unsteady but single-minded. I didn't look at the vats. I kept my eyes on the prize.

Henry offered me a chair. "Sit. Put your head between your knees," he said.

I didn't take the chair. I took his datapad.

"Amara…I don't think it's a good idea to document this," he said, his voice full of uncertainty.

"You wouldn't," I spit, striding away, feeling the self-assurance of purpose grow in me. I didn't know if he'd try to wrestle the datapad back, but I was prepared to fight for it if I had to.

He didn't. He returned to whatever he was doing in the refrigeration unit.

I captured images without looking too closely. It was the only way. But who could I send them to? I didn't know anyone in the Freelands with a datapad. Henry had been sending his images to Stella.

Stella, my Old Blood girlfriend, who was on her way if not already here by now. Thinking of her sent a stabbing pain through my chest. I ignored it and pushed on.

I looked up at a small sound. The door to the lab opened, and in came the guard who had been sleeping at his post. He wasn't sleeping anymore. He was pointing a gun at me.

Rebecca stepped into the lab behind him.

I clicked send.

"Henry?" She seemed genuinely surprised.

I froze, uncertain what I could do or should say. I waited, trusting my gut as I had ever since leaving the Freelands for this horrible place. I watched Rebecca carefully and could practically see her wheels turning. The guard kept his gun trained on me. I kept perfectly still and waited.

"Henry, is she holding Stella hostage? Is the Defiance forcing your hand?"

I didn't dare turn to see Henry's reaction, but I heard him sigh deeply before answering. "Thank you for trying to save me, my dear, but no. I'm helping them of my own free will."

Her eyes narrowed. "Where is our daughter?"

"She's safe," he replied.

I realized in that moment that *we* would be safer, though, if Rebecca thought Stella might be in danger, so I rushed to contradict him. "How safe she is depends on you, actually." She glared at me with unveiled hatred, and I could hardly blame her. "She's close. Coming to get us, in fact."

"Amara," Henry warned.

"It's true. You might want to think carefully about how you proceed, Dr. Keenan."

Rebecca tore her hateful gaze from me to Henry. "You involved our only child in this mess?"

He didn't answer, and I still didn't dare look at him.

She looked at the ceiling and breathed heavily, as if swallowing her feelings. She spared a look at the guard, then refocused on me. "When I got an alert that my alternate biometrics were used, I expected to find you and your mother, perhaps my daughter, but I never suspected you'd rope my ex-husband into your treachery. I have to say, I very much underestimated you, Amy, née Amara Rodriguez. Or maybe that should be Lopez, properly speaking. Or should I call you Bridget Kelly? Your name at birth."

The room lurched, and I was back to fearing falling in the vats.

"Henry didn't tell you your birth name? Valentina didn't bother, either? Perhaps that's why you're so misguided. You don't even know who you are. Would you like me to tell you?" She gave a freaky facsimile of a smile, and I started to tremble, my mind swimming.

"Rebecca, this isn't the time," Henry warned.

"What? You don't want your new partner in crime to know how you spearheaded that program? It was brilliant, Henry. Really helped solve the maladjust problem." She took a few steps toward me, and I automatically stepped back, moving closer to Henry and the workstation.

She halted, smiling that unnerving non-smile again. "Let me tell you what I know. You see, we had a bit of a revolt on our hands when the reproduction ban was announced. A necessary evil, the council had decided, but one that not every Old Blood could support. Some, like your adoptive mother, had trouble adjusting to the new reality. Many left Hydra to have children, despite the fact that their children would no longer have access to the Remedy, and leaving meant giving up the right to return. We needed to offer an alternative to maintain control, but we were stuck for ideas, until my brilliant husband came up with the espionage program.

"You shouldn't be shy about it, Henry. Really, it was an ingenious solution. You see, in this program, Old Blood women who still wanted to experience motherhood were offered New Blood orphans to raise in the outskirts. In exchange for a minimum fifteen-year stay outside, they would earn the right to return with their progeny. They could apply for the Remedy for their children through the usual channels. Although, to be honest, no application has won enough council votes to be granted so far. The whole point of the ban was to limit the number of new Old Bloods and maintain sustainability.

"Fifteen years is nothing. Many women jumped. We gave them new names and planted them strategically in neighborhoods where we hoped to learn more of the Defiance's movements." She took a step closer, and I didn't step back this time. I didn't know why. Maybe the need to know the truth of my past.

"Your biological mother's name was Siobhan Kelly. She didn't know or wouldn't reveal your father's name. She was a drug addict. She overdosed a few days after having you, and one of our medical scouts brought you to Hydra for the program."

Siobhan. Bridget. Siobhan. Bridget. Siobhan. Bridget. The names kept playing in my mind like some strange manic mantra. Despite the guard's gun, I turned to Henry, looking for confirmation.

He swallowed. "It's true."

I nodded and turned back to Rebecca. It seemed to take forever. It felt like I was underwater.

"When Valentina returned, it wasn't unexpected. She'd put in her time and was free to come back with or without her daughter. But then, she disappeared after her initial processing. Obviously, that raised red flags. Why would she return to Hydra and not take up residence in her old home, reconnect with her friends, rejoin society? All along, we'd feared that these maladjust implants might 'go native,' and Valentina's actions appeared to support this. We used every means at our disposal to look for her, but to no avail. Then you showed up."

She paused to look over the biovats, no doubt concerned that we'd messed with her precious research. I shuddered and was overcome with the urge to get away from her. I stepped onto the concrete between two vats. The guard adjusted, and I realized it was wiser to move toward the outer wall, away from Henry and the workstation. Rebecca only had one guard, probably because she had worried Stella might be here and wanted to keep the whole thing as under wraps as possible. Dividing the guard's attention seemed smart, and I made up my mind to edge closer to the wall while I listened.

Rebecca went on: "You can imagine what we thought. A maladjust Old Blood spy returned and disappeared into thin air. Then her adoptive daughter shows up, applying to become a BabyDoll. Everyone knew Valentina must be a threat. Well, almost everyone." She gave Henry a look, and I was left puzzled at its meaning. "Most of us understood that she'd turned and was likely working for the Defiance, planning some kind of atrocity. After all, who would return without reclaiming the rights and privileges of Hydra citizenship? Something people the world over can only dream of doing, even the most rich and powerful. But you? Were you a threat? That was the puzzle.

"Some on the council felt it was a coincidence. They thought you clueless about your adoptive mother's intentions, that you were just a lost little girl trying to find her way in the big bad world without her mother. The good-bye note in your sketchbook supported the theory that Valentina had lied to you and that you had no idea of her terrorist affiliations. But it could have been part of the ploy. Some of us couldn't dismiss the notion that you were wrapped up in her plan too. So we kept you close where we could watch you and dangle you as bait for Valentina."

Her face hardened. "I hadn't foreseen the possibility of you manipulating my daughter. Was seducing her part of your plan from the beginning?"

There was nothing I could say that would convince her our connection was real and spontaneous, but it seemed an affront to our connection to let her question go unanswered. "I love Stella." It was all I could squeak out. The thought of her hurt. Where was she right now? How would she react when she learned about what her mother was working on? She'd justified the killing at the Juvenalia until I'd pushed back. Would she justify this too? Was I being naive about her complicity?

"The relationship between the girls is real, Rebecca," Henry said. "I've seen it with my own eyes. If you can't see it, maybe it's because you've never loved anything more than your own ideas."

Rebecca actually looked hurt for a moment but quickly rallied. "My ideas are world-changing. You can understand why I might be enamored of them."

"No one will argue against that, my dear. But regardless, these girls are in love. Stella is happy."

"Stella is happy because she doesn't understand what's going on. We had a responsibility to protect her, and we failed."

"She's not a child, Rebecca."

"She is. On some level. It's what's best and worst in her, and you've gotten her all wrapped up in something far too complicated and dangerous for someone so simple."

It was strange to hear her share protective if condescending feelings about her daughter. It mixed me up inside. I needed her to remain the villain. It was easier that way. "This isn't the point," I yelled, startled by the strength of my own voice. "What the fuck is this? *This* is the point." I gestured to the freaky floating people.

"This *is* the point," Rebecca agreed. "This is *everything*. Do you even understand what you're looking at?"

"Torture? Evil? Old Blood heartlessness?" I offered, feeling my face flush with anger.

She gave me a patronizing look and shook her head. "This is groundbreaking research, the next step in biological immortality. *Regeneration*." She said the word like it was holy. She stepped between another set of vats, inspecting her subjects with something like awe. The guard didn't move except to mirror my movements every time I tried to inch farther away. "*Hydra magnipapillata*, a simple freshwater polyp, no more than half an inch in length, and yet it holds the key to not only life extension but to improved health span, giving us not only more years but better years, healthier years. They're everything a bio-gerontologist could ever dream of."

She wandered between the vats, staring at her subjects like she'd forgotten about us. "Did you know that if you chop up hydra in a blender, puree them, then just sit back and watch, you can actually see the disembodied pieces crawl back together? Tentacles reaching out of the shredded remains? It's startling and awe-inspiring the way they cling to life."

Henry gasped. "Morphallaxis. That's what you're working on."

She looked up, her eyes shining. "Yes. Tissue regeneration. Think about it, Henry. All the good we could do. Because of course, we're not actually immortal. We don't know how long the Remedy can keep us alive. Our bodies will still fail at some point, albeit far in the future. Plus, we're still susceptible to violence, accidents, and some disease. It's not like preexisting conditions just disappear if someone takes the Remedy. It's only age-related diseases it stops." She paused her pacing, then went on as though giving a footnote to a lecture. "That's no small thing, of course, given that ninety percent of people in the industrialized world die of age-related causes, dropping down to sixty in the developing world."

She had the same way of pontificating that Henry had. Was this how they'd spent their evenings together in the past? Swapping science statistics? It seemed plausible. Even in the midst of this insane danger, it struck me as somewhat funny.

"But tissue regeneration. It could help everyone," she concluded.

I had to scoff. "Yeah, except you Old Bloods aren't so good at sharing your brilliant discoveries."

Henry shook his head. "We didn't share the Remedy because it would be immoral to do so." My anger must have shown in my expression because he rushed on to explain. "I know you think it's immoral to limit the Remedy, but sharing it without strict guidelines would have catastrophic consequences for the planet. We're already pushing Mother Nature to her limit with current population and consumption patterns. We can't all live indefinitely. That's the hard truth. And Old Bloods have had to live with that hard truth as much as New Bloods. We sacrificed our fertility for it."

I hated that I understood his logic.

"Regardless, there'd be no reason not to share this particular discovery," Rebecca added. "It could benefit everyone. And its profits could lead to further research."

Of course. It was a potential moneymaker. A huge potential moneymaker.

"Hydra stem cells have the capacity for infinite self-renewal," Rebecca said. "They've achieved true agelessness. What if we could too? I've made strides…"

We all peered at the biovats. I zeroed in on the woman's hand floating in the closest vat. It sprouted fingers from all angles like a creepy sea urchin. My stomach lurched, and I had to look away. I closed my eyes and breathed deeply, focusing on Rebecca's voice as a way to distract myself from the nausea:

"I just can't figure out how to stop the tissue from hyperproliferating. If I wasn't so worried about you having moral qualms, I could have really used your assistance, Henry."

That pulled me back into my purpose. I registered the weight of the datapad in my hands. Whatever good she thought she was doing, she was doing it at my people's expense. "Who are these people?" I demanded, clicking record as surreptitiously as I could manage, thankful for the distance between us and the dim lighting of the room.

She didn't seem to notice. She was looking at Henry as if she wanted something from him. Agreement? Approval? Assistance?

"How did you pass this by ethics?" he asked, ignoring my question.

"Some understand the vital nature of the research," she answered carefully.

"By some, you mean Tabitha?"

She didn't answer. Which was an answer. Who the hell was Tabitha?

I asked my question with more vehemence this time. "Who the fuck are these people?"

Rebecca deigned to look at me. "They're test subjects. All perfectly aboveboard. Acquired through a prisoner exchange with the Confederacy. They're helping further science."

"They consented to this?" I asked doubtfully.

"Corpses don't have to give consent," she answered icily.

I started and looked at the naked woman floating in the vat beside me. "Corpses don't need breathing tubes," I said, fairly certain that was what was covering the woman's face.

"Not typically. But I assure you, they're all legally dead. We've just extended the window between life and death a bit."

I shuddered and turned off recording. I had enough. I clicked send without breaking eye contact, praying Rebecca wouldn't notice, praying even harder that Stella and Rake would come and get us out of this impossible hell.

Chapter Twenty-one

O Captain! My Captain!

Henry asked the question I was thinking: "What do you mean you've extended the window between death and life?"

Rebecca actually *shrugged.* "These were all death row prisoners, legally transferred to Hydra for lethal injection. They'll get their shot. But first, they're going to do some good for once in their lives."

"Rebecca! There's no way this should have passed ethics. It contravenes the Nuremberg Code, for God's sake."

"Does it? Medical ethicists created those rules after the Nazi experiments in order to safeguard human rights in living subjects. These people are dead. Ask our legal team. Entirely different rules apply to cadaver research."

My head was swimming. "Henry, what does she mean? Are they dead or alive?"

Rebecca spoke before he could. "Don't fret. They were treated well. Better than they treated their victims. They were all given last rites, a choice of final meal, an opportunity to say their good-byes. We ritualized the entire thing. No need to be less than humane. But instead of a lethal injection, they were sedated. They don't know what's happening. They feel no pain. They'll be disposed of respectfully when they've served their purpose."

Disposed of. I suppressed a shudder.

"But they didn't sign up for this," I yelled, angry at the thought of their families, how they would never know what was happening to these people.

"They gave up their rights when they became felony criminals." Rebecca's face flushed, and she walked to the vat with the dragon tattoo man. "Do you feel sorry for them? You wouldn't if you knew what they'd done. This one liked to rape and kill little girls. Four was his preferred age."

The datapad shook in my hands. I tried not to let her words sink in. I was going to be cursed with nightmares forever after this. If I managed to find a way out.

"And this one?" She pointed to a different vat. "This one tied his parents to their bed and set their house on fire, burning them alive when they refused to give him money for his drug habit."

I couldn't look. Who could do such a thing? It was unthinkable.

"These people wasted their own lives, and they devasted other people's lives. Now they have a chance to give back to humanity, and it costs them nothing. You want to paint me as the bad guy here, go ahead. But I'm trying to improve humanity's possibilities on a grand scale, to take us all on a magnificent leap forward. These people only ever caused themselves and others pain."

"You don't know that," I said, though the argument felt weak even to me.

"Regardless," Henry said, "the end doesn't justify the means. This is wrong, and you know it, or you wouldn't have hidden it from me."

Rebecca scoffed. "People always say that, but they gladly enjoy the end produced by the means. I'm not a philosopher. I'll leave debating the finer points of bioethics to others. I care about results. About progress. You think this is unethical research, but we use the outcomes of unethical research every single day. The hepatitis B vaccine. Retin-A cream. The invention of the speculum. The lumbar puncture procedure. I could keep going. The entire field of anatomy is indebted to grave robbers who stole corpses to keep doctors supplied with cadavers. And when that store ran dry, some committed murder to keep up the supply. You know this, Henry."

"Yes, medical history is full of…unsavory episodes. That doesn't mean we have to contribute more."

She laughed. "Yes, well, thank goodness no one asked Henrietta Lacks for consent to take her stem cells, or where would modern medicine be nowadays? But as long as it's in the past, we can overlook it, right?"

I didn't understand everything she was referring to, but I could see Henry becoming more and more uncomfortable.

"There's not always a virtuous path to progress," Rebecca said, stressing each word as if talking to a moron. "This is the ugly underside of advancement that no one wants to look at, even as they want it.

That's the harsh truth. But we're too old to pretend not to see it, Henry. Hollow, pseudo-philosophical platitudes are meant for the masses, not the innovators. War is inevitable. There have to be 'have nots' in order for there to be 'haves.' And progress requires sacrifice that will benefit some more than others. These are bitter pills of truth that you and I have lived too many decades not to swallow with our eyes wide open."

I was alarmed to see the way Henry looked thoughtful, as though he was wavering, persuaded by her logic.

"Ma'am?" the guard said, and we all looked at him. I'd forgotten he was there, which was pretty shocking, given the gun trained on me. He'd gotten closer when I wasn't paying attention.

I took a few instinctive steps back, though it didn't do much good since he followed.

"She's got something hidden in her bra. Looks like three to four vials. Most likely samples of the Remedy from the outer lab."

Shit.

Henry's face registered shock and betrayal. Rebecca's only rage. "You see who you've aligned with? Do you still think she's really in love with Stella?"

Henry took off his glasses and pinched the bridge of his nose. I felt guilty that he'd think I'd betrayed him by snagging the Remedy, but how could he expect me not to when something so priceless was sitting right there for the taking?

Rebecca sneered at me. "You little fool. Do you have any idea the kind of chaos you'd unleash if you made this available to the wider world? Life on this planet requires a balance. You might not like the way it's stacked, but it is sustainable this way."

I just barked a laugh. I didn't even know what to say.

"We could annihilate all of you," she said as she seethed. "We have immense forces that we've never brought to bear. Old Bloods simply want to be left free to pursue our own way of life."

"Live and let live, huh? Funny. Then who's pushing pop on our streets and keeping us from forming any kind of stable government?"

"Destabilization is necessary given your proximity. It could be much worse. You know it could. We've shown great restraint."

"And here I thought you weren't into philosophizing. Let's cut to the chase now that everyone knows what everyone is hiding. What are you going to do to me? You going to shoot me? Stick me in a vat, cut off my limbs, and experiment on me?"

"Don't be ridiculous. You're a living, documented BabyDoll." She looked at Henry, then back at me. I'd said the question with bravado, but now I felt the chill of dawning realization. She really did hold all the cards. My fate, my mom's, Stella's, Henry's, Rake's…everyone's fate was in her hands. This enigmatic, difficult genius of a woman. Did she care enough about her family to figure a way out of this where no one was harmed?

She sighed. "Here's how this will go. Amy, you'll be arrested for espionage and given a fair trial. You can't expect much more. Neither can our daughter. You, ex-husband of mine, are the real traitor here. You've proven to be a danger to Hydra itself. You will give up your seat on the council, resign your Asenescence credentials, and live out your days in whatever irrelevant way you see fit. But you will never be part of the Hydra elite again because you cannot be trusted."

I looked to Henry, feeling more upset at his fate than my own. He didn't make eye contact with me. He was staring intently at my hands. As though that was a message. The datapad? "I sent a recording to Stella. There's evidence of your research," I warned.

"I can handle Stella, and I can handle a leak. We have an excellent PR team here at Asenescence."

My heart dropped. I looked at Henry again, but he was still staring meaningfully at my hands. What? Why did he keep—

The glove. The fucking glove!

I eased my right hand free, weirded out that I had somehow become accustomed to the feel of the glove pulsing over my flesh. The guard seemed alarmed and looked to Rebecca for direction. On impulse, I dangled it over a vat, and Rebecca physically started.

I had her.

Adrenaline shot through me, and I got cocky. "I don't like your plan. How about if I tell you my version of how this is going to go?" Henry smiled behind Rebecca's back, and I sped on, buoyed by the success of our silent communication. "We're going to walk out of here, and you're going to let us go. Why? Because I don't think any PR team on the planet could spin what you're doing here and save the reputation of your family at the same time. Your daughter and your ex-husband both involved, but not you? Seems suspicious." I edged toward the door.

The guard looked to Rebecca. "Code green?" She shook her head.

"Tell the guard to join you by that wall. Henry, let's go. Stella's waiting for us." I was almost at the door, staying close enough to a vat to threaten the glove. It was probably the only one in existence. Years of research. She didn't want to risk it.

Henry stayed near the workstation while the guard approached Rebecca as instructed. "Well, my dear, I can't say that I agree with you on many of the points you made. But I will concede one." He stared at her across the giant space. "I can't be trusted." He pushed a few buttons on the workstation, and the bodies in the vats began to flail and thrash. Red lights blinked, and an alarm wailed. Rebecca ran to the workstation as Henry ran away from it.

The guard screamed, "Code green? Code green?" but Rebecca didn't answer; she was entirely focused on pushing buttons. "For fuck's sake, Dr. Keenan, with respect, do I shoot or not? She has the Remedy."

Henry and I were just past the door when I heard her say, "Her, not him," before the door closed behind us.

I didn't have time to be chilled by it. We pushed a desk against the door and ran. I went for the stairs, but Henry grabbed my arm. He pushed the elevator button, then pulled me into the space under the stairs. I didn't like it. We were trapped and weaponless, my heartbeat thundering in my ears so loud, I wasn't sure I'd be able to hear any footsteps.

The guard came through the door, kicking the desk away. He paused by the elevator and then stormed up the steps. Rebecca didn't follow him.

We waited, and I tried to calm my breathing. What the hell was the plan?

Henry whispered, "You have to calm yourself. She hasn't called a code white yet, so the other guards won't be alerted. We have a window to just walk out, but you have to seem natural. Are you ready?"

Why hadn't she made the call? Was she still playing it safe for Stella? Or was it Henry? Did she still care about him after all this time? Or was she trying to cover everything up to save her own ass?

Henry looked pointedly at the glove dangling from my right hand, and I promptly put it back on. He held my gaze for a minute, reassuringly, and I timed my breathing to his, slowing it down. He nodded, and we stepped out into the open and started up the stairs.

"Rebecca?" I whispered, glancing at the door to the lab.

"It'll take her a while to fix the mess I created. She won't risk losing all that data."

We finally reached the main floor. "Let me lead," Henry advised.

He walked out almost jauntily, and I stumbled beside him, probably not doing a very good job of hiding my fear.

It didn't take me long to realize I wasn't the only bad actor in the room. Stella and Rake stood by the front desk, talking to the guard, Justin, from earlier, the one watching the game.

"Dad. There you are," Stella trilled, her voice too strained.

They looked off standing side by side. Stella was holding her body unnaturally, stiff and prim-looking next to Rake, who seemed to be trying to make up for Stella's tense posture with excessive nonchalance. They didn't look like they belonged together. Weirdly enough, they were dressed in mostly white and black, just like in my dream. But it almost seemed like Rake was holding Stella hostage. She had an arm slung casually but possessively around Stella's shoulders, and Stella seemed uncomfortable and faintly desperate. I could see by his expression that Justin felt like something was off, but he didn't seem too sure what to make of it.

"Stella, what are you doing here?" Henry asked.

"You're working too hard," she replied. "It's late. You know the doctor said you need to start keeping regular hours."

"Nonsense. He doesn't understand how creativity works. You have to put in the effort when the ideas come."

Justin said, "Sir, you didn't tell me your daughter was dating a famous ring fighter. You know my cousin sometimes steps into the rings. I haven't tried it myself, but it looks fun."

Henry stiffened. "Yes, well, I have advised my daughter several times against dating such…ruffians, but what do I know?"

I winced at the term "ruffian." It wasn't current lingo. He should have said street rat. But maybe Justin would just think he was too much of a FirstGen to be in touch with the latest slang.

"With respect, sir," Rake said, "did you ever consider that maybe your daughter likes it rough?"

Justin's eyes went wide, and he looked like he was working hard to hold back laughter.

Henry harrumphed and grabbed my arm. "That's enough. We're leaving."

Stella elbowed Rake as if she was mad at her and pulled her along, following us. We had only taken a few steps when the word "Freeze!" rang out in the lobby.

I felt my heart stop.

"Don't move or I'll shoot every one of you." The guard from the basement.

I looked around wildly, seeking a way out. Having people I cared about with me made the terror worse.

"What's going on?" Justin asked.

"Code green. The BabyDoll has the Remedy. Several vials stuffed in her bra."

Next thing I heard was scuffling, sounds of surprise, then Rake's voice, "Don't be a fool."

I turned and saw Rake holding Justin hostage, a gun to his head. For a moment, I wondered how she'd gotten that into the building. She couldn't have. She must have taken it off him. How the hell had she managed that?

"Now, boys…" Henry began, holding up his hands. "There's no need for anyone to get hurt. Just give me your gun, and we won't have to watch this poor girl shoot your friend."

"Dr. Keenan?" Justin's eyes were huge and alarmed. He was probably just some soft boy from the inskirts trying to make a few credits with an easy job: watch sports all night and get paid for it. From the looks of him, he hadn't banked on any real action.

"Don't worry, Justin," Henry said. "This is all just a big misunderstanding with the missus. You know how women can be."

Rake raised her eyebrow, unimpressed. "Justin, you need to convince your friend to hand over his gun, and we'll be on our way. You can pretend you never saw us."

A choked-off sob burst out of Justin's throat. "I don't get paid enough for this."

"It's true. You make what? Fifty thousand credits a year?" Henry asked.

Justin grimaced.

"Too high? That's not worth taking a bullet for."

"Give him the gun, Ricky," Justin pleaded. He was shaking all over.

Ricky didn't move, but it was clear that he was torn and wavering.

"Give him the fucking gun, Ricky. Who cares about the stupid code green? It's the lab's fault. I don't want to die for these pricks."

Henry slowly moved toward Ricky, his hand outstretched. Ricky's hand shook, and I had a horrible feeling that approaching him was a bad idea, but he caved and offered up the gun. I heard Stella whimper in relief. "Thank you, boys. Thank you very much. Now, I'm terribly sorry, but we can't very well leave the two of you to wander about, so if you wouldn't mind squeezing into that supply closet?"

The guards stared at each other.

"Or I could have this one knock you both out, if you prefer?"

Rake grinned wickedly, and the men quickly complied. Once they were locked in the closet, Rake playfully punched Henry on the arm. "You're surprisingly good at this."

"Well, I certainly haven't felt this alive in decades," he replied, patting Stella's shoulder as she clung to him. "Now, let's get out of here. I suggest we—"

An alarm went off, blaring throughout the entire building.

"Damnit!" Henry swore.

"What does it mean?" Rake asked.

"She's initiated a code white. We have to hurry. Reinforcements will be coming. We have maybe ten minutes."

"Let's go," I said, a fresh wave of adrenaline pumping through my veins.

"We can't go out the front. Stunner drones are probably already surrounding the grounds."

"Then what do we do?" Rake asked, surprisingly calm.

"Maria said there was a friendly on the inside, a Drudge. With a code white, they'll be evacuating out the back gate. We need to disguise ourselves as them."

"Lead the way," Rake said, accepting his plan without question.

I wished I had her calm.

Henry took us along a corridor into a little staff room. Two people stood in there, both of them older, gathering their things. They froze when we burst in.

"Excuse our rudeness," Henry said, "But we need four uniforms."

Rake brought up the gun. "Now."

They were rough-looking women. One glance and I could tell they'd led a hard life. One was ballsy to boot. "Why should we help you?"

I wanted to say "Besides the gun?" but I watched the way they looked at Henry and Stella and saw the old class-resentment in their sullen, disdainful expressions. Stella looked like a supermodel in her stupid white outfit, and her dad was well-known. They were the very epitome of "the powers that be," powers that had no doubt made these women's lives so hard.

They were calling our bluff. We were fucked. I started to panic.

"Hey, you two ever been to the rings?" Rake asked. She was holding the gun with one hand and laboriously rolling up the sleeve of her shirt with the other. What was she doing? We didn't have time for freaking small talk.

"Why?"

"I fight in them. Maybe you've heard of me. They call me the Emasculator." She said it dramatically and winked. She rolled her sleeve all the way up, and I realized her purpose. The paradise fish tattoo. If either of them was aligned with the cause, she'd get the signal.

One nodded, though the other looked confused and unimpressed. "Yeah. My grandson fights in the rings. Goes by Meat Man. You know him?"

"Hell yeah. That guy's an animal. Kicks Old Blood ass on the regular." I could see she was winning them over, but the alarms were still blaring. "Look, we don't have much time. Can you help us?"

They looked doubtfully at Henry and Stella but nodded and threw us some spare uniforms, baggy jumpsuits, easy to put over our clothes.

"Muster station is by the back gate," the one with the fighting grandson said. "We're already gonna get shit for taking too long, so we best get a move on."

The door to the staff room opened. We all froze. I kept my back turned and my head down, hoping whoever it was would see the formless green uniforms and not look too closely.

"We're late. I know. I know," one of the Drudges said.

"Get your asses in gear already," a guard said with a sneer. "Code white is no time to dawdle. There are intruders, you slags."

"Yeah, yeah," the Drudge replied.

I felt Rake nudge me forward and started forward after Stella out the open back door.

"It's them," the other Drudge cried. "It's them. They forced us."

Everything became a distorted blur, things happening both too quickly and in a bizarre kind of slow motion. Stella froze. Rake pushed me. Then the ground was in my face, and there was a sharp pain in my chest. There was a loud bang. Was that before or after I fell? Screaming. More banging. Someone was yanking on my arm, hauling me painfully to my feet. I looked down and saw blood starting to soak through my uniform. Had someone shot me? Was I dying? I wobbled, leaning against someone. The alarm was blaring, and floodlights lit the grounds outside. I blinked. Dazed. Finally registered my name being yelled.

"Run! Run for the fucking gate. Amara, I'm begging you, run."

I ran. Blindly. Wildly. I didn't even know if it was the right direction. But I ran with an instinctive animal panic. I saw a whirl of color to my left and realized it was one of the Drudges running alongside me. Had she been the one to help me up?

A silver drone whined overhead. There was more screaming. I recognized the voice. Stella. I stopped and looked. Behind me, Rake was running, carrying Stella in her arms like a ragdoll.

"Dad! Dad," Stella wailed.

I looked back. Henry was sprawled out on the door stoop in a puddle of blood that was dripping slowly down the steps.

Chapter Twenty-two

Just Ourselves and Immortality

My mind could not keep up with all that was happening. It felt like I was outside myself watching a holofilm. A horror film. I wanted to switch it off.

Rake caught up to me and yelled at me to keep running. The Drudge yanked on my arm again. "Keep your head down, or the drone will scan your face and realize you're not staff," the Drudge hollered, breathing hard beside me. She yelled to Rake, "We'll have to deal with the gatekeeper."

Rake nodded and shifted Stella's weight in her arms.

I just kept running, my mind a terrible blank, letting them do all the thinking.

Henry. Blood dripping.

Keep running. Don't think.

There was another loud bang, and I stumbled, looking for the source of the sound. A flash of gray to my right made me jump. A drone smashed to the ground. More banging. I started to panic and run mindlessly, lost in the urgent instinct to get away from here, but again, the Drudge grabbed my arm and jerked me forward.

"It's friendly. Look!" She pointed to the gate.

Someone stood there, their torso jutting from the sunroof of a car just beyond the gate. Gun in hand. They were yelling, "Open the gate," before they disappeared into the car.

Rake ran ahead, shielding me, and the Drudge ran for the gatehouse. I peeked around to see a guard lying on the ground by the gate. Bullet-riddled. The sound of sirens approached and the whirling of another drone.

"Hurry!"

The gates opened, and we ran to the car. Rake pushed me inside. She dumped Stella on my lap and called for the Drudge, "Come on."

The Drudge did not look like someone I'd expect to be this calm and capable. She was an older, bigger woman, but she was keeping up with us. She'd kept me from freaking out and had hauled ass to the car. She squeezed in beside me. The car sped off before Rake even closed the door. Stella lay whimpering on my lap, and I kept smoothing her hair, trying to soothe myself as much as her. I craned my neck to see the driver. Whose fucking car was this? What was happening?

"Which of you is the best shot?" the driver asked. Definitely a female voice. Familiar.

"Me," Rake didn't hesitate to say.

The driver reached back to hand her a different gun. "With a code white, drones will follow off District grounds. You have to shoot it without letting it register your face. This gun has a flexi-scope. It doesn't have to be pretty, just quick so you don't get stunned." Rake nodded and took a second to inspect the weapon, then leaned over me to check out the position of the pursuing drone through the window.

"How did you learn how to shoot?" I asked, bewildered.

"Defiance training," she answered, still looking out the window.

"I thought you were a trader."

"I wasn't trading jellybeans."

Rake moved to the sunroof. There was a horrible, miniscule pause while she aimed. I braced for the sound of her being hit by the stun drone, but she took her shot, then dropped back into the car looking relieved.

"I don't see any more," the Drudge said, peering out the windows, holding tightly to the gun Rake had dropped in favor of the driver's.

"Okay, time to be less conspicuous. It shouldn't be too hard to avoid other vehicles this time of night, even with the code white, then we should hopefully be clear to the gate." The car slowed to a reasonable speed, and the driver's seat spun around.

I just about choked on nothing but my own surprise. "Elder Sister Dara?"

"Amara."

"Wha...How...What?"

Her eyebrows furrowed. "You're bleeding."

"Oh yeah," I said, as if so much had happened that I forgot I might have been shot. I started laughing in a twitchy, hysterical kind of way. Was this what it meant to be in shock?

Rake pushed Stella off me to rip open my jumpsuit and shirt.

In another context, that would have been really hot. None of my thoughts were making sense. Rake looked scared. And then confused.

"There's a med kit in that console, Edith," Dara said. She nudged Rake. "If you don't mind?"

Rake made way for her, and Dara examined my chest. I was too scared to look down.

"Okay, I'm going to ask everyone to look away, please," Dara said, her voice cool, her manner as efficient and businesslike as it had ever been at the academy.

Rake blanched and turned away. Stella was curled up in a ball on the floor of the car, oblivious. The Drudge, Edith, just kept looking on, nonplussed as anything.

It occurred to me that I should be in a lot more pain if I'd been shot, but maybe that was the effect of shock too? I took a breath and looked as Dara used medical scissors to cut my bra off. It was covered in blood and green goo, and there were shards of glass poking out of my chest. But I couldn't see anything that looked like a bullet hole.

I made a strange little "Oh" sound and grabbed the glass that fell away with the bra. My boobs were just hanging out for anyone to see.

Edith didn't look away. In fact, she peered closer. "What is that?" she asked.

"Can I look?" Rake asked, her voice shaky with concern.

"No," both Dara and I said at the same time.

In my hand, amidst all the shards, there were two intact vials of the Remedy, shocking in their lurid green color. The third had broken, probably when Rake had pushed me—so I wouldn't get shot like Henry…the blood dripping…*stop it*—but I wasn't shot. It was just the glass of the broken vial slicing into me. A few sizeable shards stuck out of the top of my left tit. Looking at it made my head swim, and I turned away.

"Amara, are these what I think they are?" Dara asked.

"It's the Remedy. I stole three vials and stuffed them in my bra because my pants had no pockets."

She started to laugh, and I worried maybe we were both losing it.

"She's okay? She's not shot?" Rake asked.

"She'll be fine. One of the vials broke, and she's going to have a nasty scar, but that's about it. I'll just do an initial patch-up now, and we can do a better cleaning of the wound once we get to the safe house."

Rake slumped in relief.

Dara's eyes were shining when they next met mine. "Do you have any idea what you've done?" Her words echoed Rebecca's from earlier, and I couldn't help but shudder. What had I done? Was it the right thing? Henry. I looked to Stella curled up on the floor. I was getting away with a nasty scar. It wasn't really me who'd paid the price for this.

I swallowed hard, hating myself in that moment. "Patch me up quickly, please."

Dara complied with the same brusque competence she had exhibited at the Academy. Edith assisted, and they fixed me up enough to get by. Dara cut away my shirt, and I wiggled carefully out of the jumpsuit. She gave me her hot pink BabyDoll blazer to wear as a top, the one that signaled her station as an Elder Sister. I winced putting my arm into its sleeves, but it felt good to have something on that wasn't covered in blood.

"Stella, are you okay? Do you want to come up here?" I asked, but she was lost to everything but her grief. Though it hurt, I thought it best to leave her be for the time being.

"Can I turn around now?" Rake asked.

"Yes," Dara answered, carefully replacing items in the med kit.

Rake's eyes went to my chest, which was covered with medical dressing. "You're okay? You're not in too much pain? Did you give her a painkiller?"

"Yes. What about you? Do you want me to look you over? Edith?"

"I'm fine," Edith answered. "Just want to get the fuck outta here."

Dara looked to Rake, who was still looking at me. "And you?"

"Huh? Oh, I'm fine. Don't worry about me."

I didn't want Stella to think I wasn't thinking of her, so I went to bend down to stroke her back, but it hurt too much to bend that way.

"Here," Rake offered, and she began rubbing Stella's back in comforting circles, exactly how I would have done it. Stella probably didn't even realize it wasn't me. For some reason, Rake's willingness to do this made me tear up.

I didn't want to start feeling things, or I'd fall apart, so I began to ask Dara questions instead. "Are you with the Defiance?" It seemed pretty self-evident that she was, but my mind had suffered so many shocks in the past twenty-four hours that it seemed a reasonable place to start.

"Yes. Being an Elder Sister is helpful. I have access to many Old Blood homes. I help with useful placements."

"You two know each other?" Rake asked.

"She was my teacher at the Academy."

"My name is Dara. Nice to meet you." She held out her hand in a formal gesture that seemed out of place, but Rake took it and offered her own name in return.

"Okay but how…why were you there?" I asked.

"At the gate?"

"Yes."

She sighed. "There's a micro-tracker in your IUD."

"What?"

"When Dr. Ahmed inserted the IUD, he placed a tracker too. We started paying more attention to your movements when you stopped communicating with the book."

I blinked at her, dumbfounded.

"We saw you were starting to frequent some…unusual locales and theorized you were either being exploited by your proprietor or were digging for your missing mother."

"My mom!" I said just as Rake said, "Maria." We looked at each other in panic, but so much was happening that we hadn't registered her role in this yet. "She's at Dr. Keenan's house. Henry Keenan. You have to send someone to get her."

"That's where she disappeared to," Dara mused.

"Please," I begged. "Henry…" I looked at Stella and leaned closer to Dara to whisper. "Henry's…dead. He got us in. He tried to save us. He's…His…" I couldn't get the words out.

Edith spoke up. "If he's the one who got shot, they'll be searching his house for sure. Better call that in quick."

Dara nodded and pulled up a datascreen. She opened an app that seemed to be a music composition swapping program. She pressed "New Song" and started tapping buttons like crazy as we all watched. She played back the whole thing, an odd melody full of synthetic sounds, then nodded and sent it off.

Rake gave her a look.

"Auditory code. Public app. Hidden in plain sight. Higher-level stuff."

"My mom?" I asked. "Someone will get her? Right away?"

"We'll try our best," Dara said, which hardly seemed reassuring.

"Where are we going?" Rake asked.

"The hell outta Dodge," Edith said.

"It's better if you don't know," Dara answered. "We'll pass through a lesser-used gate with friendlies, then take you to a safehouse. It's going to be a few hours' drive. Rest if you can."

"Okay, but you haven't answered my question," I reminded her.

"Why was I at the gate?"

"Yes. You saw I was at the Asenescence labs, so you thought you should show up? Just in case?"

"Essentially. I told Eldest Sister Mallory I had a family emergency. Honestly, I thought Maria was with you and the president of the Confederacy. She'd gone quiet like you, and we don't have her tracked. We tried to shake it out of Anastasia, but that woman 'deals in silence,' as she likes to say."

"Wait. You thought my mom was going through with the second part of her mission?"

"That was my working theory. I just couldn't figure out why you both went silent. But it seemed like something big was about to go down, so I thought I should see what I could find out. Edith would've helped me in if needed. Then the alarm went off, and I knew it was time to help out when I saw your tracking icon heading for the back gate."

"We went silent because I didn't want to tell you about Henry. About working with him. We didn't think the Defiance would approve of us trusting an Old Blood council member."

Edith made a sound of disdain. "I guess the fuck not."

"Why did you trust him?" Dara asked. Her tone implied curiosity, not questioning my judgment.

There was a lump in my throat, and I couldn't answer at first. "He was a good man." It was all I could get out.

Rake tried to help. "I trusted him. For the most part. He had an understandable motive. He wanted to know what his ex-wife was working on. Knew it was something top secret and potentially dangerous. I think he was sort of questioning his role in creating the Remedy in the first place, or at least, in how it all turned out after its creation. That was my impression. He did seem a decent guy. He leapt in front of us. His daughter was farthest from the shooter. Says a lot."

It said everything.

We all looked at Stella curled up on the floor. Dara looked closer. "I think she passed out."

"Is that normal? Will she be okay?" I asked, worried.

"Everyone responds differently to grief and trauma. She'll find her way. Probably just crashing from the adrenaline."

We were quiet, then. All of us probably feeling our own fatigue.

"It's not great that she's here," Dara said. "It complicates matters. Why *is* she here?"

Rake looked at me. "We're dating," I answered.

"For real?" Dara asked, surprised.

My temper flared. "Yes, for real. Why does everyone keep asking me whether this is real?"

"It's strategically advantageous. Seems suspicious," Dara answered frankly. "And she's…"

"Drop-dead gorgeous? Yes, I know. I'm very much aware that I'm the ugly one in this relationship."

Edith snorted. "If you're ugly, what does that make me?"

"I didn't actually mean that I'm ugly. I meant…" I stumbled, realizing that I'd inadvertently insulted her, but that in trying to fix it, I now sounded conceited.

"We understand what you meant," Dara reassured me.

"Yes, well, my point is that it might've been strategically smart to fall for an Old Blood council member's daughter, but that's not why I did it."

"Unfortunately," Rake muttered.

Dara turned to her. "You two know each other from the outside? I'm sorry. I've never been briefed on you."

"Yep, Amara and I go way back," she said, avoiding eye contact. "And you wouldn't have heard of me. I'm just a minor player at best." There was a bitter note to her words that I didn't expect. An awkward tension made its way around the car.

"It's a long drive," Dara said. "I don't expect it to be eventful. You should all get some rest if you can. I'll stay up and let you know if there's any trouble." She adjusted her seat to look forward once more, leaving us to our own devices.

I wouldn't have thought it possible to sleep after all that. But I did doze eventually. My poor body and mind were so utterly wasted that they just pooped out. Stella woke at one point, and I heard her crying, so I invited her to snuggle with me. I wasn't sure she'd want to, but she curled up in my lap like a little kid, and relief flooded me. Part of me had been worried that she'd blame me and would never want to be around me again. Edith and Rake watched through exhausted, half-closed eyes. Edith looked at Rake and patted her lap suggestively, inviting Rake to curl up if she wanted, which made us all smile, despite everything.

Far too many tired and hungry hours later, we pulled up outside a huge, abandoned factory building, and Dara declared that we had arrived. I was so out of sorts that our arrival passed in a blur. There were people. Defiance members. They were curious about us and stared. I had no space to care. I just wanted food and a shower and a bed.

The shower was too much to ask for, but there was an area to wash up, and a hot meal was waiting when I'd finished. I went through the motions while watching out for Stella and Rake, ensuring someone tended to their needs as well. Stella didn't want to be alone. We slept all that day in a room with random metal instruments scattered about. When I woke next, it was night again. I disentangled myself from Stella, who was still sleeping, and tiptoed from the room, feeling anxious about my mother.

The place was full of graffiti, broken windows, and odd, rusted industrial contraptions, big rollers and other machines whose purpose I couldn't imagine. Whenever I passed someone, they looked at me strangely, like they were avoiding me. Which I was happy about, honestly. I didn't think I could manage small talk. I looked around for Dara or Rake but couldn't find them anywhere. Eventually, I had to cave and ask. I picked a young guy, probably around my age, with long hair and a scraggly beard. "Do you know where I can find Dara?"

He brightened when I spoke to him. "No, but your mom is here. She arrived a few hours ago, but you were still sleeping, so the Crone said to let you be."

My mom! She was okay. We were all here.

Almost.

"Where?" I asked, breathless with eagerness to wrap my arms around her.

"She and your friend climbed to the overseer's platform," he said, pointing to a huge ladder that led to a sizeable metal platform overlooking the main factory floor. Just looking at it made my limbs ache, but I turned to go nonetheless.

"Wait, Amara?" he said, not quite daring to touch my arm.

I turned, surprised that he knew my name. "Yes?"

His eyes shone, and his grin was overlarge. "Thank you." He extended his hand formally. "Thank you for all you did for the cause."

I felt awkward. I realized with alarm that he was looking at me like I was some kind of hero or something. Was that the look everyone was giving me? It was hard to repress the bubble of laughter that wanted to burst from inside me at the thought. I felt like the farthest thing from a hero. I just wanted to go hug my mom. Then fix my girlfriend and my ex-girlfriend—or best friend or whatever the hell she was—and make sure we weren't all going to fall apart because of all of this. This wasn't how a hero for the cause felt. But I kept down the laugh and shook his hand. I didn't know what to say, so I just nodded slightly and took off, embarrassed.

Whoever had designed this factory was an asshole, I decided as I climbed the ladder to get to my mom. Hand over hand, rung after rung, I kept asking myself why I hadn't had breakfast first. A little caffeine. That would have been much more logical. But nope. Apparently, strenuous climbing was what I needed after last night. I paused near the lip of the platform, weirded out by a strange muffled sound. I peeked over the top and saw my mom comforting Rake, who was trembling and apparently crying in her arms.

I cried all the time. But Rake rarely did. It felt wrong seeing her like this when she didn't know I was here. Like I was spying on something intimate that I had no right to see. I hesitated for a moment then started to head back down.

"Amara!" My mother had spied me.

I grimaced and reluctantly made my way up. "Sorry, I didn't mean to intrude."

Rake was turned away, wiping her face on her sleeve, and my mom pulled me into an embrace. "Don't be ridiculous. Come here."

She hugged me like only my mother could. That feeling of fitting together just right. Bringing back years and years of comforting memories. She was okay. She was here. We were going to be fine.

Most of us.

Rake made a self-conscious farewell.

"You don't have to go," I argued, though I did want to be alone with my mom.

"It's okay. We'll catch up later," Rake said, making her way down the ladder.

My mom and I talked. Looking out over the expanse of the old factory floor, watching the people come and go, we told each other what had happened. We checked in carefully. She told me she'd grabbed my sketchbook before leaving, which made me clap my hands over my chest in relief. I told her about Henry, which made her do the same in sympathy. It was good. Cathartic. What I needed.

We talked about the past too. Things I'd never asked her about before, either because I didn't know enough to ask or because I was too afraid to make her feel bad. But we were both such a bizarre mix of happy and sad that it just felt right to talk it all out at last.

"Why didn't you have a kid before the reproduction ban?"

Her face pinched. "I tried. Many times. It never worked out. My mother lost a lot of children too. That's why my parents were so overprotective of me. Why they gave me everything. I was their miracle baby after so much heartbreak."

She smiled, and I wondered once again at how much I didn't know of my own mother's life story.

"I think that's part of why I became such a caretaker. We had a lot of wealth, but there was a lot of suffering in my family too."

We lapsed into comfortable silence for a bit while I thought through all her revelations. "So…but…when you first signed up for the espionage program and they gave me to you, did you plan to return to the enclave with me after the fifteen years was up? Weren't you worried they might not grant me the Remedy? You'd have to watch me grow old and die while you lived on." Her face darkened, and I rushed to add, "Sorry, I'm just curious. You don't have to—"

"No, it's fine, my girl. Ask your questions. I should've talked to you about all this years ago, but…I don't know…it seemed impossible as I changed sides, and things got more and more complicated." She looked at me and held my gaze. A lot of emotions flicked through her face before she spoke again. "I never really believed they'd grant applications for the Remedy for our children. The Remedy was already priceless. But so is motherhood." She smiled, and I smiled back. It was such a Maria answer.

"I can't believe my real name is Bridget. It sounds wrong in my mouth."

"That's because it's not your real name, just your first name," my mom said, reframing it for me. "Maybe if Siobhan had lived and raised you, you'd be a Bridget, but you're Amara. That's your real name."

I teared up and threw my arms around her, replaying the sentence in my mind, letting its import sink in. "Why'd you pick that name?" I asked when I finally pulled away.

"'Amar' means 'to love' in Spanish. And 'mar' means 'sea.' I've always lived by the sea, at least until the Freelands. I knew I would miss it on assignment. Plus, *Bridget…*" She pronounced it awkwardly. "I can't even say that properly. Amara rolls off this Spanish tongue like it was meant to be."

I laughed at the difference in the way the two names came out of her mouth. "But what about you? You don't want to go back to your birth name?"

"No, with all due respect to my wonderful parents, Valentina never felt right. It's too precious." She wrinkled her nose in distaste. "There's nothing pretentious about a Maria."

I thought about it. "Well, I mean, Maria is the Spanish form of Mary, so you're kind of referencing being the mother of the savior of the world. I'd say that's a bit pretentious."

We both laughed. "I didn't think of that." She ruffled my hair. "Eh, well, maybe there's a tiny spark of truth in that, given what you just accomplished. How did I raise such an amazing daughter, huh?"

She put her arm around my shoulder, and I tried to relax into the compliment and the love, but it was a bittersweet thing to think about. Perhaps I had done some good by getting the Remedy to the Defiance. Or perhaps, as Rebecca had warned, I'd just inadvertently initiated a series of events that could lead to a global catastrophe. No big deal.

Was this how Henry felt? Watching the consequences of his choices spin out beyond his control, wondering if the great good he thought he'd been a part of was really so good after all?

Henry was dead. Stella was traumatized. How could I possibly congratulate myself on my accomplishments? What was going to happen now? With the Remedy? With my relationship with Stella? And Rake? Where was the Defiance even going to take us? We couldn't squat here forever. How would we rebuild our lives? Would we always be on the run, forever afraid of discovery by Hydra agents?

I looked out over the abandoned factory floor, my mother's arm around my shoulders, and tried to feel brave in the face of so many heavy questions.

CHAPTER TWENTY-THREE

Sunset and Evening Star

The mirror shook as I held it up. It felt strange to look too hard at myself, but I was doing it now for a sketch. My first ever self-portrait. I'd needed to get away from everyone, but the only place I was allowed to go outside was this kind of courtyard area between the buildings, a little haven of sunshine and greenery amidst the broken-down industrial remnants of the old factory.

It wasn't exactly a flattering portrait. Or at least, half of it wasn't. It was my face, girlish and pretty enough, with huge uncertain eyes and my hair upswept, tendrils escaping to frame my features. Roses bloomed along the crown of my head. It spoke to femininity in the fresh promise of youth. The proverbial tender maiden budding into the ripe power of womanhood. At least on one side. On the other, the flesh rotted away to bone, the cavernous void of an eye socket, the rows of teeth exposed where once the fullness of lips had invited love to make itself known. The crown of roses wilting until only thorns remained. And all of it captured not inside the shimmering opalescent bubbles I once used to draw so obsessively but inside a glass vial, luminous, with a lurid green upon its edges.

The local Crone had offered me one of the two vials I'd stolen from Hydra. "You earned it. Your friend Dara argued most passionately on your behalf. Besides, we only need one to begin reverse engineering the formula."

For one foolish, fleeting moment, I imagined myself poolside with Stella back in Henry's home, free to live out my days in love and luxury.

But Henry was dead. And that dream was dead too. We were fugitives now.

I didn't know what to do. Did I want to live forever? To never get old? I liked old people, but I didn't necessarily want to be one. To physically deteriorate. Though that was far enough away and part of the natural cycle of things. But still. I had the opportunity of a lifetime before me.

So why did it freak me out whenever I thought of it? If I took it, I'd get more time with my mom. But I'd watch Rake get old and die. Then again, if I didn't take it, my mom would watch me get old and die. And I'd miss out on so many things. So I was back where I started. I didn't know what to do.

I'd asked my mom, but she'd refused to weigh in, saying it was her job to guide me until I was old enough to make my own decisions, and I was old enough by now. I'd argued with her, but she was as stubborn as always. Her words were powerful, though: "Freedom is the greatest gift we can give someone. To honor their sovereignty."

I saw that, but I needed the benefit of her wisdom. Wasn't that supposed to be the prize that came with a long life?

She'd said, "It's my job to hold open a space in the world for you to be whoever who choose to be. It's not my job to influence your choices."

Maybe that was the wisdom of her long life, but I didn't have to like it. I felt childish for wanting her to tell me what to do, but the weight of such a colossal, irreversible decision made me want to regress. I'd pushed, but she was obstinate, refusing no matter what I'd said, and I'd eventually realized I'd get nowhere with her on this point.

It really was up to me.

I sat in the courtyard on a ratty blanket underneath a pear tree just beginning to fruit. I put down the mirror and scrutinized the sketch. I liked it. It captured something I didn't know how to express any other way about what I felt and what I was struggling with. On a whim, I drew some swirling mist coming off the vial. It was beautiful and magical and creepy all at the same time. It seemed fitting.

I sighed and thought about asking Rake what to do, but how could I? I couldn't even face her. We were avoiding each other, and I honestly couldn't say why.

I'd asked Dara what she would do. She'd been the one to convince the Crone that I deserved one of the vials, after all. I'd been surprised when she'd told me that she wouldn't take the Remedy, given the chance.

"But you argued for me to have it."

"I argued for you to have the choice. Not necessarily to take it. That's up to you."

Everyone was always pushing the decision back on me when all I really wanted was for someone to decide for me. On some level, I knew I should be grateful and that they were right. But I was so conflicted that it irritated me.

Dara had called it "unnatural." When I'd pushed back on that, asking if she was secretly Amish or something, she'd pointed out that we all had to draw the line somewhere on what was natural, and that was it for her. "Look what it's done to their society," she'd said. "They have no children. It's a cold, greedy, ruthless, selfish place. The planet can't sustain more people living that way, with those values." She'd gone on a rant the way Rake sometimes had back in the Freelands. "What do you do once you've fulfilled every dream you ever had? Fucked everyone else rich and attractive enough to be fuckable? Tried every food, every hobby, every single pleasure that life has to offer? From what I've seen, you take more risks and crazier drugs, have weirder sex, get more violent. Or more depressed because you're chasing a high that is increasingly hard to get. A zest for life but life has lost its luster because it just goes on and on and on, so time and money and power limit nothing. It's already happening. Give them another couple of centuries, and who knows what depravity they'll get up to? Maybe there will be a rash of suicides, and they'll kill themselves off. But not before sucking our planet dry and killing a hell of a lot more New Bloods."

I'd never heard her talk like that. It didn't sound like her. But maybe I didn't really know her. I knew Elder Sister Dara. Not Defiance member Dara. And whoever she was before and beyond that.

I thought back to Henry. He had been a good man. He was kind and loving and selfless. But he was struggling with the legacy of his scientific discovery. There was something sad in him. Was it just this, or was he also struggling with the ennui of timelessness that Dara had alluded to? Dara talked about Old Bloods like they were insatiable parasites, clinging to life even after they'd sucked it dry of all it had to offer while ruthlessly guarding the opportunity from others. Did I want to be that? The thought of staying young and beautiful forever was pretty appealing, but I hated to think of doing it at the expense of others. Of shifting my alliances somehow. Of leaving Rake and so many others behind.

I heard a small noise and looked up, irritated to be disturbed until I realized it was Stella. Poor thing. She looked terrible. Her version of terrible was anyone else's version of okay, but still, she looked rough around the edges in a way I'd never seen before. It broke my heart to see the toll grief had taken on her face: the bags under her bloodshot eyes, the pallor of her skin, the haunted cast to her face. She was wearing a secondhand T-shirt given to her by the Defiance, bright red with an ugly corporate logo splashed across the chest. Not something she would ever choose. It was wrinkled and ill fitting, and even the color was wrong on her.

I called her, eager to give her any comfort I could. She sat beside me on the blanket, and I felt the strangeness that was always between us now. There was still love but also pain and guilt, regret and uncertainty. Nothing was the same. How could it be? I touched her knee, and she smiled weakly before reaching for my open sketchbook. She pulled it to her lap and looked over the sketch carefully.

"I thought you didn't like to sketch yourself?"

"I don't. Not usually. But…I don't know…maybe I'm changing." I didn't say that I felt compelled to sketch myself because I was lost and torn. Because I felt like I didn't know who I was anymore or who I wanted to become.

She traced the lines of the sketch. "Can I keep this?"

"What? No. I mean, if you want one, I'll draw you a nice sketch of me, but…wait, what do you mean?" I asked, afraid of what might be underneath her question.

She sighed deeply and really looked at me. "I'm leaving, Amara."

I just looked at her, dumbfounded and scared.

"I already talked it over with the Crone. We have a plan."

That shocked me into speech. "What? No. Why? What do you mean?" I almost said, "Am I coming with you?" but stopped myself before I could sound like a desperate idiot.

She took my hand and said, "My mom's all alone now. She needs me."

Fucking Rebecca. Anger flared in me. "You can't go. You'll be arrested."

"Maybe. But my mom will find a way to clear me. She's powerful and clever. You know that."

I couldn't hold her hand. I was too upset. This was idiotic. "Stella, that's a huge gamble. They know you were with us. Why would the Defiance even agree to let you return? You know too much."

"Do I? I'm just a dumb girl who got caught up in things she didn't really understand." Her face showed she was being sarcastic, but it didn't sound believable. She sighed. "It's a gamble for me and the

Defiance. But I talked to your friend Dara. She seemed to get it. Helped me convince the Crone. They know I won't do anything to endanger you. I'll just say whatever my mother's lawyers tell me to say to get off, and then I can probably do some good there. Be an ally on the inside. A voice of reason."

"No one's going to listen to you."

"Oh, I think people will be very curious about what I have to say. The LastGen fool who fell for a terrible terrorist BabyDoll? The one who ended up wrapped up in the Defiance's evil plot to overthrow the enclave and steal the Remedy? Daughter of the two most powerful people in Hydra? One of whom turned traitor? Yeah. Trust me. I'll be the object of intense interest."

"That's not necessarily a good thing."

"It's not necessarily a bad thing, either. My mom will help me spin it. There will be an open council seat now."

"You'll try for your dad's position?"

"What better way to influence not just my mom but Hydra itself?"

I felt like she was someone new. She was changing too. Henry's death had taken a toll on her. But she wasn't just a victim. She was getting stronger.

Her eyes teared up. "I know you think my mom's awful…" She hesitated a moment as though hopeful I'd contradict her.

I kept silent. I didn't know what to say about Rebecca. I couldn't really say how I felt about her in a two-second pause. It was complicated. *She* was complicated. She *was* truly awful. In both senses of the word. She was horrible and awe-inspiring at the same time. Regardless, in this moment, I was just pissed off and jealous that concern for her was going to take Stella away from me. She didn't deserve Stella. She didn't even appreciate her. I couldn't say all this, though. So I said nothing.

Stella went on: "But she's all alone now. She thinks she's lost all her family. I know her. She'll be devastated. She loved my dad. He left her, and she was gutted. That's when she got even more obsessive about her work. Honestly, if I don't go back, I'm worried she'll obsess even more. That she'll blame New Bloods and hyper-fixate on new ways to control the Freelands or infiltrate the Defiance or get revenge. Who knows? It's dangerous when powerful people lose their way. My mom needs me to keep her on a reasonable path."

I could see now why the Defiance was supporting Stella's return. They were betting on her being a steadying hand. I shook my head and looked away. "You're such a good daughter. Better than your mom deserves."

"Don't say that." She touched my knee to draw my gaze. Her eyes were pleading. "People don't understand my mother, and I get why. But I do. I get her. And I love and respect her. You think she doesn't deserve me, but there's a way in which none of us deserve her. Think of all she's given to humanity."

I made a scoffing sound.

"Really, Amara, what did I do to deserve to live for so long? Nothing. It was an accident of fate that I was born to this woman. So this is the least I can do for all that privilege, privilege you helped me see, that I can help other Old Bloods to see. I don't think people in the enclave actually understand what it's like for people on the outside. This is immoral. Allowing people to scrape by and suffer when we have so much. It doesn't have to be that way."

I didn't know whether to applaud her conviction that she could change things or dismiss it as a kind of ignorant arrogance. I did know that I didn't want her to leave. "But she was never even there for you. Why are you going back to her when you could stay here and—"

"And what? Continue my couture fashion business? Dabble in event planning and interior design on the side? I don't belong here. There's no space for who I am here."

It was true. I hated it, but it was true. Stella couldn't be her old self here. Though she could change. Adapt. I was wondering who she might become if she really tried when she interrupted my thoughts.

"My mom was never there for me because she doesn't know how to love." Stella grabbed my face and pulled it to her, forcing me to really hear her. "But I do. I know how to love. And I'm going to help her because she's lost right now. You didn't give up on your mom. And I'm not giving up on mine. It's what my dad would have wanted." Tears fell from her eyes, and I knew she was right, that I was resisting and holding on to her out of selfishness, out of grief at the thought of losing her, but it was right for her to go.

Tears fell from my eyes too. "You're right. I'm sorry. I understand. You should go. I'll just…I'll miss you." We crushed each other in a tearful embrace.

"I'll miss you too. I'm sorry," she mumbled into my hair. "You'll be okay, right?"

I pulled back to look at her. "Me? Don't worry about me. I'm a tough girl from the streets, right?" I wiped my eyes.

"You have your mom. And…Rake." She said her name shyly, implying I wasn't sure what. "They'll look after you, right?"

"Yeah. I'll be fine. Feelings are for wimps."

Her expression was uncertain. "It's just, my mom has no one, you know?"

I wanted to reassure her, make her smile, shift the tone. I'd break down later when she wasn't around to watch me crumble. "Well, I mean, she still has Magnus."

That did it. She smiled. A little one. But I counted it.

"And Huxley. We can't forget that shining paragon of kindness."

She looked at me strangely. "I like Huxley."

I laughed. "I know you do."

She looked back at the sketch that still lay in her lap. "Can I keep this, then?"

"You want a sketch of me with half my face rotted off?"

"No, I want a sketch that reminds me of what's at stake. That the Remedy has two sides and I have a responsibility to New Bloods as well as Old Bloods."

I nodded slowly. "Okay. But can I sketch you now, before you go?"

She scowled. "I look terrible." She pulled at her T-shirt. "This shirt's too big for me, and what the hell are Merritone Milk Bars anyway? Is that a kind of snack?"

I thought back to that day we'd spent by the pool before this whole thing began. To her giant, immaculate closet full of posh designer clothes. It felt like a lifetime ago. "Don't worry. I'll draw you in a pretty dress. I'd just be getting the lines of your face and body. It'll be flattering, I promise."

She trusted me, and I got her to pose by the pear tree. Usually, I only ever drew exactly what I saw. But Stella was a shadow of herself. This wasn't how I wanted to remember her. So I drew her with a combination of memory, fantasy, and what stood before me.

"Have you ever seen a pear tree in bloom?" I asked, adding profusions of blooms behind her in the sketch.

"No. I don't think so."

"They're lovely. Delicate white flowers, speckled near the heart of each blossom. The trees just burst into fluffy clouds of flowers each spring. It's something to see."

I already knew I wouldn't be adding a bubble to this one. Was I done with that? Or was it just that Stella's image didn't need a bubble because her beauty wasn't fleeting? She'd look this good forever. Though, in another way, her bubble had already burst. She wasn't the same sheltered girl I'd first met on the beach. Either way, my usual finishing touch felt wrong. It had once been my artistic signature, but I really was changing. I could see it in my drawings.

I scrutinized Stella's features, trying to capture them, knowing that I'd use this sketch to draw more later when I was missing her. I could already imagine drawing her by the ocean where I'd first laid eyes on her. I could see the broad outlines of the sketch in my mind as I worked on this one. The way she'd appear like a water goddess, a sort of nod to Aphrodite emerging from the foam. Clearly, my drawings were taking on more of a fantasy touch. At least when it came to her. Was that because this whole thing with Stella had been a kind of fantasy? Everyone seemed to imply that. It bugged me that people had kept asking me if it was real, but maybe they'd seen something I didn't. Could we have ever been for real?

I stared at Stella and sat in the question. And the answer felt like yes. Yes, there was a moment where it could have worked for us. But that future was very limited in its possibility. So many things would have to work out just so. But our hearts had been willing. That thread of connection between us was as real as anything. It was the circumstances of our lives that were against us, forces that were far beyond us. Maybe I'd draw her with a background of a sea at storm, lightning tearing apart the sky. Time would tell.

For now, I focused on adding more blossoms. More and more and more. Never too many. The tree, like Stella, a stunning example of natural, gorgeous, girlie excess.

The day was windy, and Stella was struggling to keep her hair out of her face as she posed. "It's too windy," she complained.

"No, it's perfect," I said, the wind giving me an idea. "Use your left hand to hold your hair and put your right arm out like this." I adjusted her pose. "Look off like this." I modeled how I wanted her face to be.

Except her face was strained. I wanted to see it light up again. To hear one of my five favorite laughs. But how to make her laugh?

She was looking off to the distance, her right hand lifted elegantly, following the lines of her windswept hair and the imaginary gown's long, flounced skirt. That made it easy to hide my scheming as I carefully ripped a blank page from my sketchbook, trying to make as little noise as possible. I smiled in anticipatory amusement and let it go.

"Shit. The sketch. Grab it," I yelled.

Stella startled and looked around wildly. The paper was twirling through the air, and we both raced to catch it. It skidded along the ground, then an updraft took it and blew it into a bush. We chased it, and Stella almost had it until another gust of wind blew it away from her outstretched hands.

"*No.*" She kept chasing, and I started cracking up, delighted with my own deviousness. She joined in, and I made a mental note of the way her face lit up. The paper blew up and around and all over until it landed against a brick wall. Stella slammed her hands on it triumphantly just as I slammed into her, breathless from running. Our faces pressed close together, both of us breathing heavily, and we burst out laughing. I tried to hold on to the look and the feel of it, this moment. Knowing it wouldn't last.

We leaned in to kiss, then remembered ourselves. Stella's face crumpled. "How can I be laughing over something so stupid when my dad just died?"

I didn't know what to say, so I put my arms around her and let her cry. I felt terrible. I hadn't thought of how it might hurt her to feel happy for a bit. "He'd want you to be happy, Stella. He'd love to see you laughing." I took a risk and pat, pat, patted her shoulder like Henry used to do.

She choked on a particularly large sob and held me tighter. I just kept holding her, being with her in the sadness. What else could I do? Eventually, she pulled away and used her sleeve to wipe her eyes. "Sorry."

"There's nothing to apologize for."

She looked at the paper, slightly crumpled in her hands. Her face showed confusion. "There's nothing on here." She held it up and turned it both ways.

"I know. The real sketch is in my book. I just wanted to make you laugh."

Her eyes went huge. "What?" I tried to make a sheepish, somewhat anxious face, and she hit me in partly real, partly mocking, anger. "You jerk."

I laughed, relieved she wasn't too irritated. She crumpled up the page and threw it at my face. But she smiled. "Keep smiling," I said, opening my sketchbook. "If you can. Just for a minute. I want to remember you that way."

The smile wavered, but she held it with only slight sign of strain. It was what I needed to finish. A moment of how happiness looked on her face. I walked back to the blanket and picked through my pencil crayons, looking for a pink one. "Just a few traces of color for now to give an idea." I'd fix it up later, but the essence was there. And it was perfect. I held it out for Stella to see, watching her face carefully for its reaction.

"Oh my God. You made me beautiful," she cried.

I smiled. "You like it?"

"I love it. I love that you see me this way."

It showed her standing in front of a pear tree in bloom wearing a pale pink dress with a long, ruffled skirt that billowed out away from her in the wind like an undulating wave. She held back her hair and looked off where the wind blew, a dreamy, content expression on her face.

She looked like a mythical storybook princess. But she had been real. And she had been mine. For a short but powerful time. I closed the book slowly, feeling my heart sink.

"When do you leave?"

She shifted uncomfortably. "Tonight. After dinner."

So soon? Despair flooded through me.

Stella took a step closer. "Can I…Um…Is it okay to kiss you? One last time?"

My heart leapt, and I didn't even try to answer. I pushed her up against the tree trunk and put my mouth on hers once more, eager to remember the way she tasted, to memorize the way she fit into me so perfectly. I was wilder than I should have been perhaps, hungrier, but she responded in kind, and we were breathless and entangled for a time, the wind whipping our hair about our faces as we used our hands and lips to say everything our hearts didn't know how to say. She made the little sounds of pleasure I loved to bring out in her.

This was it. She was really leaving. I wouldn't hear those sounds again. I started to choke on a sob and had to pull away. I wanted to keep kissing her every second until she had to go, but there were things I had to say. This was it. I wouldn't get another chance.

I took her face and held her gaze. "I want you to have a long, happy, good life, Stella." She smiled, her eyes shining. "Make beautiful things and don't apologize for being who you are. Your mom doesn't see it, but others will. We need beauty. It sustains and nourishes us. It's important not frivolous." I watched my words impact her. She literally brightened and stood taller. "You have a real gift. Give it away like the gift it is. Make people feel good in the clothes you make or the rooms you design. You're good, Stella. You're so good." I became overwhelmed and buried my face her neck, crying again. "I don't want to let you go."

"I know. I don't either." She was rubbing my back in a soothing gesture. I sniffed and extricated my face from her hair. She looked at me sadly. "But life is calling us in different directions. And that's okay. Right? We enriched each other's lives. We changed each other for the better. What more can you ask from a relationship?"

I scoffed and wiped at my eyes. "Um…that it last. That I get to keep you forever," I answered bitterly.

"Not even Old Bloods get forever," she said. "Not really. And maybe even less so than New Bloods because we truly see that nothing lasts. We live long enough to watch it happen."

Who was this girl? When had she gotten so wise?

"You're a lot smarter than anyone gives you credit for," I told her.

"Maybe we have that in common, being underestimated." She went up on her tippy-toes and placed her mouth on mine once more. But it was a different sort of kiss. Sadder. Gentler. More resigned.

There was a noise behind us, and we broke apart to see an older man standing awkwardly by a door. "Sorry to interrupt. Just letting you know that dinner is ready when you are." He turned and left us to ourselves.

I felt weighed down with dread, feeling the countdown to the moment that would take her away from me. I broke out in a sweat at the thought. We had so little time.

Stella took my hand. "Come share a meal with me, then see me off, okay?" She looked up at me with such sweet trust, so much love shining in her eyes that I broke down again.

"I'm never going to see you again."

"You never know. Life takes us on unexpected paths. I certainly never thought I'd fall in love with a terrorist spy." She shrugged. She was trying to be playful, but there was still that undertone of sadness that never left her eyes now.

"Come," she said, tugging gently on my arm.

I followed her into the factory, my heart devastated.

CHAPTER TWENTY-FOUR

She Has a Voice of Gladness

I didn't take the Remedy. I didn't have any deep philosophical or political reason why; it just felt wrong. Maybe I'd grow to regret it later, but it felt like a relief in the moment not to be wrestling with such a colossally impactful decision.

I asked the Crone what would happen to the second dose. She asked if I had a recommendation. I told her I was just curious, and she said it might be given to the Head Sage of the movement. I'd only met Crones, so I didn't even know what a Sage was or how high up they stood. For someone who had risked and accomplished so much, I really knew very little about the cause. I didn't care to find out more, though. I just wanted to put this all behind me.

The Crone explained, "Conroy knows our history, the strategies we've used, the players we're up against. By giving him the Remedy, we're preserving the memory of the Defiance We'd have an Old Blood of our own, admittedly a divisive idea, one we're still debating whether to share widely. Some people are only part of the cause because they want everyone to have a shot at potential immortality. Others joined because they don't think anyone should have such longevity. Would you approve giving it to the Head Sage?"

It felt odd to be asked, but I supposed the vial did belong to me somehow. The choice only existed because of my actions. "Preserving the memory of our elders. Like a living history book. Yes, I like it."

She smiled. "He's not too old. Fifty-eight. Still spry and healthy. It won't be wasted. He has a brilliant mind."

Like Henry, who had died protecting me as I stole the elixir that would make this other brilliant man immortal. It felt strange. But the Crone's plan sounded right. It might even the score a bit with Hydra, pitting one Old Blood genius against another. Though I doubted Conroy was really that smart. The plan he'd set my mother up with was just plain stupid. And no one was Rebecca-level smart. She was a lone prodigy. No one could touch her. Not even Henry, for all his intelligence. But perhaps Stella could. Not intellectually but emotionally. If Stella could reach Rebecca's heart, maybe she could soften and redirect her. That was the hope anyway.

I could see all the pieces clicking into place in the next chapter of this undeclared blood war.

The Defiance moved us to a long-term safehouse, a farm farther north in the Freelands. It was run by maladjust Old Bloods named Christina and Jacob, who'd left Hydra to continue their family. They had a whole brood of children to help run the place and another on the way. I'd never known anything but city life, so the farm had been a kind of revelation. Maria and Rake took to it quite naturally, enjoying the physical labor and caretaking involved in tending gardens, the small vineyard, and animals.

Rake dressed the part, transforming herself once again, always in work gloves and a plaid shirt or overalls and a bandana holding back her hair. She was such a chameleon and could fit in anywhere. I felt envious, since I was awkward and uncertain.

The first few weeks, I walked around in a daze. It wasn't so much the loss of Stella. Already, my time with her felt like some fantastical dream. I was sad, but it was sadness touched with a bizarre kind of incredulity that it had ever happened in the first place. Stella had given me the hair elastic from her ponytail as a parting gift, the only thing she had from home, a gift she'd been embarrassed to offer, though I'd reassured her it was perfect. I wore it around my wrist for the first couple weeks. But the white material quickly became dirty with all I had to do around the place. I threw it in with some red laundry to dye it pink so it wouldn't show the dirt as much while still being a color I could associate with Stella. But eventually, I stopped wearing it altogether because it was just getting ruined. I could have stopped trying to pretend it was jewelry and just put it in my hair, but what was the point? Pristine, pretty things didn't last in the outskirts.

My sadness ran deeper than the loss of Stella. And yet, I had every reason to be happy. I'd accomplished my goal. I'd gotten my mother back. I'd proven myself and saved the day. Was it just a sense of "now what?" It wasn't like I'd dreamed of living on a farm. But here we were. For who knew how long. It was beautiful and welcoming and alive, and I should have been grateful. But part of me missed the noise and busyness and commotion of the city. This didn't feel like home. It felt like another strange dream. And who would I end up being this time? I had so many names now. So many selves. I felt confused and lost.

My mom went out of her way to wrangle me into little tasks of caretaking that she thought would brighten my mood like they did hers. I didn't mind helping, but it didn't fill me up and give me purpose like it did for her. Still, I went along and pretended because I could see she was worried, and I didn't want concern for me to weigh her down.

Rake was different now too. At nights, when we'd enjoy a campfire and look at the stars, far more stars than I'd ever seen in the Barrio, Christina and Jacob's teenage children would tell stories and jokes and play little games. Rake listened but never took center stage. She didn't try to befriend or charm anyone. She stood apart, seemingly lost in her thoughts. Or she took off to go wandering by herself. When our eyes met, they'd sort of skitter off each other. We never talked, and it hurt, but I didn't try to do anything about it. I didn't know what to say to her. I assumed she felt the same.

When Christina went into labor, my mom insisted that I help. I tried to wiggle out of it, uncertain how I'd feel about witnessing a birth, especially of a complete stranger. But my mom urged me so passionately that I gave up. I had no clue what to expect, but my mom assured me it would likely be quick and easy since Christina had had so many kids already.

It didn't look easy. And it was messier than I had expected. But also more magical. I hadn't been prepared for that, either. All the women present gasped and cried out when the newborn slid into the neighbor's waiting hands. He was so tiny and perfect and ugly and gorgeous. Covered in blood and mucus, his head misshapen from the pushing, his little fists flailing in outrage. I couldn't stop laughing and crying. And I wasn't alone. We all seemed to feel the awe. I felt changed. Renewed. My mom squeezed me and kissed my forehead. What was this like for her? As someone who had never borne her own children? She didn't seem mournful. Only overjoyed.

Something shifted for me after that, and I couldn't say why. But I started to look at my new life differently, less as a cage and more as a playground of new possibilities. A place of rebirth. Yes, I was having to reinvent myself again, but maybe life was always a series of reinventions if we were wise enough to keep growing.

I did what I always did when I struggled. I took my sketchbook and my feelings, and I found a place to be with both: an abandoned barn on the far edge of the property that I'd discovered when wandering aimlessly. I liked how the light shone through the slats. The new barn was modern and well organized closer to the main house, but this one was all weathered wood, empty, with just a few random forgotten things scattered here and there. I sat in the middle of the floor to sketch.

I liked the quiet. I liked how vast the space felt with its high, vaulted ceiling. I liked the emptiness. The wooden slats and beams made pleasing patterns of solid sturdy brown, while the light shining through made patterns of warm ethereal white. Dust danced in the sunbeams. It made me feel calm. It was almost church-like in its silence and grandeur.

Musing on the sacred made me think of the newborn, and before I realized what I was doing, I was adding to the sketch, drawing the baby on the floor of the barn. Little Oliver. Swaddled in a blanket, tiny and vulnerable and miraculous, in the sizeable expanse of the barn.

The sketch was beautiful. This place was beautiful.

Space and light and old trees.

And life.

This barn was beautiful *because* it was old and breaking down.

Since coming to the farm, I'd seen things die, and I'd seen things born. There was a rightness in it. In the coming and going. The growing and withering. The way abundance and scarcity were all held in balance by the cycles and seasons.

I let the last of my uncertainty about not taking the Remedy go.

I ran my hand over the drawing, pleased with my efforts. I flipped through the book, noting that there weren't many blank pages left, and I'd soon need a new one. I didn't know where I'd find one or what new images would fill that book, but I felt a flicker of excitement at the thought of finding out, a renewed sense of anticipation for the possibilities of life.

I closed the book and made to go when I sensed something strange. Rake sat in the hayloft above, her legs dangling over the edge. I made a strangled little sound of surprise. "What the hell? How long have you been there?"

She didn't answer. Just shrugged.

I felt the familiar pull of discomfort urging me to get away, to avoid her, as I had been ever since our misadventure. But there was that other pull again, a pull to return to her, to fix this thing between us. She just stared, her expression difficult to read. In the quiet, I wrestled with the two impulses.

She waited. Maybe it was the stillness that helped me listen to what I actually wanted.

I wanted her. I wasn't right because we weren't right. "I'm coming up, okay?"

She moved away from the edge, and I started climbing the ladder, wondering why I was always having to climb to get to her.

I reached the top and stopped, surprised. "You've been living here?"

She was leaning against a far wall, watching me with a guarded expression. She shrugged again. "I like it here."

There was so much distance between us. It was painful, and I didn't know how to bridge it. We'd always been so easy with each other in the past. Usually, we fell into banter, and it clicked, but things were strained now. It made me want to make up some excuse and run away, but I persevered, determined to find a way back to connection.

I looked at her things, saw papers with drawings on them.

She rushed to grab them. "Oh my God. Don't look at those. I can't draw like you can." Her face was close to mine, and we both took a step back, blushing.

I hadn't been anywhere near her in forever, and remembering her energy got me all rattled. "Sorry. I didn't mean to snoop. They were sitting out."

"No, it's fine. I just..." She folded the drawings and tucked them under the mattress on the floor. "I don't want anyone to see them. It's just a dumb idea." She wasn't someone who flustered easily. In the past, I would've pounced and teased her for this, but I wasn't sure if it would go over well now. She seemed sensitive and not herself.

I decided to test the waters a bit but took a gentler tack. "Dumb ideas are my favorite." I sat cross-legged on the far edge of the mattress and watched her, waiting to see if she'd join me.

Uncertainty played across her features, but she settled on the bed, a little stiffly and as far away from me as possible. But still. She coughed like she was uncomfortable and unsure what to say. "I just...I had this idea that maybe I could fix this barn up." She looked at me sideways.

"That would be amazing."

"Yeah, well, I mean, I don't know anything about how to do it. But I figure I can learn. I'm not afraid to get my hands dirty. Jacob would probably be happy to teach me, and maybe some of the older kids might like to join." She kept looking at me as if gauging my reaction, so I kept nodding, grateful she was opening up. "They're not using it, so I figure if I put the work in, maybe they'll let me have it."

"That would be incredible."

Her face darkened. "Yeah, well, it's something to do. I need a focus."

I hated seeing her mood shift. I tried to think of how to shift it back. "You don't have to show me the sketches, but what are you thinking?"

She seemed hesitant and wary at first, but once she got going, she went on and on about how she'd go about converting the barn into a living space. It was a relief to see her energized by a new dream. I half listened to her plans and mostly paid attention to the excitement in her face as she described them.

"Check this out." She pulled open a door in the wall, revealing a huge window to the outside. I stepped closer, but she put her hand out to stop me, almost brushing my chest, something we both seemed embarrassed about. "It's not safe. There's no rail or anything. This is the door they used to bring up the hay when this was a working barn. They stored it up here."

I nodded, admiring the way the door framed the world beyond. "I can imagine. It'll be beautiful."

She closed the door, and we gravitated back to her bed, sitting a little less far apart this time. "Can I see your sketch?" she asked.

"What?"

"The one you were working on."

"Oh." I pulled my sketchbook out and handed it over. I wondered if she'd play the art critic and make obscure ridiculous comments like she used to. But she didn't. We weren't there yet.

She just looked at it carefully, her silence making me nervous.

"Don't ask me what it means because I'm not sure," I said, anxious to fill the silence.

She grinned, a ghost of the cheeky grin she used to give me all the time. "I think it means Maria is going to be happy one day when you give her lots of grandbabies."

I rolled my eyes. "You know she roped me into helping with Oliver's birth, right?"

"I heard. How was it?"

I let out a breath, struggling with how to describe it. "Intense."

We were quiet for a minute, both looking at the drawing now.

"Actually, I think I'd like that," I said, feeling oddly shy.

"What?"

"Giving Maria a bunch of grandbabies."

Her head shot back. "Really?"

I shrugged, keeping my eyes on the sketch. "I think so. Yeah. One day."

She made a little "hmm" sound in her throat.

"Yeah, I mean…" I hesitated, wondering if she'd understand what I meant. "I guess, I always sort of resist the things my mom wants for me. Just on principle, you know." I snuck a peek at her. She was watching me intently. I kept going, averting my eyes. "But I usually come around. She knows me well. Gets what would make me happy."

When I looked up, Rake's eyes were uncertain, as if she didn't know how to interpret that.

"Rake, I'm…I'm sorry I've been distant."

"It's okay. I've been distant too."

"But like…why? Why are we avoiding each other?"

She bristled and leaned away. I felt it like she'd shoved me. "You know why," she said, getting up and crossing the hayloft, putting her back to me.

"What if I don't?"

She glanced at me but kept pacing. She fiddled with the latch of the door, saying nothing for a taut moment. Then, she blurted, "I don't know how to be with you right now, Amara."

I got up and came closer, not quite daring but wanting to put my hand on her shoulder. "Just be yourself," I whispered.

She made a scoffing sound and kept running her hands through her hair, keeping her back to me. She rolled her shoulder like she was trying to shirk some of the tension. I touched her lightly, and she whirled around to face me. "I can't 'just be myself' with you," she yelled, "because you don't want me to feel the things I feel. And I don't know how to just turn it off!"

It was hard to hold still in the face of her anger. It scared me a little. And that must have shown on my face because she swore, put her face in her hands, and rushed away. I followed, even though it had freaked me out because at least now, she was being real with me.

"I'm sorry. I shouldn't have yelled."

"It's fine. You're upset. I understand."

She started crying, her hands covering her face. "I was so scared when I thought you were shot. Like *so scared*."

"I know. I'm sorry." I rubbed her arm tentatively, worried she'd shrug me away, but she didn't.

She took her hands away from her face. "I've been avoiding you because after that, I realized you're it for me. You're fucking it, Amara. I'm all in."

My heart clenched in a strange combination of fear and happiness as she looked at me, so vulnerable and certain in her feelings that it made me dizzy.

"I knew I needed to fight for you, not just for some stupid cause. But how could I fight for you when Stella's father had just fucking died saving us?" She swore again and walked away from me.

I felt my heart sink after being stirred up with hopeful possibilities.

"It was impossible. And then she left, and you were devastated, and that's not easy to watch. To sit around watching the girl you love mourn the loss of someone who's not you? That fucking sucked."

I didn't know what to say. "I'm sorry. I'm so sorry."

She sniffed and wiped her eyes, seeming embarrassed now that she'd gotten some of it out. "Don't be. I get it. She was something special."

"I thought you said she was a Barbie doll princess." I couldn't keep myself from reminding her, still hurt by the lazy simplification of all that Stella was.

"I was jealous," she said. "That was new for me. Girls tried to make me jealous in the past, and I was always like, 'joke's on you.' I didn't care. But I cared that you were with her…I cared…I…care." She waited for my reply, her eyes pained.

I didn't know what she was saying exactly. Did she want to pursue something with me? Did I want that? Was it possible for us to figure this thing out despite all the hurt I'd caused by choosing Stella? Wasn't it wrong of me to turn to Rake now that Stella was gone?

While these questions raced through my mind, Rake's face registered more pain, and I hated myself for my habit of overthinking. I was always hurting her with my indecision and hesitation. But if we went down this path, I needed to be all in like she was. Was I finally ready to do that?

"I could help you. With the renovation," I said.

She looked doubtful.

"I don't know how to do anything, either, but I tend to be most successful when I have no clue what I'm doing. I have the scar to prove it."

That made her laugh. "Who gets a scar on their tit?"

"Only the most daring spies. When I'm old and telling war stories about the time I broke into the top secret Old Blood headquarters to steal the Remedy, if people think I'm full of shit, I'll just flash 'em. That'll shut 'em up. My left boob looks very tough."

She laughed some more. "I bet." A strange mix of desire, amusement, and sadness flashed across her features. "You are the world's most unexpected badass, Amara Rodriguez."

We smiled at each other, and I appreciated the brief, precious moment. We were back in the playful easy banter I'd enjoyed so much. "I could help. If you don't mind spending time with me," I offered, feeling vulnerable.

"I'd like that." She looked at me for a loaded moment, then crossed the room and pulled me into a careful hug.

I could feel us both holding back, being prudent. Even so, it was too much. Feeling her body. Smelling her skin. I started shaking, trying hard to control myself and hold everything in, but I burst out crying, unable to help myself. She pulled me in tighter, crushing me in a good way, where I felt secure even as I felt I was falling apart. I thought I felt her shaking too. "I miss you."

"I miss you too."

There were so many things I wanted to say. There were so many things I was feeling. Regret. Desire. Confusion. Gratitude. How had I gotten so far away from the one person who'd always made me feel like I was home? I felt her grip loosen, and I sniffed. "I'm sorry. I'm all mixed up."

"I know the feeling. It's okay."

We pulled apart and looked at each other uncertainly.

Rake brightened. "Hey, I got a place I like to go when I feel mixed up. You want to check it out?"

She took me to the river that ran along one edge of the property but not to the usual swimming spot. Farther downstream than I'd ever ventured before, where there were more rocks. No one here owned a bathing suit. We all just swam in our underthings. I thought about keeping my T-shirt on, but Rake was so casual in the way she undressed that it made it seem less of a big deal.

I couldn't help but peek as she stripped. Farm labor had only added to her physique. She was tanned and super fit and had tattoos I'd never seen before, either because they were new or because I'd never seen her in so little clothing. She glanced over, and I was embarrassed to be watching her, so I looked away and rushed to remove my clothes, grateful I was wearing something relatively cute. I could just see the tip of my scar poking out from the edge of my bra. It was ugly. I was trying to adjust the bra to hide it, when I felt a hand at my elbow.

"Wear it like a badge of honor," Rake said.

My eyes teared up, and heat rushed through me. I'd been trying to downplay the intimacy of stripping together for a swim, but now I was all too aware of it, standing so close to Rake in next to nothing. She was looking at me with her hair falling in her eyes and perfect things coming out of her mouth, and just when I was feeling all squirmy like I had to get away before I did something wrong, she said, "Come on," and held out her hand to lead me into the river.

She showed me why the rocks were a plus as she lay on a particularly big one and let the water flow past her. "You can sit if you prefer. Try here." She helped me position myself against a boulder that became like a chair back. "Try to relax. Let the river flow past you. That's what I love about it. It can take everything away, and you don't have to do anything. You can just relax and be present. There's no worrying about tomorrow or obsessing about yesterday. You can let go. Just feel. Be present." She left me to attempt this and found her own spot.

I gave it an honest go. But I couldn't get comfortable, and the river flowed surprisingly fast. I kept squirming, trying to settle.

"Oh my God, Amara. How are you still this awkward?" She laughed. "Get over here."

I blushed and went to make excuses, but she grabbed me and hauled me over. She forced my body into position, pulling me between her legs and coaxing me to lean back into her. Then she wrapped her arms around me and didn't say another word.

It didn't seem so hard to relax then. To let the water take it all away while she held me safe in her arms. The sun shone gently on my face. There was birdsong in the trees above the rushing stream. Rake's face nestled in my neck, her breath warm on the tender flesh.

I let go. Of my sorrow for the loss of Henry and Stella. My uncertainty about Rake. It seemed ridiculous now, the things I'd worried about in relation to her: that she was a flirt and it didn't mean anything. That I'd ruin our friendship if we became lovers. That I'd let her and my mother down in the end. None of those things were real. They were just stories I'd made up out of fear. And I'd been afraid because my feelings for Rake were so powerful. But I'd faced much scarier things now.

This was where I belonged. In this woman's arms. Wherever we went. I felt the water flow and flow, and I thought of it as life, moving on, going where it would. But as long as I could be here, in her embrace, I would be home.

I pulled away and turned, kneeling between her legs. She opened her eyes and looked at me quizzically. I looked at her lips, then back to her eyes. I caught the moment when her breath quickened, and my whole body felt alive with tingling, nervous energy. I brought my mouth to hers for the first time since that fateful night when I'd prepared to leave for this crazy adventure.

Her lips were soft and gentle, and she made a little sound of enjoyment in her throat that I could just hear over the din of the river's coursing stream. She let me lead, and I explored her mouth tentatively, wanting to know her. Rake. The girl I grew up with. The one who knew me better than anyone.

She wrapped her hand in my hair and pulled me away for a moment, her eyes searching mine as if for confirmation of something. Whatever she was looking for, I wanted to give it to her. We came back together, our kisses more passionate now, more certain. She ran her hands down my sides to land at my hips, then forcefully pushed me away. I was still hungry for her touch and looked at her in surprise.

She was smirking.

"What?"

"Just wondering if the novelty has worn off?"

I tilted my head at her, confused, and she laughed.

"Last time we kissed, you said you liked it but warned me not to get too cocky about it since you hadn't kissed too many people. It might just be the novelty. So…do you still like it?" She brought her mouth close, and I could taste her breath, but she moved out of reach the moment I leaned in.

I tried again to reach her, but she pulled away once more, teasing, evasive.

"Answer the question," she insisted, arching her eyebrow playfully.

"Some things just get better with age," I said, pulling myself away, moving downstream so she'd have to come to me.

She growled and splashed after me, rewarding me with a

particularly searing kiss once she caught up to me. "I'm glad," she said, when we finally pulled apart. Then we both laughed. It was such an insufficient response, even as it said everything there was to say.

"You're stuck with me now," she said. "I want to be with you every day, Amara. To wake up with you and fall asleep with you and annoy you for the rest of your days." She gave me a cute little kiss on the tip of my nose and winked. She paused like she was thinking. "Or maybe I should say for the rest of *my* days, if you take the Remedy."

"I'm not taking it. I already gave it away."

"What? Why not?"

I shrugged as if giving up a shot at immortality were an inconsequential thing. "I guess one regular human life is enough for me."

Her brows furrowed. "Are you sure?"

"Not really. But it's what I chose. It feels right." A crow cawed loudly and flew across from the treetops behind Rake's head. Something stirred in me. "I'm sorry I got lost," I said quietly.

She smoothed my hair from my face. "You weren't lost. Stella was important to you. I'm sure she gave you something you needed when I wasn't there." She held my gaze, and my heart swelled with gratitude for her understanding. For this strong, devoted, fun-loving woman I would be lucky to spend my one short, precious life with.

I already knew I would work hard to make her happy too, to lessen the load she carried, to see her spark return and to help make her dreams come true.

A sly look came in her eyes. "But don't get me wrong. I'm fucking glad she's gone." We both laughed in a sudden relief of tension. She looked at my body, not hiding it, and sidled closer. "I want you to come to me now, though. With anything you need." There was a sexy edge to her words, and my body responded.

"Anything?" I asked in a suggestive tone I'd never used with her before. I wrapped my legs around her waist and my arms around her neck, wiggling coquettishly.

She reacted now. She liked it all right.

It made me want to be more playful. "What if I'm very demanding? Or have unusual and highly specific needs?"

She flashed her old devilish grin and said, "Your wish is my command."

I gave a little laugh and mumbled, "Service with civility."

"What?"

"That's the motto of the BabyDoll academy."

"Mmm, well..." She pulled me closer, adjusting my position so I was nearly grinding against her. Damn, I liked the way she just kept putting me where she wanted. It seemed rather promising. She cupped my face, and her eyes were soft and sexy as they held my gaze. "I can make you happy, Amara. You know that's all I really want."

"And all I really want is you."

We kissed and kissed and let ourselves be carried away with our feelings, no longer afraid to feel them. I still had fears, of course. But not about her. I felt deep down that this was right. That we were always meant to be and that my mother had been annoyingly correct yet again.

I remained worried, though, that maybe I'd made the wrong choice in giving the Remedy to the Defiance. I tried to let the river take that worry, as Rake had shown me. In the weeks that followed, whenever I questioned my decision, I'd return there, settle in, and try to let the water wash the fear away.

I had to "believe," as the patch on my beloved pencil case urged. Faith had gotten me through the perils of the enclave, and faith had brought my family back to me. So I had to have faith in humanity too, to trust that everything would work out, that I hadn't unleashed a curse upon the planet. If the Defiance was successful in reverse-engineering the Remedy, lots more people would be faced with this decision. Could New Bloods handle the awesome responsibility of managing its distribution and regulation any better than Old Bloods had? The fate of the planet and life itself hung in the balance.

But we deserved the right to choose. And surely, there was an honorable and ethical way forward, a better way to manage our resources, to make life sustainable and enjoyable for more people for more years. Surely, with all the accumulated wisdom of centuries, humanity could manage it, if they had to.

I decided to trust. I believed it was possible. I had faith that humanity could do better.

Perhaps I was right or perhaps I was too young to know better.

About the Author

Melissa Sky has a PhD in English literature and has always dreamed of publishing a novel like all the beloved books she enjoys savoring in her free time. She's an avid traveler and unrepentant daydreamer who works in education when she's not scribbling down stories.

Books Available From Bold Strokes Books

Curse of the Gorgon by Tanai Walker. Cass will do anything to ensure Elle's safety, but is she willing to embrace the curse of the Gorgon? (978-1-63679-395-5)

Dance with Me by Georgia Beers. Scottie Templeton mixes it up on and off the dance floor with sexy salsa instructor Marisa Reyes. But can Scottie get past Marisa's connection to her ex? (978-1-63679-359-7)

Gin and Bear It by Joy Argento. Opposites really can attract, and as Kelly and Logan work together to create a loving home for rescue cat Bear, they just might find one for themselves as well. (978-1-63679-351-1)

Harvest Dreams by Jacqueline Fein-Zachary. Planting the vineyard of their dreams, Kate Bauer and Sydney Barrett must resist their attraction while battling nature and their families, who oppose both the venture and their relationship. (978-1-63679-380-1)

The No Kiss Contract by Nan Campbell. Workaholic Davy believes she can get the top spot at her firm if the senior partners think she's settling down and about to start a family, but she needs the delightful yet dubious Anna to help by pretending to be her fiancée. (978-1-63679-372-6)

Outside the Lines by Melissa Sky. If you had the chance to live forever, would you take it? Amara Rodriguez did, and it sets her on a journey to find her missing mother and unravel the mystery of her own heart. (978-1-63679-403-7)

The Value of Sylver and Gold by Michelle Larkin. When word gets out that former Boston homicide detective Reid Sylver can talk to the dead, the FBI solicits her help on a serial murder case, prompting Reid to assemble forces once again with Detective London Gold. (978-1-63679-093-0)

When It Feels Right by Tagan Shepard. Freshly out of the closet Marlene hasn't been lucky in love, but when it comes to her quirky new roommate Abby, everything just feels right. (978-1-63679-367-2)

Lucky in Lace by Melissa Brayden. Straitlaced stationery store owner Juliette Jennings's predictable life unravels when a sexy lingerie shop and its alluring owner move in next door. (978-1-63679-434-1)

Made for Her by Carsen Taite. Neal Walsh is a newly made member of the Mancuso crime family, but will her undeniable attraction to Anastasia Petrov, the wife of her boss's sworn enemy, be the ultimate test of her loyalty? (978-1-63679-265-1)

Off the Menu by Alaina Erdell. Reality TV sensation Restaurant Redo and its gorgeous host Erin Rasmussen will arrive to film in chef Taylor Mobley's kitchen. As the cameras roll, will they make the jump from enemies to lovers? (978-1-63679-295-8)

Pack of Her Own by Elena Abbott. When things heat up in a small town, steamy secrets are revealed between Alpha werewolf Wren Carne and her human mate, Natalie Donovan. (978-1-63679-370-2)

Return to McCall by Patricia Evans. Lily isn't looking for romance—not until she meets Alex, the gorgeous Cuban dance instructor at La Haven, a newly opened lesbian retreat. (978-1-63679-386-3)

So It Went Like This by C. Spencer. A candid and deeply personal exploration of fate, chosen family, and the vulnerability intrinsic in life's uncertainties. (978-1-63555-971-2)

Stolen Kiss by Spencer Greene. Anna and Louise share a stolen kiss, only to discover that Louise is dating Anna's brother. Surely, one kiss can't change everything…Can it? (978-1-63679-364-1)

The Fall Line by Kelly Wacker. When Jordan Burroughs arrives in the Deep South to paint a local endangered aquatic flower, she doesn't expect to become friends with a mischievous gin-drinking ghost who complicates her budding romance and leads her to an awful discovery and danger. (978-1-63679-205-7)

To Meet Again by Kadyan. When the stark reality of WW II separates cabaret singer Evelyn and Australian doctor Joan in Singapore, they must overcome all odds to find one another again. (978-1-63679-398-6)